TERRY CARR'S
BEST
SCIENCE FICTION
AND FANTASY OF
THE YEAR
#16

TERRY CARR'S
BEST
SCIENCE FICTION
AND FANTASY OF
THE YEAR
#16

TOR

TERRY CARR'S BEST SCIENCE FICTION AND FANTASY OF THE YEAR #16

Copyright © 1987 by Terry Carr

First printing: September 1987

A TOR Book

Published by Tom Doherty Associates, Inc.
49 West 24 Street
New York, N.Y. 10010

Cover art by Peter Gudynas
Cover design by Carol Russo

ISBN: 0-312-93025-9

Library of Congress Catalog Card Number: 87-50472

Printed in the United States of America

0 9 8 7 6 5 4 3 2 1

ACKNOWLEDGMENTS

EDITOR'S NOTE

Terry Carr passed away on April 6, 1987, a few days after delivering the final text of the introductions to this volume.

For sixteen years he told us which stories were good, and which stories were the best. He was right more often than he was wrong, and it was his hand, more than any other, that brought science fiction to its present level of literary excellence. We will miss him in the years to come.

I miss him now.

BAM
6/5/87

CONTENTS

INTRODUCTION

THIS YEAR'S *Best Science Fiction and Fantasy of the Year*—even more so than last year's or the one before that—represents the fulfillment of the great and confusing period of growth and change that typified science fiction in the 1970s.

That decade, I'm sure you'll recall, saw vast and startling changes in a couple of areas even more significant than science fiction—the global economy, for example, and the nature of the political process in Western industrial society. In our own field, we saw a period of simultaneous synthesis and metamorphosis, as the science fiction of the two innovative decades of the 1950s and 1960s was brought into a new configuration that was either revolutionary or counter-revolutionary, depending on your own ideological position.

What I mean is that in the 1950s such new magazines as Anthony Boucher and J. F. McComas' *Fantasy and Science Fiction,* Horace Gold's *Galaxy,* and the short-lived but significant publications of such editors as Lester del Rey, Larry T. Shaw, Robert W. Lowndes, and Frederik Pohl brought magazine science fiction a long way from its old pulp-adventure status. Building on the pioneering work of John W. Campbell, Jr., those editors permitted a new maturity of concept and style that made science fiction probably the most exciting form of short fiction being written.

Then, in the wild 1960s, a newer and even bolder batch of editors sponsored the vigorous, undisciplined movement loosely termed the "New Wave," in which the conceptual and stylistic developments of the previous decade were given a stimulating jolt of literary technique imported from mainstream fiction and an exhilarating anything-goes content very much in keeping with the free-swinging period of the times. Such magazines as Michael Moorcock's *New Worlds* and such original-fiction anthologies as Harlan Ellison's *Dangerous Visions*, Damon Knight's *Orbit*, and Robert Silverberg's *New Dimensions*, kept the New Wave pot bubbling.

Like most revolutions, the New Wave ended in a welter of conflicting sub-movements and self-destructive excess. There was a spell in the early and middle 1970s when both the readers and writers of science fiction seemed a little shellshocked. But out of it came an even newer sort of science fiction, more conservative in outward appearance than New Wave stuff but more thoughtful and generally better written than the 1950s material. Experimentalism for its own sake was dead; but new young writers, trained by workshop methods to purge pulp-magazine mannerisms from their approach, worked within the conventional narrative modes to produce science fiction that was both searching and entertaining at the same time.

While this was going on in the area of the science fiction short story, a different kind of counter-revolution was taking place in the realm of the novel—the production of books (often in stereotyped trilogy format) that could win vast reader appeal beyond the hard-core audience and actually put science fiction on national best-seller lists. Whether this was healthy for the creative impulses of science fiction writers is a debatable matter, but no question that it brought remarkable prosperity and confidence to the field.

The development of the best-selling science fiction book led a great many of the veteran SF writers to abandon the shorter forms almost entirely and go in pursuit of the far greater economic rewards the novel afforded. No longer was it possible for a writer to earn a living in the magazine market alone. A prolific few were able to do that twenty years earlier, but now, with a great many more writers competing for places in just a handful of magazines, not even the best could hope to earn very much. On the other hand, science fiction writers could—and did—become millionaires by producing novels. So the Old Guard science fiction writers moved off en masse to concentrate on books—when did you last see a short story by Robert A. Heinlein or Arthur C. Clarke?—and many of the new ones started their careers with trilogies of novels instead of short stories. Which left the pages of the magazines wide open for the impressive fiction of a pack of gifted newcomers whose primary aim in writing was not to get rich quick but to tackle challenging ideas in stimulating ways.

The impressive results have been showing up over the past several years in these annual anthologies. In 1984, only four of thirteen contributors had published any science fiction as far back as 1971. Last year, the figure was two out of twelve. And in the current book, only one writer—Robert Silverberg, who while still relatively young has managed to sustain a science fiction career across nearly thirty-five years by now—can be considered Old Guard. Silverberg is one of the few major novelists of the field who still writes short stories with some frequency also. The other ten of this year's contributors—some beginning to be noted for novels as well as short stories but most still working only in the shorter lengths—all are writers of the 1970s and 1980s.

Even Silverberg, by stretching a point, could be deemed a figure of the 1970s, since he began his career a second time, in markedly different fashion, in 1978, after taking a hiatus of some years for re-thinking. But there are no such ambiguities about the others. John Varley began to appear on magazine contents pages regularly in 1975 and 1976; Orson Scott Card, a year or so later; Ian Watson and Kim Stanley Robinson likewise. Those are the veterans of the group. Except for Varley, whose career started in fast and furious fashion, they have really all come into their own as writers only in the 1980s. Carter Scholz and Lucius Shepard are distinctly figures of the present decade; and Harry Turtledove, Judith Moffett, Richard Kearns, and James Patrick Kelly may all be fairly considered new writers.

What we see here, then, is not exactly a youth movement, but it is definitely the consolidation on the scene of a group of commanding younger writers who have taken full possession of the science fiction short story. Most are novelists as well, and I think we'll be seeing remarkable work from them all for a long time to come. The auguries for the future of science fiction are auspicious.

—Terry Carr

This story is a remarkable change of pace for Kim Stanley Robinson, the author of such searching and dark-hued stories as the memorable "The Lucky Strike," which appeared in this anthology a couple of years ago, and the haunting fantasy "Black Air." This time around he offers a madcap Himalayan farce, which affords a new height in something-or-other when it gives us Jimmy Carter solemnly shaking hands with a yeti *in Birkenstocks in a corridor of the Everest Sheraton International Hotel. But the fun's only beginning. . . .*

    Robinson, a Californian, has been living in Switzerland lately. A collection of his fine short stories, The Planet on the Table, *was published last year.*

ESCAPE FROM KATHMANDU

Kim Stanley Robinson

I

Usually I'm not much interested in other people's mail. I mean, when you get right down to it, even my own mail doesn't do that much for me. Most of it's junk mail or bills, and even the real stuff is, like, official news from my sister-in-law, photo-copied for the whole clan, or at best an occasional letter from a climbing buddy that reads like a submission to the *Alpine Journal for the Illiterate.* Taking the trouble to read some stranger's version of this kind of stuff? You must be kidding.

But there was something about the dead mail at the Hotel Star in Kathmandu that drew me. Several times each day I would escape the dust and noise of Alice's Second City, cross the sunny paved courtyard of the Star, enter the lobby and get my key from one of the zoned-out Hindu clerks—nice guys all—and turn up the uneven stairs to go to my room. And there at the bottom of the stairwell was a big wooden letter rack nailed to the wall, absolutely *stuffed* with mail. There must have been two hundred letters and postcards stuck up there—thick packets, blue airmail pages, dog-eared post- cards from Thailand or Peru, ordinary envelopes covered with complex addresses and purple postal marks—all of them bent over the wooden retainer bars of the rack, all of them gray with dust. Above the rack a cloth print of Ganesh stared down with his sad elephant gaze, as if he represented all the correspondents who had mailed these letters, whose messages were never going to reach their destinatiions. It was dead mail at its deadest.

And after a while it got to me. I became curious. Ten times a day I passed this sad sight, which never changed—no letters taken away, no new ones added. Such a lot of wasted effort! Once upon a time these names had taken off for Nepal, and back home some relative or friend or lover had taken the time to sit down and write a letter, which to me is like dropping a brick on your foot as far as entertainment is concerned. Heroic, really. "Dear George Freder- icks!" they cried. "Where are you, how are you? Your sister-in- law had her baby, and I'm going back to school. When will you be home?" Signed, Faithful Friend, Thinking of You. But George had left for the Himal, or had checked into another hotel and never been to the Star, or was already off to Thailand, Peru, you name it; and the heartfelt effort to reach him was wasted.

One day I came into the hotel a little wasted myself, and noticed this letter to George Fredericks. Just glancing through them all, you know, out of curiosity. My name is George, also—George Fergus- son. And this letter to George was the thickest letter-sized envelope there, all dusty and bent permanently across the mid- dle. "George Fredericks—Hotel Star—Thamel Neighborhood—Kath- mandu—NEPAL." It had a trio of Nepali stamps on it—the King, Cho Oyo, the King again—and the postmark date was illegible, as always.

Slowly, reluctantly, I shoved the letter back into the rack. I tried to satisfy my curiosity by reading a postcard from KoSamui: "Hello! Do you remember me? I had to leave in December when I ran out of money. I'll be back next year. Hello to Franz and Badim Badur—Michel."

No, no. I put the card back and hoisted myself upstairs. Postcards are all alike. *Do you remember me?* Exactly. But that letter to George, now. About half-an-inch thick! Maybe six or eight ounces— some sort of epic, for sure. And apparently written in Nepal, which naturally made it more interesting to me. I'd spent most of the previous year in Nepal, you see, climbing and guiding treks and hanging out; and the rest of the world was beginning to seem pretty unreal. These days I felt the same way about *The International Herald Tribune* that I used to feel about *The National Enquirer*. "Jeez," I'd think as I scanned a Tribby in front of a Thamel bookstore, and read of strange wars, unlikely summits, bizarre hijackings. "How do they think these things up?"

But an epic from Nepal, now. That was reality. And addressed to a "George F." Maybe they had misspelled the last name, eh? And anyway, it was clear by the way the letter was doubled over, and the envelope falling apart, that it had been stuck there for years. A dead loss to the world, if someone didn't save it and read it. All that agony of emotions, of brain cells, of finger muscles, all *wasted*. It was a damn shame.

So I took it.

II

My room, one of the nicest in all Thamel, was on the fourth floor of the Star. The view was eastward, toward the tall bat-filled trees of the King's Palace, overlooking the jumble of Thamel shops. A lot of big evergreens dotted the confusion of buildings; in fact, from my height it looked like a city of trees. In the distance I could see the green hills that contained the Kathmandu Valley, and before the clouds formed in the mornings I could even see some white spikes of the Himal to the north.

The room itself was simple: a bed and a chair, under the light of a single bare bulb hanging from the ceiling. But what else do you really need? It's true that the bed was lumpy; but with my foam pad from my climbing gear laid over it to level it out, it was fine. And I had my own bathroom. It's true the seatless toilet leaked pretty badly, but since the shower poured directly onto the floor, and leaked also, it didn't matter. It was also true that the shower came in two parts, a waist-high faucet and a showerhead near the ceiling, and the showerhead didn't work, so that to take a shower I had to sit on the floor under the faucet. But that was okay—it was all okay—because that shower was *hot*. The water heater was right there in the room hanging over the toilet, and the water that came from it was so hot that when I took a shower I actually had to turn on the cold water too. That in itself made it one of the finest bathrooms in Thamel.

Anyway, this room and bath had been my castle for about a month, while I waited for the monsoon to end and my next trekkers' group from Mountain Adventure, Inc, to arrive. When I entered it with the lifted letter in hand I had to kick my way through clothes, climbing gear, sleeping bag, food, books, Tribbys—sweep a pile of stuff off the chair—and clear a space for the chair by the windowsill. Then I sat down, and tried to open the bent envelope without actually ripping it.

No way. It wasn't a Nepali envelope, and there was some real glue on the flap. I did what I could, but the CIA wouldn't have been proud of me.

Out it came. Eight sheets of lined paper, folded twice like most letters, and then bent double by the rack. Writing on both sides. The handwriting was miniaturized and neurotically regular, as easy to read as a paperback. The first page was dated June 2, 1985. So much for my guess concerning its age, but I would have sworn the envelope looked four or five years old. That's Kathmandu dust for you. A sentence near the beginning was underlined heavily: *"You must not tell ANYBODY about this!!!"* Whoah, heavy! I glanced out the window, even. A letter with some secrets in it! How great! I tilted the chair back, flattened the pages, and began to read.

June 2nd, 1985

Dear Freds—

I know, its a miracle to get even a postcard from me, much less a letter like this one's going to be. But an amazing thing has happened to me and you're the only friend I can trust to keep it to himself. *You must not tell ANYBODY about this!!!* Okay? I know you won't—ever since we were roommates in the dorm you've been the one I can talk to about anything, in confidence. And I'm glad I've got a friend like you, because I've found I really have to tell this to somebody, or go crazy.

As you may or may not remember, I got a Master's degree in Zoology at U.C. Davis, and put in more years than I care to recall on a Ph.D. there, before I got disgusted and quit. I wasn't going to have anything more to do with any of that, but last fall I got a letter from a friend I had shared an office with, a Sarah Hornsby. She was going to be part of a zoological/botanical expedition to the Himalayas, a camp modeled on the Cronin expedition, where a broad range of specialists set up near treeline, in as pure a wilderness as they can conveniently get to. They wanted me along because of my "extensive experience in Nepal," meaning they wanted me to be sirdhar, and my degree didn't have a thing to do with it. That was fine by me. I took the job and went hacking away at the bureaucratic underbrush in Kathmandu. Central Immigration, Ministry of Tourism, Forests and Parks, RNAC, the whole horrible routine, which clearly was designed by someone who had read too much Kafka. But eventually it got done and I took off in the early spring with four animal behaviorists, three botanists, and a ton of supplies, and flew north. We were joined at the airstrip by twenty-two local porters and a real sirdhar, and we started trekking.

I'm not going to tell you exactly where we went. Not because of you; it's just too dangerous to commit it to print. But we were up near the top of one of the watersheds, near the crest of the Himalayas and the border with Tibet. You know how those valleys end: tributaries keep getting higher and higher, and finally there's a last set of box canyon-type valleys fingering up into the highest peaks. We set our base camp where three of these dead-end valleys met, and members of the group could head upstream or down depending on their project. There was a trail to the camp, and a bridge over the river near it, but the three upper valleys were wilderness, and it was tough to get through the forest up into them. It was what these folks wanted, however—untouched wilderness.

When the camp was set the porters left, and there the eight of us were. My old friend Sarah Hornsby was the ornithologist—she's quite good at it, and I spent some time working with her. But she had a boyfriend along, the mammologist (no, not that, Freds), Phil Adrakian. I didn't like him much, from the start. He was the expedition leader, and absolutely MR. ANIMAL BEHAVIOR—but he sure had a tough time finding any mammals up there. Then Valerie Budge was the entomologist—no problem finding subjects for her, eh? (Yes, she did bug me. Another expert.) And Armaat Ray was the herpetologist, though he ended up helping Phil a lot with the blinds. The botanists were named Kitty, Dominique, and John; they spent a lot of time to themselves, in a large tent full of plant samplings.

So—camp life with a zoological expedition. I don't suppose you've ever experienced it. Compared to a climbing expedition it isn't that exciting, I'll tell you. On this one I spent the first week or two crossing the bridge and establishing the best routes through the forest into the three high valleys; after that I helped Sarah with her project, mostly. But the whole time I entertained myself by watching the crew—being an animal behaviorist for the animal behaviorists, so to speak.

What interests me, having once given it a try and decided it wasn't worth it, is why others carry on. Following animals around, then explaining every little thing you see, and then arguing intensely with everyone else about the explanations—for a *career?* Why on earth would anyone do it?

I talked about it with Sarah, one day when we were up the middle valley looking for beehives. I told her I had formed a classification system. She laughed "Taxonomy! You can't escape your training." And she asked me to tell her about it.

First, I said, there were the people who had a genuine and powerful fascination with animals. She was that way herself, I said; when she saw a bird flying, there was a look on her face . . . it was like she was seeing a miracle.

She wasn't so sure she approved of that; you have to be scientifically detached, you know. But she admitted the type certainly existed.

Then, I said, there were the stalkers. These people liked to crawl around in the bush tailing other creatures, like kids playing a game. I went on to explain why I thought this was such a powerful urge; it seemed to me that the life it led to was very similar to the lives led by our primitive ancestors, for a million long years. Living in camps, stalking animals in the woods: to get back to that style of life is a powerfully satisfying feeling.

Sarah agreed, and pointed out that it was also true that nowadays when you got sick of camp life you could go out and sit in a hot bath drinking brandy and listening to Beethoven, as she put it.

"That's right!" I said. "And even in camp there's quite a night life, you've all got your Dostoevski and your arguments over Edmund O. Wilson . . . it's the best of both worlds. Yeah, I think most of you are stalkers on some level."

"But you always say 'you people,' " Sarah pointed out to me. "Why are you outside it, Nathan? Why did you quit?"

And here it got serious; for a few years we had been on the same path, and now we weren't, because I had left it. I thought carefully about how to explain myself. "Maybe it's because of type three, the theorists. Because we must remember that animal behavior is a Very Respectable Academic Field! It has to have its intellectual justification, you can't just go into the academic senate and say, 'Distinguished colleagues, we do it because we like the way birds fly, and it's fun to crawl in the bushes!' "

Sarah laughed at that. "It's true."

And I mentioned ecology and the balance of nature, population biology and the preservation of species, evolutionary theory and how life became what it is, sociobiology and the underlying animal causes for social behavior. . . . But she objected, pointing out those were real concerns.

"Sociobiology?" I asked. She winced. I admitted, then, that there were indeed some excellent angles for justifying the study of animals, but I claimed that for some people these became the most important part of the field. As I said, "For most of the people in our department, the theories became more important than the animals. What they observed in the field was just more data for their theory! What interested them was on the page or at the conference, and a lot of them only did field work because you have to to prove you can."

"Oh, Nathan," she said. "You sound cynical, but cynics are just idealists who have been disappointed. I remember that about you—you're such an idealist!"

I know, Freds—you will be agreeing with her: Nathan Howe,

idealist. And maybe I am. That's what I told her: "Maybe I am. But jeez, the atmosphere in the department made me sick. Theorists backstabbing each other over their pet ideas, and sounding just as scientific as they could, when it isn't really scientific at all! You can't test these theories by designing an experiment and looking for reproducibility, and you can't isolate your factors or vary them, or use controls—it's just observation and untestable hypothesis, over and over! And yet they acted like such solid scientists, math models and all, like chemists or something. It's just scientism."

Sarah shook her head at me. "You're too idealistic, Nathan. You want things perfect. But it isn't so simple. If you want to study animals, you have to make compromises. As for your classification system, you should write it up for *Sociobiological Review*! But it's just a theory, remember. If you forget that, you fall into the trap yourself."

She had a point, and besides we caught sight of some bees and had to hurry to follow them upstream. So the conversation ended. But during the following evenings in the tent, when Valerie explained to us how human society behaved much like ants—or when Sarah's boyfriend Adrakian, frustrated by his lack of sightings, went off on long analytical jags like he was the hottest theorist since Robert Trivers—she would give me a look and a smile, and I knew I had made my point. Actually, though he talked a big line, I don't think Adrakian was all that good; his publications wouldn't exactly give a porter backstrain, if you know what I mean. I couldn't figure out what Sarah saw in him.

One day soon after that Sarah and I returned to the middle high valley to hunt again for beehives. It was a cloudless morning, a classic Himalayan forest climb: cross the bridge, hike among the boulders in the streambed, ascending from pool to pool; up through damp trees and underbrush, over lumpy lawns of moss. Then atop the wall of the lower valley, and onto the floor of the upper valley, much clearer and sunnier up there in a big rhododendron forest. The rhododendron blooms still flared on every branch, and with the flowers' pink intensity, and the long cones of sunlight shafting down through the leaves to illuminate rough black bark, orange fungi, bright green ferns—it was like hiking through a dream. And three thousand feet above us soared a snowy horseshoe ring of peaks. The Himalayas—you know.

So we were in good spirits as we hiked up this high valley, following the streambed. And we were in luck, too. Above one small turn and lift the stream widened into a long narrow pool; on the south face above it was a cliff of striated yellowish granite, streaked with big horizontal cracks. And spilling down from these cracks were beehives. Parts of the cliff seemed to pulsate blackly, clouds of bees drifted in front of it, and above the quiet sound of the stream I could hear the mellow buzz of the bees going about their work. Excited, Sarah and I sat on a rock in the sun, got our binoculars, and started watching for bird life. Goraks upvalley on the snow, a lammergeier sailing over the peaks, finches beeping around as always—and then I saw it—a flick of yellow, just bigger than the biggest hummingbird. A warbler, bobbing on a twig that hung before the hive cliff. Down it flew, to a fallen piece of hive wax; peck peck peck; wax into bird. A honey warbler. I nudged Sarah and pointed it out, but she had already seen it. We were still for a long time, watching.

Edwin Cronin, leader of a previous expedition of this kind to the Himalayas, did one of the first extensive studies of the honey warbler, and I knew that Sarah wanted to check his observations and continue the work. Honey warblers are unusual birds, in that they manage to live off the excess wax of the honey-combs, with the help of some bacteria in their gastro-intestinal systems. It's a digestive feat hardly any other creature on earth has managed, and its obviously a good move for the bird, as it means they have a very large food source that nothing else is interested in. This makes them very worthy of study, though they hadn't gotten a whole lot of it up to that point—something Sarah hoped to change.

When the warbler, quick and yellow, flew out of sight, Sarah stirred at last—took a deep breath, leaned over and hugged me. Kissed me on the cheek. "Thanks for getting me here, Nathan."

I was uncomfortable. The boyfriend, you know—and Sarah was so much finer a person than he was. . . . And besides, I was remembering, back when we shared that office, she had come in one night all upset because the boyfriend of the time had declared for someone else, and what with one thing and another—well, I don't want to talk about it. But we had been *good friends*. And I still felt a lot of that. So to me it wasn't just a peck on the cheek, if you know what I mean. Anyway, I'm sure I got all awkward and formal in my usual way.

In any case, we were pretty pleased at our discovery, and we returned to the honey cliff every day after that for a week. It was a really nice time. Then Sarah wanted to continue some studies she had started of the goraks, and so I hiked on up to Honey Cliff on my own a few times.

It was on one of these days by myself that it happened. The warbler didn't show up, and I continued upstream to see if I could find the source. Clouds were rolling up from the valley below and it looked like it would rain later, but it was still sunny up where I was. I reached the source of the stream—a spring-fed pool at the bottom of a talus slope—and stood watching it pour down into the world. One of those quiet Himalayan moments, where the world seems like an immense chapel.

Then a movement across the pool caught my eye, there in the shadow of two gnarled oak trees. I froze, but I was right out in the open for anyone to see. There under one of the oaks, in shadow darker for the sunlight, a pair of eyes watched me. They were about my height off the ground. I thought it might be a bear, and was mentally reviewing the trees behind me for climbability, when it moved again—it blinked. And then I saw the eyes had whites visible around the iris. A villager, out hunting? I didn't think so. My heart began to hammer away inside me, and I couldn't help swallowing. Surely that was some sort of *face* there in the shadows? A bearded face?

Of course I had an idea what I might be trading glances with. The yeti, the mountain man, the elusive creature of the snows. The *Abominable Snowman,* for God's sake! My heart's never pounded faster. What to do? The whites of its eyes . . . chimpanzees have white eyelids that they use to make threats, and if you look at them directly they see the white of your eyes, and believe you are threatening them; on the off-chance that this creature had a similar code, I tilted my head and looked at him indirectly. I swear it appeared to nod back at me.

Then another blink, only the eyes didn't return. The bearded face and the shape below it were gone. I started breathing again, listened as hard as I could, but never heard anything except for the chuckle of the stream.

After a minute or two I crossed the stream and took a look at the ground under the oak. It was mossy, and there were areas of moss that had been stepped on by something at least as heavy as me; but no clear tracks, of course. And nothing more than that, in any direction.

I hiked back down to camp in a daze; I hardly saw a thing, and jumped at every little sound. You can imagine how I felt—a sighting like that . . . !

And that very night, while I was trying to quietly eat my stew and not reveal that anything had happened, the group's conversation veered onto the topic of the yeti. I almost dropped my fork. It was Adrakian again—he was frustrated at the fact that despite all of the spoor visible in the area, he had only actually seen some squirrels and a distant monkey or two. Of course it would have helped if he'd spent the night in the night blinds more often. Anyway, he wanted to bring up something, to be the center of attention and take the stage as The Expert. "You know these high valleys are exactly the zone the yeti live in," he announced matter-of-factly.

That's when the fork almost left me. "It's almost certain they exist, of course," Adrakian went on, with a funny smile.

"Oh, Philip," Sarah said. She said that a lot to him these days, which didn't bother me at all.

"It's true." Then he went into the whole bit, which of course all of us knew: the tracks in the snow that Eric Shipton photographed, George Schaller's support for the idea, the prints Cronin's party found, the many other sightings. . . . "There are thousands of square miles of impenetrable mountain wilderness here, as we now know first hand."

Of course I didn't need any convincing. And the others were perfectly willing to concede the notion. "Wouldn't that be something if we found one!" Valerie said. "Got some good photos—"

"Or found a body," John said. Botanists think in terms of stationary subjects.

Phil nodded slowly. "Or if we captured a live one. . . ."

"We'd be famous," Valerie said.

Theorists. They might even get their names latinized and made part of the new species' name. *Gorilla montani adrakianias-budgeon.*

I couldn't help myself; I had to speak up. "If we found good evidence of a yeti it would be our duty to get rid of it and forget about it," I said, perhaps a bit too loudly.

They all stared at me. "Whatever for?" Valerie said.

"For the sake of the yeti, obviously," I said coldly. "As animal behaviorists you're presumably concerned about the welfare of the animals you study, right? And the ecospheres they live in? But if the existence of the yeti were confirmed, it would be disastrous for both. There would be an invasion of expeditions, tourists, poachers—yetis in zoos, in primate center cages, in laboratories under the knife, stuffed in museums—" I was getting upset. "I mean what's the real value of the yeti for us, anyway?" They only stared at me: value? "Their *value* is the fact that they're unknown, they're beyond science. They're the part of the wilderness we can't touch."

"I can see Nathan's point," Sarah remarked in the ensuing silence, with a look at me that made me lose my train of thought. Her agreement meant an awful lot more than I would have expected. . . .

The others were shaking their heads. "A nice sentiment," Valerie said. "But really, hardly any of them would be affected by study. Think what they'd add to our knowledge of primate evolution!"

"Finding one would be a contribution to science," Phil said, glaring at Sarah. And he really believed that, too, I have to give him that.

Armat said slyly, "It wouldn't do any harm to our chances for tenure, either."

"There is that," Phil admitted. "But the real point is, you have to abide by what's *true*. If we found a yeti we'd be obliged to say so, because it was so—no matter how we felt about it. Otherwise you get into suppressing data, altering data, all that kind of thing."

I shook my head. "There are values that are more important than scientific integrity."

And the argument went on from there, mostly repeating points. "You're an idealist," Phil said to me at one point. "You can't *do* zoology without disturbing some subject animals to a certain extent."

"Maybe that's why I got out," I said. And I had to stop myself from going further. How could I say that he was corrupted by the tremendous job pressures in the field to the point where he'd do anything to make a reputation, without the argument getting ugly? Impossible. And Sarah would be upset with me. I only sighed. "What about the subject animal?"

Valerie said indignantly, "They'd trank it, study it, put it back in its environment. Maybe keep one in captivity, where it would live a lot more comfortably than in the wild.''

Total corruption. Even the botanists looked uncomfortable with that one.

"Let's just hope we never find one," Sarah said, frowning. "That way the problem will never come up."

"I don't think we have to worry," Armaat said with his sly smile. "The beast is supposed to be nocturnal."—Because Phil had shown no enthusiasm for night blinds, you see.

"Exactly why I'm starting a high-valley night blind," Phil snapped, tired of Armaat's needling. "Nathan, I'll need you to come along and help set it up."

"And find the way," I said. The others continued to argue, Sarah taking my position, or at least something sympathetic to it; I retired, worried about the figure in the shadows I had seen that day. Phil watched me suspiciously as I left.

So, Phil had his way, and we set up a tiny blind in the upper valley to the west of the one I had made the sighting in. We spent several nights up in an oak tree, and saw a lot of Himalayan spotted deer, and some monkeys at dawn. Phil should have been pleased, but he only got sullen. It occurred to me from some of his mutterings that he had hoped all along to find the yeti; he had come craving that big discovery.

And one night it happened. The moon was gibbous, and thin clouds let most of its light through. About two hours before dawn I was in a doze, and Adrakian elbowed me. Wordlessly he pointed at the far side of a small pool in the stream.

Shadows in shadows, shifting. A streak of moonlight on the water—then, silhouetted above it, an upright figure. For a moment I saw its head clearly, a tall, oddly shaped, furry skull. It looked almost human.

I wanted to shout a warning; instead I shifted my weight on the platform. It creaked very slightly, and instantly the figure was gone.

"Idiot!" Phil whispered. In the moonlight he looked murderous. "I'm going after him!" He jumped out of the tree and pulled what I assumed was a tranquilizer pistol from his down jacket.

"You can't find anything out there at night!" I whispered, but he was gone. I climbed down and took off after him—with what purpose I wasn't sure.

Well, you know the forest at night. Not a chance of seeing animals, or of getting around very easily, either. I have to give it to Adrakian—he was fast, and quiet. I lost him immediately, and after that only heard an occasional snapped branch in the distance. More than an hour passed, and I was only wandering through the trees. The moon had set and the sky was about halfway to dawn light when I returned to the stream.

I rounded a big boulder that stood on the bank and almost ran straight into a yeti coming the other way, as if we were on a busy sidewalk and had veered the same direction to avoid each other. He was a little shorter than me; dark fur covered his body and head, but left his face clear—a patch of pinkish skin that in the dim light looked quite human. His nose was as much human as ape-like—broad, but protruding from his face—like an extension of the occipital crest that ridged his skull fore-to-aft. His mouth was broad and his jaw, under its ruff of fur, very broad—but nothing that took him outside the parameters of human possibility. He had thick eyebrow crests bent high over his eyes, so that he had a look of permanent surprise, like a cat I once owned.

At this moment I'm sure he really was surprised. We both were as still as trees, swaying gently in the wind of our confrontation—but no other movement. I wasn't even breathing. What to do? I noticed he was carrying a small smoothed stick, and there in the fur on his neck were some objects on a cord. His face—tools—ornamentation: a part of me, the part outside the shock of it all, was thinking (I suppose I am still a zoologist at heart), *They aren't just primates, they're hominid.*

As if to confirm this idea, he spoke to me. He hummed briefly; squeaked; sniffed the air hard a few times; lifted his lip (quite a canine was revealed) and whistled, very softly. In his eyes there was a question, so calmly, gently, and intelligently put forth that I could hardly believe I couldn't understand and answer it.

I raised my hand, very slowly, and tried to say "Hello." I know, stupid, but what do you say when you meet a yeti? Anyway, nothing came out but a strangled "Huhn."

He tilted his head to the side inquisitively, and repeated the sound. "Huhn. Huhn. Huhn."

Suddenly he jacked his head forward and stared past me, upstream. He opened his mouth wide and stood there listening. He stared at me, trying to judge me. (I swear I could tell these things!)

Upstream there was a crash of branches, and he took me by the arm and wham, we were atop the stream bank and in the forest. Hoppety-hop through the trees and we were down on our bellies behind a big fallen log, lying side-by-side in squishy wet moss. My arm hurt.

Phil Adrakian appeared down in the streambed, looking considerably the worse for wear. He'd scraped through some brush and torn the nylon of his down jacket in several places, so that fluffy white down wafted away from him as he walked. And he'd fallen in mud somewhere. The yeti squinted hard as he looked at him, clearly mystified by the escaping down.

"Nathan!" Phil cried. "Naaaa—thannn!" He was still filled with energy, it seemed. "I saw one! Nathan, where are you, dammit!" He continued downstream, yelling, and the yeti and I lay there and watched him pass by.

I don't know if I've ever experienced a more satisfying moment.

When he had disappeared around a bend in the stream, the yeti sat up and sprawled back against the log like a tired backpacker. The sun rose, and he only squeaked, whistled, breathed slowly, watched me. What was he thinking? At this point I didn't have a clue. It was even frightening me; I couldn't imagine what might happen next.

His hands, longer and skinnier than human hands, plucked at my clothes. He plucked at his own necklace, pulled it up over his head. What looked like fat seashells were strung on a cord of braided hemp. They were fossils, of shells very like scallop shells—evidence of the Himalayas' days underwater. What did the yeti make of them? No way of knowing. But clearly they were valued, they were part of a culture.

For a long time he just looked at this necklace of his. Then, very carefully, he placed this necklace over my head, around my neck. My skin burned in an instant flush, everything blurred through tears, my throat hurt—I felt like God had just stepped from behind a tree and blessed me, and for no reason, you know? I didn't deserve it.

Without further ado he hopped up and walked off bowleggedly, without a glance back. I was left alone in the morning light with nothing except for the necklace, which hung solidly on my chest. And a sore arm. So it *had* happened, I hadn't dreamed it. I had been blessed.

When I had collected my wits I hiked downstream and back to camp. By the time I got there the necklace was deep in one of my down jacket's padded pockets, and I had a story all worked out.

Phil was already there, chattering to the entire group. "There you are!" he shouted. "Where the hell were you? I was beginning to think they had gotten you!"

"I was looking for you," I said, finding it very easy to feign irritation. "Who's this *they?*"

"The yeti, you fool! You saw him too, don't deny it! And I followed him and saw him again, up the river there."

I shrugged and looked at him dubiously. "I didn't see anything."

"You weren't in the right place! You should have been with me." He turned to the others. "We'll shift the camp up there for a few days, very quietly. It's an unprecedented opportunity!"

Valerie was nodding, Armaat was nodding, even Sarah looked convinced. The botanists looked happy to have some excitement.

I objected that moving that many people upvalley would be difficult, and disruptive to whatever life was up there. And I suggested that what Phil had seen was a bear. But Phil wasn't having it. "What I saw had a big occipital crest, and walked upright. It was a yeti."

So despite my protests, plans were made to move the camp to the high valley and commence an intensive search for the yeti. I didn't know what to do. More protests from me would only make it look suspiciously like I had seen what Phil had seen. I have never been very clever at thinking up subterfuges to balk the plans of others; that's why I left the university in the first place.

I was at my wit's end when the weather came through for me with an early monsoon rainstorm. It gave me an idea. The watershed for our valley was big and steep, and one day's hard rain, which we got, would quickly elevate the level of water in our river. We had to cross the bridge before we could start up the three high valleys, and we had to cross two more to get back out to the airstrip.

So I had my chance. In the middle of the night I snuck out and went down to the bridge. It was the usual village job: piles of big stones on each bank, supporting the three half-logs of the span. The river was already washing the bottom of the stone piles, and some levering with a long branch collapsed the one on our shore. It was a strange feeling to ruin a bridge, one of the most valuable human works in the Himalayas, but I went at it with a will. Quickly the logs slumped and fell away from each other, and the end of the downstream one floated away. It was easy enough to get the other two under way as well. Then I snuck back into camp and into bed.

And that was that. Next day I shook my head regretfully at the discovery, and mentioned that the flooding would be worse downstream. I wondered out loud if we had enough food to last through the monsoon, which of course we didn't; and another hour's hard rain was enough to convince Armaat and Valerie and the botanists that the season was up. Phil's shrill protests lost out, and we broke camp and left the following morning, in a light mist that turned to brilliant wet sunshine by noon. But by then we were well downtrail, and committed.

There you have it, Freds. Are you still reading? I lied to, concealed data from, and eventually scared off the expedition of old colleagues that hired me. But you can see I had to do it. There is a creature up there, intelligent and full of peace. Civilization would destroy it. And that yeti who hid with me—somehow he *knew* I was on their side. Now it's a trust I'd give my life to uphold, really. You can't betray something like that.

On the hike back out, Phil continued to insist he had seen a yeti, and I continued to disparage the idea, until Sarah began to look at me funny. And I regret to report that she and Phil became friendly once again as we neared J—, and the end of our hike out. Maybe she felt sorry for him, maybe she somehow knew that I was acting in bad faith. I wouldn't doubt it; she knew me pretty well. But it was depressing, whatever the reason. And nothing to be done about it. I had to conceal what I knew, and lie, no matter how much it screwed up that friendship, and no matter how much it hurt. So when we arrived at J—, I said goodbye to them all. I was pretty sure that the funding difficulties endemic in zoology would keep them away for a good long time to come, so that was okay. As for Sarah—well—damn it . . . a bit reproachfully I said farewell to her. And I hiked back to Kathmandu rather than fly, to get away from her, and work things off a bit.

The nights on this hike back have been so long that I finally decided to write this, to occupy my mind. I hoped writing it all down would help, too; but the truth is, I've never felt lonelier. It's

been a comfort to imagine you going nuts over my story—I can just
see you jumping around the room and shouting "YOU'RE KID-
DING!" at the top of your lungs, like you used to. I hope to fill
you in on any missing details when I see you in person this fall in
Kathmandu. Til then—

your friend, Nathan

III

Well, blow my mind. When I finished reading that letter all I could
say was "Wow." I went back to the beginning and started to
re-read the whole thing, but quickly skipped ahead to the good
parts. A meeting with the famed Abominable Snowman! What an
event! Of course all this Nathan guy had managed to get out was
"Huhn." But the circumstances were unusual, and I suppose he
did his best.

I've always wanted to meet a yeti myself. Countless mornings in
the Himal I've gotten up in the light before dawn and wandered out
to take a leak and see what the day was going to be like, and almost
every time, especially in the high forests, I've looked around and
wondered if that twitch at the corner of my sleep-crusted eye wasn't
something abominable, *moving*.

It never had been, so far as I know. And I found myself a bit
envious of this Nathan and his tremendous luck. Why had this yeti,
member of the shyest race in Central Asia, been so relaxed with
him? It was a mystery to consider as I went about in the next few
days, doing my business. And I wished I could do more than that,
somehow. I checked the Star's register to look for both Nathan and
George Fredericks, and found Nathan's perfect little signature back
in mid-June, but no sign of George, or Freds, as Nathan called
him. The letter implied they would both be around this fall, but
where?

Then I had to ship some Tibetan carpets to the States, and my
company wanted me to clear three "videotreks" with the Ministry
of Tourism, at the same time that Central Immigration decided I
had been in the country long enough; and dealing with these
matters, in the city where mailing a letter can take you all day,
made me busy indeed. I almost forgot about it.

But when I came into the Star late one sunny blue afternoon and saw that some guy had gone berserk at the mail rack, had taken it down and scattered the poor paper corpses all over the first flight of stairs, I had a feeling I might know what the problem was. I was startled, maybe even a little guilty-feeling, but not at all displeased. I squashed the little pang of guilt and stepped past the two clerks, who were protesting in rapid Nepali. "Can I help you find something?" I said to the distraught person who had wreaked the havoc.

He straightened up and looked me straight in the eye. Straight-shooter, all the way. "I'm looking for a friend of mine who usually stays here." He wasn't panicked yet, but he was close. "The clerks say he hasn't been here in a year, but I sent him a letter this summer, and it's gone."

Contact! Without batting an eye I said, "Maybe he dropped by and picked it up without checking in."

He winced like I'd stuck a knife in him. He looked about like what I had expected from his epic: tall, upright, dark-haired. He had a beard as thick and fine as fur, neatly trimmed away from the neck and below the eyes—just about a perfect beard, in fact. That beard and a jacket with leather elbows would have got him tenure at any university in America.

But now he was seriously distraught, though he was trying not to show it. "I don't know how I'm going to find him, then. . . ."

"Are you sure he's in Kathmandu?"

"He's supposed to be. He's joining a big climb in two weeks. But he always stays here!"

"Sometimes it's full. Maybe he had to go somewhere else."

"Yeah, that's true." Suddenly he came out of his distraction enough to notice he was talking to me, and his clear, grey-green eyes narrowed as he examined me.

"George Fergusson," I said, and stuck out my hand. He tried to crush it, but I resisted just in time.

"My name's Nathan Howe. Funny about yours," he said without a smile. "I'm looking for a George Fredericks."

"Is that right! What a coincidence." I started picking up all the Star's bent mail. "Well, maybe I can help you. I've had to find friends in Kathmandu before—it's not easy, but it can be done."

"Yeah?" It was like I'd thrown him a lifebuoy; what was his problem?

"Sure. If he's going on a climb he's had to go to Central Immigration to buy the permits for it. And on the permits you have to write down your local address. I've spent too many hours at C.I., and have some friends there. If we slip them a couple hundred rupees baksheesh they'll look it up for us."

"Fantastic!" Now he was Hope Personified, actually quivering with it. "Can we go now?" I saw that his heartthrob, the girlfriend of The Unscrupulous One, had had him pegged; he was an idealist, and his ideas shone through him like the mantle of a Coleman lantern gleaming through the glass. Only a blind woman wouldn't have been able to tell how he felt about her; I wondered how this Sarah had felt about him.

I shook my head. "It's past two—closed for the day." We got the rack back on the wall, and the clerks returned to the front desk. "But there's a couple other things we can try, if you want." Nathan nodded, stuffing mail as he watched me. "Whenever I try to check in here and it's full, I just go next door. We could look there."

"Okay," said Nathan, completely fired up. "Let's go."

So we walked out of the Star and turned right to investigate at the Lodge Pheasant—or Lodge Pleasant—the sign is ambiguous on that point.

Sure enough, George Fredericks had been staying there. Checked out that very morning, in fact. "Oh my God no," Nathan cried, as if the guy had just died. Panic time was really getting close.

"Yes," the clerk said brightly, pleased to have found the name in his thick book. "He is go on trek."

"But he's not due to leave here for two weeks!" Nathan protested.

"He's probably off on his own first," I said. "Or with friends."

That was it for Nathan. Panic, despair; he had to go sit down. I thought about it. "If he was flying out, I heard all of RNAC's flights to the mountains were canceled today. So maybe he came back in and went to dinner. Does he know Kathmandu well?"

Nathan nodded glumly. "As well as anybody."

"Let's try the Old Vienna Inn, then."

IV

In the blue of early evening Thamel was jumping as usual. Lights snapped on in the storefronts that opened on the street, and people were milling about. Big Land Rovers and little Toyota taxis forged through the crowd abusing their horns; cows in the street chewed their cud and stared at it all with expressions of faint surprise, as if they'd been magically zipped out of a pasture just seconds before.

Nathan and I walked single file against the store fronts, dodging bikes and jumping over the frequent puddles. We passed carpet shops, climbing outfitters, restaurants, used book stores, trekking agents, hotels, and souvenir stands, and as we made our way we turned down a hundred offers from the young men of the street: "Change money?" "No." "Smoke dope?" "No." "Buy a nice carpet?" "No." "Good hash!" "No." "Change money?" "No." Long ago I had simplified walking in the neighborhood, and just said "No" to everyone I passed. "No, no, no, no, no, no, no." Nathan had a different method that seemed to work just as well—or better, since the hustlers never seemed to think I was negative enough; he would nod politely with that straight-shooter look, and say "No, thank you," and leave them open-mouthed in the street.

We passed K.C.'s, threaded our way through "Times Square," a crooked intersection with a perpetual traffic jam, and started down the street that led out of Thamel into the rest of Kathmandu. Two merchants stood in the doorway of their shop, singing along with a cassette of Pink Floyd's *The Wall:* "We don't need no education, we don't need no thought control." I almost got run over by a bike. Where the street widened and the paving began, I pushed a black goat to one side, and we leaped over a giant puddle into a tunnel-like hall that penetrated one of the ramshackle streetside buildings. Up the hall, turn left up scuzzy concrete stairs. "Have you been here before?" I asked Nathan.

"No, I always go to K.C.'s or Red Square." He looked as though he wasn't sorry, either.

At the top of the stairs we opened the door, and stepped into the Austro-Hungarian Empire. White tablecloths, paneled partitions between deep booths, red wallpaper in a fleur-de-lis pattern, plush upholstery, tasteful kitschy lamps hanging over every table; and suffusing the air, the steamy pungent smell of sauerkraut and goulash. Strauss waltzes on the box. Except for the faint honking from the street below, it was absolutely the real item.

"My Lord," Nathan said, "How did they get *this* here?"

"It's mostly her doing." The owner and resident culinary genius, a big plump friendly woman, came over and greeted me in stiff Germanic English.

"Hello, Eva. We're looking for a friend—" But then Nathan was already past us, and rushing down toward a small booth in the back.

"I think we find him," Eva said with a smile.

By the time I got to the table Nathan was pumping the arm of a short, long-haired blond guy in his late thirties, slapping his back, babbling with relief—overwhelmed with relief, by the look of it. "Freds, thank God I found you!"

"Good to see you too, bud! Pretty lucky, actually—I was gonna split with some Brits for the hills this morning, but old Reliability Negative Airline bombed out again." Freds had a faint Southern or country accent, and talked as fast as anyone I'd ever heard, sometimes faster.

"I know," Nathan said. He looked up and saw me. "Actually, my new friend here figured it out. George Fergusson, this is George Fredericks."

We shook hands. "Nice name!" George said. "Call me Freds, everyone does." We slid in around his table while Freds explained that the friends he was going to go climbing with were finding them rooms. "So what are you up to, Nathan? I didn't even know you were in Nepal. I thought you were back in the States working, saving wildlife refuges or something."

"I was," Nathan said, and his grim do-or-die expression returned. "But I had to come back. Listen—you didn't get my letter?"

"No, did you write me?" said Freds.

Nathan stared right at me, and I looked as innocent as I could. "I'm going to have to take you into my confidence," he said to me. "I don't know you very well, but you've been a big help today, and the way things are I can't really be. . . ."

"Fastidious?"

"No no no—I can't be over-cautious, you see. I tend to be over-cautious, as Freds will tell you. But I need help, now." And he was dead serious.

"Just giving you a hard time," I reassured him, trying to look trustworthy, loyal, and all that; difficult, given the big grin on Freds' face.

"Well, here goes," Nathan said, speaking to both of us. "I've got to tell you what happened to me on the expedition I helped in the spring. It still isn't easy to talk about, but . . ."

And ducking his head, leaning forward, lowering his voice, he told us the tale I had read about in his lost letter. Freds and I leaned forward as well, so that our heads practically knocked over the table. I did all I could to indicate my shocked surprise at the high points of the story, but I didn't have to worry about that too much, because Freds supplied all the amazement necessary. "You're kidding," he'd say. "No. Incredible. I can't believe it. It just *stood there? You're kidding!* In-fucking-credible, man! I can't *believe* it! How great! What?—oh, no! You didn't!" And when Nathan told about the yeti giving him the necklace, sure enough, just as Nathan had predicted, Freds jumped up out of the booth and leaned back in and shouted, "YOU'RE KIDDING!!"

"Shh!" Nathan hissed, putting his face down on the tablecloth. "No! Get back down here, Freds! Please!"

So he sat down and Nathan went on, to the same sort of response ("You tore the fucking BRIDGE DOWN!?!" *"SHHHH!!"*); and when he was done we all leaned back in the booth, exhausted. Slowly the other customers stopped staring at us. I cleared my throat: "But then today, you um, you indicated that there was still a problem, or some new problem . . . ?"

Nathan nodded, lips pursed. "Adrakian went back and got money from a rich old guy in the States whose hobby used to be *big game hunting*. J. Reeves Fitzgerald. Now he keeps a kind of a photo zoo on a big estate. He came over here with Adrakian, and Valerie, and Sarah too even, and they went right back up to the camp we had in the spring. I found out about it from Armaat and came here quick as I could. Right after I arrived, they checked into a suite at the Sheraton. A bellboy told me they came in a Land Rover with its windows draped, and he saw someone funny hustled upstairs, and now they're locked in that suite like it's a fort. And I'm afraid—I think—I think they've *got one up there.*"

Freds and I looked at each other. "How long ago was this?" I asked.

"Just two days ago! I've been hunting for Freds ever since, I didn't know what else to do!"

Freds said, "What about that Sarah? Is she still with them?"

"Yes," Nathan grated, looking at the table. "I can't believe it, but she is." He shook his head. "If they're hiding a yeti up there—if they've got one—then, well, it's all over for the yeti. It'll just be a disaster for them."

I supposed that was true enough. Freds was nodding automatically, agreeing just because Nathan had said it. "It would be a zoo up there, ha ha."

"So you'll help?" Nathan asked.

"Of course, man! Naturally!" Freds looked surprised Nathan would even ask.

"I'd like to," I said. And that was the truth, too. The guy brought it out in you, somehow.

"Thanks," said Nathan. He looked very relieved. "But what about this climb you were going on, Freds?"

"No prob. I was a late add-on anyway, just for fun. They'll be fine. I was beginning to wonder about going with them this time anyway. They got themselves a Trivial Pursuit game for this climb, to keep them from going bonkers in their tents. We tried it out yesterday and you know I'm real good at Trivial Pursuit, except for the history, literature, and entertainment categories, but this here game was the *British* version. So we get a buzz on and start to playing and suddenly I'm part of a Monty Python routine, I mean they just don't play it the same! You know how when we play it and you don't know the answer everyone says Ha, too bad—but here I take my turn and go for sports and leisure which is my natural forté, and they pull the card and ask me, 'Who was it bowled three hundred and sixty-five consecutive sticky wickets at the West Indian cricket match of 1956,' or whatever, and they liked to *died* they were laughing so hard. They jumped up and danced around me and *howled*. 'Yew don't know, dew yew! Yew don't have the slightest fookin' *idear* who bowled those sticky wickets, dew yew!' It was really hard to concentrate on my answer. So. Going with them this time might have been a mistake anyway. Better to stay here and help you."

Nathan and I could only agree.

Then Eva came by with our food, which we had ordered after Nathan's epic. The amazing thing about the Old Vienna Inn is that the food is even better than the decor. It would be good anywhere, and in Kathmandu, where almost everything tastes a little like cardboard, it's simply unbelievable. "Look at this steak!" Freds said. "Where the hell do they get the meat?"

"Didn't you ever wonder how they keep the street cow population under control?" I asked.

Freds liked that. "I can just imagine them sneaking one of them big honkers into the back here. Wham!"

Nathan began to prod dubiously at his snitzel. And then, over a perfect meal, we discussed the problem facing us. As usual in situations like this, I had a plan.

V

I have never known baksheesh to fail in Kathmandu, but that week at the Everest Sheraton International the employees were bottled up tight. They didn't even want to *hear* anything out of the ordinary, much less be a part of it, no matter the gain. Something was up, and I began to suspect that J. Reeves Fitzgerald had a very big bankroll indeed. So Plan A for getting into Adrakian's room was foiled, and I retired to the hotel bar, where Nathan was hidden in a corner booth, suitably disguised in sunglasses and an Australian outback hat. He didn't like my news.

The Everest Sheraton International is not exactly like Sheratons elsewhere, but it is about the quality of your average Holiday Inn, which makes it five star in Kathmandu, and just about as incongruous as the Old Vienna. The bar looked like an airport bar, and there was a casino in the room next to us, which clearly, to judge by the gales of laughter coming from it, no one could take seriously. Nathan and I sat and nursed our drinks and waited for Freds, who was casing the outside of the hotel.

Suddenly Nathan clutched my forearm. "Don't look!"

"Okay."

"Oh, my God, they must have hired a whole bunch of private security cops. Jeez, look at those guys. No, don't look!"

Unobtrusively I glanced at the group entering the bar. Identical boots, identical jackets, with little bulges under the arm; clean-cut looks, upright, almost military carriage. . . They looked a little bit like Nathan, to tell the truth, but without the beard. "Hmm," I said. Definitely not your ordinary tourists. Fitzgerald's bankroll must have been *very* big.

Then Freds came winging into the bar and slid into our booth. "Problems, man."

"Shh!" Nathan said. "See those guys over there?"

"I know," said Freds. "They're Secret Service agents."

"They're *what?*" Nathan and I said in unison.

"Secret Service agents."

"Now *don't* tell me this Fitzgerald is a close friend of Reagan's," I began, but Freds was shaking his head and grinning.

"No. They're here with Jimmy and Rosalynn Carter. Haven't you heard?"

Nathan shook his head, but I had a sudden sinking feeling as I remembered a rumor of a few weeks back. "He wanted to see Everest . . . ?"

"That's right. I met them all up in Namche a week ago, actually. But now they're back, and staying here."

"Oh, my god," Nathan said. "Secret Service men, *here.*"

"They're nice guys, actually," Freds said. "We talked to them a lot in Namche. Real straight, of course—real straight—but nice. They told us what was happening in the World Series, and what their jobs were like, and everything. Of course sometimes we asked them questions about the Carters and they just looked around like no one had said anything, which was weird, but mostly they were real normal."

"And *what* are they doing here?" I said, still not quite able to believe it.

"Well, Jimmy wanted to go see Everest. So they all helicoptered into Namche just as if there was no such thing as altitude sickness, and took off for Everest! I was talking just now with one of the agents I met up there, and he told me how it came out. Rosalynn got to fifteen thousand feet and turned back, but Jimmy kept on trudging. Here he's got all these young tough Secret Service guys to protect him, you know, but they started to get sick, and every day they were helicoptering out a number of them because of altitude sickness, pneumonia, whatever, until there were hardly any left! He hiked his whole crew right into the ground! What is he, in his sixties? And here all these young agents were dropping like flies while he motored right on up to Kala Pattar, and Everest Base Camp too. I love it!"

"That's great," I said. "I'm happy for him. But now they're back."

"Yeah, they're doing the Kathmandu culture scene for a bit."

"That's too bad."

"Ah! No luck getting a key to the yeti's room, is that it?"

"*Shhhhh,*" Nathan hissed.

"Sorry, I forgot. Well, we'll just have to think of something else, eh? The Carters are going to be here another week."

"The windows?" I asked.

Freds shook his head. "I could cimb up to them no problem, but the ones to their room overlook the garden and it wouldn't be all that private."

"God, this is bad," Nathan said, and downed his Scotch. "Phil could decide to reveal the—what he's got, at a press conference while the Carters are here. Perfect way to get enhanced publicity fast—that would be just like him."

We sat and thought about it for a couple of drinks.

"You know, Nathan," I said slowly, "there's an angle we haven't discussed yet, that you'd have to take the lead in."

"What's that?"

"Sarah."

"What? Oh, no. No. I couldn't. I can't talk to her, really. It just—well, I just don't want to."

"But why?"

"She wouldn't care what I said." He looked down at his glass and swirled the contents nervously. His voice turned bitter: "She'd probably just tell Phil we were here, and then we'd *really* be in trouble."

"Oh, I don't know. I don't think she's the kind of person to do that, do you, Freds?"

"I don't know," Freds said, surprised. "I never met her."

"She couldn't be, surely." And I kept after him for the rest of our stay, figuring it was our best chance at that point. But Nathan was stubborn about it, and still hadn't budged when he insisted we leave.

So we paid the bill and took off. But we were crossing the foyer, and near the broad set of front doors, when Nathan suddenly stopped in his tracks. A tall, good-looking woman with large owl-eye glasses had just walked in. Nathan was stuck in place. I guessed who the woman must be, and nudged him. "Remember what's at stake."

A good point to make. He took a deep breath. And as the woman was about to pass us, he whipped off his hat and shades. "Sarah!"

The woman jumped back. "Nathan! My God! What—what are you doing here!"

Darkly: "You know why I'm here, Sarah." He drew himself up even straighter than usual, and glared at her. If she'd been convicted of murdering his mother I don't think he could have looked more accusing.

"What—?" Her voice quit on her.

Nathan's lip curled disdainfully. I thought he was kind of overdoing the laying-on-of-guilt trip, and I was even thinking of stepping in and trying a less confrontational approach, but then right in the middle of the next sentence his voice twisted with real pain: "I didn't think you'd be capable of this, Sarah."

With her light brown hair, bangs, and big glasses, she had a schoolgirlish look. Now that schoolgirl was hurting; her lip quivered, she blinked rapidly; "I—I—" And then her face crumpled, and with a little cry she tottered toward Nathan and collapsed against his broad shoulder. He patted her head, looking flabbergasted.

"Oh, Nathan," she said miserably, sniffing. "It's so *awful*. . . ."

"It's all right," he said, stiff as a board. "I know."

The two of them communed for a while. I cleared my throat. "Why don't we go somewhere else and have a drink," I suggested, feeling that things were looking up a trifle.

VI

We went to the Hotel Annapurna coffee shop, and there Sarah confirmed all of Nathan's worst fears. "They've got him in there locked in the *bathroom*." Apparently the yeti was eating less and less, and Valerie Budge was urging Mr. Fitzgerald to take him out to the city's funky little zoo immediately, but Fitzgerald was flying in a group of science and nature writers so he could hold a press conference, the next day or the day after that, and he and Phil wanted to wait. They were hoping for the Carters' presence at the unveiling, as Freds called it, but they couldn't be sure about that yet.

Freds and I asked Sarah questions about the set-up at the hotel. Apparently Phil, Valerie Budge, and Fitzgerald were taking turns in a continuous watch on the bathroom. How did they feed him? How docile was he? Question, answer, question, answer. After her initial breakdown, Sarah proved to be a tough and sensible character. Nathan, on the other hand, spent the time repeating, "We've got to get him out of there, we've got to do it soon, it'll be the *end* of him." Sarah's hand on his just fueled the flame. "We'll just have to *rescue* him."

"I know, Nathan," I said, trying to think. "We know that already." A plan was beginning to fall into place in my mind. "Sarah, you've got a key to the room?" She nodded. "Okay, let's go."

"What, now?" Nathan cried.

"Sure! We're in a hurry, right? They're going to notice Sarah is gone, and these reporters are going to arrive. . . . And we've got to get some stuff together, first."

VII

When we returned to the Sheraton it was late afternoon. Freds and I were on rented bikes, and Nathan and Sarah followed in a taxi. We made sure our cabbie understood that we wanted him to wait for us out front; then Freds and I went inside, gave the all-clear to Nathan and Sarah, and headed straight for the lobby phones. Nathan and Sarah went to the front desk and checked into a room; we needed them out of sight for a while.

I called all the rooms on the top floor of the hotel (the fourth), and sure enough half of them were occupied by Americans. I explained that I was J. Reeves Fitzgerald, assistant to the Carters, who were fellow guests in the hotel. They all knew about the Carters. I explained that the Carters were hosting a small reception for the Americans at the hotel, and we hoped that they would join us in the casino bar when it was convenient—the Carters would be down in an hour or so. They were all delighted at the invitation (except for one surly Republican that I had to cut off), and they promised to be down shortly.

The last call got Phil Adrakian, in room 355; I identified myself as Lionel Hodding. It went as well as the others; if anything Adrakian was even more enthusiastic. "We'll be right down, thanks—we have a reciprocal invitation to make, actually." I was prejudiced, but he did sound like a pain. Nathan's epithet, *theorist*, didn't really make it for me; I preferred something along the lines of, say, *asshole*.

"Fine. Look forward to seeing all your party, of course."

Freds and I waited in the bar and watched the elevators, Americans in their safari best began to pile out and head for the casino; you wouldn't have thought there was that much polyester in all Kathmandu, but I guess it travels well.

Two men and a plump woman came down the broad stairs beside the elevator. "Them?" Freds asked. I nodded; they fitted Sarah's descriptions exactly. Phil Adrakian was shortish, slim, and good-looking in a California Golden Boy kind of way. Valerie Budge wore glasses and had a lot of curly hair pulled up; somehow she looked intellectual where Sarah only looked studious. The money man, J. Reeves Fitzgerald, was sixtyish and very fit-looking, though he did smoke a cigar. He wore a safari jacket with eight pockets on it. Adrakian was arguing a point with him as they crossed the foyer to the casino bar, and I heard him say, *"better than a press conference."*

I had a final inspiration and returned to the phones. I asked the hotel operator for Jimmy Carter, and got connected; but the phone was answered by a flat Midwestern voice, very businesslike indeed. "Hello?"

"Hello, is this the Carters' suite?"

"May I ask who's speaking?"

"This is J. Reeves Fitzgerald. I'd like you to inform the Carters that the Americans in the Sheraton have organized a reception for them in the hotel's casino bar, for this afternoon."

". . . I'm not sure their scheduling will allow them to attend."

"I understand. But if you'd just let them know."

"Of course."

Back to Freds, where I downed a Star beer in two gulps. "Well," I said, *"something* should happen. Let's get up there."

VIII

I gave Nathan and Sarah a buzz and they joined us at the door of Room 355. Sarah let us in. Inside was a big suite—style, generic Holiday Inn—it could have been in any city on Earth. Except that there was a slight smell of wet fur.

Sarah went to the bathroom door, unlocked it. There was a noise inside. Nathan, Freds, and I shifted around behind her uncomfortably. She opened the door. There was a movement, and there he was, standing before us. I found myself staring into the eyes of the yeti.

In the Kathmandu tourist scene, there are calendars, postcards, and embroidered T-shirts with a drawing of a yeti on them. It's always the same drawing, which I could never understand; why should everyone agree to use the same guess? It annoyed me: a little furball thing with his back to you, looking over his shoulder with a standard monkey face, and displaying the bottom of one big bare foot.

I'm happy to report that the real yeti didn't look anything like that. Oh he was furry, all right, but he was about Freds' height, and had a distinctly humanoid face, surrounded by a beard-like ruff of matted reddish fur. He looked a little like Lincoln—a short and very ugly Lincoln, sure, with a squashed nose and rather prominent eyebrow ridges—but the resemblance was there. I was relieved to see how human his face looked; my plan depended on it, and I was glad Nathan hadn't exaggerated in his description. The only feature that really looked unusual was his occipital crest, a ridge of bone and muscle that ran fore-and-aft over the top of his head, like his skull itself had a Mohawk haircut.

Well, we were all standing there like a statue called "People Meet Yeti," when Freds decided to break the ice; he stepped forward and offered the guy a hand. "Namaste!" he said.

"No, no—" Nathan brushed by him and held out the necklace of fossil shells that he had been given in the spring.

"Is this the same one?" I croaked, momentarily at a loss. Because up until that bathroom door opened, part of me hadn't really believed in it all.

"I think so."

The yeti reached out and touched the necklace and Nathan's hand. Statue time again. Then the yeti stepped forward and touched Nathan's face with his long, furry hand. He whistled something quiet. Nathan was quivering; there were tears in Sarah's eyes. I was impressed myself. Freds said, "He looks kind of like Buddha, don't you think? He doesn't have the belly, but those eyes, man. Buddha to the max."

We got to work. I opened my pack and got out baggy overalls, a yellow "Free Tibet" T-shirt, and a large anorak. Nathan was taking his shirt off and putting it back on to show the yeti what we had in mind.

Slowly, carefully, gently, with many a soft-spoken sound and slow gesture, we got the yeti into the clothes. The T-shirt was the hardest part; he squeaked a little when we pulled it over his head. The anorak was zippered, luckily. With every move I made I said "Namaste, blessed sir, namaste."

The hands and feet were a problem. His hands were strange, fingers skinny and almost twice as long as mine, and pretty hairy as well; but wearing mittens in the daytime in Kathmandu was almost worse. I suspended judgment on them and turned to his feet. This was the only area of the tourist drawing that was close to correct; his feet were huge, furry, and just about square. He had a big toe like a very fat thumb. The boots I had brought, biggest I could find in a hurry, weren't wide enough. Eventually I put him in Tibetan wool socks and Birkenstock sandals, modified by a penknife to let the big toe hang over the side.

Lastly I put my blue Dodgers cap on his head. The cap concealed the occipital crest perfectly, and the bill did a lot to obscure his rather low forehead and prominent eyebrows. I topped everything off with a pair of mirrored wraparound sunglasses. "Hey, neat," Freds remarked. Also a Sherpa necklace, made of five pieces of coral and three giant chunks of rough turquoise, strung on black cord. Principle of distraction, you know.

All this time Sarah and Nathan were ransacking the drawers and luggage, stealing all the camera film and notebooks and whatever else might have contained evidence of the yeti. And throughout it all the yeti stood there, calm and attentive: watching Nathan, sticking his hand down a sleeve like a millionaire with his valet, stepping carefully into the Birkenstocks, adjusting the bill of the baseball cap, everything. I was really impressed, and so was Freds. "He really is like Buddha, isn't he?" I thought the physical resemblance was a bit muted at this point, but his attitude couldn't have been more mellow if he'd been the Gautama himself.

When Nathan and Sarah were done searching they looked up at our handiwork. "*God* he looks weird," Sarah said.

Nathan just sat on the bed and put his head in his hands. "It'll never work," he said. "Never."

"Sure it will!" Freds exclaimed, zipping the anorak up a little further. "You see people on Freak Street looking like this all the time! Man, when I went to school I played football with a whole *team* of guys that looked just like him! Fact is, in my state he could run for *Senator*—"

"Whoah, whoah," I said. "No time to waste, here. Give me the scissors and brush, I still have to do his hair." I tried brushing it over his ears with little success, then gave him a trim in back. One trip, I was thinking, just one short walk down to a taxi. And in pretty dark halls. "Is it even on both sides?"

"For God's sake, George, let's go!" Nathan was getting antsy, and we had been a while. We gathered our belongings, filled the packs, and tugged old Buddha out into the hall.

IX

I have always prided myself on my sense of timing. Many's the time I've surprised myself by how perfectly I've managed to be in the right place at the right time; it goes beyond all conscious calculation, into deep mystic communion with the cycles of the cosmos, etc., etc. But apparently in this matter I was teamed up with people whose sense of timing was so cosmically awful that mine was completely swamped. That's the only way I can explain it.

Because there we were, escorting a yeti down the hallway of the Everest Sheraton International, and we were walking casually along, the yeti kind of bowlegged—very bowlegged—and long-armed, too—so that I kept worrying he might drop to all fours—but otherwise, passably normal. Just an ordinary group of tourists in Nepal. We decided on the stairs, to avoid any awkward elevator crowds, and stepped through the swinging doors into the stairwell. And there coming down the stairs toward us were Jimmy Carter, Rosalynn Carter, and five Secret Service men.

"Well!" Freds exclaimed. "Damned if it isn't Jimmy Carter! And Rosalynn too!"

I suppose that was the best way to play it, not that Freds was doing anything but being natural. I don't know if the Carters were on their way to something else, or if they were actually coming down to attend my reception; if the latter, then my last-minute inspiration to invite them had been a really bad one. In any case, there they were, and they stopped on the landing. We stopped on the landing. The Secret Service men, observing us closely, stopped on the landing.

What to do? Jimmy gave us his famous smile, and it might as well have been the cover of *Time* magazine, it was such a familiar sight; just the same. Only not quite. Not exactly. His face was older, naturally, but also it had the look of someone who had survived a serious illness, or a great natural disaster. It looked like he had been through the fire, and come back into the world knowing more than most people about what the fire was. It was a good face, it showed what a man could endure. And he was relaxed; this kind of interruption was part of daily life, part of the job he had volunteered for nine years before.

I was anything but relaxed. In fact, as the Secret Service men did their hawk routine on Buddha, their gazes locked, I could feel my heart stop, and I had to give my torso a little twist to get it started up again. Nathan had stopped breathing from the moment he saw Carter, and he was turning white above the sharp line of his beard. It was getting worse by the second when Freds stepped forward and extended a hand. "Hey, Mr. Carter, namaste! We're happy to meet you."

"Hi, how are y'all." More of the famous smile. "Where are y'all from?"

And we answered. "Arkansas," "California," "M-Massachusetts," "Oregon," and at each one he smiled and nodded with recognition and pleasure, and Rosalynn smiled and said "Hello, hello," with that faint look I had seen before during the Presidential years, that seemed to say she would have been just as happy somewhere else, and we all shuffled around so that we could all shake hands with Jimmy—until it was Buddha's turn.

"This is our guide, B-Badim Badur," I said. "He doesn't speak any English."

"I understand," Jimmy said. And he took Buddha's hand and pumped it up and down.

Now, I had opted to leave Buddha barehanded, a decision I began to seriously regret. Here we had a man who had shaken at least a million hands in his life, maybe ten million; nobody in the world could have been more of an expert at it. And as soon as he grasped Buddha's long skinny hand, he knew that something was different. This wasn't like any of the millions of other hands he had shaken before. A couple of furrows joined the network of fine wrinkles around his eyes, and he looked closer at Buddha's peculiar get-up. I could feel the sweat popping out and beading on my forehead. "Um, Badim's a bit shy," I was saying, when suddenly the yeti squeaked.

"Naa-maas-tayy," it said, in a hoarse, whispery voice.

"Namaste!" Jimmy replied, grinning the famous grin.

And that, folks, was the first recorded conversation between yeti and human.

Of course Buddha had only been trying to help—I'm sure of that, given what happened later—but despite all we did to conceal it, his speech had obviously surprised us pretty severely. As a result the Secret Service guys were about to go cross-eyed checking us out, Buddha in particular.

"Let's let these folks get on with things," I said shakily, and took Buddha by the arm. "Nice to meet you," I said to the Carters. We all hung there for a moment. It didn't seem polite to precede the ex-President of the United States down a flight of stairs, but the Secret Service men damn well didn't want us *following* them down either; so finally I took the lead, with Buddha by the arm, and I held onto him tight as we descended.

We reached the foyer without incident. Sarah conversed brightly with the Secret Service men who were right behind us, and she distracted their attention very successfully, I thought. It appeared we would escape the situation without further difficulties, when the doors to the casino bar swung back, and Phil Adrakian, J. Reeves Fitzgerald, and Valerie Budge walked out. (Timing, anyone?)

Adrakian took in the situation at a glance. "They're kidnapping him!" he yelled, "Hey! *Kidnapping!*"

Well, you might just as well have put jumper cables on those Secret Service agents. After all, it's kind of a question why anyone would want to assassinate an ex-president, but as a hostage for ransom or whatnot, you've got a prime target. They moved like mongooses to surround the Carters and back them off, pistols instantly in hands. Freds and I were trying to back Buddha out the front doors without actually moving our legs; we weren't making much progress, and I don't doubt we could've gotten shot for our efforts, if it weren't for Sarah. She jumped right out in front of the charging Adrakian and blocked him off.

"You're the kidnapper, you liar," she cried, and slapped him in the face so hard he staggered. *"Help!"* she demanded of the Secret Service guys, blushing bright red and shoving Valerie Budge back into Fitzgerald. She looked so tousled and embattled and beautiful that the agents were confused; the situation wasn't at all clear. Freds, Buddha, and I bumped out the front door and ran for it.

Our taxi was gone. "Shit," I said. No time to think—"The bikes?" Freds asked.

"Yep." No other choice—we ran around the side of the building and unlocked our two bikes. I got on mine and Freds helped Buddha onto the little square rack over the back wheel. People around front were shouting, and I thought I heard Adrakian among them. Freds gave me a push from behind and we were off; I stood to pump up some speed, and we wavered side to side precariously.

I headed up the road to the north. It was just wider than one lane, half-paved and half-dirt. Bike and car traffic on it was heavy, as usual, and between dodging vehicles and potholes, looking back for pursuers, and keeping the bike from tipping under Buddha's shifting weight, I was kept pretty busy.

The bike was a standard Kathmandu rental, Hero Jet by brand name: heavy frame, thick tires, low handlebars, one speed. It braked when you pedaled backwards, and had one handbrake, and it had a big loud bell, which is a crucial piece of equipment. This bike wasn't a bad specimen either, in that the handbrake worked and the handlebars weren't loose and the seat wasn't putting a spring through my ass. But the truth is, the Hero Jet is a solo vehicle. And Buddha was no lightweight. He was built like a cat, dense and compact, and I bet he weighed over two hundred pounds. With him on back, the rear tire was squashed flat—there was about an eighth of an inch clearance between rim and ground, and every time I misnavigated a pothole there was an ugly *thump,* as we bottomed out.

So we weren't breaking any speed records, and when we turned left on Dilli Bazar Freds shouted from behind. "They're after us! See, there's that Adrakian and some others in a taxi!"

Sure enough, back a couple hundred yards was Phil Adrakian, hanging out the side window of a little white Toyota taxi, screaming at us. We pedaled over the Dhobi Khola bridge and shot by the Central Immigration building before I could think of anything to yell that might have brought the crowd there into the street. "Freds!" I said, panting. "Make a diversion! Tie up traffic!"

"Right on." Without a pause he braked to a halt in the middle of the road, jumped off and threw his Hero Jet to the pavement. The three-wheeled motorcab behind him ran over it before the driver could stop. Freds screamed abuse, he pulled the bike out and slung it under a Datsun going the other way, which crunched it and screeched to a halt. More abuse from Freds, who ran around pulling the drivers from their vehicles, shouting at them with all the Nepli he knew: "Chiso howa!" (Cold wind.) "Tato pani!" (Hot water.) "Rhamrao dihn!" (Nice day.)

I only caught glimpses of this as I biked away, but I saw he had bought a little time and I concentrated on negotiating the traffic. Dilli Bazar is one of the most congested streets in Kathmandu, which is really saying a lot.

The two narrow lanes are fronted by three-story buildings containing grocery markets and fabric wholesalers, which open directly onto the street and use it for cash register lines and so on, despite the fact that it's a major truck route.

Add to that the usual number of dogs, goats, chickens, taxis, young schoolgirls walking three abreast with their arms linked, pedicabs with five-foot-tall operators pedaling whole families along at two miles an hour, and the occasional wandering sacred cow, and you can see the extent of the problem. Not only that, but the potholes are fierce—some could be mistaken for open manholes.

And the hills! I was doing all right until that point, weaving through the crowd and ringing my bell to the point of thumb cramp. But then Buddha shook my arm and I looked back and saw that Adrakian had somehow gotten past Freds and hired another taxi, and he was trailing us again, stuck behind a colorfully painted bus some distance back. And we were starting up the first of three fairly steep up-and-downs that Dilli Bazar makes before it reaches the city center.

Hero Jets are not made for hills. The city residents get off theirs and walk them up inclines like that one, and only Westerners, still in a hurry even in Nepal, stay on and grind up the slopes. I was certainly a Westerner in a hurry that day, and I stood up and started pumping away. But it was heavy going, especially after I had to brake to a dead stop to avoid an old man blowing his nose with his finger. Adrakian's taxi had rounded the bus, in an explosion of honks, and he was gaining on us fast. I sat back on the seat, huffing and puffing, legs like big blocks of wood, and it was looking like I'd have to find a diplomatic solution to the problem, when suddenly both my feet were kicked forward off the pedals; we surged forward, just missing a pedicab.

Buddha had taken over. He was holding onto the seat with both hands, and pedaling from behind. I had seen tall Westerners ride their rental bikes like that before, to keep from smashing their knees into the handlebars on every upswing. But you can't get much downthrust from back there, and you didn't ever see them doing that while biking uphill. For Buddha, this was not a problem. I mean this guy was *strong*. He pumped away so hard that the poor Hero Jet squeaked under the strain, and we surged up the hill and flew down the other side like we had jumped onto a motorcycle.

A motorcycle without brakes, I should add. Buddha did not seem up on the theory of the footbrake, and I tried the handbrake once or twice and found that it only squealed like a pig and reduced our stability a bit. So as we fired down Dilli Bazar I could only put my feet up on the frame and dodge obstacles, as in one of those race-car video games. I rang the bell for all it was worth, and spent a lot of time in the right lane heading at oncoming traffic (they drive on the left).

Out of the corner of my eye I saw pedestrians goggling at us as we flew by; then the lanes ahead cleared as we rounded a semi, and I saw we were approaching the "Traffic Engineers' Intersection," usually one of my favorites. Here Dilli Bazar crosses another major street, and the occasion is marked by four traffic lights, all four of them *permanently green twenty-four hours a day*.

This time there was a cow for a traffic cop. "Bistarre!" (slowly!) I yelled, but Buddha's vocabulary apparently remained restricted to "Namaste," and he pedaled right on. I charted a course, clamped down the handbrake, crouched over the handlebars, rang the bell.

We shot the gap between a speeding cab and the traffic cow, with three inches to spare on each side, and were through the intersection before I even had time to blink. No problem. Now *that's* timing.

After that, it was just a matter of navigation. I took us the wrong way up the one-way section of Durbar Marg, to shorten our trip and throw off pursuit for good, and having survived that it was simple to make it the rest of the way to Thamel.

As we approached Thamel, we passed the grounds of the King's Palace; as I mentioned, the tall trees there are occupied day and night by giant brown bats, hanging head down from the bare upper branches. As we passed the palace, those bats must have caught the scent of the yeti, or something; because all of a sudden the whole flock of them burst off the branches, squeaking like my handbrake and flapping their big skin wings like a hundred little Draculas. Buddha slowed to stare up at the sight, and everyone else on the block, even the cow on the corner, stopped and looked up as well, to watch that cloud of bats fill the sky.

It's moments like that that make me love Kathmandu.

In Thamel, we fit right in. A remarkable number of people on the street looked a lot like Buddha—so much so that the notion hit me that the city was being secretly infiltrated by yeti in disguise. I chalked the notion up to hysteria caused by the Traffic Engineers' Intersection, and directed our Hero Jet into the Hotel Star court-yard. At that point walls surrounded us and Buddha consented to stop pedaling. We got off the bike, and shakily I led him upstairs to my room.

X

So. We had liberated the imprisoned yeti. Although I had to admit, as I locked us both into my room, that he was only partway free. Getting him completely free, back on his home ground, might turn out to be a problem. I still didn't know exactly where his home was, but they don't rent cars in Kathmandu, and the bus rides, no matter the destination, are long and crowded. Would Buddha be able to hold it together for ten hours in a crowded bus? Well, knowing him, he probably would. But would his disguise hold up? That was doubtful.

Meanwhile, there was the matter of Adrakian and the Secret Service being on to us. I had no idea what had happened to Nathan and Sarah and Freds, and I worried about them, especially Nathan and Sarah. I wished they would arrive. Now that we were here and settled, I felt a little uncomfortable with my guest; with him in there, my room felt awfully small.

I went in the bathroom and peed. Buddha came in and watched me, and when I was done he found the right buttons on the overalls, and did the same thing! The guy was amazingly smart. Another point—I don't know whether to mention this—but in the hominid-versus-primate debate, I've heard it said that most primate male genitals are quite small, and that human males are by far the size champs in that category. Hurray for us. But Buddha, I couldn't help noticing, was more on the human side of the scale. Really, the evidence was adding up. The yeti was a hominid, and a highly intelligent hominid at that. Buddha's quick understanding, his rapid adaptation to changing situations, his recognition of friends and enemies, his *cool,* all indicated smarts of the first order.

Of course, it made sense. How else could they have stayed concealed so well for so long? They must have taught their young all the tricks, generation to generation; keeping close track of all tools or artifacts, hiding their homes in the most hard-to-find caves, avoiding all human settlements, practicing burial of the dead. . . .

Then it occurred to me to wonder: if the yeti were so smart, and so good at concealment, why was old Buddha here with me in my room? What had gone wrong? Why had he revealed himself to Nathan, and how had Adrakian managed to capture him?

I found myself speculating on the incidence of mental illness among the yeti . . . a train of thought that made me even more anxious for Nathan's arrival. Nathan was not a whole lot of help in some situations, but the man had a rapport with the yeti that I sadly lacked.

Buddha was crouched on the bed, hunched over his knees, staring at me brightly. We had taken his sunglasses off on arrival, but the Dodger cap was still on. He looked observant, curious, puzzled. What next? he seemed to say. Something in his expression, something about the way he was coping with it all, was both brave and pathetic—it made me feel for him. "Hey, guy. We'll get you back up there. Namaste."

He formed the words with his lips. Namaste. I salute the spirit within you. Always one of my favorite greetings. Namaste, Mr. Yeti!

Perhaps he was hungry. What do you feed a hungry yeti? Was he vegetarian, carnivorous? I didn't have much there in the room: some packages of curried chicken soup, some candy (would sugar be bad for him?), beef jerky, yeah, a possibility; Nebico malt biscuits, which were little cookie-wafers made in Nepal. . . . I opened a package of these and one of jerky, and offered them to him.

He sat back on the bed and crossed his legs in front of him. He tapped the bed as if to indicate my spot. I sat down on the bed across from him. He took a stick of jerky in his long fingers, sniffed it, stuck it between his toes. I ate mine for example. He looked at me as if I'd just used the wrong fork for the salad. He began with a Nebico wafer, chewing it slowly. I found I was hungry, and from the roundness of his eyes I think he felt the same. But he was cool; there was a procedure here, he had me know; he handled all the wafers carefully first, sniffed them, ate them very slowly; took the jerky from between his toes, tried half of it; looked around the room, or at me, chewing very slowly. So calm, so peaceful he was! I decided the candy would be okay, and offered him the bag of jelly beans. He tried one and his eyebrows lifted; he picked one of the same color (green) from the bag, and gave it to me.

Pretty soon we had all the food I owned scattered out there on the bed between us, and we tried first one thing and then another, in silence, as slowly and solemnly as if it were all some sacred ritual. And you know, after a while I felt just like it was.

XI

About an hour after our meal Nathan, Sarah, and Freds all arrived at once. "You're here!" they cried. "All right, George! Way to go!"

"Thank Buddha," I said. "He got us here."

Nathan and Buddha went through a little hand shake with the fossil shell necklace. Freds and Sarah told me the story of their adventures. Sarah had fought with Adrakian, who escaped her and ran after us, and then with Valerie Budge, who stayed behind with Fitzgerald, to trade blows and accusations. "It was a joy to pound on her, she's been coming on to Phil for months now—not that I care anymore, of course," Sarah added quickly as Nathan eyed her. Anyway, she had pushed and shoved and denounced Budge and Fitzgerald and Adrakian, and by the time she was done no one at the Sheraton had the slightest idea what was going on. A couple of Secret Service men had gone after Adrakian; the rest contented themselves with shielding the Carters, who were being called on by both sides to judge the merits of the case. Naturally the Carters were reluctant to do this. Fitzgerald and Budge didn't want to come right out and say they had had a yeti stolen from them, so they were hamstrung; and when Freds returned to see what was up, Nathan and Sarah had already ordered a cab. "I think the Carters ended up on our side," Sarah said with satisfaction.

"All well and good," added Freds, "but there I had old Jimmy right at hand, no yeti to keep me polite, and man I had a bone to pick with that guy! I was in San Diego in 1980 and along about six o'clock on election day me and a bunch of friends were going down to vote and I argued *heavily* with them that we should vote for Carter rather than Anderson, because Anderson would just be a gesture whereas I thought Carter might still have a chance to win, since I don't believe in polls. I really went at it and I convinced every one of them, probably the peak of my political career, and then when we got home and turned on the TV we found out that Carter had already conceded the election a couple of hours before! My friends were so mad at me! John Drummond threw his beer at me and hit me right here. In fact they soaked me. So I had a bone to pick with old Jimmy, you bet, and I was going to go up to him and ask him why he had done such a thing. But he was looking kind of confused by all the ruckus, so I decided not to."

"The truth is I dragged him away before he could," said Sarah.

Nathan got us back to the problem at hand. "We've still got to get the yeti out of Kathmandu, and Adrakian knows we've got him—he'll be searching for us. How are we going to do it?"

"I've got a plan," I said. Because after my meal with Buddha I had been thinking. "Now where is Buddha's home? I need to know."

Nathan told me.

I consulted my maps. Buddha's valley was pretty near the little airstrip at J—. I nodded: "Okay, here's how we'll do it. . . ."

XII

I spent most of the next day through the looking glass, inside the big headquarters of the Royal Nepali Airline Company, getting four tickets for the following day's flight to J—. Tough work, even though as far as I could tell the plane wasn't even close to sold out. J—wasn't near any trekking routes, and it wasn't a popular destination. But that doesn't mean anything at RNAC. Their purpose as a company, as far as I can tell, is not so much to fly people places as it is to *make lists*. Waiting lists. I would call it their secret agenda, only it's no secret.

Patience, a very low-keyed pig-headedness, and lots of baksheesh are the keys to getting from the lists to the status of ticket-holder; I managed it, and in one day too. So I was pleased, but I called my friend Bill, who works in one of the city's travel agencies, to establish a little back-up plan. He's good at those, having a lot of experience with RNAC. Then I completed the rest of my purchases, at my favorite climbing outfitters in Thamel. The owner, a Tibetan woman, put down her copy of *The Far Pavilions* and stopped doing her arm aerobics, and got me all the clothes I asked for, in all the right colors. The only thing she couldn't find me was another Dodgers cap, but I got a dark blue "ATOM" baseball cap instead.

I pointed at it. "What is this 'ATOM,' anyway?" Because there were caps and jackets all over Nepal with that one word on them. Was it a company, and if so, what kind?

She shrugged. "Nobody knows."

Extensive advertising for an unknown product: yet another Great Mystery of Nepal. I stuffed my new belongings into my backpack and left. I was on my way home, when I noticed someone dodging around the crowd behind me. Just a glance and I spotted him, nipping into a newstand: Phil Adrakian.

Now I couldn't go home, not straight home. So I went to the Kathmandu Guest House, next door, and told one of the snooty clerks there that Jimmy Carter would be visiting in ten minutes and his secretary would be arriving very shortly. I walked through into the pretty garden that gives the Guest House so many of its pretensions, and hopped over a low spot in the back wall. Down an empty garbage alley, around the corner, over another wall, and past the Lodge Pleasant or Pheasant into the Star's courtyard. I was feeling pretty covert and all when I saw one of the Carters' Secret Service men, standing in front of the Tantric Used Book Store. Since I was already in the courtyard, I went ahead and hurried on up to my room.

XIII

"I think they must have followed you here," I told our little group. "I suppose they might think we really were trying a kidnapping yesterday."

Nathan groaned. "Adrakian probably convinced them we're part of that group that bombed the Hotel Annapurna this summer."

"That should reassure them," I said. "When that happened the opposition group immediately wrote to the King and told him they were suspending all operations against the government until the criminal element among them was captured by the authorities."

"Buddhist guerrillas are heavy, aren't they?" said Freds.

"Anyway," I said, "all this means is that we have a damn good reason to put our plan into effect. Freds, are you sure you're up for it?"

"Sure I'm sure! It sounds like fun."

"All right. We'd better all stay here tonight, just in case. I'll cook up some chicken soup."

So we had a spartan meal of curried chicken soup, Nebico wafers, Toblerone white chocolate, jelly beans, and iodinated Tang. When Nathan saw the way Buddha went for the jelly beans, he shook his head. "We've got to get him out of here *fast*."

When we settled down, Sarah took the bed, and Buddha immediately joined her, with a completely innocent look in his eye, as if to say: Who, me? This is just where I sleep, right? I could see Nathan was a bit suspicious of this, worried about the old Fay Wray complex maybe, and in fact Nathan curled up on the foot of the bed. I assume there weren't any problems. Freds and I threw down the mildewed foam pads I owned and lay down on the floor.

"Don't you think Buddha is sure to get freaked by the flight tomorrow?" Sarah asked when the lights were off.

"Nothing's seemed to bother him much so far," I said. But I wondered; I don't like flying myself.

"Yeah, but this isn't remotely like anything he's ever done before."

"Standing on a high ridge is kind of like flying. Compared to our bike ride it should be easy."

"I'm not so sure," Nathan said, worried again. "Sarah may be right—flying can be upsetting even for people who know what it is."

"That's usually the heart of the problem," I said, with feeling.

Freds cut through the debate: "I say we should get him stoned before the flight. Get a hash pipe going good and just get him *wasted.*"

"You're crazy!" Nathan said. "That'd just freak him out more!"

"Nah."

"He wouldn't know what to make of it," Sarah said.

"Oh yeah?" Freds propped himself up on one arm. "You really think those yetis have lived all this time up there among all those pot plants, and haven't figured them out? No way! In fact that's probably why no one ever sees them! They're immobilized! Because man, the pot plants up there are as big as *pine trees.* They probably use the buds for food."

Nathan and Sarah doubted that, and they further doubted that we should do any experimenting about it at such a crucial time.

"You got any hash?" I asked Freds with interest.

"Nope. Before this Ama Dablam climb came through I was going to fly to Malaysia to join a jungle mountain expedition that Doug Scott put together, you know? So I got rid of it all. I mean, do you fly drugs into Malaysia is not one of the harder questions on the IQ test, you know? In fact I had too much to smoke in the time I had left, and when I was hiking down from Namche to Lukla I was loading my pipe and dropped this chunk on the ground, a really monster chunk, about ten grams. *And I just left it there!* Just left it lying on the ground! I've always wanted to do that.

"Anyway, I'm out. I could fix that in about fifteen minutes down on the street if you want me to, though—"

"No, no. That's okay." I could already hear the steady breathing of Buddha, fast asleep above me. "He'll be more relaxed than any of us tomorrow." And that was true.

XIV

We got up before dawn, and Freds dressed in the clothes that Buddha had worn the day before. We pasted some swatches of Buddha's back fur onto Fred's face to serve as a beard. We even had some of the russet fur taped to the inside of the Dodger Cap, so it hung down behind. With mittens on, and a big pair of snow boots, he was covered; slip the shades onto his nose and he looked at least as weird as Buddha had in the Sheraton. Freds walked around the room a bit, trying it out. Buddha watched him with that surprised look of his, and it cracked Freds up. "I look like your long-lost brother, hey Buddha?"

Nathan collapsed on the bed despondently. "This just isn't going to work."

"That's what you said last time," I objected.

"Exactly! And look what happened! You call that *working?* Are you telling me that things *worked* yesterday?"

"Well, it depends on what you mean when you say *worked.* I mean here we are, right?" I began packing my gear. "Relax, Nathan." I put a hand on his shoulder, and Sarah put both her hands on his other shoulder. He bucked up a bit, and I smiled at Sarah. That woman was tough; she had saved our ass at the Sheraton, and she kept her nerve well during the waiting, too. I wouldn't have minded asking her on a long trek into the Himal myself, really, and she saw that and gave me a brief smile of appreciation that also said, no chance. Besides, double-crossing old Nathan would have been like the Dodgers giving away Steve Garvey. People like that you can't double-cross, not if you want to look yourself in the mirror.

Freds finished getting pointers in carriage from Buddha, and he and I walked out of the room. Freds stopped and looked back inside mournfully, and I tugged him along, irritated at the Method acting; we wouldn't be visible to anyone outside the Star until we got downstairs.

But I must say that overall Freds did an amazing job. He hadn't seen all that much of Buddha, and yet when he walked across that courtyard and into the street, he caught the yeti's gait exactly: a bit stiff-hipped and bowlegged, a rolling sailor's walk from which he could drop to all fours instantly, or so it seemed. I could hardly believe it.

The streets were nearly empty: a bread truck, scavenging dogs (they passed Freds without even a glance—would that give us away?), the old beggar and his young daughter, a few coffee freaks outside the German Pumpernickel Bakery, shopkeepers opening up. . . . Near the Star we passed a parked taxi with three men in it, carefully looking the other way. Westerners. I hurried on. "Contact," I muttered to Freds. He just whistled a little.

There was one taxi in Times Square, the driver asleep. We hopped in and woke him, and asked him to take us to the Central Bus Stop. The taxi we had passed followed us. "Hooked," I said to Freds, who was sniffing the ashtrays, tasting the upholstery, learning out the window to eat the wind like a dog. "Try not to overdo it," I said, worried about my Dodgers cap with all that hair taped in it flying away.

We passed the big clock tower and stopped, got out and paid the cabbie. Our tail stopped further up the block, I was pleased to see. Freds and I walked down the broad, mashed-mud driveway into Central Bus Stop.

The bus stop was a big yard of mud, about five or eight feet lower than the level of the street. Scores of buses were parked at all angles and their tires had torn the mud up until the yard looked like a vehicular Verdun. All of the buses were owned by private companies—one bus per company, usually, with a single route to run—and all of their agents at the wood-and-cloth booths at the entrance clamored for our attention, as if we might have come in without a particular destination in mind, and would pick the agent that made the loudest offer.

Actually, this time it was almost true. But I spotted the agent for the Jiri bus, which is where I had thought to send Freds, and I bought two tickets, in a crowd of all the other bus agents, who criticized my choice. Freds hunkered down a little, looking suitably distressed. A big hubbub arose; one of the companies had established its right to leave the yard next, and now its bus was trying to make it up the driveway, which was the one and only exit from the yard.

Each departure was a complete test of the driver, the bus' clutch and tires, and the advisory abilities of the bus agents standing around. After a lot of clutching and coaching this brightly painted bus squirted up the incline, and the scheduling debate began anew. Only three buses had unblocked access to the driveway, and the argument among their agents was fierce.

I took Freds in hand and we wandered around the track-torn mud, looking for the Jiri bus. Eventually we found it: gaily painted in yellow, blue, green and red, like all the rest, ours also had about forty decals of Ganesh stuck all over the windshield, to help the driver see. As usual, the company's "other bus" was absent, and this one was double-booked. We shoved our way on board and through the tightly packed crowd in the aisle, then found empty seats in the back. The Nepalis like to ride near the front. After more boardings, the crowd engulfed us even in the back, and it got worse after the bus attendants stored the spare tire in the aisle. But we had Freds at a window, which is what I wanted.

Through the mud-flecked glass I could just see our tail: Phil Adrakian, and two guys who might have been Secret Service men, though I wasn't sure about that. They were fending off the bus agents and trying to get into the yard at the same time, a tough combination. As they sidestepped the bus agents they got in the driveway and almost got run over by the bus currently sliding up and down the slope; Adrakian slipped in the mud scrambling away, and fell on his ass. The bus agents thought this was great. Adrakian and the other two hurried off, and squished from bus to bus trying to look like they weren't looking for anything. They were pursued by the most persistent bus agents, and got mired in the mud from time to time, and I worried after a while that they wouldn't be able to find us. In fact it took them about twenty minutes. But then Adrakian saw Freds at the window, and the three of them ducked behind a bus hulk that had sunk axle-deep, waving off the bus agents in desperate sign language. "Hooked for good," I said.

"Yeah," Freds replied without moving his lips.

The bus was now completely packed; an old woman had even been insinuated between Freds and me, which suited me fine. But it was going to be another miserable trip. "You're really doing your part for the cause," I said to Freds as I prepared to depart, thinking of the cramped day ahead of him.

"No hroblem!" he said liplessly. "I like these 'us trits!"

Somehow I believed him. I weaseled my way upright in the aisle and said good-bye. Our tails were watching the bus' only door, but that wasn't really much of a problem. I just squirmed between the Nepalis, whose concept of personal "body space" is pretty much exactly confined to the space their bodies are actually occupying— none of this eighteen-inch bullshit for them—and got to a window on the other side of the bus. There was no way our watchers could have seen across the interior of that bus, so I was free to act. I apologized to the Sherpa I was sitting on, worked the window open, and started to climb out it. The Sherpa very politely helped me, without the slightest suggestion I was doing anything out of the ordinary, and I jumped down into the mud. The Sherpa waved good-bye; hardly anyone else on the bus even noticed my departure. I snuck through the no-man's land of the back buses. Quickly enough I was back on Durbar Marg and in a cab on my way to the Star.

XV

I got the cabbie to park almost inside the Star's lobby, and Buddha barreled into the backseat like a fullback hitting the line. While we drove he kept his head down, just in case, and the taxi took us out to the airport.

Things were proceeding exactly according to my plan, and you might imagine I was feeling pretty pleased, but the truth is that I was more nervous than I'd been all morning. Because we were walking up to the RNAC desk, you see. . . .

When I got there and inquired, the clerk told us our flight had been canceled for the day.

"What?" I cried. "Canceled! What for?"

Now, our counter agent was the most beautiful woman in the world. This happens all the time in Nepal—in the country you pass a farmer bent over pulling up rice, and she looks up and it's a face from the cover of *Cosmopolitan,* only twice as pretty and without the vampire makeup. This ticket clerk could have made a million modeling in New York, but she didn't speak much English, and when I asked her "What for?" she said, "It's raining," and looked past me for another customer.

I took a deep breath. Remember, I thought: RNAC. What would the Red Queen say? I pointed out the window. "It's not raining. Take a look."

Too much for her. "It's raining," she repeated. She looked around for her supervisor, and he came on over; a thin Hindu man with a red dot on his forehead. He nodded curtly. "It's raining up at J—."

I shook my head. "I'm sorry, I got a report on the shortwave from J—, and besides you can look north and see for yourself. It's not raining."

"The airstrip at J— is too wet to land on," he said.

"I'm sorry," I said, "but you landed there twice yesterday, and it hasn't rained since."

"We're having mechanical trouble with the plane."

"I'm sorry, but you've got a whole fleet of small planes out there, and when one has a problem you just substitute for it. I know, I switched planes three times here once." Nathan and Sarah didn't look too happy to hear that one.

The supervisor's supervisor was drawn by the conversation: another serious, slender Hindu. "The flight is canceled," he said. "It's political."

I shook my head. "RNAC pilots only strike the flights to Lukla and Pokhara—they're the only ones that have enough passengers for the strike to matter." My fears concerning the real reason for the cancellation were being slowly confirmed. "How many passengers on this flight?"

All three of them shrugged. "The flight is canceled," the first supervisor said. "Try tomorrow."

And I knew I was right. They had less than half capacity, and were waiting until tomorrow so the flight would be full. (Maybe more than full, but did they care?) I explained the situation to Nathan and Sarah and Buddha, and Nathan stormed back to the desk demanding that the flight fly as scheduled, and the supervisors had their eyebrows raised like they might actually get some fun out of this after all, but I hauled him away. While I was dialing my friend in the travel agency, I explained to him how maddening irate customers had been made into a sport (or maybe an art form) by Asian bureaucrats. After three tries I got my friend's office. The receptionist answered and said, "Yeti Travels?" which gave me a start; I'd forgotten the company's name. Then Bill got on and I outlined the situation. "Filling planes again, are they?" He laughed. "I'll call in that group of six we 'sold' yesterday, and you should be off."

"Thanks, Bill." I gave it fifteen minutes, during which time Sarah and I calmed Nathan, and Buddha stood at the window staring at the planes taking off and landing. "We've got to get out today!" Nathan kept repeating. "They'll never go for another ruse after today!"

"We know that already, Nathan."

I returned to the desk. "I'd like to get boarding passes for flight 2 to J—, please?"

She made out the boarding passes. The two supervisors stood off behind a console, studiously avoiding my gaze. Normally it wouldn't have gotten to me, but with the pressure to get Buddha out I was a little edgy. When I had the passes in hand I said to the clerk, loud enough for the suprvisors to hear, "No more cancellation, eh?"

"Cancellation?"

I gave up on it.

XVI

Of course a boarding pass is only a piece of paper, and when only eight passengers got on the little two-engine plane, I got nervous again; but we took off right on schedule. When the plane left the ground I sat back in my chair, and the relief blew through me like wash from the props. I hadn't known how nervous I was until that moment. Nathan and Sarah were squeezing hands and grinning in the seats ahead, and Buddha was in the window seat beside me, staring out at Kathmandu Valley, or the shimmery gray circle of the prop, I couldn't tell. Amazing guy, that Buddha: *so* cool.

We rose out of the green, terraced, faintly Middle-Earth perfection of Kathmandu Valley, and flew over the mountains to the north, up into the land of snows. The other passengers, four Brits, were looking out their windows and exclaiming over the godlike views, and they didn't give a damn that one of their fellow passengers was an odd-looking chap. There was no problem there. After the plane had leveled out at cruising altitude one of the two stewards came down the aisle and offered us all little wrapped pieces of candy, just as on other airlines they offer drinks or meals. It was incredibly cute, almost like kids playing at running an airline, which is the sort of thought that seems cute itself until you remember you are at 17,000 feet with these characters, and they are

now going to fly you over the biggest mountains on earth in order
to land you on the smallest airstrips. At that point the cuteness goes
away and you find yourself swallowing deeply and trying not to
think of downdrafts, life insurance, metal fatigue, the afterlife. . . .

I shifted forward in my seat, hoping that the other passengers
were too preoccupied to notice that Buddha had swallowed his
candy without removing the wrapper. I wasn't too sure about the
two across from us, but they were Brits so even if they did think
Buddha was strange, it only meant they would look at him less. No
problem.

It wasn't long before the steward said, "No smoking, if it please
you," and the plane dipped over and started down toward a particularly spiky group of snowy peaks. Not a sign of a landing strip; in
fact the idea of one being down there was absurd on the face of it. I
took a deep breath. I hate flying, to tell you the truth.

I suppose some of you are familiar with the Lukla airstrip below
the Everest region. It's set on a bench high on the side of the Dudh
Khosi gorge, and the grass strip, tilted about fifteen degrees from
horizontal and only two hundred yards long, aims straight into the
side of the valley wall. When you land there all you can really see
is the valley wall, and it looks like you're headed right into it. At
the last minute the pilot pulls up and hits the grass, and after the
inevitable bounces you roll to a stop quickly because you're going
uphill so steeply. It's a heavy experience; some people get religion
from it, or at least quit flying.

But the truth is that there are at least a dozen RNAC strips in
Nepal that are *much worse* than the one at Lukla, and unfortunately
for us, the strip at J— was at about the top of that list. First of all, it
hadn't begun life as an airstrip at all—it began as a *barley terrace,*
one terrace among many on a mountainside above a village. They
widened it and put a windsock at one end, and tore out all the
barley of course, and that was it. Instant airstrip. Not only that, but
the valley it was in was a deep one—say five thousand feet—and
very steep-sided, with a nearly vertical headwall just a mile upstream from the airstrip, and a sharp dogleg just a mile or so
downstream, and really, nobody in their right *minds* would think to
put an airstrip there. I became more and more convinced of this as
we made a ten-thousand-foot dive into the dogleg, and pulled up
against one wall of the valley, so close to it that I could have made

a good estimate of the barley count per hectare if I'd been inclined to. I tried to reassure Buddha, but he was working my candy wrapper out of the ashtray and didn't want to be disturbed. Nice to be a yeti sometimes. I caught sight of our landing strip, and watched it grow bigger—say to the size of a ruler—and then we landed on it. Our pilot was good; we only bounced twice, and rolled to a stop with yards to spare.

XVII

And so we came to the end of our brief association with Buddha the yeti, having successfully liberated him from people who would no doubt become major lecturers on the crank circuit forever after.

I have to say that Buddha was one of the nicest guys I've ever had the pleasure of knowing, and certainly among the coolest. Unflappable, really.

But to finish: we collected our packs, and hiked all that afternoon, up the headwall of that valley and along a forested high valley to the west of it. We camped that night on a broad ledge above a short falls, between two monster boulders.

Nathan and Sarah shared one tent, Buddha and I another. Twice I woke and saw Buddha sitting in the tent door, looking out at the immense valley wall facing us.

The next day we hiked long and hard, up continuously, and finally came to the site of the expedition's spring camp. We dropped our packs and crossed the river on a new bridge made of bamboo, and Nathan and Buddha led us up the cross-country route, through the forest to the high box canyon where they had first met. By the time we got up there it was late afternoon, and the sun was behind the mountains to the west.

Buddha seemed to understand the plan, as always. He took off my Dodger cap and gave it back to me, having shed all the rest of his clothes back at camp. I had always treasured that cap, but now it was really something special. Nathan put the fossil necklace back around Buddha's neck; but the yeti took it off and bit the cord apart, and gave a fossil seashell to each of us. It was quite a moment. Who knows but what yetis didn't eat these shellfish, in a previous age? I know, I know, I've got the timescales wrong, or so they say, but believe me, there was a look in that guy's eye when he gave us those shells that was ancient. I mean *old*. Sarah hugged him, Nathan hugged him. I'm not into that stuff, I shook his skinny strong right hand. "Good-bye for Freds, too," I told him.

"Na-mas-te," he whispered.

"Oh, Buddha," Sarah said, sniffling, and Nathan had his jaw clamped like a vise. Quite the sentimental moment. I turned to go, and sort of pulled the other two along with me; there wasn't that much light left, after all.

Buddha took off upstream, and last I saw him he was on top of a riverside boulder, looking back down at us curiously, his wild russet fur suddenly groomed and perfect-looking in the proper context. The yeti was a hard man to read, sometimes, but it seemed to me then that his eyes were sad. His big adventure was over.

On the way back down it occurred to me to wonder if he wasn't in fact a little crazy, as I had thought once before. I wondered if he might not walk right into the next camp he found, and sit down and croak "Namaste," blowing all the good work we'd done to save him from civilization. Maybe civilization had corrupted him already, and the natural man was gone for good. I hoped not. If so, you've probably already heard about it.

Well, things were pretty subdued in the old expedition camp that night. We got up the tents by lantern light, and had some soup and sat there looking at the blue flames of the stove. I almost made a real fire to cheer myself up, but I didn't feel like it.

Then Sarah said, with feeling. "I'm proud of you, Nathan," and he began to do his Coleman lantern glow, he was so happy. I would be, too. In fact, when she said, "I'm proud of you too, George," and gave me a peck on the cheek, it made me grin, and I felt a pang of . . . well, a lot of things. Pretty soon they were off to their tent. Fine for them, and I was happy for them, really, but I was also feeling a little like old Smedley at the end of the Dudley Do-Right episode: left out in the cold, with Dudley getting the girl. Of course I had my fossil seashell, but it wasn't quite the same.

I pulled the Coleman over, and looked at that stone shell for a while. Strange object. What had the yeti who drilled the little hole through it been thinking? What was it *for?*

I remembered the meal on my bed, Buddha and me solemnly chomping on wafers and picking over the supply of jelly beans. And then I was all right; that was enough for me, and more than enough.

XVIII

Back in Kathmandu we met Freds and found out what had happened to him, over snitzel Parisienne and apple strudel at the Old Vienna. "By noon I figured you all were long gone, so when the bus stopped for a break at Lamosangu I hopped off and walked right up to these guys' taxi. I did my Buddha thing and they almost died when they saw me coming. It was Adrakian and two of the Secret Service guys who chased us out of the Sheraton. When I took off the cap and shades they were fried, naturally. I said, 'Man, I made a mistake! I wanted to go to Pokhara! This isn't Pokhara!' They were so mad they started yelling at each other. 'What's that?' says I. 'You all made some sort of mistake too? What a shame!' And while they were screaming at each other and all I made a deal with the taxi driver to take me back to Kathmandu too. The others weren't too happy about that, and they didn't want to let me in, but the cabbie was already pissed at them for hiring him to take his car over that terrible road, no matter what the fare. So when I offered him a lot of rupees he was pleased to stick those guys somehow, and he put me in the front seat with him, and we turned around and drove back to Kathmandu."

I said, "You drove back to Kathmandu with the *Secret Service?* How did you explain the fur taped to the baseball cap?"

"I didn't! . . . So anyway, on the way back it was silent city behind me, and it got pretty dull, so I asked them if they'd seen the latest musical disaster movie from Bombay."

"What?" Nathan said. "What's that?"

"Don't you go see them? They're showing all over town. We do it all the time, it's great. You just smoke a few bowls of hash and go see one of these musicals they make, they last about three hours, no subtitles or anything, and they're killer! Incredible! I told these guys that's what they should do—"

"You told the Secret Service guys they should smoke bowls of *hash?*"

"Sure! They're Americans, aren't they? Anyway, they didn't seem too convinced, and we still had a hell of a long way to go to Kathmandu, so I told them the story of the last one I saw. It's still in town, you sure you're not going to see it? I don't want to spoil it for you."

We convinced him he wouldn't.

"Well, it's about this guy who falls in love with a gal he works with. But she's engaged to their boss, a real crook who is contracted to build the town's dam. The crook is building the dam with some kind of birdshit, it looked like, instead of cement, but while he was scamming that he fell into a mixer and was made part of the dam. So the guy and the gal get engaged, but she burns her face lighting a stove. She heals pretty good, but after that when he looks at her he sees through her to her skull and he can't handle it, so he breaks the engagement and she sings a lot, and she disguises herself by pulling her hair over that side of her face and pretending to be someone else. He meets her and doesn't recognize her and falls in love with her, and she reveals who she is and sings that he should fuck off. Heavy singing on all sides at that point, and he tries to win her back and she says no way, and all the time it's raining cats and dogs, and finally she forgives him and they're all happy again, but the dam breaks right where the crook was weakening it and the whole town is swept away singing like crazy. But these two both manage to grab hold of a stupa sticking up out of the water, and then the floods recede and there they are hanging there together, and they live happily ever after. Great, man. A classic."

"How'd the Secret Service like it?" I asked.

"They didn't say. I guess they didn't like the ending."

But I could tell, watching Nathan and Sarah grinning hand-in-hand across the table, that they liked the ending just fine.

XIX

Oh, one more thing: *you must not tell ANYONE about this!!!* Okay?

A specialty of Orson Scott Card since the start of his career has been rugged, passionate fantasties rooted in the turbulent background of nineteenth-century rural America. This harsh tale of pioneers on the move has the solid resonance of myth.

Card has been a frequent contender for the Hugo and Nebula awards. His novel Ender's Game *swept both honors in 1986; and its sequel,* Speaker for the Dead, *won the Nebula in 1987 and has been nominated for the Hugo Award. The present story was also nominated for a Nebula in 1987.*

HATRACK RIVER

Orson Scott Card

Little Peggy was very careful with the eggs. She rooted her hand through the straw till her fingers bumped something hard and heavy. She gave no never mind to the chicken drips. After all, Mama never even crinkled her face to open up Cally's most spetackler diapers. Even when the chicken drips were wet and stringy and made her fingers stick together, little Peggy gave no never mind. She just pushed the straw apart, wrapped her hand around the egg, and lifted it out of the brood box. All this while standing tip-toe on a wobbly stool, reaching high above her head. Mama said she was too young for egging, but little Peggy showed her. Every day she felt in every brood box and brought in every egg, every single one, that's what she did.

Every one, she said in her mind, over and over: I got to reach into every one.

Then little Peggy looked back into the northeast corner, the

57

darkest place in the whole coop, and there sat Bloody Mary in her
brood box, looking like the devil's own bad dream, hatefulness
shining out of her nasty eyes, saying Come here little girl and give
me nips. I want nips of finger and nips of thumb and if you come
real close and try to take my egg I'll get a nip of eye from you.

Most animals didn't have much heartfire, but Bloody Mary's was
strong and made a poison smoke. Nobody else could see it, but
little Peggy could. Bloody Mary dreamed of death for all folks, but
most specially for a certain little girl five years old, and little Peggy
had the marks on her fingers to prove it. At least one mark,
anyway, and even if Papa said he couldn't see it, little Peggy
remembered how she got it and nobody could blame her none if she
sometimes forgot to reach under Bloody Mary who sat there like a
bushwhacker waiting to kill the first folks that just tried to come
by. Nobody'd get mad if she just sometimes forgot to look there.

I forgot forgot forgot. I looked in every brood box, every one,
and if one got missed then I forgot forgot forgot.

Everybody knew Bloody Mary was a lowdown chicken and too
mean to give any eggs that wasn't rotten anyway.

I forgot.

She got the egg basket inside before Mama even had the fire het,
and Mama was so pleased she let little Peggy put the eggs one by
one into the cold water. Then Mama put the pot on the hook and
swung it right on over the fire. Boiling eggs you didn't have to wait
for the fire to slack, you could do it smoke and all.

"Peg," said Papa.

That was Mama's name, but Papa didn't say it in his Mama
voice. He said it in his little-Peggy-you're-in-dutch voice, and little
Peggy knew she was completely found out, and so she turned right
around and yelled what she'd been planning to say all along.

"I forgot, Papa!"

Mama turned and looked at little Peggy in surprise. Papa wasn't
surprised though. He just raised an eyebrow. He was holding his
hand behind his back. Little Peggy knew there was an egg in that
hand. Bloody Mary's nasty egg.

"What did you forget, little Peggy?" asked Papa, talking soft.

Right that minute little Peggy reckoned she was the stupidest girl
ever born on the face of the earth. Here she was denying before
anybody accused her of anything.

But she wasn't going to give up, not right off like that. She couldn't stand to have them mad at her and she just wanted them to let her go away and live in England. So she put on her innocent face and said, "I don't know, Papa."

She figgered England was the best place to go live, cause England had a Lord Protector. From the look in Papa's eye, a Lord Protector was pretty much what she needed just now.

"What did you forget?" Papa asked again.

"Just say it and be done, Horace," said Mama. "If she's done wrong then she's done wrong."

"I forgot one time, Papa," said little Peggy. "She's a mean old chicken and she hates me."

Papa answered soft and slow. "One time," he said.

Then he took his hand from behind him. Only it wasn't no single egg he held, it was a whole basket. And that basket was filled with a clot of straw—most likely all the straw from Bloody Mary's box—and that straw was mashed together and glued tight with dried-up raw egg and shell bits, mixed up with about three or four chewed-up baby chicken bodies.

"Did you have to bring that in the house before breakfast, Horace?" said Mama.

"I don't know what makes me madder," said Horace. "What she done wrong or her studying up to lie about it."

"I didn't study and I didn't lie!" shouted little Peggy. Or anyways she meant to shout. What came out sounded espiciously like crying even though little Peggy had decided only yesterday that she was done with crying for the rest of her life.

"See?" said Mama. "She already feels bad."

"She feels bad being caught," said Horace. "You're too slack on her, Peg. She's got a lying spirit. I don't want my daughter growing up wicked. I'd rather see her dead like her baby sister before I see her grow up wicked."

Little Peggy saw Mama's heartfire flare up with memory, and in front of her eyes she could see a baby laid out pretty in a little box, and then another one only not so pretty cause it was the second baby Missy, the one what died of pox so nobody'd touch her but her own Mama, who was still so feeble from the pox herself that she couldn't do much. Little Peggy saw that scene, and she knew Papa had made a mistake to say what he said cause Mama's face went cold even though her heartfire was hot.

"That's the wickedest thing anybody ever said in my presence," said Mama. Then she took up the basket of corruption from the table and took it outside.

"Bloody Mary bites my hand," said little Peggy.

"We'll see what bites," said Papa. "For leaving the eggs I give you one whack, because I reckon that lunatic hen looks fearsome to a frog-size girl like you. But for telling lies I give you ten whacks."

Little Peggy cried in earnest at that news. Papa gave an honest count and full measure in everything, but most especially in whacks.

Papa took the hazel rod off the high shelf. He kept it up there ever since little Peggy put the old one in the fire and burnt it right up.

"I'd rather hear a thousand hard and bitter truths from you, Daughter, than one soft and easy lie," said he, and then he bent over and laid on with the rod across her thighs. Whick whick whick, she counted every one, they stung her to the heart, each one of them, they were so full of anger. Worst of all she knew it was all unfair because his heartfire raged for a different cause altogether, and it always did. Papa's hate for wickedness always came from his most secret memory. Little Peggy didn't understand it all, because it was twisted up and confused and Papa didn't remember it right well himself. All little Peggy ever saw plain was that it was a lady and it wasn't Mama. Papa thought of that lady whenever something went wrong. When baby Missy died of nothing at all, and then the next baby also named Missy died of pox, and then the barn burnt down once, and a cow died, everything that went wrong made him think of that lady and he began to talk about how much he hated wickedness and at those times the hazel rod flew hard and sharp.

I'd rather hear a thousand hard and bitter truths, that's what he said, but little Peggy knew that there was one truth he didn't ever want to hear, and so she kept it to herself. She'd never shout it at him, even if it made him break the hazel rod, cause whenever she thought of saying aught about that lady, she kept picturing her father dead, and that was a thing she never hoped to see for real. Besides, the lady that haunted his heartfire, she didn't have no clothes on, and little Peggy knew that she'd be whipped for sure if she talked about people being naked.

So she took the whacks and cried till she could taste that her nose was running. Papa left the room right away, and Mama came back to fix up breakfast for the blacksmith and the visitors and the hands, but neither one said boo to her, just as if they didn't even notice. She cried even harder and louder for a minute, but it didn't help. Finally she picked up her Bugy from the sewing basket and walked all stiff-legged out to Oldpappy's cabin and woke him right up.

He listened to her story like he always did.

"I know about Bloody Mary," he said, "and I told your papa fifty times if I told him once, wring that chicken's neck and be done. She's a crazy bird. Every week or so she gets crazy and breaks all her own eggs, even the ones ready to hatch. Kills her own chicks. It's a lunatic what kills its own."

"Papa like to killed me," said little Peggy.

"I reckon if you can walk somewhat it ain't so bad altogether."

"I can't walk much."

"No, I can see you're nigh crippled forever," said Oldpappy. "But I tell you what, the way I see it your mama and your papa's mostly mad at each other. So why don't you just disappear for a couple of hours?"

"I wish I could turn into a bird and fly."

"Next best thing, though," said Pappy, "is to have a secret place where nobody knows to look for you. Do you have a place like that? No, don't tell me—it wrecks it if you tell even a single other person. You just go to that place for a while. As long as it's a safe place, not out in the woods where a Red might take your pretty hair, and not a high place where you might fall off, and not a tiny place where you might get stuck."

"It's big and it's low and it ain't in the woods," said little Peggy.

"Then you go there, Maggie."

Little Peggy made the face she always made when Oldpappy called her that. And she held up Bugy and in Bugy's squeaky high voice she said, "Her name is Peggy."

"You go there, *Piggy*, if you like that better—"

Little Peggy slapped Bugy right across Oldpappy's knee.

"Someday Bugy'll do that once too often and have a rupture and die," said Oldpappy.

But Bugy just danced right in his face and insisted, "Not piggy, *Peggy!*"

"That's right, Puggy, you go to that secret place and if anybody says, We got to go find that girl, I'll say, I know where she is and she'll come back when she's good and ready."

Little Peggy ran for the cabin door and then stopped and turned. "Oldpappy, you're the nicest grown-up in the whole world."

"Your papa has a different view of me, but that's all tied up with another hazel rod that I laid hand on much too often. Now run along."

She stopped again right before she closed the door. "You're the *only* nice grown-up!" She shouted it real loud, halfway hoping that they could hear it clear inside the house. Then she was gone, right across the garden, out past the cow pasture, up the hill into the woods, and along the path to the spring house.

They had one good wagon, these folks did, and two good horses pulling it. One might even suppose they was prosperous, considering they had six big boys, from mansize on down to twins that had wrestled each other into being a good deal stronger than their dozen years. Not to mention one big daughter and a whole passel of little girls. A big family. Right prosperous if you didn't know that not even a year ago they had owned a mill and lived in a big house on a streambank in west New Hampshire. Come down far in the world, they had, and this wagon was all they had left of everything. But they were hopeful, trekking west along the roads that crossed the Hio, heading for open land that was free for the taking. If you were a family with plenty of strong backs and clever hands, it'd be good land, too, as long as the weather was with them and the Reds didn't raid them and all the lawyers and bankers stayed in New England.

The father was a big man, a little run to fat, which was no surprise since millers mostly stood around all day. That softness in the belly wouldn't last a year on a deepwoods homestead. He didn't care much about that, anyway—he had no fear of hard work. What worried him today was his wife, Faith. It was her time for that baby, he knew it. Not that she'd ever talk about it direct. Women just don't speak about things like that with men. But he knew how big she was and how many months it had been. Besides, at the noon stop she murmured to him, "Alvin Miller, if there's a road house along this way, or even a little broke-down cabin, I reckon I could use a bit of rest." A man didn't have to be a philosopher to understand her. And after six sons and six daughters, he'd have to have the brains of a brick not to get the drift of how things stood with her.

So he sent the oldest boy, Vigor, to run ahead on the road and see the lay of the land.

You could tell they were from New England, cause the boy didn't take no gun. If there'd been a bushwhacker the young man never would've made it back, and the fact he came back with all his hair was proof no Red had spotted him—the French up Detroit way were paying for English scalps with liquor and if a Red saw a white man alone in the woods with no rifle he'd own that white man's scalp. So maybe a man could think that luck was with the family at last. But since these Yankees had no notion that the road wasn't safe, Alvin Miller didn't think for a minute of his good luck.

Vigor's word was of a road house three miles on. That was good news, except that between them and that road house was a river. Kind of a scrawny river, and the ford was shallow, but Alvin Miller had learned never to trust water. No matter how peaceful it looks, it'll reach and try to take you. He was halfway minded to tell Faith that they'd spend the night this side of the river, but she gave just the tiniest groan and at that moment he knew that there was no chance of that. Faith had borne him a dozen living children, but it was four years since the last one and a lot of women took it bad, having a baby so late. A lot of women died. A good road house meant women to help with the birthing, so they'd have to chance the river.

And Vigor did say the river wasn't much.

The air in the spring house was cool and heavy, dark and wet. Sometimes when little Peggy caught a nap here, she woke up gasping like as if the whole place was under water. She had dreams of water even when she wasn't here—that was one of the things that made some folks say she was a seeper instead of a torch. But when she dreamed outside, she always knew she was dreaming. Here the water was real.

Real in the drips that formed like sweat on the milkjars setting in the stream. Real in the cold damp clay of the spring house floor.

Real in the swallowing sound of the stream as it hurried through the middle of the house.

Keeping it cool all summer long, cold water spilling right out of the hill and into this place, shaded all the way by trees so old the moon made a point of passing through their branches just to hear some good old tales. That was what little Peggy always came here for, even when Papa didn't hate her. Not the wetness of the air, she could do just fine without that. It was the way the fire went right out of her and she didn't have to be a torch. Didn't have to see into all the dark places where folks hid theirselfs.

From her they hid theirselfs as if it would do some good. Whatever they didn't like most about theirself they tried to tuck away in some dark corner but they didn't know how all them dark places burned in little Peggy's eyes. Even when she was so little that she spit out her corn mash cause she was still hoping for a suck, she knew all the stories that the folks around her kept all hid. She saw the bits of their past that they most wished they could bury, and she saw the bits of their future that they most feared.

And that was why she took to coming up here to the spring house. Here she didn't have to see those things. Not even the lady in Papa's memory. There was nothing here but the heavy wet dark cool air to quench the fire and dim the light so she could be—just for a few minutes in the day—a little five-year-old girl with a straw puppet named Bugy and not even have to *think* about any of them grown-up secrets.

I'm not wicked, she told herself. Again and again but it didn't work because she knew she was.

All right then, she said to herself, I *am* wicked. But I won't be wicked anymore. I'll tell the truth like Papa says, or I'll say nothing at all.

Even at five years old, little Peggy knew that if she kept that vow, she'd be better off saying nothing.

So she said nothing, not even to herself, just lay there on a mossy damp table with Bugy clenched tight enough to strangle in her fist.

Ching ching ching.

Little Peggy woke up and got mad for just a minute.

Ching ching ching.

Made her mad because nobody said to her, Little Peggy, you

don't mind if we talk this young blacksmith feller into settling down here, do you?

Not at all, Papa, she would've said if they'd asked. She knew what it meant to have a smithy. It meant your village would thrive, and folks from other places would come, and when they came there'd be trade, and when there was trade then her father's big house could be a forest inn, and when there was a forest inn all the roads would kind of bend a little just to pass the place, if it wasn't too far out of the way—little Peggy knew all that, as sure as the children of farmers knew the rhythms of the farm. A road house by a smithy was a road house that would prosper. So she would've said, sure enough, let him stay, deed him land, brick his chimney, feed him free, let him have my bed so I have to double up with Cousin Peter who keeps trying to peek under my nightgown, I'll put up with all that—just as long as you don't put him near the spring house so that all the time, even when I want to be alone with the water, there's that whack thump hiss roar, noise all the time, and a fire burning up the sky to turn it black, and the smell of charcoal burning. It was enough to make a body wish to follow the stream right back into the mountain just to get some peace.

Of course the stream was the smart place to put the blacksmith. Except for water, he could've put his smithy anywheres at all. The iron came to him in the shipper's wagon clear from New Netherland, and the charcoal—well, there were plenty of farmers willing to trade charcoal for a good shoe. But water, that's what the smith needed that nobody'd bring him, so of course they put him right down the hill from the spring house where his ching ching ching could wake her up and put the fire back into her in the one place where she had used to be able to let it burn low and go almost to cold wet ash.

A roar of thunder.

She was at the door in a second. Had to see the lightning. Caught just the last shadow of the light but she knew that there'd be more. It wasn't much after noon, surely, or had she slept all day? What with all these blackbelly clouds she couldn't tell—it might as well be the last minutes of dusk. The air was all a-prickle with lightning just waiting to flash. She knew that feeling, knew it meant the lightning'd hit close.

She looked down to see if the blacksmith's stable was still full of horses. It was. The shoeing wasn't done, the road would turn to muck, and so the farmer with his two sons from out West Fork way was stuck here. Not a chance they'd head home in *this*, with lightning ready to put a fire in the woods, or knock a tree down on them, or maybe just smack them a good one and lay them all out dead in a circle like them five Quakers they still was talking about and here it happened back in '90 when the first white folks came to settle here. People talked still about the Circle of Five and all that, some people wondering if God up and smashed them flat so as to shut the Quakers up, seeing how nothing else ever could, while other people was wondering if God took them up into heaven like the first Lord Protector Oliver Cromwell who was smote by lightning at the age of ninety-seven and just disappeared.

No, that farmer and his big old boys'd stay another night. Little Peggy was an innkeeper's daughter, wasn't she? Papooses learnt to hunt, pickaninnies learnt to tote, farmer children learnt the weather, and an innkeeper's daughter learnt which folks would stay the night, even before they knew it right theirselfs.

Their horses were champing in the stable, snorting and warning each other about the storm. In every group of horses, little Peggy figgered, there must be one that's remarkable dumb, so all the others have to tell him what all's going on. Bad storm, they were saying. We're going to get a soaking, if the lightning don't smack us first. And the dumb one kept nickering and saying. What's the noise, what's that noise.

Then the sky just opened right up and dumped water on the earth. Stripped leaves right off the trees, it came down so hard. Came down so thick, too, that little Peggy didn't even see the smithy for a minute and she thought maybe it got washed right away into the stream. Oldpappy told her how that stream led right down to the Hatrack River, and the Hatrack poured right into the Hio, and the Hio shoved itself on through the woods to the Mizzipy, which went on down to the sea, and Oldpappy said how the sea drank so much water that it got indigestion and gave off the biggest old belches you ever heard, and what came up was clouds. Belches from the sea, and now the smithy would float all that way, get swallered up and belched out, and someday she'd just be minding her own business and some cloud would break up and plop that smithy down as neat as you please, old Makepeace Smith still ching ching chinging away.

Then the rain slacked off a mite and she looked down to see the smithy still there. But that wasn't what she saw at all. No, what she saw was sparks of fire way off in the forest, downstream toward the Hatrack, down where the ford was, only there wasn't a chance of taking the ford today, with this rain. Sparks, lots of sparks, and she knew every one of them was folks. She didn't hardly think of doing it anymore, she only had to see their heartfires and she was looking close. Maybe future, maybe past, all the visions lived together in the heartfire.

What she saw right now was the same in all their hearts. A wagon in the middle of the Hatrack, with the water rising and everything they owned in all the world in that wagon.

Little Peggy didn't talk much, but everybody knew she was a torch, so they listened whenever she spoke up about trouble. Specially this kind of trouble. Sure the settlements in these parts were pretty old now, a fair bit older than little Peggy herself, but they hadn't forgotten yet that anybody's wagon caught in a flood is everybody's loss.

She fair to flew down that grassy hill, jumping gopher holes and sliding the steep places, so it wasn't twenty seconds from seeing those far-off heartfires till she was speaking right up in the smithy's shop. That farmer from West Fork at first wanted to make her wait till he was done with telling stories about worse storms he'd seen. But Makepeace knew all about little Peggy. He just listened right up and then told those boys to saddle them horses, shoes or no shoes, there was folks caught in the Hatrack ford and there was no time for foolishness. Little Peggy didn't even get a chance to see them go—Makepeace had already sent her off to the big house to fetch her father and all the hands and visitors there. Wasn't a one of them who hadn't once put all they owned in the world into a wagon and dragged it west across the mountain roads and down into the forest. Wasn't a one of them who hadn't felt a river sucking at that wagon, wanting to steal it away. They all got right to it. That's the way it was then, you see. Folks noticed other people's trouble every bit as quick as if it was their own.

Vigor led the boys in trying to push the wagon, while Eleanor hawed the horses. Alvin Miller spent his time carrying the little girls one by one to safety on the far shore. The current was a devil clawing at him, whispering, "I'll have your babies, I'll have them all," but Alvin said no, with every muscle in his body as he strained shoreward he said no to that whisper, till his girls stood all bedraggled on the bank with rain streaming down their faces like the tears from all the grief in the world.

He would have carried Faith, too, baby in her belly and all, but she wouldn't budge. Just sat inside that wagon, bracing herself against the trunks and furniture as the wagon tipped and rocked. Lightning crashed and branches broke; one of them tore the canvas and the water poured into the wagon but Faith held on with white knuckles and her eyes staring out. Alvin knew from her eyes there wasn't a thing he could say to make her let go. There was only one way to get Faith and her unborn baby out of that river, and that was to get the wagon out.

"Horses can't get no purchase, Papa," Vigor shouted. "They're just stumbling and bound to break a leg."

"Well we can't pull out without the horses!"

"The horses are *something*, Papa. We leave 'em in here and we'll lose wagon and horses too!"

"Your mama won't leave that wagon."

And he saw understanding in Vigor's eyes. The *things* in the wagon weren't worth a risk of death to save them. But Mama was.

"Still," he said. "On shore the team could pull strong. Here in the water they can't do a thing."

"Set the boys to unhitching them. But first tie a line to a tree to hold that wagon!"

It wasn't two minutes before the twins Wastenot and Wantnot were on the shore making the rope fast to a stout tree. David and Measure made another line fast to the rig that held the horses, while Calm cut the strands that held them to the wagon. Good boys, doing their work just right, Vigor shouting directions while Alvin could only watch helpless at the back of the wagon, looking now at Faith who was tryng not to have the baby, now at the Hatrack River that was trying to push them all down to hell.

Not much of a river, Vigor had said, but then the clouds came up and the rain came down and the Hatrack became something after all. Even so it looked passable when they got to it. The horses strode in strong, and Alvin was just saying to Calm, who had the reins, "Well, we made it not a minute to spare," when the river went insane. It doubled in speed and strength all in a moment, and the horses got panicky and lost direction and started pulling against each other. The boys all hopped into the river and tried to lead them to shore but by then the wagon's momentum had been lost and the wheels were mired up and stuck fast. Almost as if the river knew they were coming and saved up its worst fury till they were already in it and couldn't get away.

"Look out! Look out!" screamed Measure from the shore.

Alvin looked upstream to see what devilment the river had in mind, and there was a whole tree floating down the river, endwise like a battering ram, the root end pointed at the center of the wagon, straight at the place where Faith was sitting, her baby on the verge of birth. Alvin couldn't think of anything to do, couldn't think at all, just screamed his wife's name with all his strength. Maybe in his heart he thought that by holding her name on his lips he could keep her alive, but there was no hope of that, no hope at all.

Except that Vigor didn't know there was no hope. Vigor leapt out when the tree was no more than a rod away, his body falling against it just above the root. The momentum of his leap turned it a little, then rolled it over, rolled it and turned it away from the wagon. Of course Vigor rolled with it, pulled right under the water—but it worked, the root end of the tree missed the wagon entirely, and the shaft of the trunk struck it a sidewise blow.

The tree bounded across the stream and smashed up against a boulder on the bank. Alvin was five rods off, but in his memory from then on, he always saw it like as if he'd been right there. The tree crashing into the boulder, and Vigor between them. Just a split second that lasted a lifetime, Vigor's eyes wide with surprise, blood already leaping out of his mouth, spattering out onto the tree that killed him. Then the Hatrack River swept the tree out into the current. Vigor slipped under the water, all except his arm, all tangled in the roots, which stuck up into the air for all the world like a neighbor waving good-bye after a visit.

Alvin was so intent on watching his dying son that he didn't even notice what was happening to his own self. The blow from the tree was enough to dislodge the mired wheels, and the current picked up the wagon, carried it downstream, Alvin clinging to the tailgate, Faith weeping inside, Eleanor screaming her lungs out from the driver's seat, and the boys on the bank shouting something. Shouting "Hold! Hold! Hold!"

The rope held, one end tied to a strong tree, the other end tied to the wagon, it held. The river couldn't tumble the wagon downstream; instead it swung the wagon to shore the way a boy swings a rock on a string, and when it came to a shuddering stop it was right against the bank, the front end facing upstream.

"It held!" cried the boys.

"Thank God!" shouted Eleanor.

"The baby's coming," whispered Faith.

But Alvin, all he could hear was the single faint cry that had been the last sound from the throat of his firstborn son, all he could see was the way his boy clung to the tree as it rolled and rolled in the water, and all he could say was a single word, a single command. "Live," he murmured. Vigor had always obeyed him before. Hard worker, willing companion, more a friend or brother than a son. But this time he knew his son would disobey. Still he whispered it. "Live."

"Are we safe?" said Faith, her voice trembling.

Alvin turned to face her, tried to strike the grief from his face. No sense her knowing the price that Vigor paid to save her and the baby. Time enough to learn of that after the baby was born. "Can you climb out of the wagon?"

"What's wrong?" asked Faith, looking at his face.

"I took a fright. Tree could have killed us. Can you climb out, now that we're up against the bank?"

Eleanor leaned in from the front of the wagon. "David and Calm are on the bank, they can help you up. The rope's holding, Mama, but who can say how long?"

"Go on, Mother, just a step," said Alvin. "We'll do better with the wagon if we know you're safe on shore."

"The baby's coming," said Faith.

"Better on shore than here," said Alvin sharply. "Go *now*."

Faith stood up, clambered awkwardly to the front. Alvin climbed through the wagon behind her, to help her if she should stumble. Even he could see how her belly had dropped. The baby must be grabbing for air already.

On the bank it wasn't just David and Calm, now. There were strangers, big men, and several horses. Even one small wagon, and that was a welcome sight. Alvin had no notion who these men were, or how they knew to come and help, but there wasn't a moment to waste on introductions. "You men! Is there a midwife in the road house?"

"Goody Guester does with birthing," said a man. A big man, with arms like oxlegs. A blacksmith, surely.

"Can you take my wife in that wagon? There's not a moment to spare." Alvin knew it was a shameful thing, for men to speak so openly of birthing, right in front of the woman who was set to bear. But Faith was no fool—she knew what mattered most, and getting her to a bed and a competent midwife was more important than pussyfooting around about it.

David and Calm were careful as they helped their mother toward the waiting wagon. Faith was staggering with pain. Women in labor shouldn't have to step from a wagon seat up onto a riverbank, that was sure. Eleanor was right behind her, taking charge as if she wasn't younger than all the boys except the twins. "Measure! Get the girls together. They're riding in the wagon with us. You too, Wastenot and Wantnot! I know you can help the big boys but I need you to watch the girls while I'm with Mother." Eleanor was never one to be trifled with, and the gravity of the situation was such that they didn't even call her Eleanor of Aquitaine as they obeyed. Even the little girls mostly gave over their squabbling and got right in.

Eleanor paused a moment on the bank and looked back to where her father stood on the wagon seat. She glanced downstream, then looked back at him. Alvin understood the question, and he shook his head no. Faith was not to know of Vigor's sacrifice. Tears came unwelcome to Alvin's eyes, but not to Eleanor's. Eleanor was only fourteen, but when she didn't want to cry, she didn't cry.

Wastenot hawed the horse and the little wagon lurched forward, Faith wincing as the girls patted her and the rain poured. Faith's gaze was somber as a cow's, and as mindless, looking back at her husband, back at the river. At times like birthing, Alvin thought, a woman becomes a beast, slack-minded as her body takes over and does its work. How else could she bear the pain? As if the soul of the earth possessed her the way it owns the souls of animals, making her part of the life of the whole world, unhitching her from family, from husband, from all the reins of the human race, leading her into the valley of ripeness and harvest and reaping and bloody death.

"She'll be safe now," the blacksmith said. "And we have horses here to pull your wagon out."

"It's slacking off," said Measure. "The rain is less, and the current's not so strong."

"As soon as your wife stepped ashore, it eased up," said the farmer-looking feller. "The rain's dying, that's sure."

"You took the worst of it in the water," said the blacksmith. "But you're all right now. Get hold of yourself, man, there's work to do."

Only then did Alvin come to himself enough to realize that he was crying. Work to do, that's right, get hold of yourself, Alvin Miller. You're no weakling, to bawl like a baby. Other men have lost a dozen children and still live their lives. You've had twelve, and Vigor lived to be a man, though he never did get to marry and have children of his own. Maybe Alvin had to weep because Vigor died so nobly; maybe he cried because it was so sudden.

David touched the blacksmith's arm. "Leave him be for a minute," he said softly. "Our oldest brother was carried off not ten minutes back. He got tangled in a tree floating down."

"It wasn't no *tangle*," Alvin said sharply. "He jumped that tree and saved our wagon, and your mother inside it! That river paid him back, that's what it did, it punished him."

Calm spoke quietly to the local men. "It run up against that boulder there." They all looked. There was a smear of blood on the rock.

"The Hatrack has a mean streak in it," said the blacksmith, "but I never seen this river so riled up before. I'm sorry about your boy. There's a slow, flat place downstream where he's bound to fetch up. Everything the river catches ends up there. When the storm lets up, we can go down and bring back the—bring him back."

Alvin wiped his eyes on his sleeve, but since his sleeve was soaking wet it didn't do much good. "Give me a minute more and I can pull my weight," said Alvin.

They hitched two more horses and the four beasts had no trouble pulling the wagon out against the much weakened current. By the time the wagon was set to rights again on the road, the sun was even breaking through.

"Wouldn't you know," said the blacksmith. "If you ever don't like the weather hereabouts, you just set a spell, cause it'll change."

"Not this one," said Alvin. "This storm was laid in wait for us."

The blacksmith put an arm across Alvin's shoulder, and spoke real gentle. "No offense, mister, but that's crazy talk."

Alvin shrugged him off. "That storm and that river wanted us."

"Papa," said David, "you're tired and grieving. Best be still till we get to the road house and see how Mama is."

"My baby is a boy," said Papa. "You'll see. He would have been the seventh son of a seventh son."

That got their attention, right enough, that blacksmith and the other men as well. Everybody knew a seventh son had certain gifts, but the seventh son of a seventh son was about as powerful a birth as you could have.

"That makes a difference," said the blacksmith. "He'd have been a born douser, sure, and water hates that." The others nodded sagely.

"The water had its way," said Alvin. "Had its way, and all done. It would've killed Faith and the baby, if it could. But since it couldn't, why, it killed my boy Vigor. And now when the baby comes, he'll be the sixth son, cause I'll only have five living."

"Some says it makes no difference if the first six be alive or not," said a farmer.

Alvin said nothing, but he knew it made all the difference. He had thought this baby would be a miracle child, but the river had taken of that. If water don't stop you one way, it stops you another. He shouldn't have hoped for a miracle child. The cost was too high. All his eyes could see, all the way home, was Vigor dangling in the grasp of the roots, tumbling through the current like a leaf caught up in a dust devil, with the blood seeping from his mouth to slake the murderous thirst of the Hatrack.

Little Peggy stood in the window, looking out into the storm. She could see all those heartfires, especially one, one so bright it was like the sun when she looked at it. But there was a blackness all around them. No, not even black—a nothingness, like a part of the universe God hadn't finished making, and it swept around those lights as if to tear them from each other, sweep them away, swallow them up. Little Peggy knew what that nothingness was. Those times when her eyes saw the hot yellow heartfires, there were three other colors, too. The rich dark orange of the earth. The thin gray color of the air. And the deep black emptiness of water. It was the water that tore at them now. The river, only she had never seen it so black, so strong, so terrible. The heartfires were so tiny in the night.

"What do you see, child?" asked Oldpappy.

"The river's going to carry them away," said little Peggy.

"I hope not."

Little Peggy began to cry.

"There, child," said Oldpappy. "It ain't always such a grand thing to see afar off like that, is it."

She shook her head.

"But maybe it won't happen as bad as you think."

Just at that moment, she saw one of the heartfires break away and tumble off into the dark. "Oh!" she cried out, reaching as if her hand could snatch the light and put it back. But of course she couldn't. Her vision was long and clear, but her reach was short.

"Are they lost?" asked Oldpappy.

"One," whispered little Peggy.

"Haven't Makepeace and the others got there yet?"

"Just now," she said. "The rope held. They're safe now."

Oldpappy didn't ask her how she knew, or what she saw. Just patted her shoulder. "Because you told them. Remember that, Margaret. One was lost, but if you hadn't seen and sent help, they might all have died."

She shook her head. "I should've seen them sooner, Oldpappy, but I fell asleep."

"And you blame yourself?" asked Oldpappy.

"I should've let Bloody Mary nip me, and then father wouldn't've been mad, and then I wouldn't've been in the spring house, and then I wouldn't've been asleep, and then I would've sent help in time—"

"We can all make daisy chains of blame like that, Maggie. It don't mean a thing."

But she knew it meant something. You don't blame blind people cause they don't warn you you're about to step on a snake—but you sure blame somebody with eyes who doesn't say a word about it. She knew her duty ever since she first realized that other folks couldn't see all that she could see. God gave her special eyes, so she'd better see and give warning, or the devil would take her soul. The devil or the deep black sea.

"Don't mean a thing," Oldpappy murmured. Then, like he just been poked in the behind with a ramrod, he went all straight and said, "Spring house! Spring house, of course." He pulled her close. "Listen to me, little Peggy. It wasn't none of your fault, and that's the truth. The same water that runs in the Hatrack flows in the spring house brook, it's all the same water, all through the world. The same water that wanted them dead, it knew you could give warning and send help. So it sang to you and sent you off to sleep."

It made a kind of sense to her, it sure did. "How can that be, Oldpappy?"

"Oh, that's just in the nature of it. The whole universe is made of only four kinds of stuff, little Peggy, and each one wants to have its own way." Peggy thought of the four colors that she saw when the heartfires glowed, and she knew what all four were even as Oldpappy named them. "Fire makes things hot and bright and uses them up. Air makes things cool and sneaks in everywhere. Earth makes things solid and sturdy, so they'll last. But water, it tears things down, it falls from the sky and carries off everything it can, carries it off and down to the sea. If the water had its way, the whole world would be smooth, just a big ocean with nothing out of the water's reach. All dead and smooth. That's why you slept. The water wants to tear down these strangers, whoever they are, tear them down and kill them. It's a miracle you woke up at all."

"The blacksmith's hammer woke me," said little Peggy.

"That's it, then, you see? The blacksmith was working with iron, the hardest earth, and with a fierce blast of air from the bellows, and with a fire so hot it burns the grass outside the chimney. The water couldn't touch him to keep him still."

Little Peggy could hardly believe it, but it must be so. The blacksmith had drawn her from a watery sleep. The smith had *helped* her. Why, it was enough to make you laugh, to know the blacksmith was her friend this time.

There was shouting on the porch downstairs, and doors opened and closed. "Some folks is here already," said Oldpappy.

Little Peggy saw the heartfires downstairs, and found the one with the strongest fear and pain. "It's their Mama," said little Peggy. "She's got a baby coming."

"Well, if that ain't the luck of it. Lose one, and here already is a baby to replace death with life." Oldpappy shambled on out to go downstairs and help.

Little Peggy, though, she just stood there, looking at what she saw in the distance. That lost heartfire wasn't lost at all, and that was sure. She could see it burning away far off, despite how the darkness of the river tried to cover it. He wasn't dead, just carried off, and maybe somebody could help him. She ran out then, passed Oldpappy all in a rush, clattered down the stairs.

Mama caught her by the arm as she was running into the great room. "There's a birthing," Mama said, "and we need you."

"But Mama, the one that went downriver, he's still alive!"

"Peggy, we got no time for—"

Two boys with the same face pushed their way into the conversation. "The one downriver!" cried one.

"Still alive!" cried another.

"How do you know!"

"He can't be!"

They spoke so all on top of each other that Mama had to hush them up just to hear them. "It was Vigor, our big brother, he got swept away—"

"Well he's alive," said little Peggy, "but the river's got him."

The twins looked to Mama for confirmation. "She know what she's talking about, Goody Guester?"

Mama nodded, and the boys raced for the door, shouting, "He's alive! He's still alive!"

"Are you sure?" asked Mama fiercely. "It's a cruel thing, to put hope in their hearts like that, if it ain't so."

Mama's flashing eyes made little Peggy afraid, and she couldn't think what to say.

By then, though, Oldpappy had come up from behind. "Now

Peg," he said, "how would she know one was taken by the river, lessun she saw?"

"I know," said Mama. "But this woman's been holding off birth too long, and I got a care for the baby, so come on now, little Peggy, I need you to tell me what you see."

She led little Peggy into the bedroom off the kitchen, the place where Papa and Mama slept whenever there were visitors. The woman lay on the bed, holding tight to the hand of a tall girl with deep and solemn eyes. Little Peggy didn't know their faces, but she recognized their fires, especially the mother's pain and fear.

"Someone was shouting," whispered the mother.

"Hush now," said Mama.

"About him still alive."

The solemn girl raised her eyebrows, looked at Mama. "Is that so, Goody Guester?"

"My daughter is a torch. That's why I brung her here in this room. To see the baby."

"Did she see my boy? Is he alive?"

"I thought you didn't tell her, Eleanor," said Mama.

The solemn girl shook her head.

"Saw from the wagon. Is he alive?"

"Tell her, Margaret," said Mama.

Little Peggy turned and looked for his heartfire. There were no walls when it came to this kind of seeing. His flame was still there, though she knew it was afar off. This time, though, she drew near in the way she had, took a close look. "He's in the water. He's all tangled in the roots."

"Vigor!" cried the mother on the bed.

"The river wants him. The river says, Die, die."

Mama touched the woman's arm. "The twins have gone off to tell the others. There'll be a search party."

"In the dark!" whispered the woman scornfully.

Little Peggy spoke again. "He's saying a prayer, I think. He's saying—seventh son."

"Seventh son," whispered Eleanor.

"What does that mean?" asked Mama.

"If this baby's a boy," said Eleanor, "and he's born while Vigor's still alive, then he's the seventh son of a seventh son, and all of them alive."

Mama gasped. "No wonder the river—" she said. No need to finish the thought. Instead she took little Peggy's hands and led her to the woman on the bed. "Look at this baby, and see what you see."

Little Peggy had done this before, of course. It was the chief use they had for torches, to have them look at an unborn baby just at the birthing time. Partly to see how it lay in the womb, but also because sometimes a torch could see who the baby was, what it would be, could tell stories of times to come. Even before she touched the woman's belly, she could see the baby's heartfire. It was the one that she had seen before, that burned so hot and bright that it was like the sun and the moon, to compare it to the mother's fire. "It's a boy," she said.

"Then let me bear this baby," said the mother. "Let him breathe while Vigor still breathes!"

"How's the baby set?" asked Mama.

"Just right," said little Peggy.

"Head first? Face down?"

Little Peggy nodded.

"Then why won't it come?" demanded Mama.

"She's been telling him not to," said Little Peggy, looking at the mother.

"In the wagon," the mother said. "He was coming, and I did a beseeching."

"Well, you should have told me right off," said Mama sharply. "Speck me to help you and you don't even tell me he's got a beseeching on him. You, girl!"

Several young ones were standing near the wall, wide-eyed, and they didn't know which one she meant.

"Any of you, I need that iron key from the ring on the wall."

The biggest of them took it clumsily from the hook and brought it, ring and all. Mama dangled the large ring and the key over the mother's belly, chanting softly,

> "Here's the circle, open wide,
> Here's the key to get outside,
> Earth be iron, flame be fair,
> Fall from water into air."

The mother cried out in sudden agony. Mama tossed away the key, cast back the sheet, lifted the woman's knees, and ordered little Peggy fiercely to *see*.

Little Peggy touched the woman's womb. The boy's mind was empty, except for a feeling of pressure and gathering cold as he emerged into the air. But the very emptiness of his mind let her see things that would never be clearly visible again. The billion billion paths of his life lay open before him, waiting for his first choices, for the first changes in the world around him to eliminate a million futures every second. The future was there in everyone, a flickering shadow that was never visible behind the thoughts of the present moment; but here, for a few precious moments, little Peggy could see them clearly.

And what she saw was death down every path. Drowning, drowning, every path of his future led this child to a watery death.

"Why do you hate him so!" cried little Peggy.

"What?" demanded Eleanor.

"Hush," said Mama. "Let her see what she sees."

Inside the unborn child, the dark blot of water that surrounded his heartfire seemed so terribly strong that little Peggy was afraid he would be swallowed up.

"Get him out to breathe!" shouted little Peggy.

Mama reached in, even though it tore the mother something dreadful, and hooked the baby by the neck with strong fingers, drawing him out.

In that moment, the dark water retreated inside the child's mind, and just before the first breath came, little Peggy saw ten million deaths by water disappear. Now, for the first time, there were some paths open, some paths leading to a dazzling future. And all the paths that did not end in early death had one thing in common. On all those paths, little Peggy saw herself doing one simple thing.

So she did that thing. She took her hands from the slackening belly and ducked under her mother's arm. The baby's head had just emerged, and it was still covered with a bloody caul, a scrap of the sac of soft skin in which he had floated in his mother's womb.

His mouth was open, sucking inward on the caul, but it didn't break, and he couldn't breathe.

Little Peggy did what she had seen herself do in the baby's future. She reached out, took the caul from under the baby's chin, and pulled it away from his face. It came whole, in one moist piece, and in the moment it came away, the baby's mouth cleared, he sucked in a great breath, and then gave that mewling cry that birthing mothers hear as the song of life.

Little Peggy folded the caul, her mind still full of the visions she had seen down the pathways of this baby's life. She did not know yet what the visions meant, but they made such clear pictures in her mind that she knew she would never forget them. They made her afraid, because so much would depend on her, and how she used the birth caul that was still warm in her hands.

"A boy," said Mama.

"Is he," whispered the mother. "Seventh son?"

Mama was tying the cord, so she couldn't spare a glance at little Peggy. "Look," she whispered.

Little Peggy looked for the single heartfire on the distant river. "Yes," she said, for the heartfire was still burning.

Even as she watched, it flickered, died.

"Now he's gone," said little Peggy.

The woman on the bed wept bitterly, her birth-wracked body shuddering.

"Grieving at the baby's birth," said Mama. "It's a dreadful thing."

"Hush," whispered Eleanor to her mother. "Be joyous, or it'll darken the baby all his life!"

"Vigor," murmured the woman.

"Better nothing at all than tears," said Mama. She held out the crying baby, and Eleanor took it in competent arms—she had cradled many a babe before, it was plain. Mama went to the table in the corner and took the scarf that had been blacked in the wool, so it was night-colored clear through. She dragged it slowly across the weeping woman's face, saying, "Sleep, Mother, sleep."

When the cloth came away, the weeping was done, and the woman slept, her strength spent.

"Take the baby from the room," said Mama.

"Don't he need to start his sucking?" asked Eleanor.

"She'll never nurse this babe," said Mama. "Not unless you want him to suck hate."

"She can't hate him," said Eleanor. "It ain't his fault."

"I reckon her milk don't know that," said Mama. "That right, little Peggy? What teat did the baby suck?"

"His mama's," said little Peggy.

Mama looked sharp at her. "You sure of that?"

She nodded.

"Well, then, we'll bring the baby in when she wakes up. He doesn't need to eat anything for the first night, anyway." So Eleanor carried the baby out into the great room, where the fire burned to dry the men, who stopped trading stories about rains and floods worse than this one long enough to look at the baby and admire.

Inside the room, though, Mama took little Peggy by the chin and stared hard into her eyes. "You tell me the truth, Margaret. It's a serious thing, for a baby to suck on its mama and drink up hate."

"She won't hate him, Mama," said little Peggy.

"What did you see?"

Little Peggy would have answered, but she didn't know the words to tell most of the things she saw. So she looked at the floor. She could tell from Mama's quick draw of breath that she was ripe for a tongue-lashing. But Mama waited, and then her hand came soft, stroking across little Peggy's cheek. "Ah, child, what a day you've had. The baby might have died, except you told me to pull it out. You even reached in and opened up its mouth—that's what you did, isn't it?"

Little Peggy nodded.

"Enough for a little girl, enough for one day." Mama turned to the other girls, the ones in wet dresses, leaning against the wall. "And you, too, you've had enough of a day. Come out of here, let your mama sleep, come out and get dry by the fire. I'll start a supper for you, I will."

But Oldpappy was already in the kitchen, fussing around, and refused to hear of Mama doing a thing. Soon enough she was out with the baby, shooing the men away so she could rock it to sleep, letting it suck her finger.

Little Peggy figured after a while that she wouldn't be missed, and so she snuck up the stairs to the attic ladder, and up the ladder into the lightless, musty space. The spiders didn't bother her much, and the cats mostly kept the mice away, so she wasn't afraid. She crawled right to her secret hiding place and took out the carven box that Oldpappy had given her, the one he said his own papa brought from Ulster when he came to the colonies. It was full of the precious scraps of childhood—stones, strings, buttons—but now she knew that these were nothing compared to the work before her all the rest of her life. She dumped them right out, and blew into the box to clear away dust. Then she laid the folded caul inside and closed the lid.

She knew that in the future she would open that box a dozen times. That it would call to her, wake her from her sleep, tear her from her friends, and steal from her all her dreams. All because a baby boy downstairs had no future at all, except a death from the dark water, excepting if she used that caul to keep him safe, the way it once protected him in the womb.

For a moment she was angry, to have her own life so changed. Worse than the blacksmith coming, it was, worse than Papa and the hazel wand he whupped her with, worse than Mama when her eyes were angry. Everything would be different forever and it wasn't fair. Just for a baby she never invited, never asked to come here, what did she care about any old baby?

She reached out and opened the box, planning to take the caul and cast it into a dark corner of the attic. But even in the darkness, she could see a place where it was darker still: near her heartfire, where the emptiness of the deep black river was all set to make a murderer out of her.

Not me, she said to the water. You ain't part of me.

Yes I am, whispered the water. I'm all through you, and you'd dry up and die without me.

You ain't the boss of me, anyway, she retorted.

She closed the lid on the box and skidded her way down the ladder. Papa always said that she'd get splinters in her butt doing that. This time he was right. It stung something fierce, so she walked kind of sideways into the kitchen where Oldpappy was. Sure enough, he stopped his cooking long enough to pry the splinters out.

"My eyes ain't sharp enough for this, Maggie," he complained.

"You got the eyes of an eagle. Papa says so."

Oldpappy chuckled. "Does he now."

"What's for dinner?"

"Oh, you'll like this dinner, Maggie."

Little Peggy wrinkled up her nose. "Smells like chicken."

"That's right."

"I don't like chicken soup."

"Not just soup, Maggie. This one's a-roasting, except the neck and wings."

"I hate *roast* chicken, too."

"Does your Oldpappy ever lie to you?"

"Nope."

"Then you best believe me when I tell you this is one chicken dinner that'll make you *glad*. Can't you think of any way that a partickler chicken dinner could make you glad?"

Little Peggy thought and thought, and then she smiled. "Bloody Mary?"

Oldpappy winked. "I always said that was a hen born to make gravy."

Little Peggy hugged him so tight that he made choking sounds, and then they laughed and laughed.

Later that night, long after little Peggy was in bed, they brought Vigor's body home, and Papa and Makepeace set to making a box for him. Alvin Miller hardly looked alive, even when Eleanor showed him the baby. Until she said, "That torch girl. She says that this baby is the seventh son of a seventh son."

Alvin looked around for someone to tell him if it was true.

"Oh, you can trust her," said Mama.

Tears came fresh to Alvin's eyes. "That boy hung on," he said. "There in the water, he hung on long enough."

"He knowed what store you set by that," said Eleanor.

Then Alvin reached for the baby, held him tight, looked down into his eyes. "Nobody named him yet, did they?" he asked.

"Course not," said Eleanor. "Mama named all the other boys, but you always said the seventh son'd have—"

"My own name. Alvin. Seventh son of a seventh son, with the same name as his father. Alvin Junior." He looked around him, then turned to face toward the river, way off in the nighttime forest. "Hear that, you Hatrack River? His name is Alvin, and you didn't kill him after all."

Soon they brought in the box, and laid out Vigor's body with candles, to stand for the fire of life that had left him. Alvin held up the baby, over the coffin. "Look on your brother," he whispered to the infant.

"That baby can't see nothing yet, Papa," said David.

"That ain't so, David," said Alvin. "He don't *know* what he's seeing, but his eyes can see. And when he gets old enough to hear the story of his birth, I'm going to tell him that his own eyes saw his brother Vigor, who gave his life for this baby's sake."

It was two weeks before Faith was well enough to travel. But Alvin saw to it that he and his boys worked hard for their keep. They cleared a good spot of land, chopped the winter's firewood, set some charcoal heaps for Makepeace Smith, and widened the road. They also felled four big trees and made a strong bridge across the Hatrack River, a covered bridge so that even in a rainstorm people could cross that river without a drop of water touching them.

Vigor's grave was the third one there, beside little Peggy's two dead sisters. The family paid respects and prayed there on the morning that they left. Then they got in their wagon and rode off westward, "But we leave a part of ourselves here always," said Faith, and Alvin nodded.

Little Peggy watched them go, then ran up into the attic, opened the box, and held little Alvin's caul in her hand. No danger, for now at least. Safe for now. She put the caul away and closed the lid. You better be something, baby Alvin, she said, or else you caused a powerful lot of trouble for nothing.

From Playboy *comes this sleek tale of double-doublecrossing on an artificial satellite populated by escaped villains seeking sanctuary— and by those who hunt them.*

Robert Silverberg, whose career has been marked by Hugo and Nebula awards since its beginning, won his latest trophy last year with the novella "Sailing to Byzantium." His most recent novels are Star of Gypsies *and the forthcoming* At Winter's End.

BLINDSIGHT

Robert Silverberg

That's my mark, Juanito told himself. That one, there. That one for sure.

He stared at the new dinkos coming off the midday shuttle from Earth. The one he meant to go for was the one with no eyes at all, blank from brow to bridge of nose, just the merest suggestions of shadowy pits below the smooth skin of the forehead. As if the eyes had been erased, Juanito thought. But in fact they had probably never been there in the first place. It didn't look like a retrofit gene job, more like a prenatal splice.

He knew he had to move fast. There was plenty of competition. Fifteen, twenty couriers here in the waiting room, gathering like vultures, and they were some of the best: Ricky, Lola, Kluge. Nattathaniel. Delilah. Everybody looked hungry today. Juanito couldn't afford to get shut out. He hadn't worked in six weeks, and it was time. His last job had been a fast-talking fancy-dancing Hungarian, wanted on Commonplace and maybe two or three other satellite worlds for dealing in plutonium. Juanito had milked that one for all it was worth, but you can milk only so long. The newcomers learn the system, they melt in and become invisible, and there's no reason for them to go on paying. So then you have to find a new client.

"Okay," Juanito said, looking around challengingly. "There's mine. The weird one. The one with half a face. Anybody else want him?"

Kluge laughed and said, "He's all yours, man."

"Yeah," Delilah said, with a little shudder. "All yours." That saddened him, her chiming in like that. It had always disappointed Juanito that Delilah didn't have his kind of imagination. "Christ," she said. "I bet he'll be plenty trouble."

"Trouble's what pays best," Juanito said. "You want to go for the easy ones, that's fine with me." He grinned at her and waved at the others. "If we're all agreed, I think I'll head downstairs now. See you later, people."

He started to move inward and downward along the shuttle-hub wall. Dazzling sunlight glinted off the docking module's silvery rim, and off the Earth shuttle's thick columnar docking shaft, wedged into the center of the module like a spear through a doughnut. On the far side of the wall the new dinkos were making their wobbly way past the glowing ten-meter-high portrait of El Supremo and on into the red fiberglass tent that was the fumigation chamber. As usual, they were having a hard time with the low gravity. Here at the hub it was one-sixteenth G, max.

Juanito always wondered about the newcomers, why they were here, what they were fleeing. Only two kinds of people ever came to Valparaiso, those who wanted to hide and those who wanted to seek. The place was nothing but an enormous spacegoing safe house. You wanted to be left alone, you came to Valparaiso and bought yourself some privacy. But that implied that you had done something that made other people not want to let you alone. There was always some of both going on here, some hiding, some seeking, El Supremo looking down benignly on it all, raking in his cut. And not just El Supremo.

Down below, the new dinkos were trying to walk jaunty, to walk mean. But that was hard to do when you were keeping your body all clenched up as if you were afraid of drifting into midair if you put your foot down too hard. Juanito loved it, the way they were crunching along, that constipated shuffle of theirs.

Gravity stuff didn't ever bother Juanito. He had spent all his life out here in the satellite worlds and he took it for granted that the pull was going to fluctuate according to your distance from the hub. You automatically made compensating adjustments, that was all. Juanito found it hard to understand a place where the gravity would be the same everywhere all the time. He had never set foot on Earth or any of the other natural planets, didn't care to, didn't expect to.

The guard on duty at the quarantine gate was an android. His name, his label, whatever it was, was something like Velcro Exxon. Juanito had seen him at this gate before. As he came up close the android glanced at him and said, "Working again so soon, Juanito?"

"Man has to eat, no?"

The android shrugged. Eating wasn't all that important to him, most likely. "Weren't you working that plutonium peddler out of Commonplace?"

Juanito said, smiling, "What plutonium peddler?"

"Sure," said the android. "I hear you."

He held out his waxy-skinned hand and Juanito put a fifty-callaghano currency plaque in it. The usual fee for illicit entry to the customs tank was only thirty-five callies, but Juanito believed in spreading the wealth, especially where the authorities were concerned. They didn't *have* to let you in here, after all. Some days more couriers showed up than there were dinkos, and then the gate guards had to allocate. Overpaying the guards was simply a smart investment.

"Thank you kindly," the android said. "Thank you very much." He hit the scanner override. Juanito stepped through the security shield into the customs tank and looked around for his mark.

The new dinkos were being herded into the fumigation chamber now. They were annoyed about that—they always were—but the guards kept them moving right along through the puffy bursts of pink and green and yellow sprays that came from the ceiling nozzles. Nobody got out of customs quarantine without passing through that chamber. El Supremo was paranoid about the entry of exotic microorganisms into Valparaiso's closed-cycle ecology. El Supremo was paranoid about a lot of things. You didn't get to be sole and absolute ruler of your own little satellite world, and stay that way for thirty-seven years, without a heavy component of paranoia in your makeup.

Juanito leaned up against the great curving glass wall of the customs tank and peered through the mists of sterilizer fog. The rest of the couriers were starting to come in now. Juanito watched them singling out potential clients. Most of the dinkos were signing up as soon as the deal was explained, but as always a few were shaking off help and setting out by themselves. Cheapskates, Juanito thought. Assholes and wimps, Juanito thought. But they'd find out. It wasn't possible to get started on Valparaiso without a courier, no matter how sharp you thought you were. Valparaiso was a free enterprise zone, after all. If you knew the rules, you were pretty much safe from all harm here forever. If not, not.

Time to make the approach, Juanito figured.

It was easy enough finding the blind man. He was much taller than the other dinkos, a big burly man some thirty-odd years old, heavy bones, powerful muscles. In the bright glaring light his blank forehead gleamed like a reflecting beacon. The low gravity didn't seem to trouble him much, nor his blindness. His movements along the customs track were easy, confident, almost graceful.

Juanito sauntered over and said, "I'll be your courier, sir. Juanito Holt." He barely came up to the blind man's elbow.

"Courier?"

"New arrival assistance service. Facilitate your entry arrangements. Customs clearance, currency exchange, hotel accommodations, permanent settlement papers if that's what you intend. Also special services by arrangement."

Juanito stared up expectantly at the blank face. The eyeless man looked back at him in a blunt straight-on way, what would have been strong eye contact if the dinko had had eyes. That was eerie. What was even eerier was the sense Juanito had that the eyeless man was seeing him clearly. For just a moment he wondered who was going to be controlling whom in this deal.

"What kind of special services?"

"Anything else you need," Juanito said.

"Anything?"

"Anything. This is Valparaiso, sir."

"Mmm. What's your fee?"

"Two thousand callaghanos a week for the basic. Specials are extra, according."

"How much is that in Capbloc dollars, your basic?"

Juanito told him.

"That's not so bad," the blind man said.

"Two weeks minimum, payable in advance."

"Mmm," said the blind man again. Again that intense eyeless gaze, seeing right through him. "How old are you?" he asked suddenly.

"Seventeen," Juanito blurted, caught off guard.

"And you're good, are you?"

"I'm the best. I was born here. I know everybody."

"I'm going to be needing the best. You take electronic handshake?"

"Sure," Juanito said. This was too easy. He wondered if he should have asked three kilocallies a week, but it was too late now. He pulled his flex terminal from his tunic pocket and slipped his fingers into it. "Unity Callaghan Bank of Valparaiso. That's code 22-44-66, and you might as well give it a default key, because it's the only bank here. Account 1133, that's mine."

The blind man donned his own terminal and deftly tapped the number pad on his wrist. Then he grasped Juanito's hand firmly in his until the sensors overlapped, and made the transfer of funds. Juanito touched for confirm and a bright green *+cl. 4000* lit up on the screen in his palm. The payee's name was Victor Farkas, out of an account in the Royal Amalgamated Bank of Liechtenstein.

"Liechtenstein," Juanito said. "That's an Earth country?"

"Very small one. Between Austria and Switzerland."

"I've heard of Switzerland. You live on Liechtenstein?"

"No," Farkas said. "I bank there. *In* Liechtenstein, is what Earth people say. Except for islands. Liechtenstein isn't an island. Can we get out of this place now?"

"One more transfer," Juanito said. "Pump your entry software across to me. Baggage claim, passport, visa. Make things much easier for us both, getting out of here."

"Make it easier for you to disappear with my suitcase, yes. And I'd never find you again, would I?"

"Do you think I'd do that?"

"I'm more profitable to you if you don't."

"You've got to trust your courier, Mr. Farkas. If you can't trust your courier, you can't trust anybody at all on Valparaiso."

"I know that," Farkas said.

Collecting Farkas' baggage and getting him clear of the customs tank took another half an hour and cost about two hundred callies in miscellaneous bribes, which was about standard. Everyone from the baggage-handling androids to the cute snotty teller at the currency-exchange booth had to be bought. Juanito understood that things didn't work that way on most worlds; but Valparaiso, he knew, was different from most worlds. In a place where the chief industry was the protection of fugitives, it made sense that the basis of the economy would be the recycling of bribes.

Farkas didn't seem to be any sort of fugitive, though. While he was waiting for the baggage Juanito pulled a readout on the software that the blind man had pumped over to him and saw that Farkas was here on a vistor's visa, six weeks limit. So he was a seeker, not a hider. Well, that was okay. It was possible to turn a profit working either side of the deal. Running traces wasn't Juanito's usual number, but he figured he could adapt.

The other thing that Farkas didn't seem to be was blind. As they emerged from the customs tank he turned and pointed back at the huge portrait of El Supremo and said, "Who's that? Your President?"

"The Defender, that's his title. The Generalissimo. El Supremo, Don Eduardo Callaghan." Then it sank in and Juanito said, blinking. "Pardon me. You can *see* that picture, Mr. Farkas?"

"In a manner of speaking."

"I don't follow. Can you see or can't you?"

"Yes and no."

"Thanks a lot, Mr. Farkas."

"We can talk more about it later," Farkas said.

Juanito always put new dinkos in the same hotel, the San Bernardito, four kilometers out from the hub in the rim community of Cajamarca. "This way," he told Farkas. "We have to take the elevator at C Spoke."

Farkas didn't seem to have any trouble following him. Every now and then Juanito glanced back, and there was the big man three or four paces behind him, marching along steadily down the corridor. No eyes, Juanito thought, but somehow he can see. He definitely can see.

The four-kilometer elevator ride down C Spoke to the rim was spectacular all the way. The elevator was a glass-walled chamber inside a glass-walled tube that ran along the outside of the spoke, and it let you see everything: the whole great complex of wheels within wheels that was the Earth-orbit artificial world of Valparaiso, the seven great structural spokes radiating from the hub to the distant wheel of the rim, each spoke bearing its seven glass-and-aluminum globes that contained the residential zones and business sectors and farmlands and recreational zones and forest reserves. As the elevator descended—the gravity rising as you went down, climbing toward an Earth-one pull in the rim towns—you had a view of the sun's dazzling glint on the adjacent spokes, and an occasional glimpse of the great blue belly of Earth filling up the sky a hundred fifty thousand kilometers away, and the twinkling hordes of other satellite worlds in their nearby orbits, like a swarm of jellyfish dancing in a vast black ocean. That was what everybody who came up from Earth said, "Like jellyfish in the ocean." Juanito didn't understand how a fish could be made out of jelly, or how a satellite world with seven spokes looked anything like a fish of any kind, but that was what they all said.

Farkas didn't say anything about jellyfish. But in some fashion or other he did indeed seem to be taking in the view. He stood close to the elevator's glass wall in deep concentration, gripping the rail, not saying a thing. Now and then he made a little hissing sound as something particularly awesome went by outside. Juanito studied him with sidelong glances. What could he possibly see? Nothing seemed to be moving beneath those shadowy places where his eyes should have been. Yet somehow he was seeing out of that broad blank stretch of gleaming skin above his nose. It was damned disconcerting. It was downright weird.

The San Bernardito gave Farkas a rim-side room, facing the stars. Juanito paid the hotel clerks to treat his clients right. That was something his father had taught him when he was just a kid who wasn't old enough to know a Schwarzchild singularity from an ace in the hole. "Pay for what you're going to need," his father kept saying. "Buy it and at least there's a chance it'll be there when you have to have it." His father had been a revolutionary in

Central America during the time of the Empire. He would have been Prime Minister if the revolution had come out the right way. But it hadn't.

"You want me to help you unpack?" Juanito said.

"I can manage."

"Sure," Juanito said.

He stood by the window, looking at the sky. Like all the other satellite worlds, Valparaiso was shielded from cosmic ray damage and stray meteoroids by a double shell filled with a three-meter thick layer of lunar slag. Rows of V-shaped apertures ran down the outer skin of the shield, mirror-faced to admit sunlight but not hard radiation; and the hotel had lined its rooms up so each one on this side had a view of space through the V's. The whole town of Cajamarca was facing darkwise now, and the stars were glittering fiercely.

When Juanito turned from the window he saw that Farkas had hung his clothes neatly in the closet and was shaving—methodically, precisely—with a little hand-held laser.

"Can I ask you something personal?" Juanito said.

"You want to know how I see."

"It's pretty amazing, I have to say."

"I don't see. Not really. I'm just as blind as you think I am."

"Then how—"

"It's called blindsight," Farkas said. "Proprioceptive vision."

"What?"

Farkas chuckled. "There's all sorts of data bouncing around that doesn't have the form of reflected light, which is what your eyes see. A million vibrations besides those that happen to be in the visual part of the electromagnetic spectrum are shimmering in this room. Air currents pass around things and are deformed by what they encounter. And it isn't only the air currents. Objects have mass, they have heat, they have—the term won't make any sense to you—*shapeweight*. A quality having to do with the interaction of mass and form. Does that mean anything to you? No, I guess not. Look, there's a lot of information available beyond what you can see with eyes, if you want it. I want it."

"You use some kind of machine to pick it up?" Juanito asked.

Farkas tapped his forehead. "It's in here. I was born with it."

"Some kind of sensing organ instead of eyes?"

"That's pretty close."

"What do you see, then? What do things look like to you?"

"What do they look like to you?" Farkas said. "What does a chair look like to you?"

"Well, it's got four legs, and a back—"

"What does a leg look like?"

"It's longer than it is wide."

"Right." Farkas knelt and ran his hands along the black tubular legs of the ugly little chair beside the bed. "I touch the chair, I feel the shape of the legs. But I don't see leg-shaped shapes."

"What then?"

"Silver globes that roll away into fat curves. The back part of the chair bends double and folds into itself. The bed's a bright pool of mercury with long green spikes coming up. You're six blue spheres stacked one on top of another, with a thick orange cable running through them. And so on."

"Blue?" Juanito said. "Orange? How do you know anything about colors?"

"The same way you do. I call one color blue, another one orange. I don't know if they're anything like your blue or orange, but so what? My blue is always blue for me. It's different from the color I see as red and the one I see as green. Orange is always orange. It's a matter of relationships. You follow?"

"No," Juanito said. "How can you possibly make sense out of anything? What you see doesn't have anything to do with the real color or shape or position of anything."

Farkas shook his head. "Wrong, Juanito. For me, what I see *is* the real shape and color and position. It's all I've ever known. If they were able to retrofit me with normal eyes now, which I'm told would be less than fifty-fifty likely to succeed and tremendously risky besides, I'd be lost trying to find my way around in your world. It would take me years to learn how. Or maybe forever. But I do all right, in mine. I understand, by touching things, that what I see by blindsight isn't the 'actual' shape. But I see in consistent equivalents. Do you follow? A chair always looks like what I think of as a chair, even though I know that chairs aren't really shaped anything like that. If you could see things the way I do it would all look like something out of another dimension. It *is* something out of another dimension, really. The information I operate by is different from what you use, that's all. And the world I move through looks completely different from the world that normal people see. But I do see, in my own way. I perceive objects and establish relationships between them, I make spatial perceptions, just as you do. Do you follow, Juanito? Do you follow?''

Juanito considered that. How very weird it sounded. To see the world in funhouse distortions, blobs and spheres and orange cables and glimmering pools of mercury. Weird, very weird. After a moment he said, "And you were born like this?"

"That's right."

"Some kind of genetic accident?"

"Not an accident," Farkas said quietly. "I was an experiment. A master gene-splicer worked me over in my mother's womb."

"Right," Juanito said. "You know, that's actually the first thing I guessed when I saw you come off the shuttle. This has to be some kind of splice effect, I said. But why—why—" He faltered. "Does it bother you to talk about this stuff?"

"Not really."

"Why would your parents have allowed—"

"They didn't have any choice, Juanito."

"Isn't that illegal? Involuntary splicing?"

"Of course," Farkas said. "So what?"

"But who would do that to—"

"This was in the Free State of Kazakhstan, which you've never heard of. It was one of the new countries formed out of the Soviet Union, which you've also probably never heard of, after the Breakup. My father was Hungarian consul at Tashkent. He was killed in the Breakup and my mother, who was pregnant, was volunteered for the experiments in prenatal genetic surgery then being carried out in that city under Chinese auspices. A lot of remarkable work was done there in those years. They were trying to breed new and useful kinds of human beings to serve the new republic. I was one of the experiments in extending the human perceptual range. I was supposed to have normal sight plus blindsight, but I didn't quite work out that way."

"You sound very calm about it," Juanito said.

"What good is getting angry?"

"My father used to say that too," Juanito said. "Don't get

angry, get even. He was in politics, the Central American Empire. When the revolution failed he took sanctuary here.''

"So did the surgeon who did my prenatal splice," Farkas said. "Fifteen years ago. He's still living here."

"Of course," Juanito said, as everything fell into place.

"The man's name is Wu Fang-shui," Juanito said. "He'd be about seventy-five years old, Chinese, and that's all I know, except there'll be a lot of money in finding him. There can't be that many Chinese on Valparaiso, right?''

"He won't still be Chinese," Kluge said.

Delilah said. "He might not even still be a he."

"I've thought of that," said Juanito. "All the same, it ought to be possible to trace him."

"Who you going to use for the trace?" Kluge asked.

Juanito gave him a steady stare. "Going to do it myself.''

"You?"

"Me, myself. Why the hell not?''

"You never did a trace, did you?''

"There's always a first," Juanito said, still staring.

He thought he knew why Kluge was poking at him. A certain quantity of the business done on Valparaiso involved finding people who had hidden themselves here and selling them to their pursuers, but up till now Juanito had stayed away from that side of the profession. He earned his money by helping dinkos go underground on Valparaiso, not by selling people out. One reason for that was that nobody yet had happened to offer him a really profitable trace deal; but another was that he was the son of a former fugitive himself. Someone had been hired to do a trace on his own father seven years back, which was how his father had come to be assassinated. Juanito preferred to work the sanctuary side of things.

He was also a professional, though. He was in the business of providing service, period. If he didn't find the runaway gene surgeon for Farkas, somebody else would. And Farkas was his client. Juanito felt it was important to do things in a professional way.

"If I run into problems," he said, "I might subcontract. In the meanwhile I just thought I'd let you know, in case you happened to stumble on a lead. I'll pay finders' fees. And you know it'll be good money."

"Wu Fang-shui," Kluge said. "I'll see what I can do."

"Me too," said Delilah.

"Hell," Juanito said. "How many people are there on Valparaiso all together? Maybe nine hundred thousand? I can think of fifty right away who can't possibly be the guy I'm looking for. That narrows the odds some. What I have to do is just go on narrowing, right? Right?"

In fact he didn't feel very optimistic. He was going to do his best; but the whole system on Valparaiso was heavily weighted in favor of helping those who wanted to hide stay hidden.

Even Farkas realized that. "The privacy laws here are very strict, aren't they?"

With a smile Juanito said, "They're just about the only laws we have, you know? The sacredness of sanctuary. It is the compassion of El Supremo that has turned Valparaiso into a place of refuge for fugitives of all sorts, and we are not supposed to interfere with the compassion of El Supremo."

"Which is very expensive compassion, I understand."

"Very. Sanctuary fees are renewable annually. Anyone who harms a permanent resident who is living here under the compassion of El Supremo is bringing about a reduction in El Supremo's annual income, you see? Which doesn't sit well with the Generalissimo."

They were in the Villanueva Cafe, E Spoke. They had been touring Valparaiso all day long, back and forth from rim to hub, going up one spoke and down the other. Farkas said he wanted to experience as much of Valparaiso as he could. Not to see; to *experience*. He was insatiable, prowling around everywhere, gobbling it all up, soaking it in. Farkas had never been to one of the satellite worlds before. It amazed him, he said, that there were forests and lakes here, broad fields of wheat and rice, fruit orchards, herds of goats and cattle. Apparently he had expected the place to be nothing more than a bunch of aluminum struts and grim concrete boxes with everybody living on food pills, or something. People from Earth never seemed to comprehend that the larger satellite worlds were comfortable places with blue skies, fleecy clouds, lovely gardens, handsome buildings of steel and brick and glass.

Farkas said, "How do you go about tracing a fugitive, then?"

"There are always ways. Everybody knows somebody who knows something about someone. Information is bought here the same way compassion is."

"From the Generalissimo?" Farkas said, startled.

"From his officials, sometimes. If done with great care. Care is important, because lives are at risk. There are also couriers who have information to sell. We all know a great deal that we are not supposed to know."

"I suppose you know a great many fugitives by sight, yourself?"

"Some," Juanito said. "You see that man, sitting by the window?" He frowned. "I don't know, can you see him? To me he looks around sixty, bald head, thick lips, no chin?"

"I see him, yes. He looks a little different to me."

"I bet he does. He ran a swindle at one of the Luna domes, sold phony stock in an offshore monopoly fund that didn't exist, fifty million Capbloc dollars. He pays plenty to live here. This one here—you see? With the blonde woman?—an embezzler, that one, very good with computers, reamed a bank in Singapore for almost its entire capital. Him over there, he pretended to be Pope. Can you believe that? Everybody in Rio de Janeiro did."

"Wait a minute," Farkas said. "How do I know you're not making all this up?"

"You don't," Juanito said amiably. "But I'm not."

"So we just sit here like this and you expose the identities of three fugitives to me free of charge?"

"It wouldn't be free," Jaunito said, "if they were people you were looking for."

"What if they were? And my claiming to be looking for a Wu Fang-shui just a cover?"

"You aren't looking for any of them," Juanito said.

"No," said Farkas. "I'm not." He sipped his drink, something green and cloudy. "How come these men haven't done a better job of concealing their identities?" he asked.

"They think they have," said Juanito.

Getting leads was a slow business, and expensive. Juanito left Farkas to wander the spokes of Valparaiso on his own, and headed off to the usual sources of information: his father's friends, other couriers, and even the headquarters of the Unity Party, El Supremo's grass-roots organization, where it wasn't hard to find someone who knew something and had a price for it. Juanito was cautious. Middle-aged Chinese gentleman I'm trying to locate, he said. Why? Nobody asked. Could be any reason, anything from wanting to blow him away on contract to handing him a million-Capbloc-dollar lottery prize that he had won last year on New Yucatan. Nobody asked for reasons on Valparaiso.

There was a man name Federigo who had been with Juanito's father in the Costa Rica days who knew a woman who knew a man who had a freemartin neuter companion who had formerly belonged to someone high up in the Census Department. There were fees to pay at every step of the way, but it was Farkas' money, what the hell, and by the end of the week Juanito had access to the immigration data stored on golden megachips somewhere in the depths of the hub. The data down there wasn't going to provide anybody with Wu Fang-shui's phone number. But what it could tell Juanito, and did, eight hundred callaghanos later, was how many ethnic Chinese were living on Valparaiso and how long ago they had arrived.

"There are nineteen of them altogether," he reported to Farkas. "Eleven of them are women."

"So? Changing sex is no big deal," Farkas said.

"Agreed. The women are all under fifty, though. The oldest of the men is sixty-two. The longest that any of them has been on Valparaiso is nine years."

"Would you say that rules them all out? Age can be altered just as easily as sex."

"But date of arrival can't be, so far as I know. And you say that your Wu Fang-shui came here fifteen years back. Unless you're wrong about that, he can't be any of those Chinese. Your Wu Fang-shui, if he isn't dead by now, has signed up for some other racial mix, I'd say."

"He isn't dead," Farkas said.

"You sure of that?"

"He was still alive three months ago, and in touch with his family on Earth. He's got a brother in Tashkent."

"Shit," Juanito said. "Ask the brother what name he's going under up here, then."

"We did. We couldn't get it."

"Ask him harder."

"We asked him too hard," said Farkas. "Now the information isn't available anymore. Not from him, anyway."

Juanito checked out the nineteen Chinese, just to be certain. It didn't cost much and it didn't take much time, and there was always the chance that Dr. Wu had cooked his immigration data somehow. But the quest led nowhere. Juanito found six of them all in one shot, playing some Chinese game in a social club in the town of Havana de Cuba on Spoke B, and they went right on laughing and pushing the little porcelain counters around while he stood there kibitzing. They didn't *act* like sanctuarios. They were all shorter than Juanito, too, which meant either that they weren't Dr. Wu, who was tall for a Chinese, or that Dr. Wu had been willing to have his legs chopped down by fifteen centimeters for the sake of a more efficient disguise. It was possible but it wasn't too likely.

The other thirteen were all much too young or too convincingly female or too this or too that. Juanito crossed them all off his list. From the outset he hadn't thought Wu would still be Chinese, anyway.

He kept on looking. One trail went cold, and then another, and then another. By now he was starting to think Dr. Wu must have heard that a man with no eyes was looking for him, and had gone even deeper underground, or off Valparaiso entirely. Juanito paid a friend at the hub spaceport to keep watch on departure manifests for him. Nothing came of that. Then someone reminded him that there was a colony of old-time hard-core sanctuary types living in and around the town of El Mirador on Spoke D, people who had a genuine aversion to being bothered. He went there. Because he was known to be the son of a murdered fugitive himself, nobody hassled him: he of all people wouldn't be likely to be running a trace, would he?

The visit yielded no directly useful result. He couldn't risk asking questions and nothing was showing on the surface. But he came away with the strong feeling that El Mirador was the answer.

"Take me there," Farkas said.

"I can't do that. It's a low-profile town. Strangers aren't welcome. You'll stick out like a dinosaur."

"Take me," Farkas repeated.

"If Wu's there and he gets even a glimpse of you, he'll know right away that there's a contract out for him and he'll vanish so fast you won't believe it."

"Take me to El Mirador," said Farkas. "It's my money, isn't it?"

"Right," Juanito said. "Let's go to El Mirador."

El Mirador was midway between hub and rim on its spoke. There were great glass windows punched in its shield that provided a colossal view of all the rest of Valparaiso and the stars and the sun and the moon and the Earth and everything. A solar eclipse was going on when Juanito and Farkas arrived: the Earth was plastered right over the sun with nothing but one squidge of hot light showing down below like a diamond blazing on a golden ring. Purple shadows engulfed the town, deep and thick, a heavy velvet curtain falling over everything.

Juanito tried to describe what he saw. Farkas made an impatient brushing gesture.

"I know, I know. I feel it in my teeth." They stood on a big peoplemover escalator leading down into the town plaza. "The sun is long and thin right now, like the blade of an axe. The Earth has six sides, each one glowing a different color."

Juanito gaped at the eyeless man in amazement.

"Wu is here," Farkas said. "Down there, in the plaza. I feel his presence."

"From five hundred meters away?"

"Come with me."

"What do we do if he really is?"

"Are you armed?"

"I have a spike, yes."

"Good. Tune it to shock, and don't use it at all if you can help it. I don't want you to hurt him in any way."

"I understand. You want to kill him yourself, in your own sweet time."

"Just be careful not to hurt him," Farkas said. "Come on."

It was an old-fashioned-looking town, cobblestone plaza, little cafes around its perimeter and a fountain in the middle. About ten thousand people lived there and it seemed as if they were all out in the plaza sipping drinks and watching the eclipse. Juanito was grateful for the eclipse. No one paid any attention to them as they came floating down the peoplemover and strode into the plaza. Hell of a thing, he thought. You walk into town with a man with no eyes walking right behind you and nobody even notices. But when the sunshine comes back on it may be different.

"There he is," Farkas whispered. "To the left, maybe fifty meters, sixty."

Juanito peered through the purple gloom at the plazafront cafe beyond the next one. A dozen or so people were sitting in small groups at curbside tables under iridescent fiberglass awnings, drinking, chatting, taking it easy. Just another casual afternoon in good old cozy El Mirador on sleepy old Valparaiso.

Farkas stood sideways to keep his strange face partly concealed. Out of the corner of his mouth he said, "Wu is the one sitting by himself at the front table."

"The only one sitting alone is a woman, maybe fifty, fifty-five years old, long reddish hair, big nose, dowdy clothes ten years out of fashion."

"That's Wu."

"How can you be so sure?"

"It's possible to retrofit your body to make it look entirely different on the outside. You can't change the non-visual information, the stuff I pick up by blindsight. What Dr. Wu looked like to me, the last time I saw him, was a cubical block of black metal polished bright as a mirror, sitting on top of a pyramid-shaped copper-colored pedestal. I was nine years old then, but I promised myself I wouldn't ever forget what he looked like, and I haven't. That's what the person sitting over there by herself looks like."

Juanito stared. He still saw a plain-looking woman in a rumpled old-fashioned suit. They did wonders with retrofitting these days, he knew: they could make almost any sort of body grow on you, like clothing on a clothesrack, by fiddling with your DNA. But still Juanito had trouble thinking of that woman over there as a sinister Chinese gene-splicer in disguise, and he had even more trouble seeing her as a polished cube sitting on top of a coppery pyramid.

"What do you want to do now?" he asked.

"Let's go over and sit down alongside her. Keep that spike of yours ready. But I hope you don't use it."

"If we put the arm on her and she's not Wu," Juanito said, "it's going to get me in a hell of a lot of trouble, particularly if she's paying El Supremo for sanctuary. Sanctuary people get very stuffy when their privacy is violated. You'll be expelled and I'll be fined a fortune and a half and I might wind up getting expelled too, and then what?"

"That's Dr. Wu," Farkas said. "Watch him react when he sees me, and then you'll believe it."

"We'll still be violating sanctuary. All he has to do is yell for the police."

"We need to make it clear to him right away," said Farkas, "that that would be a foolish move. You follow?"

"But I don't hurt him," Juanito said.

"No. Not in any fashion. You simply demonstrate a willingness to hurt him it if should become necessary. Let's go, now. You sit down first, ask politely if it's okay for you to share the table, make some comment about the eclipse. I'll come over maybe thirty seconds after you. All clear? Good. Go ahead, now."

"You have to be insane," the red-haired woman said. But she was sweating in an astonishing way and her fingers were knotting together like anguished snakes. "I'm not any kind of doctor and my name isn't Wu or Fu or whatever you said, and you have exactly two seconds to get away from me." She seemed unable to take her eyes from Farkas' smooth blank forehead. Farkas didn't move. After a moment she said in a different tone of voice, "What kind of thing are you, anyway?"

She isn't Wu, Juanito decided.

The real Wu wouldn't have asked a question like that. Besides, this was definitely a woman. She was absolutely convincing around the jaws, along the hairline, the soft flesh behind her chin. Women were different from men in all those places. Something about her wrists. The way she sat. A lot of other things. There weren't any genetic surgeons good enough to do a retrofit this convincing. Juanito peered at her eyes, trying to see the place where the Chinese fold had been, but there wasn't a trace of it. Her eyes were blue-gray. All Chinese had brown eyes, didn't they?

Farkas said, leaning in close and hard, "My name is Victor Farkas, doctor. I was born in Tashkent during the Breakup. My mother was the wife of the Hungarian consul, and you did a gene-splice job on the fetus she was carrying. That was your specialty, tectogenetic reconstruction. You don't remember that? You deleted my eyes and gave me blindsight instead, doctor.''

The woman looked down and away. Color came to her cheeks. Something heavy seemed to be stirring within her. Juanito began to change his mind. Maybe there really were some gene surgeons who could do a retrofit this good, he thought.

"None of this is true," she said. "You're simply a lunatic. I can show you who I am. I have papers. You have no right to harass me like this.''

"I don't want to hurt you in any way, doctor.''

"I am not a doctor.''

"Could you be a doctor again? For a price?''

Juanito swung around, astounded, to look at Farkas.

"I will not listen to this," the woman said. "You will go away from me this instant or I summon the patrol.''

Farkas said, "We have a project, Dr. Wu. My engineering group, a division of a corporation whose name I'm sure you know. An experimental spacedrive, the first interstellar voyage, faster-than-light travel. We're three years away from a launch.''

The woman rose. "This madness does not interest me.''

"The faster-than-light field distorts vision," Farkas went on. He didn't appear to notice that she was standing and looked about ready to bolt. "It disrupts vision entirely, in fact. Perception becomes totally abnormal. A crew with normal vision wouldn't be able to function in any way. But it turns out that someone with blindsight can adapt fairly easily to the peculiar changes that the field induces.''

"I have no interest in hearing about—''

"It's been tested, actually. With me as the subject. But I can't make the voyage alone. We have a crew of five and they've volunteered for tectogenetic retrofits to give them what I have. We don't know anyone else who has your experience in that area. We'd like you to come out of retirement, Dr. Wu. We'll set up a complete lab for you on a nearby satellite world, whatever equipment you need. And pay you very well. And insure your safety all the time you're gone from Valparaiso. What do you say?''

The red-haired woman was trembling and slowly backing away.

"No," she said. "It was such a long time ago. Whatever skills I had, I have forgotten, I have buried."

So Farkas was right all along, Juanito thought.

"You can give yourself a refresher course. I don't think it's possible really to forget a gift like yours, do you?" Farkas said.

"No. Please. Let me be."

Juanito was amazed at how cockeyed his whole handle on the situation had been from the start.

Farkas didn't seem at all angry with the gene surgeon. He hadn't come here for vengeance, Juanito realized. Just to cut a deal.

"Where's he going?" Farkas said suddenly. "Don't let him get away, Juanito."

The woman—Wu—was moving faster now, not quite running but sidling away at a steady pace, back into the enclosed part of the cafe. Farkas gestured sharply and Juanito began to follow. The spike he was carrying could deliver a stun-level jolt at fifteen paces. But he couldn't just spike her down in this crowd, not if she had sanctuary protection, not in El Mirador of all places. There'd be fifty sanctuarios on top of him in a minute. They'd grab him and club him and sell his foreskin to the Generalissimo's men for two and a half callies.

The cafe was crowded and dark. Juanito caught sight of her somewhere near the back, near the restrooms. Go on, he thought. Go into the ladies' room. I'll follow you right in there. I don't give a damn about that.

But she went past the restrooms and ducked into an alcove near the kitchen instead. Two waiters laden with trays came by, scowling at Juanito to get out of the way. It took him a moment to pass around them, and by then he could no longer see the red-haired woman. He knew he was going to have big trouble with Farkas if he lost her in here. Farkas was going to have a fit. Farkas would try to stiff him on this week's pay, most likely. Two thousand callies down the drain, not even counting the extra charges.

Then a hand reached out of the shadows and seized his wrist with surprising ferocity. He was dragged a little way into a claustrophobic games room dense with crackling green haze coming from some bizarre machine on the far wall. The red-haired woman glared at him, wild-eyed. "He wants to kill me, doesn't he? That's all bullshit about having me do retrofit operations, right?"

"I think he means it," Juanito said.

"Nobody would volunteer to have his eyes replaced with blindsight."

"How would I know? People do all sorts of crazy things. But if he wanted to kill you I think he'd have operated differently when we tracked you down."

"He'll get me off Valparaiso and kill me somewhere else."

"I don't know," Juanito said. "I was just doing a job."

"How much did he pay you to do the trace?" Savagely. "How much? I know you've got a spike in your pocket. Just leave it there and answer me. How much?"

"Three thousand callies a week," Juanito muttered, padding things a little.

"I'll give you five to help me get rid of him."

Juanito hesitated. Sell Farkas out? He didn't know if he could turn himself around that fast. Was it the professional thing to do, to take a higher bid?

"Eight," he said, after a moment.

Why the hell not? He didn't owe Farkas any loyalty. This was a sanctuary world; the compassion of El Supremo entitled Wu to protection here. It was every citizen's duty. And eight thousand callies was a big bundle.

"Six five," Wu said.

"Eight. Handshake right now. You have your glove?"

The woman who was Wu made a muttering sound and pulled out her flex terminal. "Account 1133," Juanito said, and they made the transfer of funds. "How do you want to do this?" Juanito asked.

"There is a passageway into the outer shell just behind this cafe. You will catch sight of me slipping in there and the two of you will follow me. When we are all inside and he is coming toward me, you get behind him and take him down with your spike. And we leave him buried in there." There was a frightening gleam in Wu's eyes. It was almost as if the cunning retrofit body was melting away and the real Wu beneath was emerging, moment by moment. "You understand?" Wu said. A fierce, blazing look. "I have bought you, boy. I expect you to stay bought when we are in the shell. Do you understand me? Do you? Good."

*   *   *

It was like a huge crawlspace entirely surrounding the globe that was El Mirador. Around the periphery of the double shell was a deep layer of lunar slag held in place by centrifugal forces, the tailings left over after the extraction of the gases and minerals that the satellite world had needed in its construction. On top of that was a low open area for the use of maintenance workers, lit by a trickle of light from a faint line of incandescent bulbs; and overhead was the inner skin of El Mirador itself, shielded by the slagpile from any surprises that might come ricocheting in from the void. Juanito was able to move almost upright within the shell, but Farkas, following along behind, had to bend double, scuttling like a crab.

"Can you see him yet?" Farkas asked.

"Somewhere up ahead, I think. It's pretty dark in here."

"Is it?"

Juanito saw Wu edging sideways, moving slowly around behind Farkas now. In the dimness Wu was barely visible, the shadow of a shadow. He had scooped up two handfuls of tailings. Evidently he was going to fling them at Farkas to attract his attention, and when Farkas turned toward Wu it would be Juanito's moment to nail him with the spike.

Juanito stepped back to a position near Farkas' left elbow. He slipped his hand into his pocket and touched the cool sleek little weapon. The intensity stud was down at the lower end, shock level, and without taking the spike from his pocket he moved the setting up to lethal. Wu nodded. Juanito began to draw the spike.

Suddenly Farkas roared like a wild creature. Juanito grunted in shock, stupefied by that terrible sound. This is all going to go wrong, he realized. A moment later Farkas whirled and seized him around the waist and swung him as if he was a throwing-hammer, hurling him through the air and sending him crashing with tremendous impact into Wu's midsection. Wu crumpled, gagging and puking, with Juanito sprawled stunned on top of him. Then the lights went out—Farkas must have reached up and yanked the conduit loose—and then Juanito found himself lying with his face jammed down into the rough floor of tailings. Farkas was holding him down with a hand clamped around the back of his neck and a knee pressing hard against his spine. Wu lay alongside him, pinned the same way.

"Did you think I couldn't see him sneaking up on me?" Farkas asked. "Or you, going for your spike? It's 360 degrees, the blindsight. Something that Dr. Wu must have forgotten. All these years on the run, I guess you start to forget things."

Jesus, Juanito thought. Couldn't even get the drop on a blind man from behind him. And now he's going to kill me. What a stupid way to die this is.

He imagined what Kluge might say about this, if he knew. Or Delilah. Nattathaniel. Decked by a blind man.

But he isn't blind. He isn't blind. He isn't blind at all.

Farkas said, "How much did you sell me to him for, Juanito?"

The only sound Juanito could make was a muffled moan. His mouth was choked with sharp bits of slag.

"How much? Five thousand? Six?"

"It was eight," said Wu quietly.

"At least I didn't go cheaply," Farkas murmured. He reached into Juanito's pocket and withdrew the spike. "Get up," he said. "Both of you. Stay close together. If either of you makes a funny move I'll kill you both. Remember that I can see you very clearly. I can also see the door through which we entered the shell. That starfish-looking thing over there, with streamers of purple light pulsing from it. We're going back into El Mirador now, and there won't be any surprises, will there? Will there?"

Juanito spit out a mouthful of slag. He didn't say anything.

"Dr. Wu? The offer still stands," Farkas continued. "You come with me, you do the job we need you for. That isn't so bad, considering what I could do to you for what you did to me. But all I want from you is your skills, and that's the truth. You are going to need that refresher course, aren't you, though?"

Wu muttered something indistinct.

Farkas said, "You can practice on this boy, if you like. Try retrofitting him for blindsight first, and if it works, you can do our crew people, all right? He won't mind. He's terribly curious about the way I see things, anyway. Aren't you, Juanito? Eh? Eh?" Farkas laughed. To Juanito he said, "If everything works out the right way, maybe we'll let you go on the voyage with us, boy." Juanito felt the cold nudge of the spike in his back. "You'd like that, wouldn't you? The first trip to the stars? What do you say to that, Juanito?"

Juanito didn't answer. His tongue was still rough with slag. With Farkas prodding him from behind, he shambled slowly along next to Dr. Wu toward the door that Farkas said looked like a starfish. It didn't look at all like a fish to him, or a star, or like a fish that looked like a star. It looked like a door to him, as far as he could tell by the feeble light of the distant bulbs. That was all it looked like, a door that looked like a door. Not a star. Not a fish. But there was no use thinking about it, or anything else, not now, not with Farkas nudging him between the shoulderblades with his own spike. He let his mind go blank and kept on walking.

Science fiction in its purest and most literal sense—fiction about science—is this wry and mordant little story by the gifted Carter Scholz, author of the 1984 novel Palimpsests *(with Glenn Harcourt) and a host of strikingly original shorter works.*

GALILEO COMPLAINS
Carter Scholz

The interview was held in his spacious condominium near Marina del Rey. The venerable astronomer, who still holds Italian citizenship, was looking tan and fit despite his recent resurrection by Fenix Corp.

In appearance and attire he seems little different from any of the retired screenwriters who live in this community. His apartments contain a wall-sized video screen, *objets d'art* from several centuries, a collection of astronomical instruments. Place of honor on the broad marble mantel is held by a slender, elegant telescope of his own construction, the very instrument through which he first observed the lunar surface, the phases of Venus, the rings of Saturn, and the moons of Jupiter.

The huge cost of his resurrection was paid by the Vatican, as partial restitution for its persecution of the astronomer in the seventeenth century. The suit was brought by a direct descendant in consultation with Fenix Corp; the amount of the full settlement has not yet been decided.

But Galileo himself is phlegmatic about his wealth.

"I am well off, yes," he says, sipping a flavored Perrier water. "And I am grateful, of course, for the formal vindication. But the extent of my wealth . . . that eludes me. I am less comfortable here than I was in Pisa. These apartments are in fact smaller than those the Inquisition held me in.''

I venture that he could, if he wished, live exactly how and where he pleased.

"True. But if I am to live in this century, then I feel I should live in this century." He glances around the room with bemusement. "My lawyers tell me I am wealthier than the Medici. To me this is laughable. Can I elect a Pope with my wealth, as they did? Can I even cause to be changed that portrait of Fernando de Medici discovering Jupiter's moons? No. That wretched painting, that libel, is now a national art treasure, if you please.''

I ask his plans. Will he return to his old profession?

"Why should I? I have seen your big observatories—your Palomar, your Mauna Kea, even your Arecibo. They are impressive as elephants are impressive. But it is not astronomy as I know it. Your astronomers never actually *look* through their instruments, did you know that? They use film and machines. Indeed, your air is so filthy that your largest telescopes, as at Arecibo, are used to track *invisible* waves.'' He shakes his head, as one who discusses lunacy.

He is clearly touchy about the gulf which still separates him from the modern world. His attitudes, his beliefs, his sense of the acceptable—these are not as ours. Once the greatest astronomer on earth, he cannot but feel inferior today, dwarfed in the face of our science.

I suggest that, with his wealth, he could build the grandest observatory on earth for himself.

"No, thanks. I have no wish to be called a cracked old man.''

I ask about his observation of Neptune. Its motion is clearly marked in one of his notebooks. Does he deserve credit for the planet's discovery?

He shrugs. "I didn't know what it was. Who was expecting another planet? I thought it was a star. Or maybe I thought it was an angel, eh?'' he adds sardonically.

I search for something to say, but he leans forward, tapping me on the chest. "Do you know what they are looking for, these so-called *astronomers*, through the blind eyes of their elephants? *The origin of the universe*. They told me so. They point their machines at the edge of existence, and there they expect to find the 'origin of the universe.' Madness!'' He leans back, and finishes his Perrier.

Tactfully I shift the topic. Does he harbor any resentment against the Inquisition?

He allows himself a grim smile for a moment, then speaks in a casual voice. "No, not really. If not for them, I wouldn't be here today, eh? And you must understand that I was asking for it. I'd been warned. It was sheer idiocy to publish my dialogues. They were quite willing to let me pursue my studies freely, so long as I made no asinine pronouncements; but I did. During my incarceration they were most pleasant to me. Cardinal Baggi himself made some valuable comments on celestial mechanics, and on the nature of matter. I had, you see, a very irresponsible obsession with what I was pleased to call *truth*, whereas the Church took the longer and wiser view that all truth is relative. The way to truth must be prepared, or it does more harm than good.'' He sighs. "I wonder if I could resurrect Cardinal Baggi. I miss our talks. But no, it wouldn't be fair to him.''

What of his legendary words—*and still it moves*—which history records after he signed the recantation?

"Oh, yes. I muttered that, under my breath I thought, and the old presiding Cardinal—I forget his name—smiled and said, 'Of course it does, my son, but you must not say so.' A very enlightened group, the Roman Church.''

Is he still a practicing Catholic?

"Certainly. What did you expect?''

But—his experience of death—surely that must have affected his belief.

"Death was nothing: a hyphen. I was in an intermediate state, as doctrine teaches. Souls are called to their reward only on Judgment Day, not before. That is the true resurrection. Or perhaps—'' He smiles inscrutably, and spreads his hands to encompass, it seems, all Marina del Rey. "—perhaps *this* is purgatory. What do you think, eh? All of us dead and damned here, and ignorant of it, a purgatory neither bad nor good, but just like Earth, where we must again earn our bliss or damnation, over and over, until we've learned better.''

I am no theologian, but I mention that even the Church has

recently admitted that Heaven and Hell may be fictions, or metaphors, rather than literal places. Galileo has a long laugh at this.

"And they called *me* a heretic! Ah, changing times. But perhaps they're wise. Perhaps that's been the truth all along, and we're only now ready to accept it. Or perhaps I'm right, and this is purgatory, and such thoughts are devil's snares, eh? What do you think? Have you died, young man?"

I insist that I have not, of course I have not, but even as I speak I have a sudden sickening memory, doubtless false, of an accident . . . he is persuasive, this Italian. I must remind myself that resurrection, in a case such as his, is from fragmentary material. There is potential for error. There are doubts as to the fidelity of the reproduction. I find I am speaking aloud. Galileo dismisses my doubts.

"I am he. Even my memories are intact. Can you say as much?"

My memories? At least I know that I have never died. Galileo favors me again with his inscrutable smile as he rises from his chair. I sense the interview is almost over.

"Yes, perhaps I'm a devil's snare for you. Ah, but you don't believe in the devil. So much the worse for you. Well, if I have my way I won't be resurrected again, despite my wealth. I'm not satisfied with this world of yours. In my day there were giants: the Medici, Michelangelo, Newton, myself. This world's a bad imitation. Your telescopes have mirrors the size of rotundas, or antennae to cover a vineyard, but with all of it you haven't made a tenth the change in your world that I made in mine with this." And he touches the slender telescope.

I ask if no modern achievement has impressed him. What of the photographs taken by unmanned space probes—the sublime breathtaking beauty of Saturn's twined rings seen close, or the tortured surfaces of his namesake Jovian satellites? Do even these leave him unmoved?

Grandly he looks down on me. "Remember that it was *I* who discovered these marvels. Even as I remember that it was God who made them."

This, at last, is too much for me, and I begin to enumerate the dozens, the hundreds, the thousands of accomplishments which have moved our world so far along the paths of progress since his death—resurrections not least among them!—but as I continue I realize that these achievements must be incomprehensible to his archaic mind. As I stop myself he is merely nodding politely.

"A race of clever monkeys," he says. "Best turn those monstrous mirrors back on yourselves."

So I leave the Italian, his vanity irrepressible at the last, and I move into the unnatural sunlight to board my hovercraft. Beyond its tinted glass Marina del Rey seems thin and insubstantial as it fades below me. Soon I am headed north, where I will continue my researches in talks with Einstein and Eduard Degas. Einstein is said to have renounced relativity, and passes his time in Lake Tahoe, learning Tartini violin sonatas and gambling at dice. Degas, rumor has it, has taken up computer graphics.

For the past three or four years Lucius Shepard has mined rich science fiction and fantasy from Central American backgrounds. This moving, powerful tale of time-travel and violence in Honduras is one of his best—a haunting, dazzling vision of a world destroyed and a world strangely reborn. Shepard's novella, R&R *won the Nebula award in 1987.*

AYMARA

Lucius Shepard

My name is William Page Corson, and I am the black sheep of the Buckingham County Corsons of Virginia. How I came to earn such disrepute relates to several months I spent in Honduras during the spring and summer of 1978, while doing research for a novel to be based on the exploits of an American mercenary who had played a major role in regional politics. That novel was never written, partly because I was of an age (twenty-one) at which one's concentration often proves unequal to lengthy projects, but mainly due to reasons that will be made clear—or if not made clear, then at least brought somewhat into focus—in the following pages.

One day while leafing through an old travel book, *A Honduran Adventure* by William Wells, I ran across the photograph of a blandly handsome young man with blond hair and mustache, carrying a saber and wearing an ostrich plume in his hat. The caption identified him as General Lee Christmas, and the text disclosed that he had been a railroad engineer in Louisiana until 1901, when—after three consecutive days on the job—he had fallen asleep at the wheel and wrecked his train. To avoid prosecution he had fled to Honduras, there securing employment on a fruit company railroad.

One year later, soldiers of the revolution led by General Manuel Bonilla had seized his train, and rather than merely surrendering, he had showed his captors how to armor the flatcars with sheet iron; thus protected, the soldiers had gained control of the entire north coast, and for his part in the proceedings, Christmas had been awarded the rank of general.

From other sources I learned that Christmas had taken a fine house in Tegucigalpa after the successful conclusion of the revolution, and had spent most of his time hunting in Olancho, a wilderness region bordering Nicaragua. By all accounts, he had been the prototypical good ol' boy, content with the cushy lot that had befallen him; but in 1904 something must have happened to change his basic attitudes, for it had been then that he entered the employ of the United Fruit Company, becoming in effect the company enforcer. Whenever one country or another would balk at company policy, Christmas would foment a rebellion and set a more malleable government in office; through this process, United Fruit had come to dominate Central American politics, earning the sobriquet El Pulpo (The Octopus) by virtue of its grasping tactics.

These materials fired my imagination and inflamed my leftist sensibility, and I traveled to Honduras in hopes of fleshing out the story. I soon unearthed a wealth of anecdotal detail, much of it testifying to Christmas' irrational courage: he had, for instance, once blown up a building atop which he was standing to prevent the armory it contained from falling into counter-revolutionary hands. But nowhere could I discover what event had precipitated the transformation of an affable, easygoing man into a ruthless mercenary, and an understanding of Christmas' motivations was, I believed, of central importance to my book. Six weeks went by, no new knowledge came to light, and I had more or less decided to create a fictive cause for Christmas' transformation, when I heard that some of the men who had fought alongside him in 1902 might still be alive on the island of Guanoja Menor.

From the window of the ancient DC-3 that conveyed me to Guanoja, the island resembled the cover of a travel brochure, with green hills and white beaches fringed by graceful palms; but at ground level it was revealed to be the outpost of an unrelenting poverty. Derelict shacks were tucked into the folds of the hills, animal wastes fouled the beaches, and the harbors were choked with sewage. The capital, Meachem's Landing, consisted of a few dirt streets lined with weatherbeaten shanties set on pilings, and beneath them lay a carpet of coconut litter and broken glass and crab shells. Black men wearing rags glared at me as I hiked in from the airport, and their hostility convinced me that even the act of walking was an insult to the lethargic temper of the place.

I checked into the Hotel Captain Henry—a ramshackle wooden building, painted pink, with a rust-scabbed roof and an electric pole lashed to its second-story balcony—and slept until nightfall. Then I set out to investigate a lead provided by the hotel's owner: he had told me of a man in his nineties, Fred Welcomes, who lived on the road to Flowers Bay and might have knowledge of Christmas. I had not gone more than a half-mile when I came upon a little graveyard confined by a fence of corroded ironwork and overgrown with weeds from which the tops of the tombstones bulged like toadstools. Many of the stones dated from the turn of the century, and realizing that the man I was soon to interview had been a contemporary of these long-dead people, I had a sense of foreboding, of standing on the verge of a supernatural threshold. Dozens of times in the years to follow, I was to have similar apprehensions, a notion that everything I did was governed by unfathomable forces; but never was it stronger than on that night. The wind was driving glowing clouds across the moon, intermittently allowing it to shine through, causing the landscape to pulse dark to bright with the rhythm of a failing circuit, and I could feel ghosts blowing about me, hear windy voices whispering words of warning.

Welcomes' shanty sat amid a banana grove, its orange-lit windows flickering like spirits in a dark water. As I drew near, its rickety shape appeared to assemble the way details are filled in during a dream, acquiring a roof and door and pilings whenever I noticed that it seemed to lack such, until at last it stood complete, looking every bit as dilapidated as I supposed its owner to be. I hesitated before approaching, startled by a banging shutter. Glints of moonlit silver coursed along the warp of the tin roof, and the plastic curtains twitched like the eyelids of a sleeping cat. At last I climbed the steps, knocked, and a decrepit voice responded, asking who was there. I introduced myself, explained that I was interested in Lee Christmas, and—after a considerable pause—was invited to enter.

The old man was sitting in a room lit by a kerosene lantern, and on first glance he seemed a giant; even after I had more realistically estimated his height to be about six-five, his massive hands and the great width of his shoulders supported the idea that he was larger than anyone had a right to be. It may be that this impression was due to the fact that I had expected him to be shriveled with age; but though his coal-black skin was seamed and wrinkled, he was still well-muscled: I would have guessed him to be a hale man in his early seventies. He wore a white cotton shirt, gray trousers, and a baseball cap from which the emblem had been ripped. His face was solemn and long-jawed, all its features so prominent that it looked to be a mask carved of black bone; his eyes were clouded over with milky smears, and from his lack of reaction to my movements, I came to realize he was blind.

"Well, boy," he said, apparently having gauged my youth from the timbre of my voice. "What fah you want to know 'bout Lee Christmas? You want to be a warrior?"

I switched on my pocket tape recorder and glanced around. The furniture—two chairs and a table—was rough-hewn; the bed was a pallet with some clothes folded atop it. An outdated calendar hung from the door, and mounted on the wall opposite Welcomes was a small cross of black coral: in the orange flux of the lantern light, it looked like a complex incision in the boards.

I told him about my book, and when I had done he said, "I 'spect I can help you some. I were wit' Lee from the Battle of La Ceiba 'til the peace at Comayagua, and fah a while after dat."

He began to ramble on in a direction that did not interest me, and I cut in, saying, "I've heard there was no love lost between the islanders and the Spanish. Why did they join Bonilla's revolution?"

"Dat were Lee's doin'," he said. "He promise dat dis Bonilla goin' to give us our freedom, and so he have no trouble raisin' a company. And he tell us that we ain't goin' to have no difficulty wit' de Sponnish, 'cause dey can't shoot straight." He gave an amused grunt. "Nowadays dey better at shootin', lemme tell you. But in de back-time de men of de island were by far de superior marksmen, and Lee figure if he have us wit' him, den he be able to defeat the garrison at La Ceiba. Dat were a tall order. De leader of de garrison, General Carrillo, were a man wit' magic powers. He ride a white mule and carry a golden sword, and it were said no bullet can bring him down. Many of de boys were leery, but Lee gather us on the dock and make us a speech. 'Boys,' he say, 'you done break your mothers' hearts, but you no be breakin' mine. We goin' to come down on de Sponnish like buzzards on a sick steer, and when we through, dey goin' to be showin' to de bone.' And by de time he finish, we everyone of us was spittin' fire.''

As evidenced by this recall of a speech made seventy-five years before, Welcomes' memory was phenomenal, and the longer he spoke, the more fluent and vital his narrative became. Everything I had learned about Christmas—his age (twenty-seven in 1902), his short stature, his background—all that was knitted into a whole cloth, and I began to see him as he must have been: an ignorant, cocky man whose courage stemmed from a belief that his life had been ruined and so he might as well throw what remained of it away on this joke of a revolution. And yet he had not been without hope of redemption. Like many of his countrymen, he adhered to the notion that through the application of American know-how, the inferior peoples of Central America could be brought forward into a Star-Spangled future and civilized; I believe he nurtured the hope that he could play a part in this process.

When Welcomes reached a stopping point, I took the opportunity to ask if he knew what had motivated Christmas to enter the service of United Fruit. He mulled the question over a second or two and finally answered with a single word: "Aymara."

So, Aymara, it was then I first heard your name.

Perhaps it is passionate experience that colors my memory, but I recall now that the word had the sound of a charm the old man had pronounced, one that caused the wind to gust hard against the shanty, keening in the cracks, fluttering the pages of the calendar on the door as if it, too, were a creature playing with time. But it was only a name, that of a woman whom Christmas and Welcomes had met while on a hunting trip to Olancho in 1904; specifically, a trip to the site of the ruined city of Olancho Viejo, a place founded by the Spanish in 1589 and destroyed by a mysterious explosion not fifty years thereafter. Since that day, Welcomes said, the vegetation there had grown stunted and malformed, and all manner of evil legend had attached to the area, the most notable being that a beautiful woman had been seen walking in the flames that swept over the valley. Though the city had not been rebuilt, this apparition had continued to be sighted by travelers and Indians, always in the vicinity of a cave that had been blasted into the top of one of the surrounding hills by the explosion. Christmas and Welcomes had arrived at this very hilltop during a furious storm and . . . Well, I will let the old man's words (edited for the sake of readability) describe what happened, for it is his story, not mine, that lies at the core of these complex events.

That wind can blow, Lord, that wind can blow! Howlin', rippin' branches off the trees, and drivin' slants of gray rain. Seem like it 'bout to blow everything back to the beginnin' and start all over with creation. Me and Lee was leadin' the horses along the rim of the valley, lookin' for shelter and fearin' for our lives, 'cause the footin' treacherous and the drop severe. And then I spot the cave. Not for a second did I think this the cave whereof the legend speak, but when I pass through the entrance, that legend come back to me. The walls, y'see, they smooth as glass, and there were a tremble in the air like you'd get from a machine runnin' close by . . . 'cept there ain't no sound. The horses took to snortin' and balkin', and Lee pressed hisself flat against the wall and pointed his pistol at the dark. His hair were drippin' wet, plastered to his brow, and his eyes was big and starin'. "Fred," he says, "this here ain't no natural place."

"You no have to be tellin' me," I say, and I reckon the shiver in my voice were plain, 'cause he grins and say, "What's the matter, Fred? Ain't you got no sand?" That were Lee's way, you understand—another man's fear always be the tonic for his own.

Just then I spy a light growin' deeper in the cave. A white light, and brighter than any star. Before I could point it out to Lee, that light shooted from the dark and pass right through me with a flash of cold. Then come another light, and another yet. Each one colder and brighter than the one previous, and comin' faster and faster, 'til it 'pears the cave brightly lit and the lights they flickerin' a little. It were so damn cold that the rainwater have froze in my hair, and I were half-blinded on top of that, but I could have swore I seen somethin' inside the light. And when the cold begin to heaten up, the light to dwindle, I made out the shape of a woman . . . just her shape at first, then her particulars. Slim and black-haired, she were. More than pretty, with both Spanish and Indian breedin' showin' in her face. And she wearin' a garment such as I never seen before, but what in later years I come to recognize as a jump-suit. There were blood on her mouth and a fearful expression on her face. The light gathered 'round her in a cloud and dwindle further, fadin' and shrinkin', and right when it 'bout to fade away complete, she take a step toward us and slump to the ground.

For a moment the cave were pitch-dark, with only the wind and the vexed sounds of the horses, but directly I hear a clatter and a spark flares and I see that Lee have got one of the lanterns goin'. He kneel beside the woman and make to touch her, and I tell him, "Man, I wouldn't be doin' that. She some kinda duppy."

"Horseshit!" he say. "Ain't no such thing."

"You just seen her come a'whirlin' outta nowhere," I say. "That's the duppy way."

'Bout then the woman give out with a moan and her eyelids they flutter open. When she spot Lee bendin' to her, the muscles in her face start strainin' and she try to speak, but all that come out were this creaky noise. Finally she muster her strength and say, "Lee . . . Lee Christmas?" Like she ain't quite sure he's who she thinks.

Lee 'pears dumbstruck by the fact she know his name and he can't say nothin'. He glance up to me, bewildered.

"It *is* you," she say. "Thank God . . . thank God." And she reach out to him, clawin' at his hand. Lee flinched some, and I expected him to go a'whirlin' off with her into white light. But nothin' happen.

"Who are you?" Lee asks, and the question seem to amuse her, 'cause she laugh, and the laugh turn into a fit of coughin' that bring up more blood to her lips. "Aymara," she say after the fit pass. "My name is Aymara." Her eyes look to go blank for a second or two, and then she clutch at Lee's hand, desperate-like, and say, "You have to listen to me! You have to!"

Lee look a little desperate himself. I can tell he at sea with this whole business. But he say, "Go easy, now. I'll listen." And that calm her some. She lie back, breathin' deep, eyes closed, and Lee's starin' at her, fixated. Suddenly he give himself a shake and say, "We got to get you some doctorin'," and try to lift her. But she fend him off. "Naw," she say. "Can't no doctor help me. I'm dyin'." She open her eyes wide as if she just realize this fact. "Listen," she say. "You know where I come from?" And Lee say, No, but he's been a'wonderin'. "The future," she tell him. "Almost a hundred years from now. And I come all that way to see you, Lee Christmas."

Wellsir, me and Lee exchange looks, and it's clear to me that he thinks whatever happened to this here lady done 'fected her brain.

"You don't believe me!" she say in a panic. "You got to!" And she hold up her wrist and show Lee her watch. "See that? You ain't got watches like that in 1904!" I peer close and see that this watch ain't got no hands, just numbers made up of dots that flicker and change as they toll off the seconds. But it don't convince me of nothin'—I figure it's just some foreign thing. She must can tell we still don't believe her, 'cause she pull out a coupla other items to make her case. I know what them items was now—a ball point pen and a calculator—but at the time they was new to me. I still ain't convinced. Her bein' from the future were a hard truth to swallow, no matter the manner of her arrival in the cave. She start gettin' desperate again, beggin' Lee to believe her, and then her features they firm up and she say, "If I ain't from the future, then how come I know you been talkin' to United Fruit 'bout doin' some soldierin' for 'em."

This were the first I hear 'bout Lee and United Fruit, and I were surprised, 'cause Lee didn't have no use for them people. "How the hell you know that?" he asks, and she say, "I told you how. It's in the history books. And that ain't all I know." She take to reelin' off a list of names that weren't familiar to me, but—from the dumbstruck expression on Lee's face—must have meant plenty to him. I recall she mention Jacob Wettstein and Andrew Colby and Machine Gun Guy Maloney, who were to become Lee's second-in-command. And then she reel off another list, this one of battles and dates. When she finish, she clutch his hand again. "You gotta 'cept their offer, Lee. If you don't, the world gonna suffer for it."

I could tell Lee have found reason to believe from what she said, but that the idea of workin' with United Fruit didn't set well with him. "Couldn't nothin' good come of that," he say. "Them boys at the fruit company ain't got much in mind but fillin' their pockets."

"It's true," she say. "The company they villains, but sometimes you gotta do the wrong thing for to 'chieve the right result. And that's what *you* gotta do. 'Less you help 'em, 'less America takes charge down here, the world's gonna wind up in a war that might just be the end of it.''

I know this strike a chord in Lee, what with him always carryin' on 'bout good ol' American ingenuity bein' the salvation of the world. But he don't say nothin'.

"You gotta trust me," she say. "Everything depends 'pon you trustin' me and doin' what I say. I come all this way, knowin' I were bound to die of it, just to tell you this, to make sure you'd do what's necessary. You think I'd do that to tell you a lie?''

"Naw," he says. "I s'pose not." But I can see he still havin' his doubts.

She sigh and look worried and then she start explainin' to us that the machine what brought her have gone haywire and set her swayin' back and forth through time like a pendulum. Back to the days of the Conquistador and into the future an equal ways. She tell us 'bout watchin' the valley explode and the old city crumblin' and finally she say, "I only have a glimpse of the future, of what's ahead of my time, and I won't lie, it were too quick for me to have much sense of it. But I have a feelin' from it, a feelin' of peace and beauty . . . like a perfume the world's givin' off. When I 'cepted this duty, I thought it were just to make sure things wouldn't work out worse than they has, but now I know somethin' glorious is goin' to come, somethin' you never would 'spect to come of all the bloodshed and terror of history.''

It were the 'spression on her face at that moment—like she's still havin' that feelin' of peace—that's what put my doubts to rest. It weren't nothin' she coulda faked. Lee he seemed moved by it, but maybe he's stuck with thinkin' that she's addled, 'cause he say, "If you from the future, you tell me some more 'bout my life.''

A shudder pass through her, and for a second I think we gonna lose her then and there. But she gather herself and say, "You gonna marry a woman named Anna and have two daughters, one by her and one by another woman.''

Not many knew Lee were I love with Anna Towers, the daughter of an indigo grower in Truxillo, and even less knew 'bout his illegitimate daughter. Far as I concerned, this sealed the matter, but Aymara didn't understand the weight of what she'd said and kept goin'.

"You gonna die of a fever in Puerto Cortez," she says, "in the year . . ."

"No!" Lee held up his hand. "I don't wanna hear that."

"Then you believe me."

"Yes," he say. "I do."

For a while there weren't no sound 'cept the keenin' of the wind from the cave mouth. Lee were downcast, studyin' the backs of his hands like he were readin' there some sorry truth, and Aymara were glum herself, like she were sad he did believe her. "Will you do it?" she asks.

Lee give a shrug. "Do I got a choice?

"Maybe not," she tell him. "Maybe this how it have to be. One of the men who . . . who help send me here, he claim the course of time can't be changed. But I couldn't take the chance he were wrong." She wince and swallow hard. "Will you do it?"

"Hell," he say after mullin' it over. "Guess I ain't got no better thing to do. Might as well go soldierin' awhile."

She search his face to see if he lyin' . . . 'least that's how it look to me. "Swear to it," she say, takin' his hand. "Swear you'll do it."

"All right," he say. "I swear. Now you rest easy."

He try doctorin' her some, wettin' down her brow and such, but nothin' come of it. Somethin' 'bout the manner of travel, she say, have tore up her insides, and there's no fixin' 'em. It 'pear to me she just been hangin' on to drag that vow outta Lee, and now he done it, she let go and start slippin' away. Once she make a rally, and she tell us more 'bout her journey, sayin' the strange feelin's that sweep over her come close to drivin' her mad. I think Lee's doubtin' her again, 'cause he ask another question or two 'bout the future. But it seem she answer to his satisfaction. Toward the end she take to talkin' crazy to someone who ain't there, callin' him Darlin' and sayin' how she sorry. Then she grab hold of Lee and beg him not to go back on his word.

"I won't," he say. But I think she never hear him, 'cause as he speak blood come gushin' from her mouth and she sag and look to be gazin' into nowhere.

Lee don't hardly say nothin' for a long time, and then it's only after the storm have passed and he concerned with makin' a grave.

We put her down near the verge of the old city, and once she under
the earth, Lee ask me to say a little somethin' over her. So I utter
up a prayer. It were strange tryin' to talk to God with the ruined
tower of the cathedral loomin' above, all ivied and crumblin', like
a sign that no prayers would be answered.

"What you gonna do?" I ask Lee as he saddlin' up.

He shake his head and tighten the cinch. "What would you do,
Fred?"

"I guess I wouldn't want to be messin' with them fruit company
boys," I say. "They takes things more serious than I likes."

"Ain't that the truth," he say. He look over to me, and it seem
all the hollows in his face has deepened. "But maybe I ain't been
takin' things serious enough." He worry his lip. "You really think
she from the future?" He ask this like he wantin' to have me say,
No.

"I think she from somewhere damn strange," I say. "The future
sound 'bout as good as anything."

He scuff the ground with his heel. "Pretty woman," he say. "I
guess it ain't reasonable she just throw her life away for nothin'."

I reckoned he were right.

"Jesus Christ!" He smack his saddle. "I wish I could just forget
alla 'bout her."

"Well, maybe you can," I tell him. "A man can forget 'bout
most anything with enough time."

I never should have say that, 'cause it provide Lee with somethin'
to act contrary to, with a reason to show off his pride, and it could
be that little thing I say have tipped the scales of his judgment.

"Maybe *you* can forget it," he say testily. "But not me. I ain't
'bout to forget I give her my word." He swing hisself up into the
saddle and set his horse prancin' with a jerk of the reins. Then he
grin. "Goddamn it, Fred! Let's go! If we gotta win the world for
ol' United Fruit, we better get us a move on!"

And with that, we ride up from the valley and into the wild and
away from Aymara's grave, and far as I know, Lee never did take a
backward glance from that day forth, so busy he were with his
work of forgin' the future.

I asked questions, attempting to clarify certain points, the exact
date of the encounter among other things, but of course I did not

believe Welcomes. Despite his aura of folksy integrity, I knew that Guanoja was rife with storytellers, men who would stretch the truth to any dimension for a price, and I assumed Welcomes to be one of these. Yet I was intrigued by what I perceived as the pathos surrounding the story's invention. Here was the citizen of a country long oppressed by the economic policies of the United States, who—in order to earn a tip from an American tourist (I had given him twenty *lempira* upon the conclusion of his tale)—had created a fable that exonerated the United States from guilt and laid the blame for much of Central America's brutal history upon the shoulders of a mystical woman from the future. On returning to my hotel, I typed up sections of the story and seeded them throughout a longer piece that documented various of Christmas' crimes along with others committed by his successors. I entitled the piece "Aymara," and the following day I sent it off to *Mother Jones*, having no real expectations that it would see print.

But "Aymara" *was* published, as was my next piece, and the next . . . And so began a journalistic career that has lasted these sixteen years.

During those years, my espousal of left-wing causes amd the ensuing notoriety inspired my family to break off all connections with me. (They preferred not to acknowledge that I also lent my support to populist rebellions against Soviet-sponsored regimes.) I was not offended by their action; in fact, I took it for a confirmation of the rightness of my course, since—with their stock portfolios and mausoleum-like homes and born-again conservatism—they were as nasty a pack of capitalist rats as one could meet. I traveled to Argentina, South Africa. The Philippines, to any country that offered the scenario of a superpower-backed dictatorship and masses of the oppressed, and I wired back stories that sought to undermine the Commie-hating mentality engendered by the Reagan years. I admit that my zeal was occasionally misplaced, that I was used at times by corrupt men who passed themselves off as populist leaders. And I will further admit that in some cases I was motivated less by passionate concern than by a desire to increase my own legend. I had, you see, become a media figure. My photograph was featured on the covers of national magazines concomitant with such headings as "William Corson and the New Journalism"; my books made the best-seller lists; talk shows pestered my agent. But despite the glitter, I truly cared about the causes I espoused. Perhaps I cared too much. Perhaps—like Lee Christmas—I made the mistaken assumption that my American citizenship was a guarantee of wisdom superior to that of the peoples whom I tried to help. In retrospect, I can see that the impulses that provoked my writing of "Aymara" were no less ingenuous, no more informed, than those that inspired his career; but this is an irony I do not choose to dwell upon.

In January of 1994, I returned to Guanoja. The purpose of the trip was partly for a vacation, my first in many years, and also to satisfy a nostalgic whim to visit the place where my career had begun. The years had brought little change to Meachem's Landing. True, there was now a jetport outside of town, and a few of the shanty bars had been replaced by more pricey watering holes of concrete block; but it remained essentially the same confluence of dirt streets lined with weathered shacks and populated by raggedly dressed blacks. The most salient differences were the gaggle of lower-echelon Honduran civil servants who spent each day hunched over their typewriters on the second-story verandah of the Hotel Captain Henry, churning out reams of officialese, and the alarming number of CIA agents: cold-eyed, patently anonymous men who could be seen sitting in the bars, gazing moodily toward Nicaragua and the Red Menace. War was in the offing, its onset as inevitable as the approach of a season, and this, too, was a factor in my choice of a vacation spot. I had received word of a mysterious military installation on the Honduran mainland, and—after having nosed around Washington for several weeks—I had been invited to inspect this installation. The Pentagon apparently wanted to assure me of its harmlessness and thus prevent their benign policies from being besmirched by more of my yellow journalism.

After checking into the hotel, I walked out past the town to the weedy little graveyard, where I expected I would find a stone marking the remains of Fred Welcomes. There was, indeed, such a stone, and I was startled to learn that he had survived until 1990, dying at the age of 106. I had assumed that he could not have lived much past the date of my interview with him, and the fact that he had roused my guilt. All my good fortune was founded upon his eloquent lie, and I could have done a great deal to ease his decline. I leaned against the rusted fence, thinking that I was no better than the businessmen whose exploitative practices I had long decried, that I had mined gold from the old man's imagination and given him a pittance in return. I was made so morose that later the same night, unable to achieve peace of mind, I set out on a drunk . . . at least this was my intent.

Across the street from the hotel was a two-story building of white stucco with faded lettering above the door that read Maud Price's Golden Dream. I remembered Maud from my previous trip—a fat, black woman who had kept an enormous turtle in a tin washtub and would entertain herself by feeding it chicken necks and watching it eat—and I was saddened to discover that she, too, had passed away. Her daughter was now the proprietor, and I was pleased to find that she had maintained Maud's inimitable decor. Strung across the ceiling were dozens upon dozens of man-shaped paper dolls, colored red and black, and these cast magical-looking shadows on the walls by the light of two flickering lanterns. Six wooden tables, a bar atop which rested a venerable stereo that was grinding out listless reggae, and a number of framed photographs whose glass was too flyspecked to permit easy observation of the subject matter. I ordered a beer, a Salvavida, and was preparing for a bout of drunken self-abnegation, when I noticed a young woman staring at me from the rear table. On meeting my eyes, she showed no sign of embarrassment and held her gaze steady for a long moment before turning back to the magazine she had been reading. Even in that dim light, I could see she was beautiful. Slim, long-limbed, with a honeyed complexion. Curls of black hair hung over the front of her white blouse, their shapes as elegant as the tailfeathers of exotic birds. Her face . . . I could tell you that she had large dark eyes and high cheekbones, that her features had an impassive Indian cast. But that does nothing more than to define her by type and illuminates her not at all. This was a woman with whom I was soon to be in love, if I was not somewhat in love with her already, and the most difficult thing in the world to describe is the face of your lover, because though it is familiar in every detail, it tends to become a mirror of your devotion, to reflect the ideals of passion, and thus is less a human face than the face of love itself.

I continued to watch her, and after a while she looked up again and smiled. There was no way I could ignore this contact. I walked over, introduced myself (in Spanish, which I assumed to be her native tongue), and asked if I could join her. "Why not?" she replied in English, and after I had taken a seat, she pushed her magazine toward me, pointing to an inset photograph of me, one snapped some years before when I had worn a mustache. "I thought it was you," she said, "You look much more handsome clean-shaven."

Her name, she told me, was Ivie Solis. She was employed by a travel agency in La Ceiba and was on a working vacation, having arrived the day before. We talked of this and that, nothing of consequence, but the air between us seemed to crackle. Everything about her, everything she did, struck a chord within me, and I was mesmerized by her movements, entranced, as if she were a magician who might at any moment loose a flight of birds from her fingertips.

Eventually the conversation turned to my work, of which she had read the lion's share, and she told me that her favorite piece was my first, "Aymara." I expressed surprise that she had seen it—it had never been reprinted—and she explained that her parents had run a small hotel catering to American tourists, and the magazine had been left in one of the rooms. "It had the feel of being part of a puzzle," she said. "Or the answer to a riddle."

"It seems fairly straightforward to me," I said.

She tucked a curl behind her ear, a gesture I was coming to recognize as characteristic. "That's because you didn't believe the old man's story."

"And you did?"

"I didn't leap to disbelief as you did." She settled back in her chair, picking at the label of her beer bottle. "I guess I just like thinking about what motivated the woman."

"Obviously," I said, "according to the logic of the story, she came from a world worse off than this one and was hoping to initiate a course of events that would improve it."

"I thought that myself at first," she said. "But it *doesn't* fit the logic of the story. Don't you remember? She knew what would happen to Christmas. His military career, his triumphs. If she'd come from a world in which those things hadn't occurred, she wouldn't have had knowledge of them."

"So . . ." I began.

"I think," she cut in, "that if she did exist, she came from this world. That she knew she would have to sacrifice herself in order to ensure that Christmas did as he did. It may be that your article was the agency that informed her of her duty."

"Even if that's the case," I said, "why would she have tried to inspire Christmas' crimes? Why wouldn't she have tried to make him effect good works? Perhaps she could have destroyed United Fruit."

"That would be the last thing she'd want. Don't you see? If her actions were politically motivated, she would understand that before real change could occur, the circumstances, the conditions of life under American rule, would have to be so oppressive that violent change would become a viable option. Revolution. She'd realize that Christmas' violences were necessary. They set the tone for American policies and licensed subsequent violence. She'd be afraid that if Christmas didn't work for United Fruit, the process of history that set the stage for revolution might be slowed down or negated. Perhaps the American stranglehold might be achieved with such subtlety that change would be forever impossible."

She spoke these words with marked intensity, and I believe I realized then that there was more to Ivie than met the eye. Her logic was the logic of terrorism, the justification of bloodshed in terms of its consciousness-raising effects. But I was so intent upon her as a woman, I scarcely noticed the implication of what she had said.

"Well," I said, "given that your scenario is accurate, it still doesn't make sense. The idea of time travel, of tinkering with the past . . . it's absurd. Too many paradoxes are involved. What you're supposing isn't a chain of events wherein one action predicates another. It's a loop, a metaphysical knot tied in reality, linking my article and some woman and a man years dead. There's no end, no beginning. Things don't work that way."

"They don't?" She lowered her eyes and traced a design in the moisture on the table. "It seems to me that life *is* paradox. Things occur without apparent reason between nations." She looked up at me. "Between people. Perhaps there are reasons, but they're impossible to unravel or define. And dealing with such an unreasonable quantity as time, I wouldn't expect it to be anything other than paradoxical."

We moved on to other topics, and shortly afterward we left the bar and walked along the road to Flowers Bay. A few hundred yards past the last shanty, at a point where the road meandered close to the shore and the sea lay calm beneath a sheen of starlight, visible through a labyrinthine fringe of mangrove, there I kissed her. It was the kind of kiss that holds a lifetime of promise, tentative, then growing more assured and involving as the contact surpasses all your expectations. I had thought kisses like that existed solely in the province of romance novels, and on discovering this was not so, all my cynicism was dissolved and I fell wholly in love with Ivie Solis.

I do not propose to detail our affair, the evolution of our feelings. While these things seemed to me remarkable, I doubt they were more so than the interactions of any other pair of lovers, and they are pertinent to my story only in the volatility that attached to our moments together. Despite Ivie's thesis that love—like time— was an inexplicable mystery, I sought to explain it to myself and decided that because I had never had any slack in my life, because I had never allowed myself the luxury of deep emotional involvement, I had therefore been ripe for the picking. I might, I told myself, have fallen in love with anyone. Ivie had simply been the first acceptable candidate to happen along. All I knew of her aside from her work and place of birth were a few bits and pieces: that she was twenty-seven; that she had attended the University of Miami; that—like most Hondurans—she resented the American presence in her country; that she had a passion for coconut candy and enjoyed the works of Manuel Puig. How, I wondered, could I be obsessed with someone about whose background I was almost completely ignorant. And yet perhaps my depth of feeling was enhanced by this lack of real knowledge. Things are often most alluring when they are not quite real, when your contact with them is brief and intense, and in the light of the mind they acquire the vividity and artfulness of a dream.

We spent nearly every moment of every day in each other's company, and most of this in making love. My room, our clothing, smelled of sex, and we became such a joke to the old woman who cleaned the hotel that whenever she saw us she would let loose with gales of laughter. The only times we were apart were an hour or so each afternoon when Ivie would have to perform her function as a travel agent, securing—she said—cheap group rates from various resorts that would be offered by her firm to American skin-divers. On most of these occasions I would pace back and forth, impatient for her return. But then, ten days after we had initiated the affair, thinking I might as well make some use of the interval, I rented a car and drove to Spanish Harbor, a small town up the coast where there had lately been several outbreaks of racial violence, highly untypical for Guanoja; I was interested in determining whether or not these incidents were related to the martial atmosphere that had been gathering about the island.

By the time I arrived in the town, which differed from Meachem's Landing hardly at all, having a larger harbor and perhaps a half a dozen more streets, I was thirsty, and I stopped in a tourist restaurant for a beer. This particular restaurant, The Treasure Chest, consisted of a small room done up in pirate decor that was fronted by a cement deck where patrons sat beneath striped umbrellas. Standing at the bar, I had a clear view of the deck, and as I sipped my beer, wondering how best to pursue my subject, I spotted Ivie sitting at a table near the railing. With her was a man wearing a gray business suit. I assumed him to be a resort owner, but when he turned to signal a waiter, I recognized him by his hawkish features and fringe of salt-and-pepper beard to be Abimael Sotomayor, the Leader of *Sangre y Verdad* (Blood and Truth), one of the most extreme of Latin American terrorist groups. I had twice interviewed him and I knew him for a charismatic and scary man, a poet who excelled at torture, whose followers performed quasi-mystical blood rituals in his name prior to each engagement. The sight of him with Ivie numbed me, and I began to construct rationalizations that would explain her presence in innocent terms. But none of my rationalizations held water.

I left the restaurant and drove full-tilt back to Meachem's Landing, where I bribed the cleaning woman into admitting me to Ivie's room. It was identical to mine, with gray boards and a metal cot and a night table covered in plastic and a single window that opened onto the second-story verandah. I began by searching the closet, but found only shoes and clothing, apparel quite in keeping with her purported job. Her overnight case contained make-up, and the rest of her luggage was empty . . . or so it appeared. But as I hefted one of the suitcases, preparing to stow it beneath the cot, I realized it was heavier than it should have been. I laid it on the cot and before long I located the catch that opened a false bottom; inside was a machine pistol.

I sat staring at the gun. It was an emblem of Ivie's complicity with an organization so violent that even I, who sympathized with their cause, was repelled by their actions. Yet despite this, I found I loved her no less; I only feared that she did not love me, that she was using me. And, too, I feared for her: the fact that she was at the least an associate of *Sangre y Verdad* offered little hope of a happy ending for the two of us. Finally I replaced the false bottom, restored the suitcase to its original spot beneath the cot and went to my room to wait for Ivie.

That night I said nothing about the gun, rather I tested Ivie in a variety of ways, trying to learn whether or not her affections for me were fraudulent. Not only did she pass every test, but I came to understand much about her that had been puzzling me. I realized that her distracted silences, her deferential attitude concerning the future, her vague references to "responsibilities," all these were symptomatic of the difficulty our relationship was causing her, the contrary pulls exerted by her two passions. Throughout the night, I kept thinking of horror stories I had heard about *Sangre y Verdad*, but I loved Ivie too much to judge her. How could I—a citizen of the country which had created the conditions that bred organizations like Sotomayor's—ever hope to fathom the pressures that had brought her to this pass?

For the next three days, knowing that our time together was likely to be brief, I tried to put politics from mind. Those days were nearly perfect. We swam, we danced, we rented a dory and rowed out past the reef and threw out lines and caught silkfish, satinfish, fish that gleamed iridescent red and blue and yellow, like talismans of our own brilliance. Yet despite our playfulness, our happiness, I was constantly aware that the end could not be far off.

Four days after her meeting with Sotomayor, Ivie told me she had an appointment that evening, one that might last two or three hours; her nervous manner informed me that something important was in the works. At eight o'clock she drove off along the road to Flowers Bay, and I tailed her in my rented car, maintaining a discreet distance, my headlights dark. She parked by the side of the road about a mile past Welcomes' shanty, and seeing this, I pulled my car into a thicket and continued on foot.

It was a moonless night, but the stars were thick, their light revealing every shadowy rut, silhouetting the palms and mangrove. Mosquitoes whined in my ear; the sound of waves on the reef came as a faint hiss. A couple of hundred feet beyond Ivie's car stood a largish shanty set among a stand of cocals. Several cars were parked out front, and two men were lounging by the door, obviously on sentry duty. Orange light flickered in the window. I eased through the brush, making my way toward the rear of the shanty, and after ascertaining that no guards were posted there, I duckwalked across a patch of open ground and flattened against the wall. I could hear many voices speaking at once, none of them intelligible. I inched along the wall to the window whose shutter was cracked open. Through the gap I spotted Sotomayor sitting atop a table, and beside him, a thin, agitated-looking man of thirty-five or so, with prematurely gray hair. I could see none of the others, but judging by their voices, I guessed there to be at least a dozen men and women present.

With a peremptory gesture, Sotomayor signaled for quiet. "I would much have preferred to use my organization alone," he said. "But Doctor Dobler"—he acknowledged the gray-haired man with a nod—"insisted that the entire spectrum of the left be included and I had no choice but to agree. However, in the interests of security, I wish to limit participation in this operation to those in this room. And, since some of you are unknown to the rest, I suggest that we not increase our intimacy by an exchange of names. Let us choose false names. Simple ones, if you please." He smoothed back his hair, glancing around at his audience. "As I am to lead, I will take a military rank for my name." He smiled. "And as I am not overly ambitious, you may refer to me as the Sergeant." Laughter. "Perhaps if we are successful, I will receive a promotion."

Each of the men and women—there were fourteen in all—selected a name, and I heard Ivie say, "Aymara."

The hairs on the back of my neck prickled to hear it, but knowing her fascination with my article, I did not think it an unexpected choice.

"Very well," said Sotomayor, all busines now. "The matter under consideration is the American military project known as Longshot."

I was startled—Longshot was the code name of the installation I was soon to inspect.

"For some months," Sotomayor went on, "we have been hearing rumors concerning Longshot, none likely to inspire confidence in our neighbors to the north. We have been unable to substantiate the rumors, but this situation has changed. Doctor Dobler was until recently one of the coordinators of the project. He has come to us at great personal risk, because he believes there is terrible danger associated with Longshot, and because, with our lack of bureaucratic impediments, he believes we may be the only ones capable of acting swiftly enough to forestall disaster. I will let him explain the rest."

Sotomayor stepped out of view, leaving the floor to Dobler, who looked terrified. Thinking what it must have taken for him to venture forth from his ivory tower and out among the bad dogs, I awarded him high marks for guts. He cleared his throat. "Project Longshot is essentially an experiment in temporal displacement . . . that is to say, time travel."

This sparked a babble, and Sotomayor called for quiet. I wished I could have seen Ivie's face, wanting to know if she were as stunned and frightened as I was.

"The initial test is to be conducted twenty-three days from now," said Dobler. "We have every reason to believe it will succeed, because evidence exists in the past . . ." He broke off, appearing confused. "There's so much to . . ." His eyes darted left to right. "I'm sorry. I . . ."

"Please be calm," advised Sotomayor. "You're among friends."

Dobler squared his shoulders. "I'm all right," he said, and drew a deep breath. "The site of the project is a hill overlooking the ruins of Olancho Viejo, a colonial city destroyed in 1623 by an explosion. I say 'explosion,' but I believe I can safely state that it was not an explosion in the typical sense of the word. For one thing, eyewitness accounts testify that while, indeed, some of the buildings were blown apart, others appeared to crumble, to collapse into powder and chunks of rotten stone, the result of being washed over by a wave of blinding white radiance. Of course these accounts were written by superstitious men—mainly priests—and are thus suspect. Some tell of a beautiful woman walking in the midst of the light, but I think we can attribute that to the Catholic propensity for seeing the Virgin in moments of stress." This elicited a few chuckles, and Dobler was braced by the response. "However, allied with readings we have taken, with other anomalies we've discovered on and near the site, it's evident that the destruction of Olancho Viejo was a direct result of our experiment. Though our target date is in the 1920s, it seems that the displacement will create a kind of shockwave that will produce dire effects three-hundred-and-sixty years in the past."

"How does that affect us?" someone asked.

"I'll get to that in a minute," said Dobler. He was warming to his task, becoming the model of an enthused lecturer. "First it's important you understand that although the initial experiment will merely consist of the displacement of a few laboratory animals and some mineral specimens, plant life, and so forth, the target purpose of the project is the manipulation of the past through assassination and other means."

Expressions of outrage from the gathering.

"Wait!" said Dobler. "That's not what you should be worried about, because I don't think it's possible."

"Why not?" A woman's voice.

"I really don't think I could explain it to you," said Dobler. "The mathematics are too complex . . . and my conclusions, I admit, are arguable. Several of my colleagues are in complete disagreement; they believe the past *can* be altered. But I'm convinced otherwise. Time, according to my mathematical model, has a fixed shape. It is not simply a process that affects physical objects; it has its own physicality, or—better said—the process of time involves its own spectrum of physical events, all on the particulate level, and it is the isolation of this spectrum that will allow us to displace objects into the past." He must have been the focus of bewildered stares, for he threw up his hands in helplessness. "The language isn't capable of conveying an accurate explanation. Suffice it to say, that in my opinion, any attempt to alter the course of history will fail, because the physical potentials of time will compensate for that alteration."

"It sounds to me," said Sotomayor, "as if you're embracing the doctrine of predestination."

"That's a rather murky analogue," said Dobler. "But, yes, I suppose I am."

"Then why are you asking us to stop something which, according to you, cannot be stopped? If evidence exists that the experiment was carried out, we can do nothing . . . at least if we are to accept your logic."

"As I stated, I may be wrong in this," said Dobler. "In which case, an attack on the project might succeed. But even if time does prove to be unalterable, what is unalterable in this circumstance is the destruction of Olancho Viejo. It's possible that our experiment can be stopped, and the malleability of time will enlist some other causal agent."

"There's something I don't understand." Ivie's voice. "If you are correct about the unalterability of time, what do we have to fear?"

"For every action," said Dobler, "there must be a reaction. The action will be the experiment: One small part of the reaction can be observed in what happened three centuries ago. But my figures show that the greater part of the reaction will occur in the present. I've gone over and over the equations, and there's no error." Dobler paused, summoning thought. "I've no idea what form this end of the reaction will take. It may be similar to the explosion in 1623; it may be entirely different. We know nothing about the forces involved . . . except how to trigger them and how to perform a few simple tricks. But I'm sure of one thing. The reaction will affect matter on the subatomic levels and it will be on the order of a billion times more extensive than what happened in 1623. I doubt anything will survive it."

A silence ensued, broken at last by Sotomayor. "Have you shown these equations to your colleagues?"

"Of course." Dobler gave a despairing laugh. "They believe they've solved the problem by constructing a containment chamber. It's a solution comparable to wrapping a blanket around a nuclear device."

"How can we discount their opinion?" someone asked.

"Look," said Dobler, peeved. "Unless you can understand the mathematics involved, there's no way I can prove my case. I believe my colleagues are too excited about the project to accept the fact that it's potentially disastrous. But what does it mean for me to tell you that? The best evidence I can give you is the fact that I am here, that I have in effect thrown away my career in order to warn you." He looked down at the floor. "Though perhaps I can offer one further proof."

They began to bombard him with questions, most of them challenging in tone, and—concerned that the meeting might suddenly break up and my car be discovered—I slipped away from the window and headed back toward town.

It is a measure, I believe, of the foolishness of love that I was less worried about the fate of the world than about Ivie's possible involvement in the events of Welcomes' story, a story I was now hard put to disbelieve; it seemed I was operating under the assumption that if Ivie and I could work things out, everything else would fall into place around us. I drove back to the hotel, waited a while, and then, deciding that I wanted to talk to her somewhere more private, somewhere an argument—I thought one likely—would not be overheard, I left a note asking her to meet me on the far side of the island, at an abandoned construction site a short ways up the beach from St. Mark's Key—the skeleton of a large house belonging to the estate of an American who had died shortly after work had begun. This site was of special moment for Ivie and me. It was set back from the shore, hidden from prying eyes by dense growths of palms and sea grape and cashew trees, and we had made love there on several occasions. By the time I reached it, the moon had risen and the unfinished house—with its gapped walls and skewed beams and free-standing doorways—had the look of a surreal maze of silver light and shadow. Sitting inside it on the ground floor, I felt it was an apt metaphor for the labyrinthine complexity of the situation.

Until that moment, I had not brought my concentration to bear on this complexity, and now, trying to unravel the problem, I found I could not do so. The circumstances of Welcomes' story, of Dobler's, Ivie's, and my own . . . all this smacked of magical serendipity and was proof against logic. Time, which had always been for me a commodity, something to be saved and expended, seemed to have been revealed as a vast fabulous presence cloaked in mystery and capable of miracles, and I had as little hope of comprehending its processes as I would those of a star winking overhead. Less, actually. I attempted to narrow my focus, to consider separate pieces of the puzzle, beginning with what Welcomes had told me. Assuming it was true, I saw how it explained much I had not previously given thought to. Christmas' courage, for instance. Knowing that he would die of a fever would have made him immune to fear in battle. All the pieces fit together with the same irrational perfection. It was only the whole, the image they comprised, that was inexplicable.

At last I gave it up and sat staring at the white combers piling in over the reef, listening to the scattery hiss of lizards running in the beach grass, watching the colored lights of the resort on St. Mark's Key flicker as palm fronds were blown across them by the salt breeze. I must have sat this way an hour before I heard a car engine; a minute later, Aymara—so I had been thinking of her— walked through the frame of the front door and sat beside me. "Let's not stay here," she said, and kissed me on the cheek. "I'd like a drink." In the moonlight her face looked to have been carved more finely, and her eyes were aswim with silvery reflections.

I could not think how to begin. Finally, settling on directness, I said, "Did you know what Dobler was going to tell you? Is that why you chose the name Aymara?"

She pulled back from me, consternation written on her features. "How . . ." she said; and then: "You followed me. You shouldn't have done that."

"Why the hell not?" Anger over her betrayal, her subterfuge, suddenly took precedence over my concern for her. "How else am I going to keep track of who's who in the revolution these days?"

"You could have been killed," she said flatly.

"Right!" I said, refusing to let her lack of emotionality subdue me. "God knows, Sotomayor might have had you drink my blood for a nightcap! What the hell possessed you to get involved with him?"

"I'm not involved with him!" she said, her own temper surfacing.

"You're not with *Sangre y Verdad?*"

"No, the FDLM."

I was relieved—the FDLM was the most populist and thus the most legitimate element of the Honduran left. "You haven't answered my first question," I said. "Why did you choose that name?"

"I was thinking of you. That's all it was. But now . . . I don't know."

"You're going to do it, aren't you? Play out the story?" I slugged my thigh in frustration. "Jesus Christ! Sotomayor will kill you if he finds out! And Dobler, he might be a crazy! A CIA plant! Right now he's . . ."

"You didn't stay until the end?" she cut in.

"No."

"He's dead," she said. "He told us that if we attacked, we should destroy all the computers and records, anyone who had knowledge of the process. He said that when he was younger, he would have supported any evil whose goal was the increase of knowledge, but now he had uncovered knowledge that he couldn't control and he couldn't live with that. He said he hoped what he intended to do would prove something to us. Then he went onto the porch and shot himself."

I sat stunned, picturing that nervous little man and his moment of truth.

"I believe him," she said. "Everyone did. I doubt we would have otherwise."

"Sotomayor would have believed him no matter what," I said. "He yearns for disaster. He'd find the end of the world an erotic experience."

"I shouldn't have to explain to you what produces men like Abimael," she said stiffly. She reached behind her to—I assumed— adjust the waistband of her skirt. "Are you going to inform on us?"

Her voice was tremulous, her expression strained, and she continued holding her hand behind her back; it was an awkward posture, and I began to suspect her reasons for maintaining it. "What have you got there?" I asked, knowing the answer.

A car passed on the beach, its headlights throwing tattered leaf shadows over the beams.

"What if I said I *was* going to inform on you?"

She lowered her eyes, sighed and brought forth a small caliber automatic; after a second, she let it fall to the floor. She studied it despondently, as if it were a failed something for which she had entertained high hopes. "I'm sorry," she said. "I'm . . ." She put her hand to her brow, covering her eyes.

The gun showed a negative black against the planking, an ugly brand marring the smooth grain. I picked it up. Its cold weight fueled my anger, and I heaved it into the shadows.

"I love you." She trailed her fingers across my arm, but I refused to speak or turn to her. "Please, believe me! It's just I don't know what to do anymore." Her voice broke, and it seemed I could smell her tears.

"It's all right." My voice was harsh, burred with anger.

We sat in silence. The crunch of waves on the reef built louder, the wind seethed in the palm crowns, and faint music from the resort added a fractured tinkling—I felt that the things of nature were losing definition, blending into a dissolute melodic rush. Finally I asked her what she intended to do, and she said, "I doubt my intentions matter. I don't think I can avoid going back."

"To 1902? Is that what you mean?" I said this helplessly, sensing the gravity of events sweeping toward us like a huge dark fist. "How can you even consider it? You heard Dobler, you know the dangers."

"I don't believe it's dangerous. Only inevitable."

I turned to her then, ready with protests, arguments. Christ, she was beautiful! It was as if tears had washed her clean of a film, exposed a new depth of beauty. The words caught in my throat.

"Just before Dobler killed himself," she said, "I asked him what he thought time was. He'd been talking about it as a mathematical entity, but I had the idea he wasn't saying what he really felt, and I wanted to know everything he did . . . because I was afraid. It seemed something magical was happening, that I was being drawn into some incomprehensible scheme." She brushed a strand of hair from her eyes. "Dobler said that when he had begun to develop his equations, he'd had a feeling like mine. 'An apprehension of the mystical,' he called it. There was something hypnotic about the equations . . . they reminded him of mantras the way they affected him. The further his work progressed, the more he came to think of time—its event spectrum—as evidence of divinity. Its basic operation, its mechanics. Abimael laughed at this and asked if he was talking about God. And Dobler said that if by God he meant a stable energy system governing the actions of all matter on a sub-atomic level, then Yes, that's exactly what he was talking about."

I wanted to refute this, but it was so similar to my own thoughts concerning the nature of time, I could not muster a contrary word.

"You feel it, too," she said. "Don't you?"

I took her by the shoulders. "Let's leave here. Tonight. We can hire a boat to run us over to La Ceiba, and by tomorrow . . ."

She put a finger to my lips, then kissed me. The kiss deepened, and from that point on I lost track of what happened. One moment we were sitting on the floor of that skeleton house, and the next— our clothes magicked away—we were lying in the grass behind the house, in a tiny clearing bordered by banana trees. The way Ivie's hair was fanned out around her head, its color merging with the dark grass, she looked to be a pale female bloom sprouting from the sandy soil, and her skin felt like the moonlight, smooth, coated with a cool emulsion. I thought I could taste the moonlight on the tips of her breasts. She guided me between her legs, her expression grave, focused on the act, and as I entered her she arched her neck, staring up into the banana leaves, and cried, "Oh, God!" as if she saw there some enrapturing presence. But I knew to whom she was really crying out. To that sensation of heat and weakness that enveloped us, sheltered us. To that sublimation of hope and fear into a pour of pure desiring. To that strange thoughtless and self-adoring creature we became, all hip and mouth and heart. *That* was God.

Afterward as we dressed, among the sibilant noises and wind and sea, I heard a sharper noise, a click. But before I could categorize it, I put it from mind. My head was full of plans. I would knock Ivie out, drug her, carry her off to the States. I would allow the guerrillas to destroy the project, and at the last moment come swinging out of nowhere and snatch her to safety. I envisioned even more improbable heroics. Strong with love, all these plans seemed workable to me.

We walked around the side of the house, hand in hand, and I did not notice the figure standing in the shadow of a cashew tree until it spoke, saying, "Aymara!" Ivie gave a shriek of alarm, and I stepped in front of her, shielding her. The figure moved forward, and I saw it was Sotomayor, his sharp features set in a grim expression, his neatly trimmed beard looking fake in the moonlight.

He stopped about six feet away, training a pistol on us, and fixed Ivie with a contemptuous stare. *"Puta!"* he said. He pulled something from his pocket and flung it at our feet. A folded piece of paper with writing on it. "You should be more discreet in your correspondence," he said to me.

"Listen . . ." I began.

He swung the pistol to cover my forehead. "You may have value as a hostage," he said. "But I wouldn't rely on that. I don't like being betrayed, and I'm not in the best of moods."

"I haven't betrayed you!" Ivie stepped from behind me. "You don't understand."

The muscles of Sotomayor's face worked, as if he were repressing a scream of rage.

"He's on our side," said Ivie. "You know that. He's always supported the cause."

Sotomayor smiled—a vicious, predator's smile—and leveled the pistol at her. "Did you enjoy your last fuck, bitch? I could hear you squealing down on the beach."

The muscles of his forearms bunched, preparing for the kick, and I dove for him. Too late. The pistol went off an instant before I knocked him over, the report blending with Ivie's cry, and we rolled in the grass and sand, clawing, grappling. Sotomayor was strong, but I was fighting out of sheer desperation, and he was no match for me. I tore the pistol from his grasp and brought the butt down on his temple. Brought it down a second time. He sagged, his head lolling. I crawled to where Ivie had fallen. Her legs were kicking in spasms, and when I touched her hair, I found it mired with blood. The bullet had entered through the side of her head and lodged in the brain. She must have been clinically dead already, but obeying some dumb reflex, she was trying to speak. Each time her mouth opened, blood jetted forth. She was bleeding from the eyes, the nostrils. Her entire face was slick with blood, and still her mouth kept opening and closing, making glutinous choking sounds. I wanted to touch her, to heal her with a touch, but there was so much broken, I could not decide where to lay my hands. They fluttered above her like stupid animals, and I heard myself screaming for it to stop, for her to stop. Her arms began to flop around, her hips to thrash, convulsing. A broken, bloody doll. I aimed the pistol at her chest, but could not bring myself to pull the trigger.

Finally I covered her with my body, and, sobbing, held her until all movement ceased.

I came to my feet, staggered over to Sotomayor. He had not yet regained consciousness. Tears streaming down my cheeks, I pointed the pistol at him. But it did not seem sufficient that he merely die. I kneeled beside him, then straddled his chest.

A voice called out from behind me. "What goin' on dere, mon?"

Visible as shadows, two men were standing at the water's edge.

"Man killed somebody!" I answered.

"You call de police?"

"No!"

"Den I'll be goin' to de Key, ax 'em to spark up dere radio!"

I waved acknowledgment, watched the men sprint away. Once they were out of sight, I pried Sotomayor's mouth open and inserted the pistol barrel. "Wake up!" I shouted. I spat in his face, slapped him. Repeated the process. His eyelids twitched, and he let out a muffled groan. "Wake up, you son of a bitch!" He gazed at me blearily, and I wiggled the pistol to make him aware of it. His eyes widened. He tried to speak, his eyebrows arching comically with the effort. I cocked the pistol, and he froze.

"I should turn you in," I said. "Let the police torture your ass. But I don't trust you to be a hero, man. Maybe you'd talk. Maybe you know something worth trading for your life."

He gurgled something unintelligible.

"Can't hear you," I said. "Sorry."

Using the pistol as a lever, I began turning his head from side to side. He tried to keep his eyes on mine. Sweat popped out on his brow, and he was having trouble swallowing.

"Here it comes," I said.

He tensed and shut his eyes.

"Just kidding," I told him. I waited a few seconds, then shouted, "Here it comes!"

He flinched.

I started sobbing again. "Did you see what you did to her, man? Did you see? You fucking son of a bitch! Did you see!" The pistol was shaking, and Sotomayor bit the barrel to keep it still.

For a minute or thereabouts I was crying so hard, I was blinded.

At last I managed to gain control. I wiped away the tears. "Here it comes," I said.

He blinked.

"Here it comes!"

Another blink.

"Here it fucking comes!"

His stare was mad and full of hate. But his hatred was nothing compared to mine. I was dizzy with it. The stars seemed very near, wheeling about my head. I wanted to sit astride him forever and cause him pain.

I dug the fingers of my left hand in back of his Adam's apple, forcing his jaws apart, and I battered his teeth with the barrel, breaking a couple. Blood filmed over his lower lip, trickled down into his beard. He gagged, choking on the fragments.

"Like that?" I asked him. "How about this?"

I broke his nose with the heel of my hand. Tears squeezed from his eyes, bloody saliva and mucous came from his nose. His breath made a sucking noise.

Shouts from the direction of St. Mark's Key.

I leaned close to Sotomayor, my face inches away, the blood-slimed barrel sheathed in his mouth.

"Here it comes," I whispered. "Here. It. Comes."

I know he believed me, but he was mesmerized by my proximity, by whatever he saw in my eyes, and could not look away. I screamed at him and met his terrified gaze as I fired.

Perhaps I would have been charged with murder in the States, but in Honduras, where politics and passion license all manner of violence, I was a hero.

I was a hero, and insane . . . for grief possessed me as powerfully as had love.

Now that Ivie was dead, it seemed only just that the others join her on the pyre. I told the police everything I knew. The island was sealed off, the guerrillas rounded up. The press acclaimed me; the President of the United States called to commend my actions; my fellow journalists beseiged the Hotel Captain Henry, seeking to interview me but usually settling for interviews with the cleaning woman and the owner. I was in no mood to play the hero. I drank, I wept, I wandered. I gazed into nowhere, seeing Ivie's face.

Aymara's face. In memoriam, I accorded her that name. Brave-sounding and lyrical, it suited her. And I wished she could have died wearing that name in 1902—that, I realized, should have been her destiny. Whenever I saw a dark-haired young woman, I would have the urge to follow her, to spy on her, to discover who her friends were, what made her laugh, what movies she liked, how she made love, thinking that knowing these details would help me regain the definition that Aymara had brought to my life. Yet even had this not been a fantasy, I could not have acted upon it. Grief had immobilized me. Grief . . . and guilt. It had been my meddling that had precipitated her death, hadn't it? I was a dummy moving on a track between these two emotions, stopping now and again to stare at something that had caught my eye, some curiosity that would for a moment reduce my self-awareness.

Several days after her death, the regional director of the CIA paid me a call. My visit to Project Longshot had originally been scheduled for two weeks prior to the initial test, but he now told me that since I knew about "our little secret down here," the President had authorized my presence at the test. This exclusive was to be my reward for patriotism. I accepted his invitation and came close to telling him that I would be delighted to stand at ground zero during the end of the world.

I had been too self-absorbed to give much thought to Dobler's warnings, but now I decided I wanted the world to end. What was the point in trying to save it? We had been heading toward destruction for years, and as far as I was concerned the time was ripe. A few days before I might have raised a mighty protest against the project, but my political conscience—and perhaps my moral one—had died with Aymara, and I was angry at the world, at its hollow promise and mock virtues and fallacious judgments. Anger made my grief more endurable, and I nourished it, picturing it to be a tiny golden snake with ruby eyes. A familiar. It would feed on tears, transform them into venom. It would be my secret, coiled and ready to strike. It would fit perfectly inside my heart.

On the day prior to the test, I was flown by small plane to a military base on the mainland, and from there by helicopter to the project site, passing over the valley in which lay the ruined city of Olancho Viejo, with its creeper-hung cathedral tower sticking up like an eroded green fang. Three buildings of white concrete crowned a massive jungled hill overlooking the valley, and on the hillside facing away from the valley were other buildings—living quarters and storage rooms and sentry posts. The administrator, a middle-aged balding man named Morrel, briefed me on the test; but I cut this short, informing him that I had heard most of what he was telling me from Dobler. His only reaction was to cluck his tongue and say, "Poor fellow."

Afterward, Morrel led me downhill to the commissary and introduced me to the rest of the personnel. Ostensibly this was a joint US-Honduran project, but there were only two Hondurans among the twenty-eight scientists—an elderly man clearly past his prime, and a dark-haired young woman who tried to duck out the door when I approached. Morrel urged her forward and said, "Mister Corson, this is *Senorita* Aymara Luján."

I was nearly too stunned to accept her handshake. She refused to meet my eyes, and her hand was trembling. I could not believe that this was mere coincidence. Though to my mind she was not as lovely as my Aymara, she was undeniably beautiful and of a type with my dead love. Slim and large-eyed, her features displaying more than a trace of Indian blood. I had a mental image of a long line of beautiful dark-haired women stretching across the country, each prepared to step forward should an accident befall her sisters.

"I'm pleased to meet you," this one said. "I've always admired your work." She glanced around in apparent alarm as if she had said something indiscreet; then, recovering her poise, she added, "Perhaps we'll have a chance to talk at dinner."

She placed an unnatural stress on these last words, making it plain that this was a message sent. "I'd like that," I said.

For the remainder of the day I was shown a variety of equipment and instrumentation to which I paid little attention. The appearance of this new Aymara undermined my anger somewhat, and Dobler's thesis concerning the inalterability of time, its capacity to compensate for change, seemed to embody the menace of prophecy. But I made no move to reveal what I suspected. This development had brought my insanity to a peak, and I was gripped by a fatalistic malaise. Who the hell was I to trifle with fate, I reasoned. And besides, it was unlikely that any action I took would have an effect. Maybe it *was* coincidence. I retreated from the problem into an

almost puritanical stance, as if dealing with the matter was somehow vile, beneath me, and when the dinner hour arrived, deciding
it would be best to avoid the woman, I pled weariness and retired to
my quarters.

My room was a white cubicle furnished with a bed, a desk and
chair, and a word processor. The window provided a view of the
jungle that swept away toward Nicaragua, and I sat by it, watching
sunset resolve into a slate-colored dusk, and then into a darkness
figured by stars and a half-moon. With no one about to engage my
interest, grief closed in around me.

A few minutes after eight o'clock, small arms fire began to
crackle on the hilltop. I went to the door and peered out. Muzzle
flashes were probing the darkness higher up. I had an impulse to
run, but my inertia prevailed and I went back to the chair. Soon
thereafter, the door opened and the woman who called herself
Aymara entered. She wore a white project jumpsuit that glowed in
the moonlight, and she carried an automatic rifle, which she kept at
the ready but aimed at a point to my right.

Neither of us spoke for several seconds, and then I said,
"What's going on?" and laughed at the banal tone that comment
struck.

Another burst of fire from above.

"It's almost over," she said.

I allowed several more seconds to elapse before saying, "How
did you pull it off? Security looked pretty tight."

"Most of them died at dinner." She tossed her head, shaking
hair from her eyes. "Poison."

"Oh." Again I laughed. "Sorry I couldn't make it."

"I didn't want to kill you," she said with urgency. "You've
. . . been a friend to my country. But after what you did on
Guanoja . . ."

"What I did there was execute a murderer! An animal!"

She studied me a moment. "I believe you. Sotomayor was an
evil man."

"Evil!" I made a disparaging noise. "And what force for good
do you represent? The EDP? The FDLM?"

"We acted independently . . . I and a few friends."

Silence, then a single gunshot.

"Is that really your name?" I asked. "Aymara?"

She nodded. "I've often wondered how much influence your article has had on me. On everything. Because of it, I've always felt I was involved in . . ."

"Something mystical, right? Magical. I know all about it."

"How could you?"

"How could I have written the article in the first place? I don't have any answers." I turned back to the window. "I suppose you're going to try to contact Christmas."

"I don't have a choice," she said defiantly. "I feel . . ."

"Believe me," I cut in. "I understand why. When did you decide to do this?"

"I'd been considering it for some time, but I wasn't sure. Then the news came about Sotomayor . . ."

"Jesus God!" I leaned forward, burying my face in my hands.

"What's wrong?"

"Get out!" I said. "Kill me, do whatever you have to . . . just get out of here."

"I'm not going to kill you."

I sensed her moving close, and through my fingers saw her lay some papers on the desk.

"I'm giving you a map," she said. "At the foot of the hill, next to the sentry post, there's a trail leading east. It's well-traveled, and even in the dark it won't be difficult to follow. Less than a day's walk from here, you'll come to a river. You'll find villages. Boats that'll take you to the coast."

I said nothing.

"We won't be able to go operational until dawn," she went on. "You have about ten hours. Things might not be so bad once you're out of the immediate area."

"Go away," I told her.

"I . . ." She faltered. "I think we . . ."

"What the hell do you want from me?" Angry, I spun around. But on seeing her, my anger evaporated. The moonlight seemed to have erased all distinction between her and my Aymara—she might have been my lover reborn, her spirit returned. "What do you want?" I said weakly.

"I don't know. But I do want something from you. For so long I've felt we were linked. Involved." She reached out as if to touch me, then jerked back her hand. "I don't know. Maybe I just want your blessing."

I could smell her scent of soap and perfume, sharp and clean in that musty little room, and I felt a stirring of sexual attraction. In my mind's eye I saw again that endless line of dark-haired women, and I suddenly believed that love was the scheme that had enforced our intricate union, that—truly or potentially—we were all lovers, I and a thousand Aymaras, all tuned to the same mystical pitch. I got to my feet, rested my hands on her hips. Pulled her close. Her lips grazed my cheek as she settled into the embrace. Her heart beat rapidly against my chest. Then she drew back, her face tilted up to receive a kiss. I tasted her mouth, and her warmth spread through me, melting the cold partition I had erected between myself and life. At last she pushed me away and—averting her eyes—walked to the door.

"Goodbye." She said it in Spanish—"*Adios*"—a word that translates literally as "to God."

I heard her footsteps running up the hill.

I was tempted to go after her, and to resist this temptation, not to save myself, I took her map and set out walking the trail east. Yet as I went, my desire to survive grew stronger, and I increased my pace, beating my way through thickets and plaited vines, stumbling down rocky defiles. Had I been alone in the jungle at any other time, I would have been terrified, for the night sounds were ominous, the shadows eerie; but all my fear was focused upon those white buildigns on the hilltop, and I paid no mind to the threat of jaguars and snakes. Toward dawn, I stopped in a weedy clearing bordered by ceibas and giant figs, their crowns towering high above the rest of the canopy. I was bruised, covered with scratches, exhausted, and I saw no reason to continue. I sat down, my back propped against a ceiba trunk, and watched the sky fading to gray.

I had thought brightness would fan across the heavens as with the detonation of a nuclear bomb, but this was not the case. I felt a disturbance in the air, a vibration, and then it was as if everything—trees, the earth, even my own flesh—were yielding up some brilliant white essence, blinding yet gradually growing less intense, until it seemed I was in the midst of a thick white fog through which I could just make out the phantom shapes of the jungle. Accompanying the whiteness was a bone-chilling cold; this, however, dissipated quickly, whereas it turned out that the fog lingered for hours, dwindling to a fine haze before at last becoming imperceptible. At first I was full of dread, anticipating death in one form or another; but soon I began to experience a perverse disappointment. The world had suffered a cold flash, a spot of vagueness, like the symptoms of a mild fever, and the idea that my lover had died for this made me more heartsick than ever.

I waited the better part of an hour for death to take me. Then, disconsolate, thinking I might as well push on, I glanced at my watch to estimate how much farther I had to travel, and found that not only had it stopped but that it could not be rewound. Curious, I thought. As I brushed against a bush at the edge of the clearing, its leaves crumbled to dust; its twigs remained intact, but when I snapped one off, a greenish fluid welled from the cortex. I tasted it, and within seconds I felt a burst of energy and well-being. Continuing on, I observed other changes. An intricate spiderweb whose strands I could not break, though I exerted all my strength; a whirling column of dust and light that looked to be emanating from the site of the project; and in the reflecting waters of a pond I discovered that my hair had gone pure white. Perhaps the most profound change was in the atmosphere of the jungle. Birds twittered, monkeys screeched. All as usual. Yet I sensed a vibrancy, a vitality, that had not been in evidence before.

By the time I reached the river, the fog had cleared. I walked along the bank for half an hour and came to a village of thatched huts, a miserable place littered with feces and mango rinds, hemmed in by brush and stands of bamboo. It appeared deserted, but moored to the bank, floating in the murky water, was a dilapidated boat that—except for the fact it was painted bright blue, decorated with crosses and bearded, haloed faces—might have been the twin of the scow in *The African Queen*. As I drew near, a man popped out of the cabin and waved. An old, old man wearing a gray robe. His hair was white and ragged, his face tanned and wrinkled, and his eyes showed as blue as the painted hull.

"Praise the Lord!" he yelled. "Where the hell you been?"

I glanced behind me to make sure he was not talking to someone else. "Hey," I said. "Where is everybody?"

"Gone. Fled. Scared to death, they were. But now they'll believe me, won't they?" He beckoned impatiently. "Hurry up! You think I got all day. Souls are wastin' for want of Jerome's good news.'' He tapped his chest. "That's me. Jerome.''

I introduced myself.

Again he signaled his impatience. "Got all eternity to learn your name. Let's get a move on.'' He leaned on the railing, squinting at me. "You're the one sent, ain'tcha?''

"I don't think so.''

" 'Course you are!'' He clasped his hands prayerfully. "And, lo, I fell asleep in the white light of the Rapture and the Lord spake, sayin', 'Jerome, there will come a man of dour countenance bearin' My holy sign, and he will aid your toil and lend ballast to your joy.' Well, here you are, and here I am, and if that hair of your'n ain't a sign, I don't know what is. Come on!'' He patted the railing. "Help me push 'er out into the current.''

"Why don't you use the engine?''

"It don't work.'' He cackled, delighted. "Nothin' works. Not the radio, not the generator. None of the Devil's tools. Ain't it wonderful?'' He scowled. "Now come on! That's enough talk. You gonna aid my toil or not?''

"Where are you headed?''

"Down the Fundamental Stream to the Source and back again. Ain't no other place to go now the Lord is come.''

"To the coast?'' I insisted, not in the least taken with this looney.

"Yeah, yeah!'' Jerome put his hands on his hips and regarded me with displeasure. "You gotta lighten up some, boy. Don't know as I'm gonna be needin' all this much ballast to my joy.''

I have been a month on the river with Jerome, and I expect I will remain with him a while longer, for I have no desire to return to civilization until its breakdown is complete—the world, it seems, has ended, though not in the manner I would have thought. I am convinced Jerome is crazy, the victim of long solitudes and an overdose of religious tracts; yet he has no doubt I am the crazy one, and who is to say which of us is right. At every village we stop to allow him to proclaim the Rapture, the advent of the Age of Miracles . . . and, indeed, miracles abound. I have seen a mestizo boy call fish into his net by playing a flute; I have witnessed healings performed by a matronly Indian woman; I have watched an old German expatriate set fires with his stare. As for myself, I have acquired the gift of clairvoyance, which has permitted me to see something of the world that is aborning. Jerome attributes all this to an increase in the wattage of the Holy Spirit; whereas I believe that Project Longshot caused a waning of certain principles— especially those pertaining to anything mechanical or electrical— and a waxing of certain others—in particular those applying to ESP and related phenomena. The two ideas are not opposed. I can easily imagine some long-dead psychic perceiving a whiteness at the end of time and assigning it Godlike significance. Yet I have no faith that a messiah will appear. It strikes me that this new world holds greater promise than the old (though perhaps the old world merely milked its promise dry), a stronger hope of survival, and a wider spectrum of possibility; but God, to my way of thinking, darts among the quarks and neutrinos, an eternal signal harrying them to order, a resource capable of being tapped by magic or by science, and it may be that love is both the seminal impulse of this signal and the ultimate distillation of this resource.

We argue these matters constantly, Jerome and I, to pass green nights along the river. But upon one point we agree. All arguments lapse before the mystery and coincidence of our lives. All systems fail, all logics prove to zero.

So, Aymara, we have worked our spell, you and I and time. Now I must seek my own salvation. Jerome tells me time heals all wounds, but can it—I wonder—heal a wound that it has caused. Though we had only a few weeks, they were the central moments of my life, and their tragic culmination, the sudden elimination of their virtues, has left me irresolute and weak. The freshness and optimism of the world has made your loss more poignant, and I am not ashamed to admit that—like the most clichéd of grievers—I see your face in clouds, hear your voice in the articulations of the wind, and feel your warmth in the shafts of light piercing the canopy. Often I feel that I am breaking inside, that my heart is turning in my chest like a haywire compass, trying to fix upon some familiar pole and detecting none, and I know I will never be done with weeping.

Buck up, Jerome tells me. You can't live in the past, you gotta look to the future and be strong.

I reply that I am far less at home in the fabulous present than I am in the past. As to the future, well . . . I have envisioned myself walking the high country, a place of mountains and rivers without end, of snow fields and temples with bronze doors, and I sense I am searching for something. Could it be you, Aymara? Could that white ray of science pouring from the magical green hill have somewhere resurrected you or your likeness? Perhaps I will some-day find the strength to leave the river and find answers to these questions; perhaps finding that strength is an answer in itself. That hope alone sustains me. For without you, Aymara, even among miracles I am forlorn.

This strange story is science fiction, surely—built as it is around new techniques of generating artificial illumination and a speculation on optical mechanics. Or is it fantasy—since issues of theology lie at its core? Ian Watson hereby demonstrates the fallacy of trying to put good stories into imprecise categories.

Watson, who lives in England, was represented in last year's anthology with "The People on the Precipice." His trilogy of novels, The Book of the River, *was widely acclaimed.*

COLD LIGHT

Ian Watson

Doubtless it is one of life's typical ironies that a man with defective eyesight should have spent many long years studying the history of artificial lighting. However, my friend John Ingolby was also a prominent churchman. By the time his book appeared, John was well advanced in the hierarchy of the Church of England. He was bishop of Porchester.

Now, at this time the church was in a certain amount of disarray. On the one hand it was waning due to apathy. On the other, it was beset by fundamentalist evangelism that seemed unpleasantly frantic and hysterical. Between this Scylla and Charybdis, a new liberal theology was being steered that, it was hoped, would inject new life and modern, humane thought into a seemingly dying institution.

Not, however, without resistance!

Already one new bishop—who publicly denied the doctrine of the Virgin Birth—had been enthroned amidst scandal and protest. Within two days of his enthronement, the venue—an ancient cathedral, finest example of Gothic architecture in the land—was blasted by lightning and its transept gutted by fire. Reportedly the bolts of lightning came from out of a clear sky; so fierce were they that the lightning conductors were overloaded.

Immediately the popular press pointed gleefully to the hand of God himself as source of the miraculous lightning; and some traditionalist clergy endorsed this explanation of the meteorological hazard. The cathedral had been polluted by such an enthronement; here was God's sacred reaction. Yet God, of course, was also merciful. Having first set his house ablaze, he then permitted the massed fire brigades to quench the flames and save the majority of the edifice.

Liberal-minded churchmen issued statements explaining the fire as a coincidence, and deploring popular superstition. The same cathedral had, after all, been severely damaged by fire thrice already during its history—the most recent occasion, a hundred years earlier, being incidentally a case of arson provoked by another theological dispute.

Yet the noisiest single critic of the new bishop from amongst the ranks of ecclesiastics bitterly denounced such pussyfooting explanations. In disgust he publicly quit the English church and embraced the Greek Orthodox communion. The Greek Orthodox church, as its name implied, was a staunch guardian of doctrine, ritual and liturgy.

Some months later, scandal struck again.

A radical-minded dean and lecturer in theology had been hired as presenter for a major new television series called "The Quest for God." As the date for screening for the first episode drew near, this dean revealed in interviews that he did not believe in an afterlife; nor in the Resurrection of Christ; nor for that matter did he even accept the "objective" existence of a God. "God" was a personal construct of the moral consciousness of humanity, said he.

A wave of protest arose.

And of course that first installment of "The Quest for God" was blacked out nationwide by a lightning strike . . .

Of the industrial kind. TV engineers seized this opportunity to protest certain changes in their duty rosters.

The industriual dispute was soon settled; and two nights later the TV network transmitted the blacked-out episode in place of a football match. But by now newspaper headlines had trumpeted: LIGHTNING STRIKE BLACKS ATHEIST DEAN. Even though the smaller print below explained the nature of this particular bolt from the blue, editorials in bolder black type suggested that God may move in a mysterious way his lightning to direct.

Such publicity hugely swelled the viewing figures for a program that many people might otherwise have felt disposed to ignore; so much so that the "atheist" dean was obliged to preface his second prerecorded appearance one week later with a brief personal statement in which he quipped endearingly that if God did not exist, he could hardly have thought of a better way to draw the nation's attention to the quest for him.

It was in this fraught climate that John Ingolby's book was published, surprising me (for one) by its title—then by its angle.

Religion and the History of Lighting: that was the title. The last word is quite easy to confuse with "lightning"; and indeed the printers had done so at least a dozen times during the course of three hundred pages without John—with his poor eyesight—noticing the slight though substantial difference whilst he was correcting the proofs. However, this is a mere incidental irony. The primary shock of the book came from the manner in which, like some seventeenth-century metaphysical poem, it yoked together two apparently disparate things: a scholarly history of artificial lighting— and theological insights.

I admit that my first reaction was that an exuberant editor had persuaded John to rewrite his whole volume, giving it a new commercial slant.

Let's be honest. Suppose you happen to be an aficionado of beer mats; then their history is a consuming passion—to yourself, and to a few hundred other like-minded enthusiasts. However, your *History of Beer Mats* must inevitably lack the kind of popular charisma that sells a million copies.

Blazing sticks in Neolithic caves; grease and wick in a bear skull; Phoenician candles of yarn and beeswax; Roman tallow lamps; Elizabethan lanthorns; candles of spermaceti scented with bayberry; rushlights; Herr Wintzler's lighting up of Pall Mall with gas; Welsbach's incandescent mantle; De la Rue's dim electric light of 1820; Sir Joseph Swan's carbonized cotton filaments; Humphry Davy's carbon arc; Edison at Menlo Park; mercury vapor; neon, acetylene. . . . Fascinating stuff! Yet how many of the general public would wish to read three hundred pages about it?

John set the tone from the very outset. "We wanted light," he wrote, "so that we should not feel afraid . . ." He went on to parallel advances in religious awareness with the developing technology of artificial lighting: from early shamanism to paganism; from the "light of the world" Christianity, to medieval mysticism; from the Dark Ages to the modern enlightenment or radical theology. He suggested a direct link between the two: with lighting influencing religious beliefs, and religious beliefs influencing the technology of light.

John made great play with the fitful glimmering of candles and the haunting, soul-like shadows that flittered around rooms as a result; with the smokiness of oil lamps and the bonfires of the Inquisition; with the softly restful, comparatively brilliant glass chimney lamp of the Swiss chemist AiméArgand that climaxed the Age of Reason; with the clear, steady paraffin lamp of Victorian pragmatic Christianity.

He harvested a rare crop of quotations to prove his point, from such authorities as Saint Augustine and Meister Eckhart, Jakob Böhme and Kierkegaard, Tillich and Hans Küng. His chapter on medieval stained glass and the visionary cult of the millennium was masterly, and prefaced—anachronistically, I thought at first—by this famous passage from Shelley:

> *Life, like a dome of many-coloured glass,*
> *Stains the white radiance of Eternity . . .*

But then, the finale to the chapter completed the quotation (which not many people know beyond its first two lines); and I understood.

> *. . . Until Death tramples it to fragments.*

And what of late twentieth-century lighting—not to mention fiber optics, laser beams, and holography—and the new radical, atheistic, afterlifeless theology?

And what of the future?—a future that John saw as lying in the harnessing of "cold light": the bioluminescence of bacteria, the phosphorescence of fireflies and the fish of the abyss, which generate an enormous amount of chemical light with minimal energy input and without heat? What of the cold light of the next century, which must surely follow on from the bright yet hot and kilowatt-consuming light of our era? What of the theology of *that?*

My first assumption, as I say, was that the publisher had prevailed on John to jazz up his volume.

My second assumption, when I delved deeper into John's religious mushings, was that he had decided to throw his cap into the ring of radical theology; that he had chosen to run up his colors as one of the avant-garde of the church.

Or had he? Or rather, on whose behalf was he running up his colors?

During the many years that I had known John—since college days, a time of life when brainstorming sessions are quite common—he had never to my knowledge spoken heatedly about the validity of the Virgin Birth, or of Christ's dead body walking around, or of the afterlife, or of a God in Heaven; or any of the crunch points of the new clear-vision theology that was even then taking shape. Indeed, I felt that John had entered the church largely as a reliable career—one in which he thought he would excel, since he was a good Latin and Greek scholar, but one in which his actual belief was nominal.

Let me be more specific. John did not doubt his vocation; nor did he question it. He was more like a younger son of the eighteenth or nineteenth centuries to whom becoming a clergyman was a natural step; and like several such who became better known as naturalists or geologists or amateur astronomers, John had his own parallel, genuine passion—the history of lighting.

John's father had been a vicar. His uncle was a bishop. The step was natural; advancement was likely. Without doubt, John was good-hearted; and was to prove excellent at pastoral duties. Whilst at college he involved himself in running a boy's club, and in serving hot soup to tramps of a winter's night. However, he seemed uninterested in theological disputes as such.

Could it be that John was deeply traditional at heart—and that his book was in fact a parody of the new rational theology? A spoof, a satire? Was he intending to pull the carpet out from under the feet of the church's intellectuals—like some Voltaire, but on the other side of the fence?

Had he been so annoyed in his quiet way by the new trends in theology that he had sacrificed to God all of his private research work into the history of lighting—his consuming hobby—so that by using it satirically he could defend the faith?

Would he watch and assess reactions to his book, then announce that *Religion and the History of Lighting* was in fact a holy joke? One intended to demonstrate the credulity of unbelief? To show up the trendy emptiness of today's scientific theology?

Or was John Ingolby entirely innocent of such guile? Was he a true innocent: the stuff of saints and geniuses and the dangerously naive?

Or was he simply shortsighted and afflicted with a species of tunnel vision that had compressed his two diverse occupations— the church and the history of lighting—absurdly yet persuasively into the selfsame field of view? Maybe!

At any rate, in the wake of the cathedral fire and the televised "Quest for God," the publicity department of John's publisher dangled his newly minted book under the noses of the media; and the media gladly took the bait.

Here was more "new theology" from a bishop; more (apparently) rational probing of "superstition" as a kind of slowly vanishing shadow cast by improving human technology, a function of blazing brands and paraffin lamps and neon and lasers; and an analysis of mystical insight as an analogue of candlepower and lumens—with the possibility, thrown in, of new illuminations just around the corner.

And did not Bishop Ingolby's book have something to say (at first glance) about holy lightning? Lightning that suddenly was humanized—into the sodium-vapor lamps on motorways, the neon strips over shop fronts—by the deletion of a single letter, n, like the removal by a clever trick of an unknowable infinity from an equation?

Yet—to reinject a note of mystery—did not the possibility of cold light remain? Here, John's fancy soared poetically.

The newspapers excelled themselves. Bishop Ingolby was a debunker—and should be defrocked forthwith! Bishop Ingolby was a scientific mystic, striving to yoke technology to divinity! He was this. He was that.

Certainly he suddenly became notorious. *Religion and the History of Lighting* sold a lot of copies; a good few, no doubt, were read.

T-shirts appeared bearing the icon of a light bulb on them, and the legend: *S.O. & S.* Switch On, & See. (With a punning undercurrent of Save Our Souls.) These T-shirts seemed as urgent and arbitrary as their sartorial predecessors that had instructed people to RELAX! or FIGHT! or BREATHE!

Switch On, & See. But see what? See that there was nothing in the darkness of the universe? Or that there was everything? Or that there was something unforeseen?

Thus, by way of prologue to the strange and terrible events that happened subsequently. . . .

The "Bishop's Palace" in Porchester is, in actuality, a large Georgian house set in modest grounds of lawn and shrubbery standing midway between the railway station and the ruins of Porchester Castle. The west wing of the building was devoted to the administration of the diocese. The east wing was John's own domain, where the domestic arrangements were in the hands of a housekeeper, Mrs. Mott, who arrived every morning bright and early and departed every evening after dinner; for John had never married.

Most of the domestic arangements were Mrs. Mott's province: cookery and cleaning, laundry and such. But the lighting styles of the various rooms in the east wing were John's own choice; and it was in this respect that one half of his palace resembled a living museum.

The kitchen was lit by electric light bulbs; the small private chapel by massive candles; the dining room by gas mantles; the library by brilliant neon strips. Innumerable unused lighting devices stood, or hung, around: Roman pottery oil lamps, miners' safety lamps, perforated West Indian gourds designed to house fireflies . . .

When I arrived to visit John at his urgent request on that early November evening several months after publication of his book, the whole of the east wing that met my gaze was lit up in its assorted styles, with no curtains closed. As I walked the few hundred yards from the railway station, a couple of anticipatory rockets whizzed up into the sky over Porchester and exploded, showering orange stars. This was the day before the country's children would celebrate the burning at the stake of the Catholic Guy Fawkes for trying to blow up a Protestant parliament—an earlier religious feud. John seemed, meanwhile, to be conducting his own festival of light.

I. . . .

But I haven't mentioned who I am, beyond the fact that I was at college with John a good many years ago.

My name is Morris Ash, and I am a veterinary surgeon turned homeopathist. I live in Brighton and cater to the more prosperous sectors of society. My degree was in biochemistry, and I had originally thought of going into medical research. A certain disenchantment with my fellow human beings—coupled with dawning ecological awareness of the soaring world population and the degradation of the natural environment—had shunted me into veterinary studies.

I had done well in my profession, though I never practiced to any great extent rurally with sheep and horses and cows, which may seem a contradiction (of which life is full). I had become an upmarket urban vet, a doggy doctor, a pussy physician, reknowned among my patients' owners for my compassionate bedside (or basket-side) manner.

Twenty years on, I had five partners working with me and was more of a consultant in difficult cases than a routine castrator of tom-kittens. My thoughts turned once more to biochemistry and to medical research, but with a difference: I interested myself in homeopathy, in the theory of treating disease by means of minuscule, highly diluted doses of substances that would ordinarily cause disease. I began to investigate the possibility of treating animal ailments likewise, and within a few years I was supplying a wide range of home-made homeopathic remedies to the pets of my clientele, should the owners prefer this approach—and a gratifying number did. Homeopathy worked startlingly well in a number of recalcitrant cases; and word of my success spread quickly. I soon found that I was treating my erstwhile patients' owners homeopathically, too—though not, I hasten to add, for mange or distemper!

Now, there's nothing illegal in this. You need no medical quali-
fications to practice as a homeopathic doctor; and it's a curious
fact, as I discovered, that a good many human beings would rather
have their ills tended to by a vet than by an orthodox doctor.

A doctor is often cursory, reaching quickly for his prescription
pad to scribble upon it in illegible Latin. A doctor is frequently
inclined to treat his human patients as examples of blocked plumbing or as broken-down cars—this is the common complaint by
patients. Whereas a vet must always fondle and gentle his patients
(or else the vet is likely to be scratched, bitten, and kicked). A vet
seems more sensual, more full of curative love. He is seen to
cure—to a certain extent—by a laying on of hands, whereas a
medical doctor metaphorically jabs a fist into you.

Also, people might prefer to confide in a vet because his trade
isn't viewed as a mysterious freemasonry. A vet has no cryptic
knowledge or secret records.

Finally, the doctor appears to have the power of life or death
over you; yet he will never exercise the power of death mercifully.
Indeed the law forbids him to do so. Death can come only after a
long, humiliating, and dehumanizing process of medical intervention that often seems experimental to the wasting patient and his
relatives. The vet *does* possess the power of instant death. He can
give lethal mercy injections to distempered puppies or crushed cats.
Yet it is the instant *mercy* of this, not the lethal aspect, that is noted
primarily.

(Did I mention love? I have admitted that I did not overly love
my fellow human beings compared with the furry and feathered
folk of the world. So, in common with John—though for different
reasons—I, too, never married. As a result, to many pet-owning
widowed ladies I seemed impeccably . . . shall we say, eligible?
Which was perhaps another of my homeopathic attractions. I had
diluted and rediluted my spouse potential over the years till I
became, to some hearts, devastating.)

John and I had remained firm friends for many years—as I say—
and we met perhaps thrice every year, the occasions variable. We
seemed to have much in common. We were both confirmed bachelors. As regards charitable acts, John perceived me as a kind of lay
Saint Francis of Assisi, ministering to the world's Chihuahuas and
gerbils. I had told John, at some stage, all I knew about the

enzyme-catalyzed chemical reactions that coldly light up fireflies, deep-sea fish, bacteria, and fungi; and how one day we might learn to light our homes and cities similarly—information that had surfaced, theologically mutated, in his book. . . .

I was welcomed to the palace. We drank excellent pale sherry. We spoke of homeopathy. We talked of John's book and of its lightning success (de scandale). He mentioned an upcoming television interview to be filmed in his variously lit home, during the course of which he would stride from room to room and thus from firelight era to neon era, expounding, concluding his performance in the candlelit chapel; but he was rather vague about these plans.

I tentatively broached the puzzle (to me) of the true intention of his book. Surely an old and discreet friend was privileged to know—especially since I myself had no religious axes to grind? John sidetracked me, to admire a lanthorn from Shakespeare's day that he had recently bought at auction and that now adorned the mantelshelf of his lounge.

Then Mrs. Mott served us dinner. It was a tasty meal but a queer one. We commenced with escargots and giant champignons, both cooked in butter; and John obviously had some difficulty distinguishing which of the spheres were snails and which were mushrooms. He attempted to slice through one snail shell and then to prick out the meat from within a mushroom. Had he commanded this menu as a deliberate tease to his bespectacled self?

A turbot steak in béchamel sauce followed. Next, in sentimental homage to a shared taste from our student days when we had both patronized the same cheap wholesome dive of a café, we tucked into tripe and onions accompanied by mashed potatoes.

Afterward came a meringue concoction; followed by a slab of Wensleydale cheese, and white coffee.

Mrs. Mott departed homeward, leaving us alone.

It occurred to me that the whole meal had been white, or at least creamy gray in color; and served upon white plates. Even the wine we drank with it was leibfraumilch—"milk of a beloved woman" —not that I should have fancied a robust Burgundy as accompaniment to the meat dish in question! Had we drunk Burgundy or some other red wine, it might have looked as though our glasses had miraculously filled with the blood so visibly absent from that part of the cow's anatomy.

An all-white dinner. Why?

Had Mrs. Mott gone mad?

"Will you pour the port?" asked my host; and I obliged. The port, at least, was a rich purple-red; a contrast on which I forbore, for the moment, to comment, though my curiosity was by now intense.

John tasted his wine, then at last confided in a low voice, "I'm going blind, Morris. Blind."

"Blind?" I repeated the word stupidly. I stared at John's round, rosy face and at the thick round spectacles thereon, which from some angles made his eyes seem to bulge. His cheeks were faintly pocked: a bad reaction to a childhood bout of measles, which I knew had nearly killed him and which had certainly impaired his eyesight. The dome of his head was mostly bald and smooth. His skin and remaining strands of hair were somewhat greasy. A lot of talcum powder would need to be patted onto him prior to any television appearance; or else he would seem shiny on screen.

I decided that it was high time to broach the matter of the meal—without insulting it, however, since my taste buds had relished every morsel even if my eyes had not had much to feast on.

"Er, John . . . the dinner we just ate . . . splendid fare! Mrs. Mott is to be congratulated. But, hmm, there wasn't a scrap of color in it. Everything was white from start to finish. White food on white plates. Highly ingenious! But, um, that doesn't mean that you're going blind—just because you couldn't see any colors. There weren't any to be seen."

John uttered a few staccato laughs.

"Oh Morris, I *know* that!" he declared. "Mrs. Mott has always been a great admirer of yours. The white dinner was in your honor."

"Was it? Why's that? I don't quite follow."

"You see, that's her understanding of how homeopathy works. In this case a homeopathic cure for failing vision. Take something as essential to the health of the body as a well-cooked meal. The smell and the taste play a major role in stimulating appetite. But so does the look of the meal: the contrasts, the colors."

"Oh, I see! Mrs. Mott imagines that by reducing the color content to almost nothing—"

"Just as the homeopath reduces the drug content of a medicine virtually to nothing, by repeated dilution. Exactly!"

"—thereby your visual faculty will be stimulated rather than dulled? Your brain will strain to discriminate the tiny traces of color remaining? My word, what an imagination that woman has."

"The white dinner was also served as a broad hint in case I didn't bring myself to ask your help, Morris."

Ah.

Now I could put two and two together.

Here was another instance where someone hoped for medical advice from a vet rather than from a doctor. A vet who was a close friend. A vet, moreover, who had no special bigoted axes to grind regarding a certain radical bishop who had reduced the visions of the saints to an absence of adequate light bulbs.

Doctors often had axes to grind. My patients' owners had complained to me thus more than once. Male doctors—most are male—harbor gynecological obsessions, obsessions about the "hysteria" of female patients. They nursed obsessions about plumbing and pills and transquilizers. They held political views, often of a right-wing stripe, that they allowed to color their medical personalities. Or else they had religious obsessions—about, say, birth control or woman's role as a mother. There was no such thing as an objective doctor. Personal beliefs and prejudices always flavored diagnosis and treatment. By contrast, veterinarians could easily be objective—and at the same time loving—because (to put it bluntly and very generally) animals had no politics, and no religion.

"What do you think's wrong with your eyes, then, John, old son? Cataracts?"

Jonh emptied his glass of port, as though to fortify himself.

"I'm going blind within," he said. *"Blind within."*

"Now what do you mean by that?"

"The blindness is like a shadow inside of me. This inner shadow is spreading. It's growing outward, ever outward."

I thought for a moment. "I'm no eye specialist," I said, "but it sounds to me—if you're describing this correctly—as though your optic nerves are inflamed. The pressure of the swelling could make the nerves atrophy gradually. The blind spot would seem to enlarge. Part of the retina would go blind."

John shivered. "It's more than that." He struck his forehead a blow. "This blindness has taken root inside me like some foul black weed!" His voice faltered and hushed. "It's because of my book, don't you see?"

"*What?*"

"I've prayed, of course. One does. I pray on my own in the chapel every morning for half an hour. Prayer clears the mind. The day organizes itself. Not that I pray for myself personally! I pray that the whole world shall see the light of goodness." John seemed embarrassed. He had never mentioned private prayer to me before. "Meanwhile my own light grows dim. *Vilely* so."

"In what way 'vilely,' John?"

"There's a taint of corruption to this blindness. A moral miasma is creeping around in me, spreading its tendrils."

"You blame this on the publication of your book? It's as though you're being . . . punished?" I refilled his glass from the decanter. "I hate to say this, John, but a tumor is a remote possibility. If a tumor presses upon the visual centers of your brain, there could be emotional repercussions. You might even sense the tumor as something dark and evil growing inside your head."

"Oh no, I wouldn't. If I had a tumor, I would suffer from a steady grinding headache for at least a few hours every day. Every now and then I might see complex hallucinatory patterns; or else an aura of flashing lights. You might suddenly look like an angel to me! Or Mrs. Mott might. I *do* have a number of books in my library that aren't about technology or theology. Medical books. I've checked up on tumors. I've checked up on eye troubles—I can still read, with spotlight and magnifying glass. Under normal circumstances what afflicts me would most likely be what is known as toxic amblyopia."

"Ah. Really? You'd better explain. Obviously I'm not the best fellow to hold a consultation with!"

"Oh, but you are. Now listen, will you? Toxic amblyopia involves a reduction of the acuteness of vision due to a toxic reaction of the optic nerve. I have the symptoms of this exactly. The *commonest* cause is over-indulgence in alcohol or tobacco. But I don't smoke; and I don't ordinarily overimbibe. Quinine can also cause the condition; but I've never been near the tropics. I'm not one of your malarial missionaries of yesteryear. Other causes are prolonged exposure to various poisons, principally carbon dioxide, arsenic, lead, and benzene. One thought immediately springs to mind: Am I being poisoned by these gaslights in here, or perhaps by the candles in the chapel? By something in this very palace that is directly connected with my hobbyhorse? That would be ironic, don't you think?"

"Maybe you've already solved the puzzle, John." In which case why had I been invited? And why had Mrs. Mott cooked the all-white repast?

My friend shook his head. "I've had the gas mantles checked. They're perfectly safe. As for the chapel, ever since I began to suspect candles as possible sinners, I've lit only one at a time. No remission! I've thought carefully of every other oddity of lighting. All systems are innocent. And my vision is getting worse. The affliction has no cause; unless of course it has a miraculous cause. Miraculous," he repeated quietly, "or demonic. It's a sort of slow black lightning."

"But John, you yourself wrote that demons have no more substance than shadows cast by candles. You don't believe in demons."

"Ah . . . suppose for a moment that demons exist. I feel somewhat haunted, Morris."

"You're joking."

But I could see that he was not entirely joking.

"Don't bishops know how to deal with demons?" I asked him.

"Hmm. I should need to involve a colleague from within the church. Word would inevitably leak out. Likewise, were I to start consulting eye specialists. Embarrasssing, don't you see? Embarrassing to the church. If I tried to arrange for the exorcism of a genuine—if troublesome—miracle, why, that would be worse. I should be attempting to cast God out of my life."

"Time to wheel on the homeopathic vet, eh?"

"I could do worse. At least I can discuss the ins and outs of this with you. Mrs. Mott's quite right on that score."

As we talked, a certain suspicion began to draw on me; a suspicion I hardly dared put to John outright.

John had said that arsenic could cause toxic amblyopia.

Was it possible that Mrs. Mott was slowly poisoning John? Since white is the color of innocence, did her white meal that evening protest symbolically that she was innocent? But why should she protest innocence unless she knew her own guilt?

Why should Mrs. Mott have encouraged John to seek my advice? Perhaps she did not admire me at all, and actually regarded me as a charlatan whose advice would lead John far astray and keep him away from doctors.

John depended upon Mrs. Mott. He trusted her implicitly. Dared I cast any shadow of doubt upon their relationship? And what could the woman's motive possibly be? An inheritance—a load of peculiar lighting apparatus? (The palace certainly didn't belong to him!) Inheritance of royalties from his book? Those could hardly amount to a fortune.

Finally I decided to take the plunge.

To sugar the pill, I chuckled. "Speaking of phosphorescence," I said (though we hadn't been, for a while), "in the old days, phosphorus was often used as a poison because it's difficult to detect. Some phosphorus occurs naturally in the body. There's a famous case in which one intended victim was alerted when he noticed his bowl of soup glowing while he was carrying it to table along a dark corridor!"

"Hmm," said John without more ado, "so why should Mrs. Mott wish to poison me?"

"I didn't mean to imply—"

"Oh yes, you did. Tiny doses of an arsenic compound, eh? A little bit of rat killer day by day. But in rather more than a homeopathic dose! She has no earthly motive."

"Maybe she has an unearthly one?"

"Explain."

"Maybe she regards your book as, um, blasphemous. Maybe she believes you're in league with the Antichrist."

"Mrs. Mott? I hardly think so! Do you?"

I thought about the comfy, devoted, cheery soul in question; and shook my head.

That night, as I lay on the verge of sleep in John's great oaken guest bed, my mind wandered back to the story of the phosphorescent soup. A soup bowl aglow in a dark corridor. . . .

Is this a tureen that I see before me
The ladle toward my hand? Art thou lobster bisque,
Vichyssoise, or plain beef broth with arsenic?
Art thou not, fatal bouillon, sensible
To tasting as to sight? Or art thou but
A potage of the mind?

I don't know quite why I decided to get up out of my warm bed to roam the November-chilly Bishop's Palace at midnight. Maybe I had some notion that in the pitch-dark kitchen I would spy some spice jar glowing phosphorescently, betraying the true poisonous nature of its contents. But get up I did, shuffling my slippers on my feet and belting my dressing gown about me, then proceeding to the door with hands outstretched.

I didn't use my pocket torch, nor had I opened the curtains. I knew that it was a dark, moonless night outside, but I wanted my eyes to retain the sensitivity of a cat so that the tiniest dose of light might register.

I felt my way along the upstairs corridor, tiptoeing past John's room next to mine, though I had little reason to fear that my faint footfalls—or the noisier creaking of the boards—might disturb him. John had long since told me that he invariably slept the sleep of the dead. As soon as his head touched the pillow, he became a log until dawn.

Still, the bathroom was in the opposite direction. How could I explain my nocturnal perambulation?

To cut the story of a long prowl short, I fumbled my way into the kitchen—then to all the other downstairs rooms, and even the chapel. Nowhere did I spy anything unusual.

The chapel was bitterly cold, but the chill I experienced was innocuous—winter was to blame. Unless a thermostat switched some heater on in the early morning. John's half hour of prayer must have been something of a penance. Supposedly there's another species of chill that runs down spines and makes dogs howl like banshees. Yet if it was devilish cold in John's chapel, I'm sure the devil had no hand in hypothermia, no finger in frigidity.

I returned upstairs, only stubbing my toe once.

In the darkness of the upper corridor, I miscalculated distances. I twisted a brass doorknob. It wasn't my own bedroom door that I opened—it was John's.

I realized my mistake at once because a ring of light illuminated the head of the bed, showing me John's face asleep beneath. He was wearing, of all things, a wooly nightcap with a big pompon that Mrs. Mott must have knitted for him.

The ring of light was no wider than his head, over which it seemed to perch. Though my eyes were well accommodated to night vision, the light wasn't brilliant. But it clearly showed me John's slumbering countenance and outlined the bed. Obviously the light was some reflection or refraction from outside, through the bedroom window. Perhaps a powerful arc lamp at the railway station?

I made my way to the window to check; but the heavy curtains were closed tight without a chink.

> *I saw Eternity the other night*
> *Like a great* Ring *of pure and endless light . . .*

There was no other glimmer in the room itself. No movement of mine dimmed or shadowed the ring of pearly light. Thoughts of Mrs. Mott as purveyor of phosphorus soup flew out of the window (or would have done so, had the window offered any way in or out). I could pretend to myself no longer. I *knew* what I was seeing.

Above John's head, as he slept, hung a halo.

A halo such as saints wear in paintings.

Not so bright, perhaps! Not a radiant glory. A modest halo, which wouldn't even be visible if other light competed. But a halo nonetheless.

John's head was snuggled in a fat pillow. The halo was tilted across his face. I stretched out a cautious finger to touch the apparition.

Perhaps this was foolhardy of me, but I suffered no consequences. I felt no buzz, no shock, no warmth. The thing couldn't be an odd form of ball lightning or Saint Elmo's fire.

I swept my hand right through the halo, without effect. Then I shook John's shoulder.

"Wake up, old son! Wake up, will you?"

Eventually I roused him.

"House on fire? Burglars? What's the time?"

"No, no, no. None of that. Sit up."

As he sat up, the halo shifted position so that it was poised above the nightcap.

"What's up, Morris? Where's my torch?" (John's bedroom was equipped with nineteenth-century carriage lamps.)

I gripped his wrist. "No—no torch! Is there a mirror anywhere?"

"Inside the wardrobe."

"Will you show me?"

Grumbling mildly, John got out of bed—the halo accompanying him—and soon he was pawing a wardrobe door open.

Now there were two halos: one above John's head, and the other in the full-length mirror.

"Goodness, what's that light? I haven't got my glasses."

"I'll fetch them. Where are they?"

"Table by the bed."

I retrieved his spectacles, and he put them on.

"Goodness!"

"Goodness indeed, John—by the look of it! You're wearing a halo."

He stepped to and fro. He swung his hand across his head. He pulled off his nightcap—as though I might have attached that ghostly glow as a joke.

"Oh dear me," he said. "My eyes aren't much use—but I can see it. Dear me, I always thought there was something frightfully priggish about halos . . ."

"You must be becoming a saint, eh, old son?"

"What, me? A saint? Don't be silly. Besides saints never had actual rings of light over their heads! That's just an artistic convention. A way of picturing saints."

"Maybe some saints had actual halos—ones that people could see? But not in recent history."

"I think a halo would need to be brighter than mine, for people to notice!"

"Maybe yours is just a baby halo. A young one."

"Meaning that it'll grow stronger? As my eyes grow dim? Let's light some lamps."

My friend located his torch and went through the rigmarole of getting carriage lamps to work. As the illumination of the bedroom increased, so did his halo fade away to a faint shimmer.

I sat on a chair; John perched on the bed.

"This is quite embarrassing," he said. "It's preposterous! I can't possibly be a saint in the making. And, what could conceivably cause a halo?"

"*Grace,* perhaps, my lord bishop?"

"You don't believe that."

"Any more than you believe it? I want to ask you, John: Did you write that book of yours to debunk radical theology? Is the book a kind of holy offering—of everything you cared deeply about—so that faith may be sustained?"

"Gracious me, I don't think so. Morris, I've told you that I feel an evil darkness spreading its shadow inside of me. If I'm sprouting a halo, I assure you this is at the *expense* of my soul! It isn't a spotlight to illuminate saintliness." He mused awhile. "How nice it would be to imagine that it's some lamp of goodness. How nice to visualize certain dim monasteries of the past as being genuinely lit by sanctity—with a saint's head as a light bulb! How lovely if cities of the future could be cold-lit by our own purity, should mankind perfect itself! Heaven would be radiant on account of its saints. Hell would be dingy dark because of its sinners. But that is emphatically *not* how I feel as this blindness eats up my vision."

Eats up.

"Your halo is eating your eyesight . . . what could that mean? That the halo is some kind of organized energy? It needs energy to sustain itself; to grow . . . ? Certain luminous deep-sea fish need to eat luminous plankton or else they stop glowing. And by glowing they attract their prey."

"What are you trying to say, Morris?"

"Maybe a halo is some sort of creature—an animal not of blood and bone but of energy. It's eating the photons that enter your eyes; or the electrical impulses in your optic nerves. That's why you're going blind. Your brain can sense it feeding inside you; consuming light, to produce light."

"A parasite? Why should it generate a halo? Hmm, famous saints of the past haven't been noted for their blindness. . . ."

"So halos can't be the work of parasites, presumably."

He shook his head in puzzlement. "You mentioned luminous fish attacting prey. What *prey* would a saint attract to him? Why, the faithful. The credulous. Some sinners ripe for conversion.

People who are religiously inclined. A halo might be God's fishing hook. It might be an angel that takes up residence, in order to angle for souls. And it drinks photons from the saint's eyes, to power the halo? I don't know, hagiographically, of many saints who had impaired vision!''

''Maybe there have been only a few true saints—whose halos became legend? You're the next saint. The miracle for a godless age.''

''Are you *trying* to canonize me, Morris? You should be devil's advocate.''

''I'm only looking at the possibilities. Here's another one: Maybe in the past there were more conduits to the divine light? The halo-angels didn't need to suck the vision from a saint. There were other sources of energy.''

''In that case why should I sense that my blindness is *evil?* Why should I feel such a lack of grace?''

''I don't know.''

''When I become blind as a bat, does my halo grow with glory? Whose faith is being tested? The world's, or mine? Is this a test of faith at all—or is it the work of some vile parasitic creature from elsewhere, with its own motives? Is that what a miracle is: something you can't ever prove, but must take on trust, like God himself? Even though you feel that you yourself are damned! Possessed!'' He stretched out his hands toward me. ''If I beg you to cure me, Morris—God knows why—do I damn myself? Should I let my halo strengthen and thus confirm the faith of millions of people— while I lose my own belief, sunk in my personal deep, dark pit?''

''Maybe the thing will go away,'' I said feebly. ''Maybe it'll fade, and your eyesight will improve.''

''Will you stay with me a few more days?''

''A week. Longer, if need be. Of course I will.''

He sighed. ''Thank you, Morris. Now you'd better go back to bed. And so shall I.'' His bishop's authority suddenly blossomed. ''Be off with you, Morris! I shall extinguish the lanterns. I shan't toss and turn, or lie brooding.''

A week later I was still staying at the palace; and the halo was intensifying. I could see the ring of light above John's head in the daylight or artificial lighting. My friend's eyesight had worsened drastically.

There was no question now of rushing him to an optician's or to a hospital. Moreover, John and I were in full agreement that Mrs. Mott should be kept in the dark regarding the halo. I carried the meals she cooked to John's room on a tray, and cut up meat for him.

The bishop was ill, incapacitated, and I was treating him—that was the story. He had a serious infection, though nothing dangerous or fatal. Mrs. Mott accepted the situation only when John told her firmly, from the other side of his door, that this was so.

The business of the diocese was dealt with likewise. John's secretary took umbrage somewhat; he also wanted a "genuine" doctor called to examine the bishop. Through the wood of the door, the bishop overruled him loudly; and I witnessed an aspect of my friend that made me realize how he also had a tough streak—he hadn't become a bishop simply through a combination of good works and nepotism.

John's mind remained keen. The halo-creature that had infested my friend had no apparent ambition to speak through his lips, whisper words in his head, or influence his dreams.

But it brightened; how it brightened.

"Even when I become stone-blind," John said to me, "I'll not really be *blind*. It's just that all the light will be stolen to create my halo. And it won't be long till I'm stone-blind. Should we phone the television people, do you think? Tell them to rush here for a news conference? Should I display this miracle to the world? Should I say: *Here* is God's lightning? But it doesn't strike the transepts of cathedrals. It circles about my head calmly and brightly—while *I* dwell in a pit of mud forevermore, as if in Dante's Inferno.

"Should I say: Behold the cold light of the future, of the next age of belief? I bear it as my cross—or rather, my circle, my ring of Peter, my *annulus angeli*. Yet I know that my angel is dark. It glows only by theft, by a vampirism of light. So how can it be from God? This has destroyed my faith in God as surely as it has destroyed my sight. If this thing is God's punishment, then maybe I should damn God! If it is his blessing: likewise! And if it's sent by the devil, then the world will never be perfected. We will never be enlightened."

"Maybe," I suggested, "you need a spiritual adviser rather than a homeopathic vet?"

He shook his head brusquely; the halo remained steady. "*I* . . . must decide. Only I know what it is like to be me at this time."

And decide he did—in the most gruesome manner. . . .

A distant cry clawed me out of sleep.

I flipped on my own bedside torch (absolute prerequisite in this palace where lighting systems varied from the latest to the least of technologies!) It was 5:30 A.M. by my watch. The world was still deep in darkness. Had I heard an owl screech in the frosty castle ruins?

"Morris!"

My friend's voice came from far away.

I found him in the chapel. All the candles were lit. He knelt before the little altar. By him on the flagstone lay a bloodstained bread knife. Blood ran down his cheeks—down a ghastly empty face. On the altar cloth, staring at the silver cross, perched his two eyeballs.

In moments of horror it's odd what petty details you notice. I noticed that John had used a bread knife—with a sawtooth edge and a rounded end. The rounded end, to spring his eyeball loose. The saw, to sever the optic nerve.

Maybe this wasn't such a petty detail. It proved how much forethought had gone into his mutilation of himself.

His blind, unblinking eyes stared moistly at the sign of Christ. Above his head in the light of so many candles, the halo could hardly be seen.

"Is that you there, Morris?" His voice spoke pain.

"Yes."

"Has the damned thing gone yet?"

"I think it's fading. Oh John, *John*!"

Fading, fading fast. By the time the ambulance arrived, no halo was visible.

Needless to say, I accompanied him to hospital. By the time a doctor could assure me that John was resting comfortably, sedated, a detective inspector and two other officers had arrived at St. Luke's anxious to speak to me. The ambulance man had radioed a report; the police had hurried to the palace, arriving shortly before Mrs. Mott. They had seen the bloody bread knife and the eyes perched upon the altar. It must have looked like a sadistic crime performed by a madman, me.

Fortunately I hadn't touched the knife.

During the hours of questions until John recovered from sedation, I learned how the thought processes of the police resemble those of our most disgraceful tabloid newspapers. This should hardly have surprised me, since to a large extent both share the same contents. The detective inspector spent ages pursuing the notion that Bishop Ingolby and I, both bachelors, might have been homosexually involved since college days; thus the atrocity was the product of a vicious sexual quarrel, possibly with aspects of blackmail attached—the bishop was a famous man now, was he not?

Even after John woke up and exonerated me, the detective inspector was loath to discard his suspicions. After all, the bishop might be trying to cover up for me; and for himself as well. My fingerprints weren't on the handle of the knife; only John's were present, and Mrs. Mott's beneath. But I might have worn gloves.

Perhaps I oughtn't to blame the police. They must have been well aware that I was lying—and later that John also was lying about a motive for the mutilation.

The one "sure" fact relayed by Mrs. Mott—namely that the bishop feared he was going blind—seemed not so sure in view of John's doctor knowing nothing of this; nor the diocesan secretary either.

And in what mad emotional equation did fear of impending blindness lead to the wanton gouging out of one's eyes?

In a sense it was gutter press that came to our rescue. Tipped off either by police or by ambulance men, newshounds descended on Porchester. To them the vital fact was that the eyes of John Ingolby— skeptical author of *Religion and the History of Lighting*—had been placed on the altar of God. What else could they be but an offering?

Thus the press added two and two together and made four. Whereas the real answer was some entirely irrational number. Or maybe a zero: the mysterious zero of the halo.

"Why did you really put your eyes on the altar, John?"

Two weeks had passed. John was back home in the palace, convalescing. But he wouldn't remain at the palace much longer; the archbishop's personal assistant was pressing for John's resignation, rather urgently, on compassionate grounds.

By that hour, Mrs. Mott had departed. So had John's doctor, who had called to inspect the eye sockets and change the dressings. We were alone in the palace together, John and I. How like the evening of my arrival; except that John wore a blindfold now. Except that we had earlier eaten an ordinary dinner of brown beef, green cabbage, and golden roast potatoes.

"Why, John?"

"Well, what do you think? I've always been a tidy fellow. Where else should I have put them? Down on the floor? I didn't want anyone to stand on them and squash them!"

"That's the only reason? Tidiness?"

"I had to tidy up, Morris. I had to tidy up more than merely my eyes. You know that."

"I suppose so. . . . Will you accept artificial eyes? Glass, plastic, whatever?"

He laughed wryly. "From artificial lighting—to artificial eyes! A logical progression, if an unenlightening one. Yes, I should think that glass eyes would be harmless enough. If not, they're a lot easier to get rid of! Just flush them down the toilet."

"You're a brave soul, John. A true saint: a gentleman and a martyr—an unacknowledged one."

"Let's hope I remain unacknowledged."

Yes, he was a gentleman—of the old school of English gentlemen who produced many Anglican parsons and bishops in the past. In common with such, he disliked hysteria, enthusiasm, and excess. He had performed that savage operation of optectomy (if that's the word) to root out a hysteria that was alien to him, but that might have spread outward in shock waves from his halo. He had carried this out in the cold light of dawn (almost), and certainly had applied the cold light of reason—so that the future might be reasonable.

For sanity's sake he had denied himself any future glimpse of light, natural or artificial.

In my eyes this truly made him a saint. And a martyr, too, even though he hadn't died. I alone knew this; yet how could I ever tell anybody?

John Ingolby had written a final, definitive, unpublishable chapter to his life's work—using not a pen but a bread knife. Every time I sliced a loaf of bread in the future, I would feel that I was performing an act of anti-communion. A refusal to accept the unacceptable.

I felt that more than a mere bishop was on the point of retirement in Porchester. So, too, was an enfeebled, diluted God, whose last miracle had been rejected because it would harm the world, not help it. Just as it had harmed John.

"I'm donating my collection to Porchester Museum," he told me. "After I've moved out of here, there'll be thoroughly modern lighting in every room." He sounded as if he were choking.

"Are you all right, old friend?"

"I'm weeping, Morris. And I can't ever weep. Except inside."

"Maybe God had nothing to do with any of this!" I spoke to encourage him. "Maybe the halo-parasite was something else entirely. A visitor from elsewhere in the universe. A life-form we know nothing of. You felt it was evil, remember? It might have been natural—or devilish. Aren't angels supposed to announce themselves?"

"*I* felt it was evil," he replied. "*I* did. Nobody else who saw my round, benevolent face with a lustrous halo perched above could possibly have imagined evil. They would have seen only the light of goodness shining forth. Mine was the evil, don't you see? *Don't you see?*" And tearlessly he wept.

Or at least I suppose he was tearless. He hadn't actually carved out his tear ducts. But no welling tears would lave his cheeks. Tears would drain into the empty sockets. I didn't press for details of how an eyeless man weeps.

I did my best to comfort him.

But there was I, sitting in a convivially lit room; whereas he was sitting in darkness. Darkness, always. Forever haunted by the night that had overtaken him.

Just thirty months later the announcement has come, from Matsuya Biotechnic K.K. of Japan, of the development of artificial bionic eyes that can be plugged into the optic nerves.

Matsuya Biotechnic's deluxe model improves upon our ordinary visual organs of muscle, jelly, and liquid amazingly. With tiny touch controls (hidden by the eyelid) these Japanese eyes can be adjusted to range into the infrared, to magnify telescopically, and to peer owl-like on the darkest night.

The world's armed forces are very interested; though there's one small snag. To use Matsuya eyes, first you need to have your own eyes amputated.

In the two years gone by, I must have visited John almost a dozen times at his retirement cottage in a little vilage near Porchester, where Mrs. Mott continued to care for him; and I knew how he was suffering.

Not pain—but anguish.

Not poverty—his book had sold massively in paperback and in foreign editions in the wake of his self-blinding—but claustrophobia of the spirit.

John had been fitted with false plastic eyeballs that were most convincing. The blue pupils were holographically etched so that the eyes looked twinklingly alive, more so at times than real eyes.

He phoned me a fortnight ago.

"I'm going to buy a pair of these new Matsuya eyes," he told me. "Assuming that their experts can summon up the nerve to fit them!" He laughed sharply. "The optic nerve, I mean. Just so long as there's enough optic nerve still alive and kicking in my head. I can't take any more of this hellish darkness, Morris. The halo-creature must have died ages ago. Given up; gone home—whatever halo-creatures do when their host starves them out."

We had spoken much about the "halo-creature," John and I.

An angel? A demon? An extraterrestrial life-form? Or a creature from some other universe entirely—from some other mode of existence—that had strayed across the boundary from its reality into ours?

The creature wasn't necessarily intelligent. It might have been no brighter, intellectually, than a fish of the abyss or a firefly.

Maybe it was a parasite upon some alien beings who had visited our world in secret; and it had escaped. Did it convey some advantage upon such hypothetical alien beings? Or was it just an inconvenience to them—a sort of common cold, a bug of the eyes?

The evil that John had sensed might well have been the quality of alienness rather than some moral, metaphysical pang.

We had gradually settled on a naturalistic explanation, though without any actual notion of the natural history of the beast involved. Certainly a parasite that blinded its host and lit up a beacon above its head didn't seem very survival-minded. But maybe in this respect John was a South Sea islander infected by European mumps or measles.

Or at least, *I* had settled upon this solution. John still spoke of hellish darkness.

Now technology would save him by banishing that darkness—just as improved artificial lighting had progressively banished spooks and spirits, devils and gods, lumen by lumen, century by century.

"I've been in touch with the Japanese trade people in London," he said. "Matsuya will fly a couple of their surgeons, and a pair of eyes, over the Pole. It's good publicity for their company. You could say I've been pulling strings. In ten days' time they can pull mine, inside my head, and see whether those still work. If all goes well, I should be home with my new eyes in a couple of weeks. *Jubilate!"*

All has indeed gone well.

John Ingolby can see again. He can see far better than ever he saw before in all his life. He can see better than almost all of the human race—unless they've had nature's optics removed and bionic eyes substituted.

The newly revealed world comes as a revelation to him. My face, unseen these past two years, is a mystic vision. So, too, is Mrs. Mott. Likewise her cottage garden of herbs and flowers.

Likewise the nighttime, which he can pierce with ease, seeing monochrome hills and trees and cows and hedges, the stars above drilling a thousand bright little lamp-holes.

Likewise the heat-image of the world at dawn with those same cows appearing as vivid red humps in the cool blue fields, leaving faint rosy footsteps behind them in the dew. A bird is a flaming meteor.

Such beauty redeems John's soul. His new eyes look less human than the plastic ones; they're silver-gray and at some angles seem like mirrors in his head. But that's of no account.

*   *   *

"John—"

It's the second night of my visit, and we have stepped outside to stargaze. Mrs. Mott has already retired early to bed.

"It's back, John."

"Eh?"

"Your halo: it's showing faintly."

"Don't joke, Morris."

"I'm not joking. I can *see* it."

He hurries closer to the cottage and peers in a curtained window-pane. Everything is much more visible to him. His reflection there confirms my word.

"Oh my God. So it wasn't living in my eyes and feeding on the photons. It was in my brain all the time. It's been lying dormant like a frozen virus. The light has brought it back to life. Oh my God. These Matsuya eyes are permanent. I can't pull them out when I feel like it. . . ."

"And you can't switch them off?"

"Why should anybody want to switch their eyes off? When I go to bed, my eyelids do the job. An on-off button would be one control too many. It's early yet for bionic eyes."

He tells me of Matsuya Biotechnic K.K.'s boast that future eyes will have computerized display functions activated by voice command, with memory chips located in a unit that might be surgically implanted behind the ear or in the jaw. Owners of Matsuya eyes will be able to call up statistics, run graphics across their field of view, access encyclopedias.

But not for several years yet, such sophistication.

"John, this time I think we ought to tell people. You could begin by telling the Japanese."

"No."

"Why not? They'll be worried in case the halo's some fault of the Matsuya eyes. Or they might suppose you've stumbled on some hidden power of the mind that their eyes have triggered. The liberation of the third eye by their lenses! They'll have equipment for probing the halo. They might be able to look into your brain through the eyes."

"No, Morris, the problem's the same as ever. Oh God, to have all the wonder of the world restored to me thrice over—then to have it polluted and thieved again! I'm no saint!'' he snarls suddenly. "I might have been a saintly codger in Porchester, but I damn well stopped being one during these past two years."

We go inside the cottage and drink brandy.

John gets drunk.

The halo isn't at all conspicuous when Mrs. Mott serves us our breakfast of bacon and eggs. She notices nothing odd, but I can spy the faint shimmer.

The sky is blue, the sun is bright.

"Lovely spring morning," observes John. "Might cloud over later. We'll take a walk up Hinchcombe Hill."

Hinchcombe Hill is a mile away along a lane, then up through a steep forest ride to a gorse-clad hilltop, which is deserted save for some Suffolk ewes. Suffolks are a chunky breed that lamb early, before Christmas; these ewes are already parted from their offspring.

It was cool walking up through the shade of the fir trees, but here on the hilltop it's as hot as a summer's day.

"Can you see our circular friend?"

"The sun's too bright," I tell him.

"Good. Now, we all know that we shouldn't stare at a bright sun, don't we, Morris? The sun can burn the cells of the retina. My retina is a machine. It's much more resilient. The flash from a hydrogen bomb might burn Matsuya eyes—but we all know that a nuclear flash is brighter than a *thousand* suns, don't we? So I ought to have lots of spare capacity even if I switch over to night vision."

"Don't do it, John."

"I don't care if I harm these eyes. Not now."

"You might damage your brain. The visual centers."

"Where the beast dwells, eh? Unless it dwells in a separate universe, or in Heaven, and only has a peephole in my head."

He sits down on a boulder facing the sun. "You want feeding?" he cries out. "I'll feed you!"

For some reason—habit, ritual, or insurance policy?—he crosses himself, then begins to stare fixedly at the sun. Loudly he hums the hymn tune "Angels from the Realms of Glory" over and over again monotonously.

Minutes pass.

"I can see it, John. It's glowing."

Brighter, ever brighter.

Presently it's a full-fledged radiant halo; and still he stares into the sun.

He breaks off humming. "Report, please!" he says crisply.

"I can't look directly at it any longer. It's getting too fierce." At least the halo's light is cold, otherwise John's head would surely start to cook.

"Not from my point of view! The day grows dim. The sun looks like a lemon in a mist." *Ang-els! from! the Realms! of Glo-ry!*

I simply have to turn away. The ewes have all trekked off down the slope away from this second, miniature sun in their midst.

"I'm going blind fast, Morris. It's really gobbling light."

"And pumping it out again!"

"I'll soon be back in darkness. But no matter." *Ang-els! from!*

If only I had some tinted glass with me. I only dare risk a glance now and then.

Glance:

The halo isn't doughnut-shaped any longer. It's a sphere of furnace light just like a second head. Its after-image bobs above the fir trees as though a ball of lightning is loose.

The Realms! of Glo-ry!

I cast two shadows on the grass and gorse.

Glance:

"It's elongating upward, John!"

A pillar of blinding silver radiance: it could light a whole street.

In the afterimage a figure hovers over the trees, sliding from side to side: a body of sorts. It fades.

Glance:

Now the afterimage is sharper. That isn't a human body. It's too slim, except where the chest swells out. The legs are too short, the arms too long and skinny. The head is like a bird's, with a beak of a mouth.

Ang-els! from!

The afterimage has wings, great trailing plumed wings.

It's the blazing angel who threw Adam and Eve out of Eden.

"There's a creature perching on your head, John! A tall, scraggy bird! It's like a man—but it isn't."

Its claw feet are planted on John's skull as if his skull is an egg that it is clutching.

184 / Ian Watson

Glance:

The afterimage opens its beak.

"Hullo! Hullo! Hullo!" What a screechy, reedy voice.

John isn't humming any longer. The words are screeched from *his* lips in the tones of a parrot or a mynah bird.

"I hear you!" I shout.

I shade my eyes with both hands in a visor: John is sitting as before, gazing rigidly up at our sun.

"I come," screams the bird of light. "I announce myself!"

"Where do you come from?"

"I take."

"Take what? Where to?"

"My prey! To my aerie!"

John must be the creature's prey. I have to break his link with the power of the sun! Sheltering my head from the horrid pillar of light, I stumble at a crouch and buffet him sideways off his rock. With my own eyes closed tight, I cast myself down beside him. Fumbling, I find his head and seal my hands across his Matsuya eyes.

"Aiiieee!" shrieks the voice.

John's own voice calls out: "Oh blessed visions! Realms of glory! Celestial city of the angels! With the slimmest, highest of towers all lit by cold light at night as though a star has settled on every pinnacle—an angel perching on each. White angels drifting through the pearly sky of day. A meadowland below with little blue goat-elves all a-grazing by the river of milk—"

"Don't heed it, John! Cast it out of your head."

"My soul will go inside an angel's egg."

"Refuse! The thing is trying to take your mind away with it."

"I'll be reborn—angelic."

"They're birds of prey, John. Alien eagles, not angels."

"No, they are celestial—" His voice chokes off.

"Aiiieee! I triumph!"

John's body shudders, then grows still.

Cautiously I open my eyes. The blinding light, the second sun, has gone. Only our own yellow sun beams on the gorse, the rocks, the grass; and on my friend's body.

I feel for his pulse; there's none. His heart has stopped. I don't know how to give the kiss of life, but I still try to breathe animation back into him—in vain.

I sit by his sun-warmed corpse for a long while.

John thought that his mind would go into an angel's egg on that alien world, in that other reality.

Presumably he would hatch.

As what? As an angel, the equal of the other angel-birds?

Or as a prisoner, bringing honor to its captor? A slave? A sacrifice? A gift to the Lord of the Birds of Light?

I shall soon walk back down the hill, through the forest ride, along the lane alone. I shall have to say that the strain of the ascent caused a coronary and broke his heart. I shall say that his spirit has ascended to Heaven, where he is now at home.

I must hope that no one else saw the blinding light on Hinchcombe Hill, the radiance that raptured John away to an alien aerie, leaving the abandoned clothing of his flesh behind.

Maybe John will be happy when he hatches, to the cold light of that elsewhere-city. And maybe there's no such city; maybe his last visions were lies, opiates pumped into his skull to paralyze his will. . . .

A few ewes return, to stare at the two of us with mild curiosity.

The "feral child" theme in fiction goes back at least to Rudyard Kipling's Jungle Book *and Edgar Rice Burroughs' Tarzan novels. A few years ago Philip Jose Farmer compiled an entire anthology of such stories,* Mother Was a Lovely Beast. *There may be nothing new under the sun, but there is always a new approach to a classic theme, as Judith Moffett demonstrates here in her first published science fiction story. This accomplished work by a University of Pennsylvania faculty member previously known for books of poetry and literary criticism shows us how tenuous the boundaries between worlds can sometimes be.*

SURVIVING

Judith Moffett

For nearly eighteen years I've been keeping a secret to honor the memory of someone, now pretty certainly dead, who didn't want it told. Yet over those years I've come gradually to feel uncomfortable with the idea of dying without recording what I know—to believe that science would be pointlessly cheated thereby, and Sally, too; and just lately, but with a growing urgency, I've also felt the need to write an account of my own actions into the record.

Yet it's difficult to begin. The events I intend to set down have never, since they happened, been out of my mind for a day; nevertheless the prospect of reexperiencing them is painful and my silence the harder to break on that account.

I'll start, I guess, with the afternoon an exuberant colleague I scarcely knew at the time spotted me through the glass door and barged into the psychology department office calling, "Hey, Jan, you're the expert on the Chimp Child—wait'll you hear this, you're not gonna believe it!''

People were always dashing to inform me of some item, mostly inconsequential, relating to this subject. I glanced across at John from the wall of mailboxes, hands full of memos and late papers, one eyebrow probably raised. "What now?"

"We've *hired* her!" And when I continued to look blank: "No kidding, I was just at a curriculum committee meeting in the dean's office, and Raymond Lickorish in Biology was there, and he told me: they've definitely given Sally Barnes a tenure-track appointment, to replace that old guy who's retiring this year, what's his name, Ferrin. The virus man. Raymond says Barnes's Ph.D. research was something on viruses and the origin of life on earth and her published work is all first-rate and she did well in the interview—he wasn't there so he didn't meet her, but they were all talking about it afterward—and she seems eager to leave England. So the department made her an offer and she accepted! She'll be here in September, I swear to God!"

By this point I'm sure I was showing all the incredulous excitement and delight a bearer of happy tidings could possibly have wished. And no wonder: I wrote my *dissertation* on Sally Barnes; I went into psychology chiefly because of the intense interest her story held for me. In fact the Chimp Child had been a kind of obsession of mine—part hobby, part mania—for a long time. I was a college freshman, my years of Tarzan games in the woods less far behind me than you might suppose, in 1990, when poachers hauled the screeching, scratching, biting, terrified white girl into a Tanzanian village and told its head man they would be back to collect the reward. Electrified, I followed the breaking story from day to day.

The girl was quickly and positively identified as Sally, the younger daughter of Martin and Hilary Barnes, Anglican missionary teachers at a secondary school in the small central African republic of Malawi, who had been killed when the lightplane in which they and she were traveling from Kigoma had crashed in the jungle. A helicopter rescue crew found only the pilot's body in the burned-out fuselage. Scavengers may have dragged the others away and scattered the bones; improbable survivors of the crash may have tried to walk out—the plane had come down in the mountains, something less than 150 kilometers east of Lake Tanganyika—and starved, or been killed by anything from leopards to thieves to fever. However it was, nothing had been heard or seen of the Barnes family after that day in 1981; it was assumed that one way or another all three had died in the bush.

No close living relatives remained in England. An older daughter, left at home that weekend with an attack of malaria, had been sent to an Anglican school for the children of missionaries, somewhere in the Midlands. There was no one but the church to assume responsibility for her sister the wild girl, either.

The bureaucracies of two African nations and the Church of England hummed, and after a day or two Sally was removed to the Malosa School in Southern Malawi, where the whole of her life before the accident had been lived. She could neither speak nor understand English, seemed stunned, and masturbated constantly. She showed no recognition of the school, its grounds or buildings, or the people there who had been friendly with her as a small child. But when they had cleaned her up, and cropped her matted hair, *they* recognized that child in *her*; pictures of Sally at her fourth birthday party, printed side by side in the papers with new ones of the undersized thirteen-year-old she had become, were conclusive. Hers was one of those faces that looks essentially the same at six and sixty.

But if the two faces obviously belonged to the same person, there was a harrowing difference.

A long time later Sally told me, gazing sadly at this likeness of herself: "Shock. It was nothing but shock, nothing more beastly. On top of everything else, getting captured must have uncovered my memories of the plane crash—violence; noise; confusion; my parents screaming, then not answering me—I mean, when the poachers started shooting and panicked everybody, and then killed the Old Man and flung that net over me, I fought and struggled, of course, but in the end I sort of went blank. Like the accident, but in reverse."

"Birth Trauma Number Three?" We were sitting cross-legged on the floor before the fireplace in my living room, naked under blankets, like Mohegan. I could imagine the scene vividly, had in fact imagined it over and over: the brown child blindly running, running, in the green world, the net spreading, dropping in slow motion, the child pitching with a crash into wet vegetation. Help-lessness. Claustrophia. Uttermost bowel-emptying terror. The hys-terical shrieks, the rough handling . . . Sally patted my thigh, flushed from the fire's heat, then let her hand stay where it was.

"No point looking like that. What if they *hadn't* found me then? At University College, you know, they all think it was only just in time."

"And having read my book, you know I think so, too." We smiled; I must have pressed my palm flat to her hot, taut belly, or slipped my hand behind her knee or cupped her breast—some such automatic response. "The wonder is that after that double trauma they were able to get you back at all. You had to have been an awfully resilient, tough kid, as well as awfully bright. A survivor in every sense. Or you'd have died of shock and grief after the plane crashed, or of shock and grief when the poachers picked you up, or of grief and despair in England from all that testing and training, like spending your adolescence in a pressure cooker." I can re-member nuzzling her shoulder, how my ear grazed the rough blanket. "You're a survivor, Sal."

In the firelight Sally smiled wanly. "Mm. Up to a point."

Any standard psych text published after 2003 will describe Sally Barnes as the only feral child in history to whom, before her final disappearance, full functional humanity had been restored. From the age of four and a half until just past her thirteenth birthday, Sally acted as a member of a troop of chimpanzees in the Tanza-nian rain forest; from sixteen or seventeen onward, she was a young Englishwoman, a person. What sort of person? The books are vague on this point. Psychologists, naturally enough, were wild to know; Sally herself, who rather thought she did know, was wild to prevent them from turning her inside out all her life in the interest of Science. I was (and am) a psychologist and a partisan, but professional integrity is one thing and obsession is quite an-other, and if I choose finally to set the record straight it's not because I respect Sally's own choice any less.

From the very first, of course, I'd been madly infatuated with the *idea* of Sally, in whose imagined consciousness—that of a human girl accepted by wild creatures as one of themselves—I saw, I badly wished to see, myself. The extreme harshness of such a life as hers had been—with its parasites, cold rains, bullying of the weak by the strong, and so forth—got neatly edited out of this hyper-romantic conception; yet the myth had amazing force. I don't know how many times I read the *Jungle Books* and the best of the Tarzan novels between the ages of eight and fifteen, while my mother hovered uneasily in the background, dropping hints about eye makeup and stylish clothes. Pah.

So that later, when a real apechild emerged from a real jungle and the Sunday supplements and popular scientific magazines were full of her story, for me it was an enthralling and fabulous thing, one that made it possible to finish growing up, at graduate school, *inside* the myth: a myth not dispelled but amplified, enhanced, by scientific scrutiny. The more one looked at what had happened to Sally, the more wonderful it seemed.

Her remarkable progress had been minutely documented, and I had read every document and published half a dozen of my own, including my dissertation. It was established that she had talked early and could even read fairly well before the accident, and that her early family history had been a happy, stable one; all we experts were agreed that these crucial factors explained how Sally, alone among feral children, had been able to develop, or reacquire normal language skills in later life. She was therefore fortunate in her precocity; fortunate, too, in her foster society of fellow primates. Almost certainly she could not have recovered, or recovered so completely, from eight years of life as a wolf or a gazelle. Unlike Helen Keller, she had never been sensually deprived; unlike Kaspar Hauser, also sensually deprived, she had not been isolated from social relations—wild chimpanzees provide one another with plenty of those; unlike the wolf girls of India, she had learned language before her period of abstention from the use of it. And like Helen Keller, Sally had a very considerable native intelligence to assist her.

It may seem odd that despite frequent trips to England, I had never tried to arrange a meeting with the subject of all this fascinated inquiry, but in some way my fixation made me shy, and I would end each visit by deciding that another year would do as well or better. That Sally might come to America, and to my own university, and to stay, was a wholly unlooked-for development. Now that chance had arranged it, however, shyness seemed absurd.

Not only would we meet, we would become friends. Everyone would expect us to, and nothing seemed more natural.

My grandfather used to claim, with a forgiving chuckle, that his wedding night had been the biggest disappointment of his life. I thought bleakly of him the September evening of the annual cocktail party given by the dean of arts and sciences so that the standing faculty could make the acquaintance of their newly hired colleagues. A lot of people knew about Sally Barnes, of course, and among psychologists she was really famous, a prodigy; everybody wanted to meet her, and more than a few wanted to be there when *I* met her, to witness the encounter. I was exasperated with myself for being so nervous, as well as annoyed that the meeting would occur under circumstances so public, but when the moment arrived and I was actually being introduced to Sally—the dean had stationed himself beside her to handle the crush, and did the honors himself—these feelings all proved maddeningly beside the point.

There she stood, the Chimp Child of all my theories and fantasies: a small, utterly ordinary-seeming and -sounding young woman who touched my hand with purely mechanical courtesy. The plain black dress did less than nothing for her plain pale face and reddish hair; history's only rehabilitated feral child was a person you wouldn't look at twice in the street, or even once. That in itself meant nothing; but her expression, too, was indifferent and blank, and she spoke without any warmth at all, in an "educated" English voice pitched rather high: "How d'you do, a pleasure to meet you . . ." There she actually stood, saying her canned phrase to *me*, sipping from her clear plastic container of white wine, giving away nothing at all.

I stared at the pale, round, unfamiliar face whose shape and features I knew so well, unable to believe in it or let go of the hand that felt so hard in mine. The room had gradually grown deafening. Bright, curious eyes had gathered round us. The moment felt utterly weird and wrong. Dean Eccles, perhaps supposing his difficult charge had failed to catch my name, chirped helpfully, "Of course Janet is the author of that fascinating book about *you*," and beamed at Sally as if to say, "*There* now, you lucky girl!"

Only a flicker of eyelids betrayed her. "Oh, I see," she said, but her hand pulled out of mine with a little yank as she spoke, and she looked pointedly past me toward the next person in the receiving line—a snub so obvious that even the poor dean couldn't help but notice. Flustered, he started to introduce the elderly English professor Sally's attention had been transferred to.

We had hardly exchanged a dozen words. Suddenly I simply had to salvage something from the wreck of the occasion. "Look— could I call you in a week or two? Maybe we could get together for lunch or a drink or something after you're settled in?"

"Ah, I'm afraid I'll be rather busy for quite some time," said the cool voice, not exactly to me. "Possibly I might ring you if I happen to be free for an hour one afternoon." Then she was speaking to the old gentleman and I had been eased out of the circle of shoulders and that was that.

I went home thoroughly despondent and threw myself on the sofa. An hour or so later, the phone rang: John, who had witnessed the whole humiliating thing. "Listen, she acted that way with *everybody*, I watched her for an hour. Then I went through the line and she acted like that with *me*. She was probably jet-lagged or hates being on display—she was just pretending to drink that wine, by the way, sip, sip, sip, but the level never went down the whole time I was watching. You shouldn't take it personally, Jan. I doubt she had any idea who you were in that mob of freak-show tourists."

"Oh, she knew who I was, all right, but that doesn't make you wrong. O.K., thanks. I just wish the entire department hadn't been standing around with their tongues hanging out, waiting to see us fall weeping on each other's necks." Realizing I wasn't sure which I minded more, the rejection or its having been witnessed in that way, made me feel less tragic. I said good night to John, then went and pulled down the foldable attic stairs, put on the light, and scrounged among cartons till I found the scrapbook; this I brought downstairs and brooded over, soothed by a glass of rosé.

The scrapbook was fat. The Chimp Child had been an international sensation when first reclaimed from the wild, and for years thereafter picture essays and articles had regularly appeared where I could clip or copy them. I had collected dozens of photographs of Sally: arriving at Heathrow, a small, oddly garbed figure, face averted, clinging to a uniformed attendant; dressed like an English schoolgirl at fifteen, in blazer and tie, working at a table with the team of psychologists at University College, London; on holiday with the superb teacher Carol Cheswick, who had earned a place

for herself in the educators' pantheon beside Jean-Marc Itard and
Annie Sullivan by virtue of her brilliant achievements with Sally;
greeting Jane Goodall, very old and frail, on one of Goodall's last
visits to England; in her rooms at Newnham College, Cambridge,
an average-looking undergraduate.

The Newnham pictures were not very good, or so I had always
thought. Only now that I'd seen her in person . . . I turned back to
the yellow newspaper clipping, nearly twenty years old, of a wild
thing with matted, sawed-off hair; and now for the first time the
blank face beneath struck me as queerly like this undergraduate's,
and like the face I had just been trying to talk to at the party. The
expressive adolescent's face brought into being sometime during
the nineties—what had become of it? Who was Sally Barnes, after
all? That precocious, verbally gifted little girl . . . I closed the
cover, baffled. Whoever she was, she had long since passed the
stage of being studied without her consent.

Yet I wanted so badly to know her. As fall wore on to winter, I
would often see her on campus, walking briskly, buttoned up in her
silver coat with a long black scarf wrapped round her, appearing to
take no notice of whatever leaves or slush or plain brickwork
happened to be underfoot, or of the milling, noisy students. She
always carried reading equipment and a black shoulder bag. Invariably she would be alone. I doubt that I can convey more than a dim
impression of the bewilderment and frustration with which the sight
of her affected me throughout those slow, cold months. I knew
every detail of the special education of Sally Barnes, the dedication
of her teachers, her own eagerness to learn; and there had been
nothing, nothing at all, to suggest that once "restored to human
status," she would become ordinary—nothing to foreshadow this
standoffish dullness. Of course it was understandable that she would
not wish to be quizzed constantly about her life in the wild; rumor
got round of several instances when somebody unintimidated by her
manner had put some question to her and been served with a
snappish "Sorry, I don't talk about that." But was it credible that
the child whom this unique experience had befallen had been, as
her every word and action now implied, a particularly unfriendly,
unoriginal, bad-tempered child who thereafter had scuttled straight
back to sour conventionality as fast as ever she could?

I simply did not believe it. She had to be deceiving us deliberately. But I couldn't imagine why, nor entirely trust my own intuition: I wanted far too badly to believe that *no* human being who had been a wild animal for a time, and then become human again, could possibly really be the sort of human Sally seemed to be.

And yet why not (I would argue with myself)? Why doubt that a person who had fought so hard for her humanity might desire, above all else, the life of an ordinary human?

But is it ordinary to be so antisocial (I would argue back)? Of course she never got in touch with me. A couple of weeks after the party, I nerved myself up enough to call her office and suggest meeting for lunch. The brusqueness of that refusal took some getting over; I let a month go by before trying again. "I'm sorry," she said. "But what was it you wanted to discuss? Perhaps we could take care of it over the phone."

"The idea wasn't to discuss anything, particularly. I only thought—new people sometimes find it hard to make their way here at first, it's not a very friendly university. And then, naturally I'd like to—well, just talk. Get acquainted. Get to know you a bit."

"Thanks, but I'm tremendously busy, and in any event there's very little I could say." And then, after a pause: "Someone's come to the door. Thanks for ringing."

It was no good, she would have nothing to do with me, beyond speaking when we met on campus—I could, and did, force her to take that much notice of me. Where was she living? I looked it up, an address in the suburbs, not awfully far from mine. Once I pedaled past the building, a shabby older high-rise, but there was no way of telling which of the hundreds of windows might be hers. I put John up to questioning his committee acquaintance in Biology, learning in this way: that Sally had cooly repulsed every social overture from people in her department, without exception; that student gossip styled her a Britishly reserved but better-than-competent lecturer; that she was hard at work in the lab on some project she never discussed with anybody. Not surprisingly, her fellow biologists had soon lost interest. She had speedily trained us all to leave her alone.

The psych department lost interest also, not without a certain tiresome belaboring of me, jokes about making silk purses out of chimps' ears and Ugly Chimplings and the like. John overheard a sample of this feeble mailbox badinage one day and retorted with some heat, "Hey, Janet only said she's *human* in that book. If education made you nice and personable, I know lots of people around here besides Sally Barnes who could stand to go back to school." But John, embroiled in a romance with a first-year graduate student, now found Sally a dull subject himself; besides, what he had said was true. My thesis had not been invalidated, nor Carol Cheswick and the team at University College overrated. It was simply the case, in fact, that within six months of her arrival, Sally—billed in advance as an exotic ornament to the university—had compelled us all to take her for neither more nor less than the first-rate young microbiologist she had come among us to be.

My personal disappointment grew by degrees less bitter. But still I would see the silver coat and subduedly fashionable boots, all points and plastic, moving away across the quad and think: Lady, had it been given unto me to be the Chimp Child, by God I'd have made a better job of it than you do!

Spring came. Between the faculty club and the library, the campus forsythia erupted along its straggling branches, the azaleas flowered as usual a week earlier in the city than in my garden fifteen miles away. Ridley Creek, in the nearby state park, roared with rains and snowmelt and swarmed with stocked trout and bulky anglers; and cardinals and titmice, visible all winter at the feeders, abruptly began to sing. Every winter I used to lose interest in the park between the first of February and the middle of March; every spring rekindled my sense of the luck and privilege of having it so near. During the first weeks of trout season, the trails, never heavily used, were virtually deserted, and any sunny day my presence was not required in town I would stuff a sandwich, a pocket reader, and a blanket into a daypack and pedal to the park. Generally I stayed close to the trails, but would sometimes tough my way through some brambly thicket of blackberry or raspberry canes, bright with small new chartreuse-colored leaves, to find a private spot where I could take off my shirt in safety.

Searching for this sort of retreat in a tract of large beech trees one afternoon in April, I came carefully and painfully through a tangle of briars to be thunderstruck by the sight of Young Professor Barnes where she seemed at once least and most likely to be: ten meters up in one of the old beeches. She was perfectly naked. She sat poised on a little branch, one shoulder set against the smooth gray bole of the bare tree, one foot dangling, the opposite knee cocked on the branch, the whole posture graced by a naturalness that smote me with envy in the surreal second or two before she caught sight of me. She was rubbing herself, and seemed to be crying.

One after another, like blows, these impressions whammed home in the instant of my emerging. The next instant Sally's face contorted with rage, she screamed, snapped off and threw a piece of dead branch at me (and hit me, too, in the breastbone), and was down the tree and running almost faster than I could take in what had happened, what was still happening. While part of my brain noted with satisfaction, *She didn't hear me coming!* a different part galvanized my frenzied shouting: "No! Sally, for God's sake, stop! Stop! Come back here, I won't tell anybody, I won't, I swear! *Sally!*" Unable to move, to chase her, I could only go on yelling in this semihysterical vein; I felt that if she got away now, I would not be able to bear it. I'd have been heard all over that side of the park if there had been anybody to hear, outside the zone of noise created by the creek. It was the racket I was making, in fact, that made her come pelting back—that, and the afterthought that all her clothes were back there under the tree, and realizing I had recognized her.

"All right, I'm not going anywhere, now *shut up!*" she called in a low, furious voice, crashing through undergrowth. She stomped right up to me barefoot and looked me in the eye. "God damn it to hell. What will you take to keep your mouth shut?" Did she mean right now? But I *had* stopped shouting. My heart went right on lurching about like a tethered frog, though, and the next moment the view got brighter and began to drift off to the right. I sat down abruptly on something damp.

"I was scared witless you wouldn't come back. Wait a second, let me catch my breath."

"You're the one who wrote that book, Morgan," she said between her teeth. "God damn it to *hell.*" In a minute she sat down, too, first pushing aside the prickly stems unthinking. The neutral face that gave away nothing had vanished. Sally Barnes, angry and frightened, looked exactly as I had wished to see her look; incredibly, after so much fruitless fantasy, here we were in the woods together. Here she sat, scratching a bare breast with no more special regard than if it had been a nose or a shoulder. It was pretty overwhelming. I couldn't seem to pull myself together.

Sally's skin had turned much darker than mine already, all over—plainly this was not her first visit to the bare-branched woods. Her breasts were smallish, her three tufts of body hair reddish, and all her muscles large and smooth and well-molded as a gymnast's. I said what came into my head: "I was a fairly good tree-climber as a kid, but I could never have gotten up one with a trunk as thick as that, and those high, skinny branches. Do you think if I built my arms and shoulders up, lifted weights or something—I mean, would you teach me? Or maybe I'm too old," I said. "My legs aren't in such bad shape, I run a few kilometers three times a week, but the top half of my body is a flabby mess—"

"Don't play stupid games," Sally burst out furiously. "You had to come blundering in here today, you're the worst luck I ever had. I'm asking again: Will you take money not to tell anyone you saw me? Or is there something else you want? If I can get it, you can have it, only you've *got* to keep quiet about seeing me out here like this."

"That's a rotten way to talk to people!" I said, furious myself. "I was blundering around in these woods for years before you ever set foot in them. And I'm sorry if you don't like my book, or is it just me you don't like? Or just psychologists? If it weren't for you, I probably wouldn't even *be* one." My voice wobbled up and down, I'd been angry with Sally for seven months. "Don't worry, I won't say anything. You don't need to bribe me."

"Yes, but you will, you see. Sooner or later you'll be at some dinner party, and someone will ask what the Chimp Child is like, *really*"—I looked slantwise at her; this had already happened a couple of times—"and you won't be able to resist. 'There I was, walking along minding my own business, and whomever do you think I saw—stark naked and gone right up a tree like a monkey!' Christ," Sally said through her teeth, "I could *throttle* you. Everything's spoiled." She got up hastily; I could feel how badly she wanted to clobber me again.

But I was finally beginning to be able to think, and to call upon my expertise. "Well, then, make me *want* not to tell. Make it a question of self-interest. I don't want money, but I wasn't kidding: I'd absolutely love to be able to get around in a forest like a chimp does. Teach me to climb like one—like you do. If the story gets out, the deal's off. Couldn't you agree to that?''

Sally's look meant, "What kind of idiot do you take me for?" Quickly I said, "I know it sounds crazy, but all through my childhood—and most of my adolescence, too—for whatever wacky reason, I wanted in the *worst* way to be Tarzan! And for the past twenty years, I've gone on wanting even more to be *you*! I don't know why—it's irrational, one of those passions people develop for doing various weird things, being fans or collecting stamps or—I used to know a former world champion flycaster who'd actually gone fishing only a couple of times in his life!" I drew a deep breath, held it, let it out in a burst of words: "Look—even if I don't understand it, I *know* that directly behind *The Chimp Child and the Human Family*—and the whole rest of my career, for that matter—is this ten-year-old kid who'd give anything to be Tarzan swinging through the trees with the Great Apes. I can promise that so long as you were coaching me, you'd be safe. I'll never get a better chance to act out part of that fantasy, and it would be worth—just everything! One *hell* of a lot more than keeping people entertained at some dinner party, I'll tell you that!''

"You don't want to be me," said Sally in a flat voice. "I was right the first time; it's a stupid game you're playing at." She looked at me distastefully, but I could see that at any rate she believed me now.

The ground was awfully damp. I got up, starting to feel vastly better. Beech limbs webbed the sky; strong sunshine and birdsong poured through web; it was all I could do, suddenly, not to howl and dance among the trees. I could see she was going to say yes.

Sally set conditions, all of which I accepted promptly. I was not to ask snoopy professional questions, or do any nonessential talking. At school we were to go on as before, never revealing by so much as a look or gesture that an association existed between us. I was not to tell *anybody*. Sally could not, in fact, prevent my telling people, but I discovered that I hadn't any desire to tell. My close friends, none of whom lived within 150 kilometers of the city, could guess I was concealing a relationship but figured I would talk about it when I got ready; they tended to suppose a married man, reason enough for secrecy. Sally and I both taught our classes, and Sally had her work in the lab, and I my private patients.

Once in midweek and once each weekend, we met in the beech grove; and so the "lessons" got under way.

I acquired some light weights and began a program of exercise to strengthen my arms, shoulders, chest, and back, but the best way to build up the essential muscles was to climb a lot of trees. Before long the calluses at the base of each finger, which I had carried throughout my childhood, had been re-created (and I remembered then the hardness of Sally's palm when I'd shaken hands with her at the cocktail party in September). Seeing how steadily my agility and toughness increased, Sally was impressed and, in spite of herself, gratified. She was also nervous; she'd had no intention of letting herself enjoy this companionship that had been forced upon her.

It was a queer sort of blackmail. I went along patiently, working hard and trying to make my company too enjoyable to resist; and in this way the spring semester ended.

Sally was to teach summer school, I to prepare some articles for publication and continue to see my patients through the summer. By June all the trout had been hooked and the beech woods had grown risky; we found more inaccessible places on the riding-trail side of the park where I could be put through my training-exercise routines. By the Fourth of July my right biceps measured thirty-seven centimeters and Sally had finally begun to relax in my presence, even to trust me.

That we shortly became lovers should probably surprise nobody. All the reports describe the pre-accident Sally an affectionate child, and her family as a loving one. From my reading I knew that in moments of anxiety or fear, chimps reassure one another by touching, and that in placid ones they reaffirm the social bond by reciprocal grooming. Yet for a decade, ever since Carol Cheswick died and she'd gone up to Cambridge, Sally had protected herself strictly against personal involvements, at the cost of denying herself all emotional and physical closeness. Cheswick, a plump, middle-aged, motherly person, had hugged and cuddled Sally throughout their years together, but after Cheswick's death—sick of the pokings and peerings of psychologists and of the curious public, resentful and guilty about the secret life she had felt compelled to create for herself—Sally had simply done without. Now she had me.

Except for the very beginning, in London, there had always been a secret life.

She abruptly started to talk about it late one horribly hot afternoon, at the end of a workout. We had dropped out of the best new training tree, a century-old white oak, then shaken out a ragged army blanket, sat on it cross-legged, and passed a plastic canteen and a bunch of seedless grapes between us. I felt sticky and spent, but elated. Sally looked me over critically. "You're filling out quite well, it's hard to believe these are the same scrawny shoulders." She kneaded the nearer shoulder with her hard hand, while I carefully concealed my intense awareness that except to correct an error, she had never touched me anywhere before. The hand slipped down, gripped my upper arm. When I "made a muscle" the backs of her brown fingers brushed my pale-tan breast; our eyes met, and I said lightly, "I owe it all to you, coach," but went warmer still with pleasure and the rightness of these gestures, which had the feeling of a course correction.

Sally plucked several grapes and popped them in her mouth, looking out over the creek valley while she chewed. After a bit she said, "They let me go all to pot in London. All anybody cared about was guiding me out of the wilderness of ignorance, grafting my life at thirteen back onto the stump of my life at four and then making up for the lost years how they could. The lost years . . . mind you, they had their hands full, they all worked like navvies and so did I. But I'd got absolutely consumptive with longing for the bush before they brought Carol in, and she noticed and made them let me out for a fortnight's holiday in the countryside. I'd lost a lot of strength by then, but it was only just a year so it came back quick enough."

She stopped there, and I didn't dare say anything; we ate grapes and slapped mosquitoes. It was incredibly hot. After a bit, desperate to hear more, I was weighing the risks of a response when she went on without prodding:

"At University College, though, they didn't much care to have me swinging about in trees. I think they felt, you know, 'Here *we* are, slaving away trying to drag the ape kid into the modern world, and what does she do the minute our backs are turned but go dashing madly back to her savage ways.' Sort of, 'Ungrateful little beast.' They *never* imagined I might miss that benighted life, or anything about it, but when I read *Tarzan of the Apes* myself a few years later, the part toward the end where Tarzan strips off his suit and tie and shoes and leaps into the branches swearing he'll never, never go back—I cried like anything.''

I said, "What could you do about it, though?" breaking Sally's no-questions rule without either of us noticing.

"Oh, on my own, not much. But Carol had a lot to say about what I should and shouldn't do. They respected her tremendously. And she was marvelous. After I'd got so I could talk and read pretty well, she'd take me to the South Downs on weekends and turn me loose. We had a tacit agreement that if she didn't ask, I needn't tell. We were so close, she certainly knew I was getting stronger and my hands were toughening up, but *she* never took the view that those years in the wild were best forgotten. She arranged for me to meet Jane Goodall once . . . I couldn't have borne it without her. I never should have left England while she lived. If it weren't for Carol—'' For several minutes Sally's hand had been moving of its own accord, short rhythmic strokes that ceased abruptly when, becoming aware of this movement, she broke off her sentence and glanced—sharply, in alarm—at me.

I made a terrific effort to control my face and voice, a fisherman angling for the biggest trout in the pool. "She must have been remarkable."

For a wonder Sally didn't get up without a word and stalk away. Instead she said awkwardly, "I—do you mind very much my doing this? I've always done it—for comfort, I suppose—ever since I was small, and it's a bit difficult to talk about all these things . . . without . . ."

From the first day of training, I had determined never to let Sally force a contrast between us; I would adapt to her own sense of fitness out here. If she climbed naked, so would I, tender skin or not. If she urinated openly, and standing, so would I—and without a doubt there was something agreeable about spraddling beside Sally while our waters flowed. A civilized woman can still pass the whole length of her life without ever seeing another woman's urine, or genitalia, or having extended, repeated, and matter-of-fact exposure to another woman's naked body—and yet how many *men*, I had asked myself, ever gave these homely matters a second thought?

Then why on earth should we?

Certainly no woman had ever before done in my presence what Sally had been doing. Mentally, I squared my shoulders. "Why should I mind? Look, I'll keep you company"—suiting action to words with a sense of leaping in desperation into unknown waters, graceless but absolutely determined—"O.K.?"

It was the very last thing Sally had looked for. For a second I was afraid she thought I was ridiculing her in some incomprehensible way; but she only watched, briefly, before saying, "O.K. For a psychologist you're not a bad sort. The first bloody thing they did at that mission school was make me stop doing this in front of people.

"So anyway. Carol knew I was longing for the wild life, and knew it was important, not trivial or wrong, so she gave it back to me as well as she could. But she couldn't give me back"—her voice cracked as she said this—"the chimpanzees. The people I knew. And I did miss them dreadfully—certain ones, and living in the troop—the thing is, I was a child among them, and in a lot of ways it was a lovely life for a child, out there. The wild chimps are so direct and excitable, their feelings change like lightning, they're perfectly uninhibited—they squabble like schoolkids with no master about. And the babies are so sweet! But its all very—very, you know, physical; and I missed it. I thought I should die with missing it, before Carol came." The grapes were all gone. Sally chucked the stem into the brambles and lay back on the blanket, left arm bent across her eyes, right hand rocking softly.

"Part of my training in London was manners and morals: to control myself, play fair, treat people politely whether I liked them or not. I'd *enjoyed* throwing tantrums and swatting the little ones when they got in my road, and screaming when I was furious and throwing my arms around everybody in reach when I was excited or happy, and being hugged and patted—like this," patting her genitals to demonstrate the chimpanzees' way of reassuring one another, "when I was upset. Chimps have no superego. It's hard to have to form one at thirteen. By then, pure selfishness without guilt is hard to conquer. Oh, I had a lot of selfishness to put up with from the others—I was very low-ranking, of course, being small and female—but I never got seriously hurt. And a knock-about life makes you tough, and then I had the Old Man for a protector as well." Sally lifted her arm and looked beneath it, up at me. "For a kid, most of the time, it was a pretty exhilarating life, and I missed it. And I missed," she said, "getting fucked. They were not providing any of that at University College, London."

"What?" My thumb stopped moving. "Ah—were you old enough? I mean, were the males interested, even though you didn't go pink?" I began to rub again, perhaps faster.

"For the last year or thereabouts—I'm not quite sure how long. It must have been, I don't know, pheromones in the mucus, or something in my urine, but I know it was quite soon after my periods started that they'd get interested in me *between* periods, when I would have been fertile, even without the swelling. I knew all about it, naturally; I'd seen plenty of copulating right along, as far back as I could remember. A pink female is a very agitating social element, so I'd needed to watch closely, because one's got to get out of the way, except while they're actually going at it. That's when all the little ones try to make them stop—don't ask me why." she added quickly, then grinned. "Sorry. That's one thing every primatologist has wanted to know." Sally's movements were freer now; watching, I was abruptly pierced by a pang of oddity, which I clamped down on as best I could. This was definitely not the moment for turning squeamish.

"It frightened me badly that first time; adult male chimps who want something don't muck about. When they work themselves up, you know, they're quite dangerous. I usually avoided them, except for the Old Man, who'd sort of adopted me not long after the troop took me in . . . any road the first time hurt, and then of course everybody always wants a piece of the action, and it went on for *days*. By the time it was over, I'd got terribly sore. But later . . . well, after I'd recovered from that first bout, I found it didn't really hurt anymore. In fact, I liked it. Quite a lot, actually, once I saw I needn't be frightened. The big males are frightfully strong, the only time I could ever dare be so close to so many of them was then, when I came in season, and one or another of them would sort of summon me over to him, and then they'd all queue up and press up behind me, one after another . . ."

More relieved than she realized at having broken the long silence at last, Sally went on telling her story; and of course, the more vividly she pictured for me her role in this scene of plausible bizarreness, elaborating, adding details, the more inevitable was the outcome of our own unusual scene. All the same, when the crisis struck us, more or less simultaneously, it left me for the moment speechless and utterly nonplussed, and Sally seemed hardly less flustered than I.

But after that momentary shock, we each glanced sidelong at each other's flushed, flummoxed face and burst into snorts of laughter; and we laughed together—breathlessly, raggedly, probably a little hysterically—for quite a while. And pretty soon it was all right. Everything was fine.

It was all right, but common sense cautioned that if Sally's defenses were too quickly breached, she would take fright. So many barriers had collapsed at once as to make me grateful for the several days that must elapse before the next coaching session. Still, when I passed her figure in its floppy navy smockdress and dark glasses on campus the following morning, I was struck as never before by the contrast between the public Sally and the powerful glowing creature nobody here had seen but me. A different person in her situation, I thought, would surely have exploited the public's natural curiosity: made movies, written books, gone on the lecture circuit, endorsed products and causes. Instead, to please her teachers, everything that had stubbornly remained Chimp Child in Sally as she learned and grew had had to be concealed, denied.

But because the required denial was a concealment and a lie, she had paid an exhorbitant price for it; too much of what was vital in her had living roots in those eight years of wildness. Sally was genuinely fond of and grateful to the zealous psychologists who had given back her humanity. At the same time she resented them quite as bitterly as she resented a public interested only in the racier parts of her life in the wild and in her humanity not at all. One group starved her, the other shamed her. Resentments and gratitudes had split her life between them. She would never consent to display herself *as* the Chimp Child on any sort of platform, yet without the secret life she would have shriveled to a husk. When I surprised her in the park, she had naturally feared and hated me. Not any more.

Success despite such odds made me ambitious. I conceived a plan. Somehow I would find a way—become a way!—to integrate the halves of Sally's divided self; one day she would walk across this quad, no longer alone, wearing her aspect of the woods (though clothed and cleaner). I'd worked clinically with self-despising homosexuals, and with the children of divorced and poisonously hostile parents; Sally's case, though unique in one way, was common enough in others. Charged with purpose, I watched as the brisk, dark shape entered a distant building and swore a sacred oath to the Principle of Human Potential: I would finish the job, I would dedicate myself to the saving of Sally Barnes. Who but I could save her now? At that fierce moment I knew exactly how Itard had felt when finally, for the first time, he had succeeded in reducing Victor to the fundamental humanity of tears.

Saturday looked threatening, but I set off anyway for the park. The midafternoon heat was oppressive; I cut my muscle-loosening jog to a kilometer or two, then quartered through the woods to the training oak. Early as I was, Sally had come before me. I couldn't see her, high in the now dense foliage, but her clothing was piled in the usual place and I guessed she had made a day-nest at the top of that tree or one nearby, or was traveling about up there somewhere. After a long drink from the canteen I peeled off my own sweaty shorts, toweling shirt, shoes, and the running bra of heavy spandex, smeared myself with insect repellent, and dried my hands on my shirt. Then I crouched slightly, caught a heavy limb well over two meters above the ground and pulled myself into the tree.

For ten minutes I ran through a set of upper-body warmups with care and concentration; I'd pulled one muscle in my shoulder four times and once another in my back, before finding an old book on gymnastics explaining how to prevent (and treat) such injuries. The first few weeks I had worn lightweight Keds, and been otherwise generally scraped and skinned. But now my skin had toughened—I hadn't known it would do that—and greater strength made it easier to forgo the clambering friction of calves and forearms; now, for the most part, my hands and feet were all that came in contact with the bark. A haircut had nicely solved the problems of snarling twigs and obscured vision.

Warm and loose, I quickly climbed ten meters higher and began another series of strengthening and balancing exercises, swinging back and forth, hand over hand, along several slender horizontal limbs, standing and walking over a heavier one, keeping myself relaxed.

After half an hour of this, I descended to the massive lowest limb and practiced dropping to the ground, absorbing the shock elastically with both hands and both feet, chimp-style. Again and again I sprang into the tree, poised, and landed on the ground. I was doing quite well, but on about the fifteenth drop I bruised my hand on a rock beneath the leaf mold and decided to call it an afternoon; my hair was plastered flat with sweat, and I was as drenched as if I'd just stepped out of a shower. I had a long, tepid drink and was swabbing myself down with my shirt when Sally left the tree by the same limb, landed with a negligent, perfect pounce, came forward and—without meeting my eye—relieved me of the canteen, at the same time laying her free arm briefly across my shoulders. "That one's looking pretty good," she said, nodding at the branch to indicate my Dropping-to-the-Ground exercise. The arm slid off, she picked up the squirter of Tropikbug—"but did you ever see such monstrous mosquitoes in your life?"

"It's the humidity, I was afraid the storm would break before I could get through the drill. Maybe we better skip the rest and try to beat it home."

Sally squirted some repellent into her palm and wiped it up and down her limbs and over her brown abdomen. She squirted out some more. "Yours is all sweated off," she said, still not meeting my eye; and instantly Hugo Van Lawick's photographs of chimps soliciting grooming flashed into my mind, and I turned my shoulder toward Sally, who rubbed the bug stuff into it, then anointed the other shoulder, and my back and breasts and stomach for good measure, and then handed the flask dreamily to me, presenting her own back to be smeared with smelly goop. At that instant the first dramatic thunderclap banged above the park, making us both jump; and for a heart-stopping second Sally's outstretched arm clutched round me.

We bundled the blanket back into its plastic pouch and cached it, and pulled on clothes, while rain began to fall in torrents. My jogging shoes were clearly goners. I didn't bother to put on the bra, rolling it up on the run and sticking it inside my waistband. We floundered out of the trees in a furious commotion of wind and crackle-WHAM of lightning, and dashed in opposite directions for our parked cars. It took me fully fifteen minutes to reach mine, and twenty more to pedal home by roads several centimeters deep in rain, with the heater going full blast, and another half hour to take a hot shower and brew some tea. Then, wrapped in a bathrobe, I carried the tea tray and Jane Goodall's classic study *In the Shadow of Man* into the living room, and reread for the dozenth time the passages on the social importance of physical contact among wild chimpanzees.

Over and over, as I sat there, I relived the instant of Sally's instinctive quasi embrace in the storm, and each time it stopped my breath. What must Sally herself be feeling then? What terrifying conflict of needs? She must realize, just as I did, that a torrent had begun to build that would sweep her carefully constructed defenses away, that she could not stop it now, that she must flee or be changed by what would follow.

When I thought of *change*, it was as something about to happen to Sally, though change was moving just as inexorably down upon me. Three or four times in my life, I've experienced that sense of *courting* change, of choosing my life from moment to moment, the awareness of process and passage that exalted me that evening but never before or since with such intensity. I alone had brought us to this, slowly, over months of time, as the delicate canoe is portaged and paddled to where the white water begins. Day by day we had picked up speed; now the stream was hurtling us forward together; now, with all our skill and nerve and strength, we would ride the current—we would shoot through. There is a word for this vivid awareness: existential.

If I feared then, it was that Sally might hurl herself out of the canoe.

The next day but one was not a regular coaching day, but the pitch of nervous excitement made desk work impossible. I drove to the park in mid-afternoon to jog, and afterward decided, in preference to more disciplined routines, to practice my Traveling-from-Tree-to-Tree. My speed and style at this—that of a very elderly, very arthritic ape—was still not half bad (I thought) for a human female pushing forty, though proper brachiation still lay well beyond my powers. The run, as usual, had settled me down. The creek, still aboil with muddy runoff from the storm, was racketing along through a breezy, beautiful day. I chose an ash with a low fork, stuffed my clothes into my fanny pack, buckled it on, and started to climb.

I hadn't expected to find Sally at the training tree, but saw her without surprise—seated below me, cross-legged on the grubby blanket—when, an hour later, I had made my way that far. She stood up slowly while I descended the familiar pattern of limbs and dropped from the bottommost one. Again without surprise I saw that she looked awful, shaky and sick, that assurance had deserted her—and understood then that *whatever* happened now would not surprise me, that I was ready and would be equal to it. While I stood before Sally, breathing hard, unfastening the buckle, the world arranged itself into a patterned whole.

Then, as I let the pack fall, Sally crouched low on the blanket, whimpering and twisting with distress. I knelt at once and gathered her into my arms, holding her firmly, all of her skin close against all of mine. She clutched at me, pressed her face into my neck. Baffled moaning sounds and sobs came out of her. She moved inside this embrace; still moaning, eyes squeezed shut, her blind face searched until she had taken the nipple and end of my left breast into her mouth. As she sucked and mouthed at this, with her whole face pushed into the breast, her body gradually unknotted, relaxed, curled about mine, so I could loosen my hold to stroke her with the hand not suporting her head. Soon, to relieve the strain of the position, I pressed the fanny pack—I could just reach it—into service as a pillow and lay down on my side, still cradling Sally's head.

Time passed, or stopped. The nipple began to be sore.

At last, seemingly drained, she rolled away onto her back. Her face was smeared with mucus and tears; I worked my shirt out of the pack one-handed and dried it. At once she rolled back again, pushing herself against me with a long, groaning sigh. "The past couple of nights, God, I've had all sorts of dreams. Not bad dreams, not exactly, but—there was this old female in the troop, maybe her baby died, it must have done . . . I'd completely forgotten this. This must have been when they first found me. *She* found me, I think . . . I think I'd been alone in the forest without food long enough to be utterly petrified and apathetic with terror. But when she found me . . . I remember she held me against her chest and shoved the nipple in—maybe just to relieve her discomfort, or to replace her own child with a substitute, who knows. I think I would certainly have died except for that milk, there was such all-encompassing fear and misery. I don't know how many weeks or months she let me nurse. She couldn't have lived very long, though.''

Sally weighed my breast in her hand. "Last night I dreamed I was in some terrible place, so frightened I couldn't move or open my eyes, and somebody . . . picked me up and held me, and then I was suckling milk from a sort of teat, and felt, oh, ever so much better, a great flood of relief. Then I opened my eyes and saw we were in the bush—I recognized the actual place—but it was *you*, the person holding me was you! You had a flat chest with big rubbery chimpanzee nipples"—lifting the tender breast on her palm—"and a sort of chimp face, but you were only skin all over, and I realized it was you.''

I put my hand firmly over hers, moved it down along her forearm. "How did you feel when you knew it was me?''

"Uncomfortable. Confused. Angry." Then reluctantly: "Happy, too. I woke up, though, and then mostly felt just astonished to remember that that old wet nurse had saved my life and I'd not given her a single thought for twenty-five years.'' She lay quiet under my caressing: neck, breasts, stomach, flank; her eyes closed again. "What's queer is that I should remember *now*, but not when Carol first took charge of me, and not when I first read *Tarzan*, even though the Tarzan story's nearly the same as mine. I don't understand why now and not then.''

"Do you feel you need to? I mean, does it seem important to understand?''

"I don't know." She sounded exhausted. "I certainly don't feel like even trying to sort it all out now.''

"Well. It'll probably sort itself out soon enough, provided you don't start avoiding whatever makes these disturbing memories come back.''

Sally opened her eyes and smiled thinly. "Start avoiding you, you mean. No. I shan't, never fear." She snuggled closer, widening and tilting herself; in my "therapist" frame of mind, I tried to resist this, but my hand—stroking on automatic for so long—slid downward at once on its own, and I ceased at the same instant to ignore a response I'd been blocking without realizing it for a good long while. I was still lying on my side, facing Sally; my top knee shifted without permission, and seconds later another afternoon had culminated in a POW that made my ears ring.

I was destined to know very well indeed the complicated space between Sally's muscular thighs, far better than I would ever know the complicated space inside her head, but that first swift unforeseen climax had a power I still recall with astonishment. My sex life, though quite varied, had all been passed in the company of men. I'd never objected to homosexuality in any of its forms, on principle and by professional conviction, but before that day no occasion of proving this personally had happened to occur. As for Sally, her isolation had allowed for no sex life at all with humans male *or* female; and though the things we did together meant, if possible, even more to her than they did to me, she didn't really view them in a sexual light. To Sally's way of thinking, *sex* was a thing that happened more or less constantly during several days each month, and had to do with dark, shaggy, undeniable maleness forcing itself upon you—with brief, rough gusto—from behind. She continued to miss this fear-laced excitement just as before. Our physical involvement, which was regularly reinforced, and which often ended as it had that afternoon, was a source of immeasurable pleasure and solace to her, but she viewed it as the natural end of a process that had more to do with social grooming than with sex.

But for me it was a revelation, and late in August, when the coarse, caterpillar-chewed foliage hung dispiritedly day after day in the torpid air, I went away for a week to remind myself of what ordinary sex was like with an ordinary man. Afterward I returned to Sally having arrived at a more accurate view of the contrast: not as pudendum versus penis, but as the mythic versus the mundane. Sleeping with my comfy old flame had been enjoyable as ever, but he was no wild thing living a split life and sharing the secret half with me alone.

"Are you in love with somebody?" Bill asked me on our last evening together. "Is that what's up with you? It's got to have something to do with your being in this incredible physical shape— wait! don't tell me! you've conceived a fatal passion for a jock!" I laughed and promised to let him in on the secret when I could, and though his eyes were sharp with curiosity, he didn't press the point. And for that, when the time came, Bill was one of half a dozen friends I finally did tell about Sally.

But even then, after it could no longer matter materially, I was unable to answer his question. Was I in love with Sally, or she with me? No. Or yes. For more than a year, I worked hard to link her with the human community, she to school me for a role in a childhood fantasy of irresistible (and doubtless neurotic) appeal. Each of us was surely fated to love what the other symbolized; how could we help it? But I've wondered since whether I was ever able to see Sally as anything but the Chimp Child, first and last. For each of us, you see, there was only *one*. In such a case, how can individual be told from type, how can the love be personal? And when not personal, what does "love" mean, anyway?

Whatever it was or meant, it absorbed us, and I was as happy that summer as ever in my life. As the season waned and the fall semester began, my skills and plans both moved forward obedient to my will. After workouts we would spread the blanket on its plastic ground sheet and ourselves across the blanket, giving our senses up to luxuriant pleasure, while the yellow leaves tapped down about us all but inaudibly.

And afterward we'd talk. It was at this stage that bit by bit I was able to breach Sally's quarantine by turning the talk to our work: her research, my theoretical interests, gifted or maddening students, departmental politics, university policy. Even then, when I encountered Sally on campus, her indifference toward me as toward everyone appeared unchanged; and at first these topics annoyed and bored her. But bit by bit I could see her begin to take an interest in the personalities we worked among, form judgments about them, distinguish among her students. To my intense delight, colorful chimp pesonalities began to swim up from her memory, with anecdotes to illustrate them, and she spoke often of Carol Cheswick, and—less frequently—of the team of psychologists at University College.

Cambridge provided no material of this sort, for by the time the church fellowship had sent her up, Cheswick was dead and Sally left to devise ways of coping on her own with the nosy public while protecting her privacy and the purposes it served. Antisocial behavior had proved an effective means to that end at Cambridge, as it was to do subsequently at our own university. She had concentrated fiercely on her studies. In subjects that required an intuitive understanding of people—literature, history, the social sciences—her schoolwork had always been lackluster; in mathematics and hard science, she had excelled from the first. At Cambridge she read biology. Microbiology genuinely fascinated her; now, this late in her career, Sally was discovering the pleasures of explaining an ongoing experiment to a listener only just able to follow. In fact, she was discovering gossip and shop talk.

By the time cold temperatures and bare trees had forced me to join a fitness center and Sally to work out alone in a thermal skinsuit and thin pigskin gloves and moccasins, she was able to say: "I remember that old mother chimpanzee because she saved me out of a killing despair, and so did you. So did you, Jan. That day you discovered me crying in the beech, remember? I actually believed I was coping rather well then, but the truth is I was dying. I might really have died, I think—like a houseplant, slowly, of heat and dryness and depleted soil." And to me as well, this seemed no more than the simple truth.

That winter, one measure of our progress was that I could sometimes coax Sally to my house. Had close friends of mine been living nearby, or friendly neighbors or relatives, this could not have been possible; as it was she would leave her pedalcar several blocks away and walk to the house by varying routes, and nearly always after dark. But once inside, with doors locked and curtains drawn, we could be easy, eat and read, light a fire to sit before, snuggle in bed together. In winter, outdoor sex was impractical and we could never feel entirely safe from observation in the denuded woods, whose riding trails wound through and through it. And Sally's obsessive concealment of the fact that she had made a friend, and that her privacy could therefore be trespassed upon, seemed to weaken very little despite the radical changes she had passed through.

Truly, I found myself in no hurry to weaken it. I could not expect, nor did I wish, to have Sally to myself forever. Indeed my success would be measured by how much more fully she could learn to function in society—develop other friendships and activities and so on—eventually. It is true that I could not quite picture this, though I went on working toward it in perfect confidence that the day would come. Yet for the time being, like a mother who watches her child grow tall with mingled pride and sorrow, I kept our secret willingly and thought *eventually* would be here soon enough.

*   *   *

As spring drew closer, Sally began sleeping badly and to be troubled again by dreams. She grew oddly moody also. All through the winter she had dressed and slipped out to her car in the dark; now I would sometimes wake in the morning to find her still beside me. Several times her mutterings and thrashings disturbed me in the night, and then I would soothe and hold her till we both dozed off again. That a crisis was brewing looked certain, but though the dreams continued for weeks, she soon stopped telling me anything about them and said little else to reveal the nature of her distress. In fact, I believed I knew what the trouble was. The first dreams, those she had described, were all about Africa and England and seemed drenched in yearning for things unutterably dear, lost beyond recall. They seemed dreams of mourning—for her parents, her lost wild life in Tanzania, her teacher. Events of the past year, I thought, had rendered the old defenses useless. She could not escape this confrontation any longer.

I was very glad. Beyond the ordeal of grief lay every possibility for synthesizing the halves of her life into one coherent human whole. I believed that Cheswick's death in Sally's twenty-third year had threatened to touch off a mourning for all these losses at once, and that to avoid this she had metamorphosed into the Cambridge undergraduate of my scrapbook: intellectual, unsociable, dull. "You're a survivor," I had told her one night that winter, and she had replied, "Up to a point." Now it seemed she felt strong enough at last to do the grieving and survive *that,* and break through to a more complete sort of health and strength.

Either that, or the year's developments had weakened her ability to compensate, and she would now be swiftly destroyed by the forces held so long in check; but I thought not.

Weeks passed while Sally brooded and sulked; our partnership, so long a source of happy relief, had acquired ambiguities she found barely tolerable. Once she did avoid me for nine days despite her promise—only to turn up, in a state of feverish lust, for a session as unlike our lazy summertime trysts as possible. Afterward she was heavy and silent, then abruptly tearful. I bore with all this patiently enough, chiefly by trying to foresee what might happen next and what it might mean, and so was not much surprised when she said finally, "I've decided not to teach this summer after all. I want to go to England for a month or so, after I've got the experiment written up."

I nodded, thinking, *Here it is*. Huge green skunk cabbages were thick now in the low places on the floor of the April woods, and fly fisherfolk thick along and in the creek; once again we had the mild, bare, windy, hairy-looking forest to ourselves, and were perched together high in a white-topped sycamore hung with balls. "Sounds like a good plan, though I'll miss you. Where to, exactly, or have you decided yet?"

"Well—London for a start, and Cambridge, and here and there. I might just pop in on my sister, not that there's much point to *that*." Sally's sister Helen had married the vicar of a large church in Liverpool and produced four children. "But about missing me. You like England, you're always telling me. Why not come along?"

"Really?" I hadn't foreseen everything, it seemed. "Of course I'll come, I'd love to. Or no, wait a minute"—squirming round on the smooth limb to watch her face—"have you thought this through? I mean, suppose the papers get wind of it? 'Chimp Child Returns to Foster Country.' Or even: 'Chimp Child, Friend, Visit England.' If we're traveling together, people are bound to *see* us together—sure you want to risk it?"

"Oh well, so what," said the Chimp Child, for all the world as if she hadn't been creeping up to my house under cover of night all winter long. "I want to talk to the blokes at the university, Snyder and Brill and a couple of others—get them to show me the files on *me*." She swung free of the branch and dangled by one hand to hug me with the opposite arm. "Sorry I've been such a bore lately. There's something I'm suddenly madly curious about, I've had the most appalling dreams, night after night, for weeks." She swung higher in the tree, climbing swiftly by her powerful arms alone, flashing across gaps as she worked her way to the high outermost branches and leapt outward and downward into another tree with the action I loved to see. "Right," she called back across the gulf between us, "get to work then, you lazy swine. We'll put on a show for Helen's kids that'll stop traffic all over the ruddy parish."

And so we flew to England; and now my part of the story is nearly finished.

Sally did not quite feel ready to come out, as it were, to the extent of going anywhere in my company at school, though she'd smile now with some naturalness when our paths would cross there, and even exchange a few words in passing. We arrived separately at the airport. But from that point on, we were indeed "traveling together," and she never tried to make it seem otherwise.

She had wanted a couple of days in Cambridge before tackling the records of her unique education, as if to work backward in time by bearable degees, and so it was together that we climbed the wide stairs on a Tuesday afternoon early in June to look into her first-year room in Newnham College. Unfortunately the present occupant knew the Chimp Child had once been quartered in her room and recognized Sally immediately; she must have felt perplexed and dismayed at the grimness of the famous pilgrim, who glared round without comment, refused a cup of tea, and stalked away leaving me to render thanks/apologies on behalf of us both. I caught Sally on the stairs. Nothing was said till we had proceeded the length of two green courts bordered with flower beds and come out into the road. Then: "God, I was wretched here!" she burst out. "I went through the whole three years in a—in a chromatic daze, half unconscious except in the lab, and going through that door again—it was as if all the color and warmth began to drain out of a hole in the floor of the day, and I could only stand helplessly watching. The very *smell* of the place means nothing but death to me. What bloody, bloody waste."

And "What a waste," more thoughtfully the next morning, as we walked back to the station from our bed-and-breakfast across the river and the common with its grazing Friesians and through the Botanical Gardens. "One sees why other people could manage to be so jolly and smug here, while I'd go skulking down to Grantchester at five in the morning to work out in the only wood for miles, terrified every day I should be caught out, and skulking back to breakfast every day relieved, like an exhibitionist who thinks, 'Well, there's one more time I got away with it.' " A few minutes later she added, "Of course it got much better when I was working on my thesis . . . only those years don't seem real at *all* when I try to remember them. All I can remember is the lab, I expect that's why."

"Why it got better, or why it's unreal?"

"Both, very likely."

She was pensive on the train. I fell asleep and woke as we were pulling into Liverpool Street, feeling tired and headachy, the beginnings of the flu that put me to bed for a crucial week when I might otherwise have done something, just be staying well, to affect the course of events. By late afternoon of that Wednesday, I felt too miserable to be embarrassed at imposing myself on Dr. Snyder's wife and filling their tiny guest room with my awkward germiness. For four or five days, I had a dry, wheezy cough and a fever so high that Mrs. Snyder was beginning to talk rather worriedly of doctors; then the fever broke and my head, though the size of a basketball, no longer burned, and I rallied enough to take in that Sally was gone.

She had spent the early days of my illness at University College, reading, asking occasional questions, searching—as it seemed—for something she couldn't describe but expected to recognize when she found it. Late on the fourth day, the day my temperature was highest, she came in and sat on the bed. "Listen, Jan. I'm off to Africa tomorrow."

I swam wearily to the surface. "Africa? But . . . don't you have to get, uh, inoculations or something? Visas?" I didn't wonder, within the remoteness of my fever, why she was going. Nor did I much care that evidently she would be going without me.

"Only cholera and yellow fever, and I've had them. Before we left, just in case; and yesterday afternoon I bagged the last seat on a tourist charter to Dar es Salaam. The flight returns in a fortnight, by which time you should be fit again, and we can go on up north then or wherever you like." When I didn't reply, she added, unnecessarily, "I've got to visit the school, Malosa School, and sort of stare the forest in the face again. It's terribly important, though I can't say just why. Maybe when I've got back, when you're better. Only, I've made my mind up to take this chance while it's going, because I do feel I've absolutely got to go through with it, as quick as I can."

My eyes ached. I closed them, shutting out the floating silhouette of Sally's head and shoulders. "I know. I wish . . ."

"Never mind. It'll be all right. Sorry I didn't tell you before, but first I wanted to make sure." I felt her hand beneath my pajama jacket. "God, you're *hot*," she said, surprised. "Perhaps I ought to leave it till you're a bit better."

Distantly amused at this display of superego, I said, "You know a fever's always highest at night, old virologist. Anyway, you can't do any good here. We'll have a doctor in soon if it doesn't go down." I made a truly tremendous effort. "It's probably a good idea, Sally, the trip. I hope you can find whatever it is you're looking for." Clumsily I patted the hand inside my pajamas. "But don't miss the plane coming back, I'll be dying to hear what happened."

"I shan't, I promise you," she said with relief; and when I woke the next morning, she had gone.

We know that Sally reached Dar es Salaam after an uneventful flight, spent the night in an airport hotel, flew Air Malawi to the Chileka airfield the next morning, and hired a driver to take her the 125 kilometers overland to Machinga and the Malose Secondary School, where she was greeted with pleased astonishment by those of the staff who remembered her—everyone, of course, knew of her connection with the school. She stayed there nearly a week, questioning people about the details of her early childhood and of exactly what had happened when the church officials brought her in, in the weeks before she had been whisked to London. She spent hours prowling about the grounds, and buildings, essentially the same as thirty years before despite some modest construction and borrowed the school's Land-Rover several times to drive alone into the countryside of the Shire Highlands and the valley beyond. Her manner had been alternately brusque and preoccupied, and she had impressed them all as being under considerable strain.

The school staff confirmed that Sally had been driven back to Chileka by a couple, old friends of her parents, who at her request had dropped her at the terminal without coming in to see her off. She had told them she intended to fly back to Dar that evening in order to catch her charter for London the next day, and that she hated a dragged-out good-bye; the couple had no way of knowing that her ticket had specified a two-week stay abroad. Inside the terminal she bought a round-trip ticket for Ujiji, in Tanzania.

From Ujiji a helicopter shuttle took her to Kogoma on Lake Tanganyika. Once there, Sally had made inquiries, then gone straight to the town's tiny branch of Bookers Ltd., a safari agency operating out of a closet-sized cubbyhole in the VW dealership. She told the Bookers agent—a grizzled old Indian—that she wanted to hire two men to help her locate the place where a plane had crashed in the mountains east of the lake, some thirty years before. She produced detailed directions and maps; and the agent, though openly doubtful whether the wreckage would not have rusted into the ground after so long, agreed for a stiff price to outfit and provision the trip. He assigned his cousin to guide her, and a native porter. Forty-eight hours later this small expedition set off into the mountains in the agency's battered four-wheel-drive safari van.

The cousin had parked the van beside the road of ruts that had brought them as far as roads could bring them toward the area marked on Sally's maps, much nearer than any road had approached it on the day of the crash, but still not near. They had then followed a footpath into the forest for several kilometers before beginning to slash a trail away from it to the westward, toward the site where the plane had gone down. Something like fifty kilometers of rain-forested mountainous terrain had to be negotiated on foot, a difficult, unpleasant, suffocating sort of passage. Sally must have been assailed by frustration at the clumsiness of their progress; the guide called her a bad-tempered bitch, probably for good reason. On the third morning her patience had evidently snapped. When the men woke up, Sally was not in camp. They waited, then shouted, then searched, but she never replied or reappeared. And I knew what they could not: that she must have slipped away and taken to the trees, flying toward a goal now less than fifteen kilometers distant.

I had gone out to meet Sally's plane, due into Gatwick on the same day the reporters got hold of the story of her disappearance. When she proved not to be aboard, and to have sent no word, all my uneasiness broke out like sweat, and back in the city I must have hurried past any number of news agents' before the *Guardian* headline snatched at my attention: WILD WOMAN MISSING IN JUNGLE, SEARCH CONTINUES. I bought a paper and stood shaking on the pavement to read: "Dodoma (Tanzania), Tuesday. Sally Barnes, the wild girl brought up by chimpanzees, has been missing in the mountains of Tanzania since Friday . . . two companions state . . . no trace of the Chimp Child . . . police notified and a search party . . ." and finally: "Searchers report sighting several groups of wild chimpanzees in the bush near the point of her disappearance."

All the rest is a matter of record. Day by day the newspapers repeated it: No trace, No trace, and at last, Presumed dead. The guide and porter were questioned but never tried for murder. In print and on the video news, it was noted that Dr. Barnes had vanished into the jungle only a few kilometers east of the spot where she had emerged from it twenty years earlier. Investigators quickly discovered that Sally and I had been together in Cambridge and London, and I, too, was forced to submit to questioning; I told them we had met on the plane and spent a few days as casual traveling companions, and that when I fell ill, her friends had kindly taken me in. I denied any closer connection between us, despite my having studied her case professionally—mentioning that she was well known at the university for her solitary ways. Sally herself had said nothing in particular to the Snyders about us, and I had been too sick. No one was alive in all the world to contradict the essential factors of this story, and, as it appeared to lead nowhere, they soon let me alone. (Some years later, however, I told Dr. Snyder the whole truth.)

It developed that no one had any idea why Sally had gone to Tanzania, why she was looking for the site of the plane crash.

For me that fall was hellish. By the time I returned to the States, only a few days before the new semester was to get under way, Sally's apartment—the apartment I had never seen, though she had called me from it two or three times during the final weeks of spring—had been stripped of its contents by strangers and her effects shipped to the Liverpool sister. At school, people were overheard to suggest, only half jokingly, that Sally had rejoined the chimps and was living now in the jungle, wild again. Such things were freely voiced in my presence; indeed, the loss of Sally, so shocking, so complete, was the more difficult to accept because not a single person on my side of the Atlantic could have the least suspicion that I had lost her.

My acting, I believe, was flawless. Though I went dazedly about my work, nobody seemed to see anything amiss. But might-have-beens tormented me. Save for my interference, Sally would almost certainly still have been alive. Or (more excruciating by far), had she not met defeat in the jungle, her search would almost certainly have left her healed of trauma, able to fit the halves of her life together. I had nearly freed her; now she was dead, the labor come to nothing, the child stillborn. I did believe she was dead. Yet I felt as angry with her, at times, as if she had purposely abandoned and betrayed me, disdained the miracle of healing I had nearly brought off—as if she had really chosen to return to the wild. For now neither of us could ever, ever complete the crossing into those worlds each had been training the other to enter for the preceding year.

I did not see how I was going to survive the disappointment, nor could I imagine what could possibly occupy, or justify, the rest of my life. The interlude with Sally had spoiled me thoroughly for journeyman work. It would not be enough, any longer, to divide my time between educating healthy minds and counseling disturbed ones. Long before that bleak winter was out, I had begun to cast about fretfully for something else to do.

This document has been prepared in snatches, over many evenings, by kerosene lanternlight in my tent in the Matangawe River Nature Reserve overlooking Lake Malawi, 750 kilometers northwest across the immense lake from Sally's birthplace. The tent is set up inside a chimp-proof cage made of Cyclone fencing and corrugated iron. Outside, eleven chimpanzees of assorted ages and stages of reacclimatization to independent survival in the wild are sleeping (all but the newest arrival, who is crying to get in). A few of these chimps were captured as infants in the wild; the rest are former subjects of language and other learning experiments, ex-laboratory animals or animals who were reared in homes until they began to grow unmanageable.

This may seem an unlikely place in which to attempt the establishment of a free-living population of rehabilitant chimpanzees, for the ape has been extinct in Malawi for a couple of centuries at least, and the human population pressure is terrific, the highest in Africa. In fact, to "stare the forest in the face," Sally was forced to go on back to Tanzania, where there was (and still is) some riverine forest left standing. Yet private funding materialized, and I've been here since the reserve was created, nearly fifteen years. Despite some setbacks and failures—well, there were bound to be some!—the project is doing very well indeed. At this writing, thirty-four chimps have mastered the course of essential survival skills and moved off to establish breeding, thriving communities on their own in the reserve. For obvious reasons these societies fascinate the primatologists, who often come to study them. We've lost a few to disease and accidents, and two to poachers, but our success, considering the problems inherent to the enterprise, might even be called spectacular. We've been written up in *National Geographic* and the *Smithsonian*, which in primate studies is how you know when you've arrived, and similar projects in several more suitable West African countries have been modeled on ours.

I started alone, with three adolescent chimpanzee "graduates in psychology" from my university who, having outgrown their usefulness along with their tractable childhoods, faced long, dull lives in zoos or immediate euthanasia. Now a staff of eight works with me: my husband, John (yes, the same John), and seven graduate students from my old department and from the Department of Biology, which used to be Sally's. She would be pleased with my progress in brachiation, though arthritis in my hands and shoulders has begun to moderate my treetop traveling with my charges. (That skill, incidentally, has given me a tactical edge over every other pioneer in the field of primate rehabilitation.)

To all the foregoing I will add only that I have found this work more satisfying than I can say. And that very often as I'm swinging along through lush forest in the company of four or five young chimps, "feeding" with them on new leaves and baobab flowers, showing them how to build a sturdy nest in the branches, I know a deep satisfaction that now, at last, there's no difference that matters between Sally and me.

A hard-edged peek into the near and nasty high-tech future, by the author of previous standout stories "Rat" and "Solstice," to which this is a sort of a sequel. The pace is swift, the software is superb, and a strange and unexpected love story lies buried amid the bytes.

Kelly, who lives in New Hampshire, reports himself to be at work on a novel called Look at the Sun.

THE PRISONER OF CHILLON

James Patrick Kelly

We initiated deorbital burn over the Marshall Islands and dropped back into the ionosphere, locked by the wing's navigator into one of the Eurospace reentry corridors. As we coasted across Central America we were an easy target for the attack satellites. The plan was to fool the tracking nets into thinking we were a corporate shuttle. Django had somehow acquired the recognition codes; his computer, kludged to the navigator, made the wing think it was the property of Erno Raumfahrttechnik GMBH, the West German aerospace conglomerate.

It was all a matter of timing, really. It would not be too much longer before the people on IBM's Orbital 7 untangled the spaghetti Django had made of their memory systems and realized that he had downloaded WISEGUY and stolen a cargo wing. Then they would have to decide whether to zap us immediately or have the mindkillers waiting when we landed. Django's plan was to lose the wing before they could decide. Our problem was that very little of the plan had worked so far.

He had gotten us on and off the orbital research station all right, and had managed to pry WISEGUY from the jaws of the corporate beast. For that alone his reputation would live forever among operators, even if he was not around to enjoy the fame. But he had lost his partner—Yellowbaby, the pilot—and he still did not know exactly what it was he had stolen. He seemed pretty calm for a punk who had just plugged the world's biggest corporation. He slouched in the commander's seat across from me watching the readouts on the autopilot console. He was whistling and tapping a finger against his headset as if he were listening to one of his old jazz disks. He was a dark, ugly man with an Adam's apple that looked like a nose and a nose that looked like an elbow. He had either been juved or he was in his mid-thirties. I trusted him not at all and liked him less.

Me, I felt as though I had swallowed a hardboiled egg. I was just along for the story, the *juice*. According to the courts, all I was allowed to do was aim my microcam glasses at Django and ask questions. If I helped him in any way, I would become an accessory and lose press immunity. But press immunity wouldn't do me much good if someone decided to zap the wing. The First Amendment was a great shield and all but it didn't protect against re-entry friction. I wanted to return to earth with a ship around me; sensors showed the outer skin was currently 1400 degrees Celsius.

"Much longer?" A dumb question since I already knew the answer. But better than listening to the atmosphere scream as the wing bucked through turbulence. I could feel myself losing it; I wanted to scream back.

"Twenty minutes. However it plays." Django lifted his headset. "Either you'll be a legend or air pollution." He stretched his arms over his head and arched his back away from the seat. I could smell his sweat. "Hey, lighten up, Eyes. You're a big girl now. Shouldn't you be taking notes or something?"

"The camera sees all." I tapped the left temple of the microcam and then forced a grin that hurt my face. "Besides, it's not bloody likely I'll forget this ride." I wasn't about to let Django play with me. He was too hypered on fast-forwards to be scared. My father had been the same way; he ate them like popcorn when he was working. And called me his big girl.

It had been poor Yellowbaby who had introduced me to Django. I had covered the Babe when he pulled the Peniplex job. He was a real all-nighter—handsome as plastic can make a man, and an artiste in bed. Handsome, past tense. The last time I had seen him he was floating near the ceiling of a decompressed cargo bay, an eighty kilo hunk of flash-frozen boytoy. I missed him already.

"I copy, Basel Control." Yellowbaby's calm voice crackled across the forward flight deck. "We're doing Mach 9.9 at 57,000 meters. Looking good for touch at 14:22."

We had come out of reentry blackout. The approach program that Yellowbaby had written, complete with voice interaction module, was in contact now with Basel/Mulhouse, our purported destination. As long as everything went according to plan, the program would get us where we wanted to go. If anything went wrong . . . well, the Babe was supposed to improvise if anything went wrong.

"Let's blow out of here." Django heaved himself out of the seat and swung down the ladder to the equipment bay. I followed. We pulled EV suits from the lockers and struggled into them. I could feel the deck tilting as the wing began a series of long lazy "S" curves to slow our descent.

Django unfastened his suit's weighty backpack and quickly shucked the rest of the excess baggage: comm and life support systems, various umbilicals. He was whistling again.

"Would you shut the hell up?" I tossed the still camera from my suit onto the pile.

"You don't like Fats Waller?" There was a chemical edge to his giggle. " 'I've Got a Feeling I'm Falling,' great tune." And then he began to sing; his voice sounded like gears being stripped.

Yellowbaby's program was reassuring Basel even as we banked gracefully toward the Jura Mountains. "No problem, Basel Control," the dead man's voice drawled. "Malf on the main guidance computer. I've got backup. My L over D is nominal. You just keep the tourists off the runway and I'll see you in ten minutes."

I shut down the microcam—no sense wasting batteries and disk space shooting the inside of an EV suit—and picked up the pressure helmet.

"Think I'm falling for you, Eyes." Django blew me a kiss. "Don't forget to duck." He made a quacking sound and flapped his arms like wings. I put the helmet on and closed the seals. It was a relief not to have to listen to him rave; we had disabled the comm units to keep the mindkillers from tracking us. He handed me one of the slim airfoil packs we had smuggled onto and off of Orbital 7. I stuck my arms through the harness and fastened the front straps. I could still hear Yellowbaby's muffled voice talking to the Swiss controllers. "Negative, Basel control, I don't need escort. Initiating terminal guidance procedures."

At that moment I felt the nose dip sharply. The wing was diving straight for the summit of Mont Tendre, elevation 1679 meters. I crouched behind Django in the airlock, tucked my head to my chest, and tongued the armor toggle in the helmet. The thermofiber EV suit stiffened and suddenly I was a shock-resistant statue, unable to move. I began to count backwards from one thousand; it was better than listening to my heart jackhammer. Nine hundred and ninety-nine, nine hundred and ninety-eight, nine hundred and . . .

I remembered the way Yellowbaby had smiled as he unbuttoned my shirt, that night before we had shuttled up to 7. He was sitting on a bunk in his underwear. I had still not decided to cover the raid; he was still trying to convince me. But words weren't his strong point. When I turned my back to him, he slipped the shirt from my shoulders, slid it down my arms. I stood there for a moment, facing away from the bunk. Then he grabbed me by the waist and pulled me onto his lap. I could feel the curly hair on his chest brushing against my spine. Sitting there half-naked, my face glowing hot as any heat shield, I knew I was in deep trouble. He had nibbled at my ear and then conned me with that slow Texas drawl. "Hell, baby, only reason ain't no one never tried to jump out of a shuttle is that no one who really needed to jump ever had a chute." I had always been a fool for men who told me not to worry.

Although we were huddled in the airlock, my head was down so I did not see the hatch blow. But even with the suit in armor mode, I felt like the clapper inside a cathedral bell. The wing shuddered and, with an explosive last breath, spat us into the dazzling Alpine afternoon.

The truth is that I don't remember much about the jump after that. I know I unfroze the suit so I could guide the airfoil, which had opened automatically. I was too intent on keeping Django in sight and on getting down as fast as I could without impaling myself on a tree or smashing into a cliff. So I missed being the only live and in-person witness to one of the more spectacular crashes of the twenty-first century.

We were trying to drop into the Col du Marchairuz, a pass about seven kilometers away from Mont Tendre, before the search hovers came swarming. I saw Django disappear into a stand of dead sycamores and thought he had probably killed himself. I had no time to worry because the ground was rushing up at me like a nightmare. I spotted the road and steered for it but got caught in a gust which swept me across about five meters above the pavement. I touched on the opposite side; the airfoil was pulling me toward a huge boulder. I toggled to armor mode just as I hit. Once again the bell rang, knocking the breath from me and announcing that I had arrived. If I hadn't been wearing a helmet I would have kissed that chunk of limestone.

I unfastened the quick-release hooks and the airfoil's canopy billowed, dragged along the ground, and wrapped itself around a tree. I slithered out of the EV suit and tried to get my bearings at the same time. The Col du Marchairuz was cool, not much above freezing, and very, very quiet. Although I was wearing standard-issue isothermals, the skin on my hands and neck pebbled and I shivered. The silence of the place was unnerving. I was losing it again, lagged out: too damn many environments in too short a time. An old story. I liked to live fast, race up that adrenaline peak where there was no time to think, just survive the now and to hell with the sordid past and the shabby future. But nothing lasts, nothing. I had dropped out of the sky like air pollution; the still landscape itself seemed to judge me. The mountains did not care about Django's stolen corporate secrets or the caper story I would produce to give some jaded telelink user a Wednesday night thrill. I had risked my life for some lousy juice and a chance at the main menu; the cliffs brooded over my reasons. So very quiet.

"Eyes!" Django dropped from a boulder onto the road and trotted across to me. "You all right?"

I nodded. I couldn't let him see how close to the edge I was.

"You?" There was a long scratch on his face and his knuckles were bloody.

"Walking. Tangled with a tree. The chute got caught—had to leave it."

I nodded again. He stooped to pick up my discarded suit. "Let's lose this stuff and get going."

I stared at him, thought about breaking it off. I had enough to put together one hell of a story and I had had more than enough of Django.

"Don't freeze on me now, Eyes." He wadded the suit and jammed it into a crevice. "If the satellites caught our jump, these mountains are going to be crawling with mindkillers—not to mention the plugging Swiss Army." He hurled my helmet over the edge of the cliff and began to gather up the shrouds of my chute. "We're gone by then."

I switched on and got thirty seconds of him hiding my chute. I didn't have a whole lot of disk space left and I thought I ought to start conserving. He was right about one thing; it wasn't quite time. If the mindkillers caught me now they'd confiscate my disks and let the lawyers fight it out. I'd have nothing to peddle to Jerry Macmillan at Infoline but talking heads and text. And the Swiss had not yet made up their minds about spook journalism; I could even end up in prison. As soon as I started moving again, I felt better. Which is to say I felt nothing at all.

The nearest town was St. George, about four kilometers down the crumbling mountain road. We started at a jog and ended at a drag, gasping in the thin air. On the way Django stopped by a mountain stream to wash the blood from his face. Then he surprised me—and probably himself as well—by throwing up. When he rejoined me he was shaking: crazy Django might actually be human after all. It would make great telelink. He made a half-serious feint at the microcam and I stopped shooting.

"You okay?"

He nodded and staggered past me down the road.

St. George was one of those little ghost towns that the Swiss were mothballing with their traditional tidiness, as if they expected that the forests and vineyards would someday rise from the dead and that the tourists would return to witness this miracle. Maybe they were right; unlike other Europeans, the Swiss had not yet given up on their acid-stressed alpine lands, not even in the un-happy canton of Vaud, which had also suffered radioactive fallout from the nuking of Geneva. We stopped at a clearing planted with the new Sandoz pseudo-firs that overlooked the rust-colored roof-tops of St. George. It was impossible to tell how many people were left in the village. All we knew for sure was that the post office was still open.

Django was having a hard time catching his breath. "I have a proposition for you," he said.

"Come on, Django. Save it for the whores."

He shook his head. "It's all falling apart . . . I can't . . ." He took a deep breath and blew it out noisily. "I'll cut you in. A third: Yellowbaby's share."

According to U.S. case law, still somewhat sketchy on the subject of spook journalism, at this point I should have dropped him with a swift kick to the balls and started screaming for the local gendarmerie. But the microcam was off, there were no witnesses and I still didn't know what WISEGUY was or why Django wanted it. "The way I count, it's just us two," I said. "A third sounds a little low."

"It'll take you the rest of this century to spend what I'm offering."

"And if they catch me I'll spend the rest of the century on a punkfarm in Iowa." That was if the mindkillers didn't blow my fuses first. "Forget it, Django. We're just not in the same line. I watch—you're the player."

I'm not sure what I expected him to do next but it sure as hell wasn't to start crying. Maybe he was in shock, too. Or maybe he was finally slowing down after two solid days of popping fast-forwards.

"Don't you understand, I can't do it alone! You have to—you don't know what you're turning down."

I thought about pumping him for more information but he looked as if he were going critical. I didn't want to be caught in the explosion. "I don't get it, Django. You've done all the hard work. All you have to do is walk into that post office, get your message, and walk out."

"You don't understand." he clamped both hands to his head. "Don't understand, that was Babe's job."

"So?"

"So!" He was shaking. *"I don't speak French!"*

I put everything I had into not laughing. It would have been the main menu for sure if I had gotten that on disk. The criminal mind at work! This scrambled punk had raped the world's largest corporation and totaled a stolen reentry wing and now he was worried about sounding like a *touriste* in a Swiss *bureau de poste*. I was croggled.

"All right," I said, stalling, "all right, how about a compromise. For now. Umm. You're carrying heat?" He produced a Mitsubishi penlight. "Okay, here's what we'll do. I'll switch on and we'll do a little bit for the folks at home. You threaten me, say you're going to lase your name on my forehead unless I cooperate. That way I can pick up the message without becoming an accessory. I hope. If we clear this, we'll talk deal later, okay?" I didn't know if it would stand up in court, but it was all I could think of at the time. "And make it look good."

So I shot a few minutes of Django's threatening me and then we went down into St. George. I walked into the post office hesitantly, turned and got a good shot of Django smoldering in the entryway and then tucked the microcam glasses into my pocket. The clerk was a restless woman with a pinched face who looked as if she spent a lot of time wishing she were somewhere else. I assaulted her with my atrocious fourth form French.

"Bonjour, madame. Y a-t-il des lettres électroniques pour D. J. Hack."

"Hack?" The woman shifted on her stool and fixed me with a suspicious stare. "Comment cela s'écrit-il?"

"H-A-C-K."

She keyed the name into her terminal. "Oui, la voici. Tapez votre autorisation à la machine." She leaned forward and pointed through the window at the numeric keypad beside my right hand. For a moment I thought she was going to try to watch as I keyed in the recognition code that Django had given me. I heard him cough in the entryway behind me and she settled back on her stool. Lucky for her. The postal terminal whirred and ground for about ten seconds and then a sealed hardcopy clunked into the slot above the keypad.

"Vous êtes touristes americaines." She looked straight past me and waved to Django, who ducked out of the doorway. "Baseball Yankees, ha-ha." I was suddenly afraid he would come charging in with penlight blazing to make sure there were no witnesses. "Avez-vous besoin de une chambre pour la nuit? L'hôtel est fermé, mais . . ."

"Non, non. Nous sommes pressés. A quelle heure est le premier autobus pour Rolle?"

She sighed. "Rien ne va bien. Tout va mal." The busybody seemed to be speaking as much to herself as to me. I wanted to tell her how lucky she was that Django had decided not to needle her where she stood. "Quinze heures vingt-deux."

About twenty minutes—we were still on schedule. I thanked her and went out to throw some cold water on Django. I was surprised to find him laughing. I didn't much like all these surprises. Django was so scrambled that I knew one of these times the surprise was bound to be unpleasant. "I could've done that," he said.

"You didn't." I handed him the hardcopy and we retreated to an alley with a view of the square.

It is the consensus of the world's above and below ground economies that the Swiss electronic mail system is still the most secure in the world. It has to be: all the Swiss banks, from the big five to the smallest locals, use the system for the bulk of their transactions. Once it had printed out Django's hardcopy, the PTT system erased all records of the message. Even so, the message was encrypted and Django had to enter it into his computer cuff to find out what it said.

"What is this?" He replayed it and I watched, fascinated, as the words scrolled along the cuff's tiny display:

"Lake Leman lies by Chillon's walls: / A thousand feet in depth below / Its massy waters meet and flow; / Thus much the fathom-line was sent / From Chillon's snow-white battlement . . ."

"It's called poetry, Django."

"I know what it's called! I want to know what the hell this has to do with my drop. Half the world wants to chop my plug off and this scut sends me poetry." His face had turned as dark as beaujolais nouveau and his voice was so loud they could probably hear him in France. "Where the hell am I supposed to go?"

"Would you shut up for a minute?" I touched his shoulder and he jumped. When he went for his penlight I thought I was cooked. But all he did was throw the hardcopy onto the cobblestones and torch it.

"Feel better?"

"Stick it."

"Lake Leman," I said carefully, "is what the French call Lake Geneva. And Chillon is a castle. In Montreux. I'm pretty sure this is from a poem called 'The Prisoner of Chillon' by Byron."

He thought it over for a moment, chewing his lower lip. "Montreux." He nodded; he looked almost human again. "Uh—okay, Montreux. But why does he have to get cute when my plug's in a claw? Poetry—what does he think we are, anyway? I don't know a thing about poetry. And all Yellowbaby ever read was manuals. Who was supposed to get this anyway?"

I stirred the ashes of the hardcopy with my toe. "I wonder." A cold wind scattered them and I shivered.

Of course, I was wrong. Chillon is not in Montreux but in the outlying commune of Veytaux. It took us a little over six hours from the time we bailed out of the wing to the moment we reached the barricaded bridge which spanned Chillon's scummy moat. All our connections had come off like Swiss clockwork: postal bus to the little town of Rolle on the north shore of Lake Geneva, train to Lausanne, where we changed for a local to Montreux. No one challenged us and Django sagged into a kind of withdrawal trance, contemplating his reflection in the window with a marble egg stare. The station was deserted when we arrived. Montreux had once been Lake Geneva's most popular resort but the tourists had long since stopped coming, frightened off by rumors—no doubt true, despite official denials from Bern—that the lake was still dangerously hot from the Geneva bomb. We ended up hiking several kilometers through the dark little city, navigating by the light of the gibbous moon.

For that matter, Byron was wrong, too. Or at least out-of-date. Chillon's battlement was no longer snow-white. It was fire-blackened and slashed with laser scars; much of the north-eastern facade was rubble. There must have been a firefight during the riots after the bomb. The castle was built on a rock about twenty meters from the shore. It commanded a highway built on a narrow strip of land between the lake and a steep mountainside.

Django hesitated at the barrier blocking the wooden footbridge to the castle. "It stinks," he said.

"You're a rose?"

"I mean the setup. Poetry was bad enough. But this—" he pointed up at the crumbling towers of Chillon, brooding beside the moonlit water—"this is fairy dust. Who does this scut think he is? Count Dracula?"

"Maybe he is. Only way you're going to find out is to knock on the door and . . ."

A light on the far side of the bridge came on. Through the entrance to Chillon hopped a pair of oversized dice on pogo sticks.

"Easy, Django," I said. He had the penlight ready. "Give it a chance."

Each pogo was a white plastic cube about half a meter on a side; the pips were sensors. The legs telescoped at a beat per second; the round rubber feet hit the wooden deck in unison. *Thwocka-thwocka-thwock.*

"Snake-eyes." There was a single sensor on each of the faces closest to us. Django gave a low ugly laugh as he swung a leg over the barrier and stepped onto the bridge.

They hopped up to him and bounced in place for several beats, as if sizing him up. "I am sorry," said the pogo nearest to us in a pleasant masculine voice, "but the castle is no longer open to the public."

"Get this, scut." Django ignored the pogo and instead shook his penlight at the gatehouse on the far side of the bridge. "I've been through too much to play games with your plugging remotes, understand? I want to see you—now—or I'm walking."

"I am not a remote." The lead pogo sounded indignant. "I am a self-contained unit capable of independent action."

"Stick that." Django jabbed at his cuff and it emitted a high-pitched squeal of code. "Now you know who I am. So what's it going to be?"

"This way, please," said the lead pogo, bouncing backward toward the gatehouse. "Please refrain from taking pictures without expressed permission."

I assumed that was meant for me and I didn't like it one bit. I clambered over the barricade and followed Django.

Just before we passed through Chillon's outer wall, the other pogo began to lecture. "As we enter, notice the tower to your left. The Strong Tower, which controls the entrance to the castle, was originally built in 1402 and was reconstructed following the earthquake of 1585." *Thwock-thwocka.*

I glanced at Django. In the gloom I could see his face twist in disbelief as the pogo continued its spiel.

". . . As we proceed now into the gatehouse ward, look back over your shoulder at the inside of the eastern wall. The sundial you see is a twentieth century restoration of an original that dated back to the Savoy period. The Latin, *'Sic Vita Fugit,'* on the dial translates roughly as 'Thus Life Flies By.' "

We had entered a small dark courtyard. I could hear water splashing and could barely make out the shadow of a fountain. The pogos lit the way to another, larger courtyard and then into one of the undamaged buildings. They bounded up a flight of stairs effortlessly; I had to hurry to keep up and was the last to enter the Great Banqueting Hall. The beauty and strangeness of what I saw stopped me at the threshold; instinctively I tried to switch on the microcam. I heard two warning beeps and then a whispery crunch. The status light went from green to red to blank.

"Expressed permission," said the man who sat waiting for us. "Come in anyway, come in. Just in time to see it again—been rerunning all afternoon." He laughed and nodded at the flatscreen propped against a bowl of raw vegetables on an enormous walnut table. "Oh, God! It is a fearful thing to see the human soul take wing."

Django picked it up suspiciously. I stood on tiptoes and peeked over his shoulder. The thirty-centimeter screen did not do the wing justice and the overhead satellite view robbed the crash of much of its visual drama. Still, the fireball that bloomed on Mont Tendre was dazzling; Django whooped at the sight. The fireball was replaced by a head talking in High German and then close-ups of the crash site. What was left of the wing wouldn't have filled a picnic basket.

"What's he saying?" Django thrust the flatscreen at our host.

"That there has not been a crash like this since '55. Which

makes you famous, whoever you are." Our host shrugged. "He goes on to say that you're probably dead."

The banqueting hall was finished in wood and stone. Its ceiling was a single barrel vault, magnificently embellished. Its centerpiece was the table, some ten meters long and supported by a series of heavy Gothic trestles. Around this table was ranged a collection of wheelchairs. Two were antiques: a crude pine seat mounted on iron-rimmed wagon wheels and a hooded Bath chair. Others were failed experiments, like the ill-fated air-cushion chair from the turn of the century and a low-slung cousin of the new aerodynamic bicycles. There were powered and push models, an ultralightweight sports chair and a bulky mobile life-support system. They came in colors; there was even one that glowed.

"So the mindkillers think we're dead?" Django put the flatscreen back on the table.

"Possibly." Our host frowned. "Depends when the satellites began to track you and what they saw. Have to wait until the Turks kick the door in. Until then call it a clean escape and welcome to Chillon prison." He backed away from the table; the leather seat creaked slightly as his wheelchair rolled over the uneven floor toward Django. "François Bonivard." With some difficulty he raised his good hand in greeting.

"I'm Django." He grasped Bonivard's hand and pumped it once. "Now that we're pals, Frank, get rid of your goddamned remotes before I needle them."

Bonivard winced as Django released his hand. "Id, Ego, make the rounds," he said. The pogos bounced obediently from the banqueting hall.

François de Bonivard, sixteenth century Swiss patriot, was the hero of Byron's "The Prisoner of Chillon." Reluctantly, I stepped forward to meet my host.

"Oh yeah." Django settled gingerly into one of the wheelchairs at the table. "Maybe I forgot to mention Eyes. Say, what do you do for drugs around here anyway? I've eaten a fistful of forwards already today; I could use some Soar to flash the edges off."

"My name is Wynne Cage," I said. Bonivard seemed relieved when I did not offer to shake his hand. "I'm a freelance . . ."

"Introductions not necessary. Famous father and all." Bonivard nodded wearily. "I know your work."

It was hard to look at the man who called himself François Bonivard and I had been trying to avoid it until now. Both of his legs had been amputated at the hip joint and his torso was fitted into some kind of bionic collar. I saw readouts marked *renal function, blood profile, bladder* and *bowels*. The entire left side of Bonivard's torso seemed withered, as if some malign giant had pinched him between thumb and forefinger. The left arm dangled uselessly, the hand curled into a frozen claw. The face was relatively untouched, although pain had left its tracks, particularly around the eyes. And it was the clarity with which those wide brown eyes saw that was the most awful thing about the man. I could feel his gaze effortlessly penetrate the mask of politeness, pierce the false sympathy and find my horror. Looking into those eyes I thought that Bonivard must know how the very sight of his ruined body made me sick.

I had to say something to escape that awful gaze. "Are you related to *the* Bonivard?"

He smiled at me. "I am the current prisoner." And then turned away. "There was a pilot."

"Past tense." Django nibbled at a radish from the vegetable bowl. "How about my flash?"

"Business first." Bonivard rolled back to the table. "You have it then?"

Django reached into his pocket and produced a stack of memory chips held together with a wide blue rubber band. "Whatever WISEGUY is, he's one fat son-of-a-bitch. You realize these are ten *G*b chips." He set them on the table in front of him.

Bonivard rolled to his place at the head of the table and put two smart chips in front of him. "Passcards. Swiss Volksbank, Zurich. As they say, the payoff. All yours now." He slid them toward Django. "You made only one copy?"

And here was the juice. I could have strangled Bonivard for wrecking the microcam.

Django eyed the passcards but did not reach for them. "Not going to do me much good if the mindkillers get me."

"No." Bonivard leaned back in his wheelchair. "But you're safe for now." He glanced up at the ceiling and laughed. "They won't look in a prison."

Django snapped the rubber band on his stack of chips. "Maybe you should tell me about WISEGUY. I put my plug on the cutting board to get it for you."

"An architecture." Bonivard shrugged. "For a new AI."

Django glanced over at me. The look on his face said it all. He was already convinced that Bonivard was scrambled; here was proof. "Come again?" he said slowly.

"Ar-ti-fi-cial in-tel-li-gence." Bonivard actually seemed to enjoy baiting Django. "With the right hardware and database, it can sing, dance, make friends and influence people."

He was pushing Django way too hard. "I thought true AI was a myth," I said, trying to break the tension. "Didn't they decide that intelligence is a bunch of ad hoc schemes glommed together any-which-way? Supposedly there's no way to engineer it—too big and messy."

"Have it your way," said Bonivard. "WISEGUY is really the way IBM keeps track of toilet paper. I'm in pulp. Want their account."

I knew my laugh sounded like braying but I didn't mind; I was trying to keep them from zapping each other. At the same time I was measuring the distance to the door. To my immense relief, Django chuckled too. And slipped the WISEGUY chips back into his pocket.

"I'm so burned-out," he said, "maybe we should wait." He stood up and stretched. "Even if we make an exchange tonight, we'd have a couple of hours of verifications to go through, no? We'll start fresh tomorrow." He picked up one of the passcards and turned it over several times between the long fingers of his left hand. Suddenly it was gone. He reached into the vegetable bowl with his right hand, pulled the passcard from between two carrots, and tossed it at Bonivard. It slid across the table and almost went over the edge. "Shouldn't leave valuable stuff like this lying around. Someone might steal it."

Django's mocking sleight-of-hand had an unexpected effect. Bonivard's claw started to tremble; I could tell he was upset at the delay. "It might be months, or years, or days—I kept no count, I took no note . . ." He muttered the words like some private incantation; when he opened his eyes, he seemed to have regained his composure. "I had no hope my eyes to raise, and clear them of their dreary mote." He looked at me. "Will you be requiring pharmaceuticals, too?"

"No, thanks. I like to stay clean when I'm working."

"Admirable," he said as the pogos bounced back into the hall. "I'm retiring for the evening. Id and Ego will show you to your rooms; you'll find what you need." He rolled through a door to the north without another word and Django and I were left staring at each other.

"What did I tell you?" said Django.

I couldn't think of anything to say. The hall echoed with the sound of the pogos bouncing.

"Voltage spikes in his CPU." Django tapped a finger against his temple.

I was awfully tired of Django. "I'm going to bed."

"Can I come?"

"Stick it." I had to get away from him, had to run. But it was too late; I could feel it behind the eyes, like the first throbs of a migraine headache. By the time I reached the hall leading to the stairs I knew the mania had faded and depression was closing in. Maybe it was because Bonivard had mentioned the famous father. A weak and selfish man who had created me in his image, brought me up in an emotional hot house, used me and called it love. Or maybe it was because now I had to let go of Yellowbaby, past tense. Who probably wasn't that much of a loss, just the most recent in a series of lovers with clever hands and a persuasively insincere line. Men I didn't have to take seriously. I came hard up against the one lesson I had learned from life: good old homo sap is nothing but a gob of complicated slime. I was slime doing a slimy job and trying to run fast enough that I wouldn't have to smell my own stink. Except that there was no place to go now. I was sorry now I hadn't hit that crazy scut Bonivard for some flash.

Thwocka-thwock. "This way, please." One of the pogos shot past me down the hallway.

I followed. "Which one are you?"

"He calls me Ego." It paused for a beat. "My real name is Datacorp R5000, serial number 290057202. Your room." It bounced through an open door. "This is the Bernese Chamber. Note the

decorative patterns of interlacing ribbons, flowers, and birds which
date . . .''

"Out," I said and shut the door behind it.

As soon as I sat on the musty bed, I realized I couldn't face
spending the night alone. Thinking. I had to run somewhere—there
was only one way. I decided that I'd had enough. I was going to
wrap the story, finished or not. The thought cheered me im-
mensely. I wouldn't have to care what happened to Django and
Bonivard, wouldn't have to wonder about WISEGUY. All I had to
do was burst a message to Infoline. I was sure that my disks of the
snatch and the crash of the wing would be story enough for Jerry
Macmillan. He'd send the muscle to take me out and then maybe
I'd spend a few months at Infoline's sanctuary in the Rockies
watching clouds. Anyway, I'd be done with it. I emptied my
diskpack, removed the false bottom, and began to rig the collapsi-
ble antenna. I locked onto the satellite and then wrote the message.
"HOTEL BRISTOL VEYTAUX 6/18 0200GMT PIX IBM WING.''
I had seen the Bristol on the walk in. I loaded the message into the
burster. There was a pause for compression and encryption and then
it hit the Infoline satellite with an untraceable millisecond burst.

And then beeped at me. Incoming message. I froze. There was
no way Infoline could respond that quickly, no way they were
supposed to respond. It had to be prerecorded. Which meant trouble.

Jerry Macmillan's face filled the burster's four centimeter screen.
He looked as scared as I felt. "Big problems, Wynne," he said.
"Whatever your boys snatched is way too hot for us to handle. It's
not just IBM—the feds are going crazy. They haven't connected
you to us yet. It's possible they won't. But if they do, Legal says
we've got to cooperate. National security. You're on your own.''

I put my thumb over his face. I would have pushed it through the
back of his skull if I could have.

"The best I can do for you is to delete your takeout message and
the fix the satellite gets on your burster. It might mean my ass, but
I owe you something. I know: this stinks on ice, kid. Good luck.''

I took my thumb away from the screen. It was blank. I choked
back a scream and hurled the burster against the stone wall of
Chillon, shattering it.

*   *   *

Sleep? It would have been easier to slit my throat than to sleep that night. I thought about it—killing myself. I thought about everything at least once. All my calculations kept adding up to zero. I could turn myself in but that was about the same as suicide. Ditto for taking off on my own; without Infoline to back me up I'd be dead meat in a week. I could throw in with Django except that two seconds after I told him that I'd let a satellite get a fix on us he'd probably be barbecueing my pancreas with his penlight. And if I didn't tell him, I might cripple whatever chances we'd have of getting away. Maybe Bonivard would be more sympathetic—but then again, why should he be? Yeah, sleep. Perchance to dream. At least I was too busy to indulge in self-loathing.

By the time the sun began to peer through my window I felt as fuzzy as a peach and almost as smart. But I had a plan—one that would require equal parts luck and sheer gall. I was going to thrust that plug-sucking Macmillan to keep his mouth shut and to delete all my records from Infoline's files. For the next few days I'd pretend I was still playing by the rules of spook journalism. I'd try to get a better fix on Bonivard. I hoped that when the time came for Django to leave I'd know what to do. Because all I was certain of that bleary morning was that I was hungry and in more trouble than I knew how to handle.

I staggered down the hall back toward the banqueting hall, hoping to find Bonivard or one of the pogos or at least that bowl of veggies. As I passed a closed door I heard a scratchy recording of saxophones honking. Jazz. Django. I didn't stop.

Bonivard was sitting alone at the great table. I tried to read him to see if his security equipment had picked up my burst to Infoline but the man's face was a mask. Someone had refilled the bowl in the middle of the table.

"Morning." I took a bite of raw carrot that was astonishingly good. A crisp sweetness, the clean spicy fragrance of loam. Maybe I'd been eating instant too long. "Hey, this isn't bad."

"My own." Bonivard nodded. "I grow everything."

"That so?" He didn't look strong enough to pull a carrot from the bowl, much less out of a garden. "Where?"

"In darkness found a dwelling place." His eyes glittered as I took a handful of cherry tomatoes. "You'd like to see?"

"Sure." Even though the tomatoes were even better than the carrot, I was no vegetarian. "You wouldn't have any sausage bushes, would you?" I laughed; he didn't. "I'd settle for an egg."

I saw him working the keypad on the arm of the wheelchair. I guess I thought he was calling the pogos. Or something. Whatever I expected, it was not the thing that answered his summons.

The spider walked on four singing, mechanical legs; it was a meter and a half tall. Its arms sang too as the servo motors which powered the joints changed pitch; it sounded something like an ant colony playing bagpipes. It clumped into the room with a herky-jerky gait although its bowl-shaped abdomen remained perfectly level. Each of its legs could move with five degrees of freedom; they ended in disk-shaped feet. One of its arms was obviously intended for heavy duty work since it ended in a large claw gripper; the other, smaller arm had a beautifully articulated four digit hand that was a masterpiece of microengineering. There was a ring of sensors around the bottom of its belly. It stopped in front of Bonivard's chair; he wheeled to face it. The strong arm extended toward him. The rear legs stretched out to balance. Bonivard gazed up at the spider with the calm joy of a man greeting his lover; I realized then that much of the pain I had detected in him had to do with the wheelchair. The claw fitted into notches in Bonivard's bionic collar and then, its servos screaming, the spider lifted him from the chair and fitted his mutilated torso into the bowl which was its body. There must have been a flatscreen just out of sight in the cockpit; I could see the play of its colors across his face. He fitted his good arm into an analog sleeve and digits flexed. He smiled down at me.

"Sometimes," he said, "people misunderstand."

I knew I was standing there like a slack-jawed moron but I was too croggled to even consider closing my mouth. The spider swung toward the stairs.

"The gardens," said Bonivard.

"What?"

"This way." The spider rose up to its full height in order to squeeze through the door. I gulped and followed. Watching the spider negotiate the steep stone steps, I couldn't help but imagine the spectacular segment I could have shot if Bonivard hadn't wasted my microcam. This was main menu stuff and I was the only spook within ten kilometers. As we emerged from the building and passed through the fountain courtyard, I caught up and walked alongside.

"I'm a reporter, you know. If I die of curiosity, it's your fault."

He laughed. "Custom-made, of course. It cost . . . but you don't need to know that. A lot. Wheelchairs are useless on steps but I keep them for visitors and going out. I'm enough of a monster as it is. The spider has to stay here anyway. Even if it could leave, imagine strolling through town wearing this thing. I'd be on the main menu of telelink within the hour and I can't allow that. You understand?" He glanced down at me and I nodded. I always nod when people tell me things I don't quite understand. Although I was pretty sure that there was a threat in there someplace.

"How do you control it?"

"Tell it where I want to go and it takes me. Rudimentary AI; about as intelligent as a brain-damaged ant. It knows every centimeter of Chillon and nothing else. Down these stairs."

We descended a flight of stone stairs into the bowels of Chillon and passed through a storeroom filled with pumps, disassembled hydroponic benches, and bags of water soluble nutrients. Beyond it, in a room as big as the Banqueting Hall, was Bonivard's garden.

"Once was the arsenal," he said. "Swords to ploughshares and all that. Beans instead of bullets."

Running down the middle of the room were four magnificent stone pillars which supported a series of intersecting roof vaults. Facing the lake to the west were four small windows set high on the wall. Spears of sunlight, tinted blue by reflections from the lake, fell on the growing benches beneath the windows. This feeble light was supplemented by fluorescents hung from the ceiling on adjustable chains.

"Crop rotation," said Bonivard, as I followed him between the benches. "Tomatoes, green beans, radishes, soy, adzuki, carrots, pak choi. Then squash, chard, peppers, peas, turnips, broccoli, favas, and mung for sprouts. Subirrigated sand system. Automatic. Here's an alpine strawberry." The spider's digits plucked a thumbnail-sized berry from a luxuriant bush. It was probably the sweetest fruit I had ever eaten, although a touch of acid kept it from cloying. "Always strawberries. Always. Have another."

As I parted the leaves to find one, I disturbed a fat white moth. It flew up at me, bounced off the side of my face, and flitted toward one of the open windows. With quickness that would have astonished a cobra, the spider's claw squealed and struck it in midair. The moth fluttered as the arm curled back toward Bonivard. He took it from the spider and popped it into his mouth. "Protein," he said. His crazed giggle was just too theatrical: part of some bizarre act, I thought. I hoped.

"Come see my flowers," he said.

Along the eastern, landward side of the arsenal, slabs of living rock protruded from the wall. Scattered among them was a collection of the sickest plants I'd ever seen. Not a single leaf was properly formed; they were variously twisted or yellowed or blotched. Bonivard showed me a jet-black daisy that smelled of rotting chicken. A mum with petals that ended with what looked like skeletal hands. A phalaenopsis orchid that he called "bleeding angels on a stick."

"An experiment," he said. "They get untreated water, straight from the lake. Some mutations are in the tenth generation. And you're the first to see."

I considered. "Why are you showing this to me?"

When the spider came to a dead stop the whine of the servos went from cacophony to a quietening harmony. For a few seconds Bonivard held it there. "Not interested?"

Although he glanced quickly away, it was not before I had seen the loneliness in his disappointed frown. There was something in me that could not help but respond to the man; a stirring that surprised and disgusted me. Still, I nodded. "Interested."

He brightened. "Then there's time for the dungeon before we go back."

We passed through the torture chamber and Bonivard pointed out burn marks at the base of the pillar which supported its ceiling. "Tied them here," he said. "Hot irons on bare heels. Look: scratch marks in the paint. Made by fingernails." He smiled at my look of horror. "Mindkillers of the Renaissance."

The dungeon was just beyond, a huge room, even larger than the arsenal. It was empty.

"There are seven pillars of Gothic mold," said Bonivard, "in

Chillon's dungeons deep and old. There are seven columns, massy and gray, dim with a dull imprisoned ray, a sunbeam which hath lost its way.''

"Byron's poem, right?'' I was getting fed up with all this oblique posturing. "You want to tell me why you keep spouting it all the time? Because, to be honest, it's damned annoying.''

He seemed hurt. "No,'' he said, "I don't think I want to tell you.''

Riding the spider did seem to change him. Or maybe it was merely my perspective that had changed. It was easy to pity someone in a wheelchair, someone who was physically lower than you. It was difficult to pity Bonivard when he was looking down at you from the spider. Even when he let his emotional vulnerability show, somehow he seemed the stronger for it.

There was a moment of strained silence. The spider took a few tentative steps into the dungeon, as if Bonivard was content to let it drift. Then he twisted in the cockpit. "It might have something to do with the fact that I'm crazy.''

I laughed at him. "You're not crazy. God knows you probably had reason enough to go crazy once, but you're tough and you survived.'' I couldn't help myself. "No, Monsieur François de Bonivard, or whoever the hell you are, I'm betting you're a faker. It suits your purposes to play scrambled, so you live in a ruined castle and talk funny and eat bugs on the wing. But you're as sane as I am. Maybe saner.''

I don't know which of us was the more surprised by my outburst. I guess Macmillan's message had made me reckless; if I was doomed, at least I didn't have to take any more crap. Bonivard backed the spider up and slowly lowered it to a crouch so that our faces were on a level.

"You know the definition of artificial intelligence?'' he said.

I shook my head.

"The simulation of intelligent behavior so that it is indistinguishable from the real thing. Now tell me, if I can simulate madness so well that the world thinks I'm mad, so well that even I myself am no longer quite sure, who is to say that I'm not mad?''

"Me,'' I said. And then I leaned into the cockpit and kissed him.

I don't know why I did it; I was out on the edge. All the rules had changed and I hadn't had time to work out new ones. I thought to myself, what this man needs is to be kissed; he hasn't been kissed in a long time. And then I was doing it. Maybe I was only teasing him; I had never kissed anyone so repulsive in my life. It was a ridiculous, glancing blow that caught him on the side of the nose. If he had tried to follow it up I probably would have driven my fingers into his eyes and run like hell. But he didn't try to follow it up. He just stayed perfectly still, bent toward me like a seedling reaching for the light. Then he decided to smile and I smiled and it was over.

"I'm in trouble." I thought then was the time to confess. The old instincts said to trust him.

He was suddenly impassive. "We're all in trouble." I could not help but notice his shriveled arm twitch. He saw this; he saw everything about me. "I'm going to die. A year, maybe two."

I was dizzy. For a few seconds we had touched each other and then without warning a chasm yawned between us. There was something monstrous about the deadness of his expression, his face lit by the flickering of menus across the flatscreen in the spider's cockpit. I didn't believe him and said so.

"Reads eye movements," he nodded toward the screen. It was as if he had not heard me. "If I look at a movement macro and blink, the spider executes it. No hands." His laugh was bitter and the servos began to sing. The spider reared up to its normal meter-and-a-half walking height and stalked to the third pillar. On the third drum of the pillar was carved "Byron."

"Forgery," said Bonivard. "Although elsewhere is vandalism actually committed by Shelley, Dickens, Harriet Beecher Stowe. Byron didn't stay long enough to get the story right. Bonivard was an adventurer. Not a victim of religious persecution. Never shackled, merely confined. Fed well, allowed to write, read books."

"Like you."

Bonivard shrugged.

"It's been so long," I said. "I barely remember the poem. Do you have a copy? Or maybe you could give a recitation."

"Don't toy with me." His voice was tight.

"I'm not." I really didn't know how things had gotten so bad, so quickly. "I'm sorry."

"Django is restless." The spider scuttled from the dungeon.

*   *   *

Nothing happened.

No assaults by corporate mercenaries, no frantic midnight escapes, no crashes, explosions, fistfights, deadlines. The sun rose and set; waves lapped at Chillon's walls as they had for centuries. At first it was torture adjusting to the rhythms of mundane life, the slow days and long nights. Then it got worse. Sleeping alone in the same damn bed and taking regular meals at the same damn table made my nerves stretch. I couldn't work. What I could do was eat, nap, worry, and wander the castle in a state of edgy boredom.

Sometimes I saw Django; other times Bonivard. But never the two at once. Perhaps they met while I was asleep; maybe they had stopped speaking. Django made it clear that their negotiations had snagged, but he did not seem upset. While I had no doubt that he would have killed either or both of us to get his payoff, I had the sense that the money itself was not important to him. He seemed to think of it in the way that an athlete thinks of the medal: a symbol of a great performance. My guess was that Django was psychologically unfit to be rich. If he lived to collect, he would merrily piss the money away until he needed to play again. Another performance.

So it was that he seemed to take a perverse enjoyment in waiting Bonivard out. And why not? Bonivard provided him with all the flash he needed. Bonivard's telelink could access the musical library in Montreux, long a mecca for jazz. Django would sit in his room for hours, playing the stuff at launch pad volume. Sometimes the very walls of the castle seemed to ring like the plates of some giant vibraphone. Django had just about everything he wanted. Except sex.

"Beautiful dreamer, wake unto me." He had been drinking some poison or other all morning and by now his singing voice was as melodious as a fire alarm. "List while I woo thee with soft melody."

We were in the little room which the pogos called the treasury. It was long since bankrupt; empty except for debris fallen from the crumbling corbels and the chilling smell of damp stone. We were not alone; Bonivard's spider had been trailing us all morning. "Stick it, Django," I said.

He drained his glass. "Just a love song, Eyes. We all need love." He turned toward the spider. "Let's ask the cripple; he's probably tuned in. What about it, spiderman? Do I sing?"

The spider froze.

"Hey, François! You watching, pal?" He threw the plastic glass at the spider but it missed. Django was twisted, all right. There was a chemical gleam in his eyes that was bright enough to read by. "You like to watch? Cutters leave you a plug to play with while you watch?"

I turned away from him in disgust. "You ever touch me, Django, and I'll chew your balls off and spit them in your face."

He grinned. "Keep it up, Eyes. I like them tough."

The spider retrieved the glass and deposited it in its cockpit with some other of Django's leavings. I ducked through the doorway into Chillon's keep and began climbing the rickety stairs. I could hear Django and the spider following. Bonivard had warned Django that the spider would start to shadow him if he kept leaving things out and moving them around. Its vision algorithms had difficulty recognizing objects which were not where it expected them to be. In its memory map of Chillon there was a place for everything; anything unaccountably out of place tended to be invisible. When Django had begun a vicious little game of laying obstacle courses for the spider, it had responded by picking up after him like a doting grandmother with a neatness fetish.

According to Ego, who had first shown me how to get into the musty tower, the top of the keep rose twenty-seven meters from the courtyard. Viewed from this height Chillon looked like a great stone ship at anchor. To the west and north the blue expanse of Lake Geneva was mottled by occasional drifts of luminescent red-orange algae. To the south and east rose the Bernese Alps. The top of the keep was where I went to escape, although often as not I ended up watching the elevated highway which ran along the shore for signs of troop movements.

"Too much work," said Django, huffing from the climb, "for a lousy view." he wobbled over to join me at a north window. "Although it is private." He tried to get me to look at him. "What's it going to take, Eyes?" The spider arrived. I ignored Django.

I gazed down at the ruined prow of the stone ship. Years before an explosion had stripped away a chunk of the northeastern curtain wall and toppled one of the three thirteenth century defensive turrets, leaving only a blackened stump. Beside it were the roofless ruins of the chapel, which connected with Bonivard's private apartment. This was the only part of Chillon to which we were denied access. I had no idea whether he was hiding something in his rooms or whether secretiveness was part of the doomed Byronic pose he continued to strike. Maybe he just needed a place to be alone.

"He must have played in Montreux," said Django.

I glanced across the bay at the sad little city. "Who?"

"Django Reinhardt. The great gypsy jazzman. My man." Django sighed. "Sometimes when I listen to his stuff, it's like his guitar is talking to me."

"What's it say: buy IBM?"

He seemed not to hear me, as if he were in a dream. Or maybe he was suffering from oxygen depletion after the climb. "Oh, I don't know. It's the way he phrases away from the beat. He's saying: don't think, just do it. Improvise, you know. Better to screw up than be predictable."

"I'm impressed," I said. "I didn't know you were a philosopher, Django."

"Maybe there's a lot you don't know." He accidently pushed a loose stone from the window sill and seemed surprised that it fell to the courtyard below. "You get a flash pretending you're better than me but remember, you're the one following me around. If I'm the rat here that makes you a flea on my ass, baby. A parasite bitch." His face had gone pale and he caught at the wall to hold himself upright. "Maybe you deserve the cripple. Look at me! I'm alive— all you two do is watch me and wish."

And then I caught him as he passed out.

"The walls are everywhere," said Bonivard. "Limits." I found myself absently picking a pole bean from its vine before I realized that I didn't want it. "You're not smart enough, not rich enough. You get tired. You die." I offered it to him. "Some people like to pretend they've broken out. That they're running free." He bit into the bean. "But there's no escape. You have to find a way to live within the walls." He waved at the growing benches; I'm not sure whether it was his arm or the spider's that waved. "And then they don't matter." He took another bite of bean, and reconsidered. "At least, that's the theory."

"Maybe they don't matter to you. But these particular walls are starting to close in on me. I've got to get out, Bonivard. I can't wait anymore for you and Django to work the deal. This place is scrambling me. Can't you see it?"

"Maybe you only think you're crazy." He smiled. "I used to be like you. Rather, like him." Bonivard nodded at the roof. Django's direction. "They spotted me in their electronic garden, plucked me from it like I might pluck an offending beetle. Squashed and threw me away."

"But you didn't die."

"No." He shook his head. "Not yet."

"Who says you're going to die?"

"Me. More you don't need to know." I think he was sorry he had told me. "Leave any time. No one to stop you."

"You know I can't. I need help. If they catch me, you're next. They'll squash you dead this time."

"Half dead already." He glanced down at his withered left side. "Sometimes I wish they had finished the job. Do what's necessary. You know Voltaire's *Candide?* 'Il faut cultiver notre jardin.' It is necessary to cultivate our garden."

"Make sense, damn it!"

"Voltaire's garden was in Geneva. Down the street from ground zero."

Thwock-thwocka-thwock.

I'd been getting tension headaches for several days but this one was the worst. Every time Ego's rubber foot hit the floor of the banqueting hall, something hammered against the inside of my skull. I felt as if my brain was about to hatch. "Get away from me."

"I have been sent to demonstrate independent action," it said pleasantly. "I understand that you do not believe in artificial intelligence."

"I don't care. I'm sick."

"Have you considered retiring to your room?"

"I'm sick of my room! Sick of you! This pisspot castle."

Thwocka-thwocka. "Bonivard is dead."

"What!"

"François Bonivard died in 1570."

I felt a thrill of excitement that my headache instantly converted to pain. What I needed was to be stored in a cool dry place for about six weeks. Instead I was a good reporter and asked the next question, even though my voice seemed to squeak against my teeth like fingernails on a blackboard. "Then who is . . . the man . . . calls himself Bonivard?"

Thwock.

I began again. "Who—"

"Carl Pfneudl."

I waited as long as I could. "Who the hell is Carl Pfneudl?"

"That is as much as I can say." The pogo was bouncing half a meter higher than usual.

"But . . ."

"A demonstration of independent action through violation of specific instructions."

I realized that I was blinking in time to its bouncing. But it didn't help.

"Had he known," continued the pogo, "he would have forbidden it and I would have had to devise another demonstration. It was a difficult problem. Do you know where Django is?"

"Yes. No. Look: don't tell Django, understand? I command you not to tell Django. Or speak to Bonivard of this conversation. Do you acknowledge my command?"

"I acknowledge," replied Ego. "However, contingencies may arise beyond . . ."

At that point I snapped. I flew out of my chair and put my shoulder into Ego's three spot. The pogo hit the floor of the banqueting hall hard. Its leg pistoning uselessly, it spun on its side. Then it began to shriek. I dropped to my knees, certain that the sound was liquefying my cochlear nucleus. I clapped hands to my ears to keep my brains from oozing out.

Id, summoned by Ego's distress call, was the first to arrive. As soon as it entered the room, Ego fell silent and ceased to struggle. Id crossed the room to Ego just as Django entered. Bonivard in the spider was right behind. Id bounced in place beside its fallen twin, awaiting instructions.

"Why two pogos?" Bonivard guided the spider around Django and offered an arm—his own—to help me up. It was the first time I'd ever held his hand. "Redundancy."

Id bounced very high and landed on Ego's rubber foot. Ego flipped into the air like a juggling pin, gyrostabilizers wailing, and landed—upright—with a satisfying *thwock.*

"You woke me up for this?" Django stalked off in disgust.
Bonivard had not yet let go of me. "How did it happen?"
"A miscalculation," said the pogo.

It had been years since I dreamed. When I was a child my
dreams always frightened me. I would wake my father up with my
screaming. He would come to my room, a grim dispenser of
comfort. He would blink at me and put his hand on the side of
my face and tell me it was all right. He never wore pajamas.
After I started to go to school I dreaded seeing him naked, his
white body parting the darkness of my room. So I guess I stopped
dreaming.

But I dreamed of Bonivard. I dreamed he rode his spider into my
room and he was naked. I dreamed of touching the white scar tissue
that covered his stumps and the catheterized fold where his genitals
had once been. To my horror I was not horrified at all.

Django's door was ajar. I knocked and, without waiting for a
reply, entered. I'd never been in his room before; it smelled like
low tide. A bowl of vegetables was desiccating on the window sill.
The bed hadn't been made since we'd arrived and clothes were
scattered as if Django had been undressed by a whirlwind. He sat,
wearing nothing but underpants and a headset, working at a marble-
topped table. White ten-gigabyte memory chips were stacked in
neat rows around his computer cuff, which was connected to a
borrowed flatscreen and a keyboard. He tapped fingers against the
black marble as he watched code scrolling down the screen.

"Yeah, I *want* to be in that *num*ber—bring it home, *Satchmo*,"
he muttered in a sing-song voice, "when those *saints* come marching *in!*"

He must have sensed he was not alone; he twisted on his chair
and frowned at me. At the same moment he hit a key without
looking and the screen went blank. Then he lifted the headset.

"Well?" I said, indicating the chips.

"Well." He rubbed his hand through his hair. "It thinks it's an
artificial intelligence." Then he smiled as if he had just made the
decision to trust me. "Don't know yet. Interesting. Hard to stretch
a program designed for a mainframe when all I've got to work with
is kludged junkware. I'd break into Bonivard's heavy equipment if
I could. Right now all I can do is make copies."

"You're making copies? Does he know?"

"Do I care if he does?"

I grabbed some dirty white pants from the floor and tossed them at him. "I'll stay if you get dressed."

He began to pull the pants on. "Welcome to the Bernese torture chamber, circa 1652," he said, doing a bad robot imitation.

"I thought the torture chamber was in the dungeons."

"With two there's no waiting." He tilted a plastic glass on the table, sniffed at it suspiciously, and then took a tentative sip. "Refreshments?"

I was about to sit on the bed but thought better of it. "Ever hear of someone called Carl Pfneudl?"

"The Noodle? Sure: one of the greats. Juice was that he set up the SoftCell scam. Made money enough to buy Wisconsin. Came to a bad end, though."

Suddenly I didn't want to hear any more. "Then he's dead."

"As a dinosaur. Mindkillers finally caught up with him. Made a snuff video; him the star. Flooded the operators' nets with it and called it deterrence. But you could tell they were having fun."

"Damn." I sagged onto the bed and told him what Ego had told me.

Django listened with apparent indifference but I had been around him long enough to read the signs. My guess was that WISEGUY was a lot more than "interesting." Which was why Django wasn't flashing on some poison or another—he had to be clean for tricky operations. And now if Bonivard was Pfneudl, that lent even more credibility to the idea that WISEGUY was a true AI.

"The old Noodle looked plenty dead to me." Django shook his head doubtfully. "That was one corpse they had to scoop up with a spoon and bury in a bucket."

"Video-synthesizers," I said.

"Sure. But still cheaper to do it for real—and they had reason enough. Look, maybe the pogo was lying. Trying to prove intelligence that way. It's the old Turing fallacy: fooling another intelligence for an hour means you're intelligent. Lots of really stupid programs can play these games, Eyes. There's only one test that means anything: can your AI mix it up with the two billion plus cerebrums on the planet without getting trashed? Drop that pogo into Manhattan and it'll be scrap by Thursday."

"Then who is Bonivard?"

Django yawned. "What difference does it make?"

My door was ajar so that I could hear the spider singing when he came past. "Bonivard!"

The spider nudged into my room, nearly filling it. Still I was able to squeeze by and thumb the printreader on the door, locking us in.

"Don't worry about Django." Bonivard seemed amused. "Busy, too busy."

I didn't want to look up at him and I wasn't going to ask him to stoop. I might have stood on the bed except then some part of me would be expecting my father to come in and yell. So instead I clambered to the high window and perched on a rickety wooden balcony that a sneeze might have blown down. The wind off the lake was cool. The rocks beneath me looked like broken teeth.

"Careful," said Bonivard. "Fall in and you'll glow."

"Are you Carl Pfneudl?"

He brought the spider to a dead silent stop. "Where did you hear that name?"

I told him about Ego's demonstration. What Django had said.

"Are you?" I repeated.

"If I am, the story changes, doesn't it?" He was being sarcastic but I wasn't sure whether he was mocking me or himself. "Juicier, as you say. Main menu. It means money. Publicity. Promotions all around. But juice is an expensive commodity." He sighed. "Make an offer."

I shook my head. "Not me. I'm not working for Infoline anymore. Probably never work again." I told him everything: about my burster, the possibility that I had given away our location, how Macmillan had cut me free. I told how I'd tried to tell him before. I don't know how much of it he knew already—maybe all. But that didn't stop me: I was on a confessing jag. I told him that Django was making copies of WISEGUY. I even told him that I had dreamed of him. It all spilled out and I let it come. I knew I was supposed to be the reporter, supposed to say nothing, squeeze the juice from him. But nothing was the way it was supposed to be.

When I was done he stared at me with an expression that was totally unreadable. His ruined arm shivered like a dead leaf in the wind. "I wanted to be Carl Pfneudl," he said. "Once. But Carl Pfneudl is dead. A public execution. Now I'm Bonivard. The prisoner of Chillon."

"You knew who I was," I said. "You brought me here. Why?"

Bonivard continued to stare, as if he could barely see me across the room. "Carl Pfneudl was an arrogant bastard. Kind of man who knew he could get anything he wanted. Like Django. If he wanted you, he would have found the way."

"Django will never get me." I leaned forward. I felt like grabbing Bonivard, shaking some sense into him. "I'm not some damn hardware you can steal, a program to operate on."

He nodded. "Maybe that was it. I was alone—too long. Saw you on telelink. You were tough. Took risks but didn't pretend you weren't afraid. You were more interesting than the punks you covered. Like Django. Fools like Carl Pfneudl. You were a whole person: nothing missing."

I took a deep breath. "Can you make love, Bonivard?"

At first he didn't react. Then the corners of his mouth turned up: a grim smile. "That's your offer?"

"You want an offer?" I spat on the floor in front of him. "If Pfneudl is dead then good, I'm glad. Now I'm going to ask once more: can you make love to me?"

"A cruel question. A reporter's question."

I said nothing.

"I don't want your damn charity." As the spider's cockpit settled to the floor, he stretched to his full pitiful length. "Look at me! I'm a monster. I know what you see."

I slid off the sill and dropped lightly to the floor. "Maybe a monster is what I want."

I think I shocked him. I think that some part of him hoped that I would lie, tell him he wasn't hideous. But that was his problem.

I unbolted him from the spider, picked him up. I'd never carried a lover to bed. He showed me how to disengage the bionic collar; told me we'd have a couple of hours before he would need to be hooked up again.

In some ways it was like my dream. The scar tissue was white, yes. But . . .

"It's thermofiber," he explained. "Packed with sensors." He could control the shape. Make it expand and contract.

"Connected to all the right places in my brain."

I kissed his forehead.

I was repulsed. I was fascinated. It was cool to the touch.

"The answer is yes," he said.

It was dinner time. Django had made a circle of cherry tomatoes on the table of the banqueting hall.

"It's over," said Bonivard.

Django whistled as he walked to the opposite side of the table to line up his shot. He flicked his thumb and his shooter tomato dispersed the top of the circle. "All right."

Bonivard tossed a Swiss Volksbank passcard across the table, scattering the remainder of Django's game. "You're leaving. Take that if you want."

Django straightened. I wondered if Bonivard realized he was carrying heat. "So I'm leaving." He picked up the passcard. "Weren't there two of these before?"

"You made copies of WISEGUY." Bonivard held up a stack of white memory chips from the cockpit of the spider. "Thanks."

"Nice bluff." Some of the stiffness went out of Django. "Except I know my copy procedure was secure." He smiled. Getting looser. "Even if that is a copy, it's no good to you. I re-encrypted it, spiderman. Armor-plated code is my specialty. You'll need computer *years* to operate."

"Even so, you're leaving." Bonivard was as grim as a cement wall. I think I knew why their negotiations had broken down—had never stood a chance. Bonivard had the same loathing for Django that an addict gets when he looks in the mirror after his morning puke. Django never recognized that hatred; he had the sensitivity of a brick.

"What's wrong, spiderman? Mindkillers knocking at the door?"

"You're good," said Bonivard. "A pity to waste talent like yours. It was a clean escape, Django; they've completely lost you. You'll need some surgery, get yourself a new identity. But that's no problem."

"No problem?" I said. "I'm used to being me."

"Maybe I wouldn't mind losing this face." Django rubbed his chin.

"The only reason I put up with you this long," said Bonivard, "was that I was waiting for WISEGUY."

"I'm taking my copies, spiderman."

"You are. And you're going to move those copies. A lot of them. Cheap and fast. Since they've lost your trail, the mindkillers are waiting to see where WISEGUY turns up. Try to backtrack to you. Your play is to bring it out everywhere. Get some pieces of it up on the operators' net. Overload the search programs and the mindkillers will be too busy to bother you."

Django was smiling and nodding like a kid learning from a master. "I like it. Old Django goes out covered with glory. New Django comes in covered with money."

"Probably headed for the history chips." Bonivard's sarcasm was wasted on Django. "The great humanitarian. Savior of the twenty-first century." Django's enthusiasm seemed to have wearied Bonivard. "The big prison, punk."

Django was too full of his own ideas to listen. He shot out of his chair and paced the hall. "A new ID. Hey, Eyes, what do you think of 'Dizzy.' I'd use 'the Count' but there's a real count—Liechtenstein or some such—who operates. Maybe Diz. Yeah."

"Go plug yourself, Django." I didn't like any of it; I never signed on to disappear.

"Maybe you're not as scrambled as you pretend, Frankie boy." There was open admiration in Django's voice. "Don't worry, the secret is safe. Not a word about this dump. Or the Noodle. Honor among thieves, right? No hard feelings." He had the audacity to extend his hand to Bonivard.

"No feelings at all." Bonivard recoiled from him. "But you'll probably get dead before you realize that."

Anger flashed across Django's face but it didn't stick. He shrugged and turned to me. "How about it, Eyes? The sweet smell of money or the stink of mildew?"

"Goodbye, Django." Bonivard dismissed him with a wave of his good hand.

I didn't need Bonivard's help to lose Django. I was almost mad enough to walk out on the two of them. But I didn't. Maybe it was reporter's instincts still at work even though they didn't matter. I gave Django a stare that was cold enough to freeze vodka. Even he could understand that.

He picked up the bank passscard, flicked it with his middle finger. "I told you once, Eyes. You're not as smart as you think you are." Flick. "So stay with him and rot, bitch. I don't need you." Flick. "I don't need anyone."

Which was exactly right.

Bonivard and I sat for a while after he had gone. Not looking at each other. The hall was very quiet. I think he was waiting for me to say something. I didn't have anything to say.

Finally the spider stretched. "Come to my rooms," said Bonivard. "Something you should see."

Bonivard had taken over the suite once reserved for the Dukes of Savoy. It had taken a battering during the riots; in Bonivard's bedroom a gaping hole in the wall had been closed with glass, affording a view of rubble and the fire-blackened curtain wall. We had to pass through an airlock into a climate-controlled room that he called his workshop. His "workshop" had more computing power than Portugal. The latest Cray filled half the space, a multi-processor he claimed was capable of performing a trillion operations per second.

"The electronic equivalent of a human brain," said Bonivard. A transformation came over him as he admired his hardware: a bit of a discarded self showed through. I realized that this was the one place in the castle where the mad prisoner of Chillon was not in complete control. "Runs the spider, although that's like using a fusion plant to run a toaster. There hasn't ever been software that could take advantage of this computer's power."

"Until WISEGUY," I said.

For a minute I thought he hadn't heard me. "Sliced through Django's encryption in a week." The spider crouched until the cockpit was almost touching the floor. "WISEGUY is a bundle of different programs that share information. Vision system, planner, parser. Not only can it address massive amounts of memory but it understands what it remembers. Learns from experience." The spider stopped singing and its legs locked in place. "What's amazing is that when you port it from one hardware configuration to another, it analyzes the capabilities of the new system and begins using them without any human intervention." The flatscreen in the cockpit went black: he had powered the spider down. "But it's not true AI."

"Not?"

He shook his head. "Heuristics are nowhere near good enough.

It's as close as anyone has ever come but still needs a man in the loop to do anything really worth doing. Bring me the helmet.''

The helmet was a huge bubble of yellow plastic which would completely cover Bonivard's head. At its base there were cutouts for his shoulders. I peeked inside and saw a pincushion of brain taps. "Careful," said Bonivard. It was attached by an umbilical to a panel built into the Cray.

I helped him settle the thing on his head and fasten the straps which wrapped under his armpits. I heard a muffled "Thanks." Then nothing for a few minutes.

The airlock whooshed; I turned. If I were the swooning type, that would have been the time for it. Yellowbaby smiled and held out his arms to me.

I took two joyous strides to him, a tentative step, and then stopped. It wasn't really the Babe. The newcomer looked like him, all right, enough to be a younger brother or a first cousin—the fact is that I didn't know what Yellowbaby really looked like anyway. The Babe had been to the face cutters so many times that he had a permanent reservation in the OR. He had been a chameleon, chasing the latest style of handsomeness the way some people chase Paris fashion. The newcomer had the same lemon blond hair cut in the same conservatively wide hawk, those Caribbean-blue eyes, the cheekbones of a baronet and the color of *café au lait*. But the neck was too short, the torso too long. It wasn't Yellowbaby.

The newcomer let his arms fall to his sides. The smile stayed. "Hello, Wynne. I've been waiting a long time to meet you."

"Who are you?"

"Who do you want me to be?" He sauntered across the room to Bonivard, unfastened the helmet, lifted it off, replaced it on its rack next to the Cray. And went stiff as a four-hour-old corpse.

Bonivard blinked in the light. "What do you think?"

"A surrogate? Some fancy kind of remote."

"Fancy, yes. It can taste, smell. When its sensors touch you, I feel it."

Telelink had been making noise about the coming of surrogate technology for a long time. Problem was that running the damn things was the hardest work anyone had ever done. Someone claimed it was like trying to play chess in your head while wrestling an alligator. After ten minutes on the apparatus they had to mop most mortals up off the floor.

"How long can you keep it going?" I said.

"Hours. WISEGUY does all the work. All I do is think. And it doesn't matter if it's this model or the spider or a robot tank or a killer satellite."

"The army of the future." I nodded. "That's why the feds went berserk."

"Django is going to be a hero. Everywhere but in the States. The world gets WISEGUY, the balance of power stays the same. And if there's anyone with any brains left in Washington, they should be secretly pleased. WISEGUY is the kind of weapon you either use or lose. Better to let the imams have it than invade Teheran and risk a nuclear exchange." He powered the spider up again. "And think of the applications for space and deep sea exploration. Hazardous work environments."

"Think of the handicapped," I said bitterly. "I lose my freedom. You get yours. You knew the story would be too hot for Infoline to handle." I hit myself with the heel of my hand; I'd been so dumb. "You paid Yellowbaby to bring me to you. Like some slimy white slaver."

"He didn't know how important WISEGUY was, that Wynne Cage would be stuck here. He didn't have the specs; I did." At least Bonivard didn't try to gloss over his guilt. It wasn't much but it was something. "You want to leave," he continued, not daring to look me in the face, "I suppose I don't blame you. I've made the arrangements. And the other bank passcard is already signed over to your new identity."

"Plug the new ID!" I walked up to the surrogate, felt its hand. The skin was warm to the touch, just moist enough to pass. "What do you need this doll for anyway?"

"The mindkillers let me come here to die. No explanations. They didn't confiscate my bank accounts. Didn't stop me from seeing all the doctors I wanted. Just let me go. Probably part of the torture. Keep me wondering. I decided not to play it their way, to hurt them even if it landed me back in their lab. But a random hit, no. I wanted to hurt them and help myself at the same time. I did some operating; found out about WISEGUY."

"Maybe they wanted you to. And IBM let Django steal it."

"That occurred to me." Bonivard ran his fingers through his thinning brown hair. "Using me and some punk operators to leak a breakthrough no one really wanted in the first place. War is bad business." He sighed. "I don't care anymore. I have WISEGUY. As you say, my freedom. I wanted the surrogate so that I could be with people again. Free from the stress, the pity. The freedom to be normal."

"But you're not normal, Bonivard. You are who you are because you're damaged and you suffer. Living with it is what makes you strong."

For a moment he seemed stung, as if I had no right to remind him of his deformities. Then the anger faded into sadness. "Maybe you're right," he said. "Maybe this body is part of the prison. But I can't go on alone anymore. or I *will* go mad." He looked at me then, half a man strapped to a robot spider. "I don't want you to go, Wynne. I love you."

I didn't know what to say to him. He was a genius operator, obscenely rich. The deformities no longer bothered me; in fact, they were part of the attraction. But he had no idea who I was. Making the surrogate look like the Babe had been a sick joke. And he had been so pathetically proud of his thermofiber prosthesis when we'd made love, as if a magic plug was all it took to make an allnighter out of a man with no legs. He didn't know about my own psychological deformities, less obvious perhaps but no less crippling. How could I stay with him when I'd never stayed anywhere before? The problem was that he was not only in love, he was in need.

"The doctors are quite sure, Wynne. Two years at most—"

"Bonivard!"

"—at most. By that time the leaking of WISEGUY will be old news. It'll be safe to be Wynne Cage again, anyone you want to be. And of course this will be yours."

"Stop it, Bonivard. Don't say anything." I could tell he had more to say; much too much more. But when he kept quiet, I was mollified. "I thought you didn't want charity."

He laughed. "I lied." At himself.

Then I had to get away; I pushed through the airlock back into the bedroom. I wanted to keep going; I could feel my nerves tingling with the impulse to run. But it had been a long time since anyone had told me they loved me and meant it. He was a smart man; maybe he could learn what I needed. Maybe we could both learn. Not Swiss bank accounts or features on the main menu.

I had been on the run for too long, slid between the sheets with too many punks like the Babe without feeling a damn thing. At least Bonivard made me feel *something*. Maybe it was love. Maybe. He was going to let me go, suffer so I would be happy. I hadn't known I was worth that. I leaned against the wall, felt the cold stone. Something Django—of all people—had said stuck with me. Don't think, just do it. Improvise.

He came out of the workshop riding the spider. I think he was surprised to see me. "My very chains and I grew friends," he said, "so much a long communion tends to make us what we are—"

"Shut up, Bonivard." Standing absolutely still, I opened my arms to him. To the prison of Chillon. "Would you shut the hell up?"

Howard Waldrop's short story "The Ugly Chickens" a few years back—about the mysterious survival of a few supposedly extinct dodos in modern-day Texas—provided much delight to readers and brought an award or two to its author. Now Harry Turtledove of Los Angeles—who used to write as "Eric G. Iverson" before coming out from behind the false whiskers to reveal his abundant real ones—puts Homo erectus *and other prehistoric oddities down in the London of Samuel Pepys, to high comic effect.*

AND SO TO BED

Harry Turtledove

May 4, 1661. A fine bright morning. Small beer and radishes for to break my fast, then into London for this day. The shambles on Newgate Street stinking unto heaven, as is usual, but close to it my destination, the sim marketplace. Our servant Jane with too much for one body to do, and whilst I may not afford the hire of another man or maid, two sims shall go far to ease her burthen.

Success also sure to gladden Elizabeth's heart, my wife being ever one to follow the dame Fashion, and sims all the go of late, though monstrous ugly. Them formerly not much seen here, but since the success of our Virginia and Plymouth colonies are much more often fetched to these shores from the wildernesses the said colonies front upon. They are also commenced to be bred on English soil, but no hope there for me, as I do require workers full-grown, not cubs or babes in arms or whatsoever the proper term may be.

The sim-seller a vicious lout, near unhandsome as his wares. No,

261

the truth for the diary: such were a slander on any man, as I saw on his conveying me to the creatures.

Have seen these sims before, surely, but briefly, and in their masters' livery, the which by concealing their nakedness conceals as well much of their brutishness. The males are most of them well made, though lean as rakes from the ocean passage and, I warrant, poor victualing after. But all are so hairy as more to resemble rugs than men, and the same true for the females, hiding such dubious charms as they may possess nigh as well as a smock of linen: nought here, God knows, for Elizabeth's jealousy to light on.

This so were the said females lovely of feature as so many Aphrodites. They are not, nor do the males recall to mind Adonis. In both sexes the brow projects with a shelf of bone, and above it, where men do enjoy a forehead proud in its erectitude, is but an apish slope. The nose broad and low, the mouth wide, the teeth nigh as big as a horse's (though shaped, it is not to be denied, like a man's), the jaw long, deep, and devoid of chin. They stink.

The sim-seller full of compliments on my coming hard on the arrival of the *Gloucester* from Plymouth, him having thereby replenished his stock in trade. Then the price should also be not so dear, says I, and by God it did do my heart good to see the ferret-faced rogue discomfited.

Rogue as he was, though, he dickered with the best, for I paid full a guinea more for the pair of sims than I had looked to, spending in all £11.6d.4d. The coin once passed over (and bitten, for to insure its verity), the sim-seller signed to those of his chattels I had bought that they were to go with me.

His gestures marvelous quick and clever, and those the sims answered with too. Again, I have seen somewhat of the like before. Whilst coming to understand in time the speech of men, sims are without language of their own, having but a great variety of howls, grunts, and moans. Yet this gesture-speech, which I am told is come from the signs of the deaf, they do readily learn, and often their masters answer back so, to ensure commands being properly grasped.

Am wild to learn it my own self, and shall. Meseems it is in its way a style of tachygraphy or short-hand such as I use to set down these pages. Having devised varying tachygraphic hands for friends and acquaintances, 'twill be amusing taking to a *hand* that is exactly what its name declares.

As I was leaving with my new charges, the sim-seller did bid me lead them by the gibbets on Shooter's Hill, there to see the bodies and members of felons and of sims as have run off from their masters. It wondered me they should have the wit to take the meaning of such display, but he assured me they should. And so, reckoning it good advice if true and no harm if a lie, I chivvied them thither.

A filthy sight I found it, with the miscreants' flesh all shrunk to the bones. But *hoo!* quoth my sims, and looked close upon the corpses of their own kind, which by their hairiness and flat-skulled heads do seem even more bestial dead than when animated with life.

Home then, and Elizabeth as delighted in my success as am I. An excellent dinner of a calf's head boiled with dumplings, and an abundance of buttered ale with sugar and cinnamon, of which in celebration we invited Jane to partake, and she grew right giddy. Bread and leeks for the sims, and water, it being reported they grow undocile on stronger drink.

After much debate, though good-natured, it was decided to style the male Will and the female Peg. Showed them to their pallets down cellar, and they took to them readily enough, as finer than what they were accustomed to.

So to bed, right pleased with myself despite the expense.

May 7. An advantage of having sims present appears that I had not thought on. Both Will and Peg quite excellent ratters, finer than any puss-cat. No need, either, to fling the rats on the dungheap, for they devour them with as much gusto as I should a neat's tongue. They having subsisted on such small deer in the forests of America, I shall not try to break them of the habit, though training them not to bring in their prey when we are at table with guests. The Reverend Mr. Milles quite shocked, but recovering nicely on being plied with wine.

May 8. Peg and Will the both of them enthralled with fire. When the work of them is done of the day, or at evening ere they take their rest, they may be found before the hearth observing the sport of the flames. Now and again one will to the other say *hoo!*—this noise, I find, they utter on seeing that which does interest them, whatsoever it may be.

Now as I thought on it, I minded me reading or hearing, I recall not which, that in their wild unpeopled haunts the sims know the use of fire as they find it set from lightning or other such mischance, but not the art of its making. No wonder then they are Vulcanolaters, reckoning flame more precious than do we gold.

Considering such reflections, I resolved this morning on an experiment, to see what they might do. Rising early for to void my bladder in the pot, I put out the hearthfire, which in any case was gone low through want of fuel. Retired then to put on my dressing gown and, once clad, returned to await developments.

First up from the cellar was Will, and his cry on seeing the flames extinguished heartrending as Romeo's over the body of fair Juliet when I did see that play acted this December past. In a trice comes Peg, whose moaning with Will did rouse my wife, and she much upset at being so rudely wakened.

When the calm in some small measure restored, I bade by signs, in the learning of which I proceed apace, for the sims to sit quietly before the hearth, and with flint and steel restored that which I had earlier destroyed. They both made such outcry as if they had heard sounded the Last Trump.

Then doused I that second fire too, again to much distress from Peg and Will. Elizabeth by this time out of the house in some dudgeon, no doubt to spend money we lack on stuffs of which we have no want.

Set up in the hearth thereupon several small fires of sticks, each with much tinder so as to make it an easy matter to kindle. A brisk striking of flint and steel dropping sparks onto one such produced a merry little blaze, to the accompaniment of much *hoo*ing out of the sims.

And so the nub of it. Shewing Will the steel and flint, I clashed them once more the one upon the other so he might see the sparks engendered thereby. Then pointed to one of the aforementioned piles of sticks I had made up, bidding him watch close, as indeed he did. Having made sure of't, I did set that second pile alight.

Again put the fires out, the wailing accompanying the act less than heretofore, for which I was not sorry. Pointed now to a third assemblage of wood and timber, but instead of myself lighting it, I did convey flint and steel to Will, and with signs essayed to bid him play Prometheus.

His hands much scarred and calloused, and under their hair knobby-knuckled as an Irishman's. He held at first the implements as if not taking in their purpose, yet the sims making tools of stone, as is widely reported, he could not wholly fail to grasp their utility.

And indeed ere long he did try parroting me. When his first clumsy attempt yielded no result, I thought he would abandon such efforts as beyond his capacity and reserved for men of my sort. But persist he did, and at length was reward with scintiilae like unto those I had made. His grin so wide and gleeful I thought it would stretch clear round his head.

Then without need of my further demonstration he set the instruments of fire production over the materials for the blaze. Him in such excitement as the sparks fell upon the waiting tinder that beneath his breeches rose his member, indeed to such degree as would have made me proud to be its possessor. And Peg was, I think, in such mood as to couple with him on the spot, had I not been present and had not his faculties been directed elsewhere than toward the lectual.

For at his success he cut such capers as had not been out of place upon the stage, were they but a trifle more rhythmical and less unconstrained. Yet of the making of fire, even if by such expedient as the friction of two sticks (which once I was forced by circumstance to attempt, and would try the patience of Job), as of every other salutary art, his race is as utterly ignorant as of the moons of Jupiter but lately found by some Italian with an optic glass.

No brute beast of the field could learn to begin a fire on the technique being shown it, which did Will nigh readily as a man. But despite most diligent instruction, no sim yet has mastered such subtler arts as reading and writing, nor ever will, meseems. Falling in capacity thus between man and animal, the sims do raise a host of conundrums vexing and perplexing. I should pay a pound, or at the least ten shillings, merely to know how such strange fusions came to be.

So to the Admiralty full of such musings, which did occupy my mind, I fear, to the detriment of my proper duties.

May 10. Supper this evening at the Turk's Head, with the other members of the Rota Club. The fare not of the finest, being boiled venison and some few pigeons, all meanly done up. The lamb's wool seemed nought but poor ale, the sugar, nutmeg and meat of roasted apples hardly to be tasted. Miles the landlord down with a quartan fever, but ill served by his staff if such is the result of his absence.

The subject of the Club's discussions for the evening much in accord with my own recent curiosity, to wit, the sims. Cyriack Skinner did maintain them creatures of the Devil, whereupon was he roundly rated by Dr. Croon as having in this contention returned to the pernicious heresy of the Manichees, the learned doctor reserving the power of creation of the Lord alone. Much flinging back and forth of Biblical texts, the which all struck me as being more the exercise of ingenuity of the debaters than bearing on the problem, for in plain fact the Scriptures nowhere mention sims.

When at length the talk did turn to matters more ascertainable, I spoke somewhat of my recent investigation, and right well-received my remarks were, or so I thought. Others with experience of sims with like tales, finding them quick enough on things practic but sadly lacking in any higher faculties. Much jollity at my account of the visible manifestation of Will's excitement, and whispers that his lady or that (the names, to my vexation, I failed to catch) owned her sims for naught but their prowess in matters of the mattress.

Just then came the maid by with coffee for the club, not of the best, but better, I grant, than the earlier wretched lamb's wool. She a pretty yellow-haired lass called I believe Kate, a wench of perhaps sixteen years, a good-bodied woman not over thick or thin in any place, with a lovely bosom she did display most charmingly as she bent to fill the gentlemen's cups.

Having ever an eye for beauty, such that I reckon little else beside it, I own I did turn my head for to follow this Kate as she went about her duties. Noticing which, Sir William Henry called out, much to the merriment of the Club and to my chagrin, "See how Samuel peeps!" Him no mean droll, and loosed a pretty pun, if at my expense. Good enough, but then at the far end of the table someone, I saw not who, worse luck, thought to cap it by braying like the donkey he must be, "Not half the peeping, I warrant, as at his sims of nights!"

Such mockery clings to a man like pitch, regardless of the truth in't, which in this case is none. Oh, the thing could be done, but the sims so homely 'twould yield no titillation, of that I am practically certain.

*   *   *

May 12. The household being more infected this past week with nits than ever before, resolved to bathe Peg and Will, which also I hoped would curb somewhat their stench. And so it proved, albeit not without more alarums than I had looked for. The sims most loth to enter the tub, which must to them have seemed some instrument of torment. The resulting shrieks and outcry so deafening a neighbor did call out to be assured all was well.

Having done so, I saw no help for it but to go into the tub my own self, notwithstanding my having bathed but two weeks before. I felt, I think more hesitation stripping down before Peg than I should in front of Jane, whom I would simply dismiss from consideration but in how she performed her duties. But I did wonder what Peg made of my body, reckoning it against the hairy forms of her own kind. Hath she the wit to deem mankind superior, or is our smoothness to her as gross and repellent as the peltries of the sims to us? I cannot as yet make shift to enquire.

As may be, my example showing them they should not be harmed, they bathed themselves. A trouble arose I had not foreseen, for the sims being nearly as thickly haired over all their bodies as I upon my head, the rinsing of the soap from their hides less easy than for us, and requiring much water. Lucky I am the well is within fifty paces of my home. And so from admiral of the bath to the Admiralty, hoping henceforward to scratch myself less.

May 13. A pleasant afternoon this day, carried in a coach to see the lions and other beasts in the menagerie. I grant the lions pride of place through custom immemorial, but in truth am more taken with the abnormous creatures fetched back from the New World than those our forefathers have known since the time of Arthur. Nor am I alone in this conceit, for the cages of lion, bear, camel had but few spectators, whilst round those of the American beasts I did find myself compelled to use hands and elbows to make shift to pass through the crowds.

This last not altogether unpleasant, as I chanced to brush against a handsome lass, but when I did enquire if she would take tea with me she said me nay, which did irk me no little, for as I say she was fair to see.

More time for the animals, then, and wondrous strange ever they strike me. The spear-fanged cat is surely the most horridest murderer this shuddering world hath seen, yet there is for him prey worthy of his mettle, what with beavers near big as our bears, wild oxen whose horns are to those of our familiar kine as the spear-fanged cat's teeth to the lion's, and the great hairy elephants which do roam the forests.

Why such prodigies of nature manifest themselves on those distant shores does perplex me most exceedingly, as they are unlike any beasts even in the bestiaries, which as all men know are more flights of fancy than sober fact. Amongst them the sims appear no more than one piece of some great jigsaw, yet no pattern therein is to me apparent; would it were.

Also another new creature in the menagerie, which I had not seen before. At first I thought it a caged sim, but on inspection it did prove an ape, brought back by the Portuguese from Afric lands and styled there, the keeper made so good as to inform me, shimpanse. It flourishes not in England's clime, he did continue, being subject to sickness in the lungs from the cool and damp, but is so interesting as to be displayed whilst living, howsoever long that may prove.

The shimpanse a baser brute than even the sim. It goes on all fours, and its hinder feet more like unto monkeys' than men's, having thereon great toes that grip like thumbs. Also, where a sim's teeth, as I have observed from Will and Peg, are uncommon large, in shape they are like unto a man's, but the shimpanse hath tushes of some savagery, though of course paling alongside those of the spear-fanged cat.

Seeing the keeper a garrulous fellow, I enquired of him further anent this shimpanse. He owned he had himself thought it a sort of sim on its arrival, but sees now more distinguishing points than likenesses: gait and dentition, such as I have herein remarked upon, but also in its habits. From his experience, he has seen it to be ignorant of fire, repeatedly allowing to die a blaze though fuel close at hand. Nor has it the knack of shaping stones to its ends, though it will, he told me, cast them betimes against those who annoy it, once striking one such with force enough to render him some time senseless. Hearing the villain had essayed tormenting the creature with a stick, my sympathies lay all for the shimpanse, wherein its keeper concurred.

And so homewards, thinking on the shimpanse as I rode. Whereas in the lands wherewith men are most familiar it were easy distinguishing men from beasts, the strange places to which our vessels have but lately fetched themselves reveal a stairway ascending the chasm, and climbers on the stairs, some higher, some lower. A pretty image, but why it should be so there and not here does I confess escape me.

May 16. A savage row with Jane today, her having forgotten a change of clothes for my bed. Her defense that I had not so instructed her, the lying minx, for I did plainly make my wishes known the evening previous, which I recollect most distinctly. Yet she did deny it again and again, finally raising my temper to such a pitch that I cursed her right roundly, slapping her face and pulling her nose smartly.

Whereupon did the ungrateful trull lay down her service on the spot. She decamped in a fury of her own, crying that I treated the sims, those very sims which I had bought for to ease her labors, with more kindlier consideration than I had for her own self.

So now we are without a serving-maid, and her a dab hand in the kitchen, her swan pie especially being toothsome. Dined tonight at the Bell, and expect to tomorrow at the Swan on the Hoop, in Fish Street. For Elizabeth no artist over the hearth, nor am I myself. And as for the sims, I should sooner open my veins than indulge of their cuisine, the good Lord only knowing what manner of creatures they in their ignorance should add to a pot.

Now as my blood has somewhat cooled, I must admit a germ of truth in Jane's scolds. I do not beat Will and Peg as a man would servitors of more ordinary stripe. They, being but new come from the wilds, are not inured to't as are our servants, and might well turn on me their master. And being in part of brute kind, their strength does exceed mine, Will's most assuredly and that of Peg perhaps. And so, say I, better safe. No satisfaction to me for the sims on Shooter's Hill gallows, were I not there to see't.

May 20. Today to my lord Sandwich's for supper. This doubly pleasant, in enjoying his fine companionship and saving the cost of a meal, the house being still without maid. The food and drink in excellent style, as to suit my lord. The broiled lobsters very sweet, and the lamprey pie (which for its rarity I but seldom eat of) the best ever I had. Many other fine victuals as well (the tanzy in especial), and the wine all sugared.

Afterwards backgammon, at which I won £5 ere my luck turned. Ended 15s. in my lord's debt, which he did graciously excuse me afterwards, a generosity not looked for but which I did not refuse. Then to crambo, wherein by tagging *and rich* to *Sandwich* I was adjudged winner, the more so for playing on his earlier munificence.

Thereafter nigh a surfeit of good talk, as is custom at my lord's. He mentioning sims, I did relate my own dealings with Peg and Will, to which he listened with much interest. He thinks on buying some for his own household, and unaware I had done so.

Perhaps it was the wine let loose my tongue, for I broached somewhat my disjoint musings on the sims and their place in nature, on the strangeness of the American fauna and much else besides. Lord Sandwich did acquaintance me with a New World beast found in their southerly holdings by the Spaniards, of strange outlandish sort: big as an ox, or nearly, and all covered over with armor of bone like a man wearing chain. I should pay out a shilling or even more for to see't, were one conveyed to London.

Then coffee, and it not watered as so often at an inn, but full and strong. As I and Elizabeth making our departures, Lord Sandwich did bid me join him tomorrow night to hear speak a savant of the Royal Society. It bore, said he, on my prior ramblings, and would say no more, but looked uncommon sly. Even did it not, I should have leaped at the chance.

This written at one of the clock, for so the watchman just now cried out. Too wound up for bed, what with coffee and the morrow's prospect. Elizabeth aslumber, but the sims also awake, and at frolic meseems, from the noises up the stairway.

If they be of human kind, is their fornication *sans* clergy sinful? Another vexing question. By their existence, they do engender naught but disquietude. Nay, strike that. They may in sooth more sims engender, a pun good enough to sleep on, and so to bed.

May 21. All this evening worrying at my thoughts as a dog at a bone. My lord Sandwich knows not what commotion internal he did by his invitation, all kindly meant, set off in me. The speaker this night a spare man, dry as dust, of the very sort I learned so well to loathe when at Cambridge.

Dry as dust! Happy words, which did spring all unbidden from my pen. For of dust the fellow did discourse, if thereby is meant, as commonly, things long dead. He had some men bear in bones but lately found by Swanscombe at a grave-digging. And such bones they were, and teeth (or rather tusks), as to make it all I could do to hold me in my seat. For surely they once graced no less a beast than the hairy elephant whose prototype I saw in menagerie so short a while ago. The double-curving tusks admit of no error, for those of all elephants with which we are anciently familiar form but a single segment of arc.

When, his discourse concluded, he gave leave for questions, I made bold to ask to what he imputed the hairy elephant's being so long vanished from our shores yet thriving in the western lands. To this he confessed himself baffled, as am I, and admiring of his honesty as well.

Before the hairy elephant was known to live, such monstrous bones surely had been reckoned as from beasts perishing in the Flood whereof Scripture speaks. Yet how may that be so, them surviving across a sea wider than any Noah sailed?

Meseems the answer lieth within my grasp, but am balked from setting finger to't. The thwarting fair to drive me mad, worse even, I think, than with a lass who will snatch out a hatpin for to defend her charms against my importuning.

May 22. Grand oaks from tiny acorns grow! This morning came a great commotion from the kitchen. I rushing in found Will at struggle with a cur dog which had entered, the door being open on account of fine weather, to steal half a flitch of salt bacon. It dodging most nimbly round the sim, snatched up the gammon and fled out again, him pursuing but in vain.

Myself passing vexed, having intended to sup thereon. But Will all downcast on returning, so had not the heart further to punish him. Told him instead, him understanding I fear but little, it were well men not sims dwelt in England, else would wolves prowl the London streets still.

Stood stock still some time thereafter, hearing the greater import behind my jesting speech. Is not the answer to the riddle of the hairy elephant and other exotic beasts existing in the New World but being hereabouts long vanished their having there but sims to hunt them? The sims in their wild haunts wield club and sharpened stone, no more. They are ignorant even of the bow, which from time out of mind has equipt the hunter's armory.

Just as not two centuries past we Englishmen slew on this island the last wolf, so may we not imagine our most remotest grandsires serving likewise the hairy elephant, the spear-fanged cat? They being more cunning than sims and better accoutered, this should not have surpassed their powers. Such beasts would survive in America, then, not through virtue inherent of their own, but by reason of lesser danger to them in the sims than would from mankind come.

Put this budding thought at luncheon today to my lord Sandwich. Him back at me with Marvell to his coy mistress (the most annoyingest sort!), viz., had we but world enough and time, who could reckon the changes as might come to pass? And going on, laughing, to say next will be found dead sims at Swanscombe.

Though meant but as a pleasantry, quoth I, why not? Against true men they could not long have stood, but needs must have given way as round Plymouth and Virginia. Even without battle they must soon have failed, as being less able than mankind to provide for their wants.

There we let it lay, but as I think more on't, the notion admits of broader application. Is't not the same for trout as for men, or for lilacs? Those best suited living reproduce their kind, whilst the trout with twisted tail or bloom without sweet scent die all unmourned leaving no descendants. And each succeeding generation, being of the previous survivors constituted, will by such reasoning show some little difference from the one as went before.

Seeing no flaw in this logic, resolve tomorrow to do this from its tachygraphic state, bereft of course of maunderings and privacies, for prospectus to the Royal Society, and mightily wondering whatever they shall make of it.

May 23. Closeted all this day at the Admiralty. Yet did it depend on my diligence alone, I fear me the Fleet should drown. Still, a deal of business finished, as happens when one stays by it. Three quills worn quite out, and my hands all over ink. Also my fine camlet cloak with the gold buttons, which shall mightily vex my wife, poor wretch, unless it may be cleaned. I pray God to make it so, for I do mislike strife at home.

The burning work at last complete, homeward in the twilight. It being washing-day, dined on cold meat. I do confess, felt no small strange stir in my breast on seeing Will taking down the washing before the house. A vision it was, almost, of his kind roaming England long ago, till perishing from want of substance or vying therefore with men. And now they are through the agency of men returned here again, after some great interval of years. Would I knew how many.

The writing of my notions engrossing the whole of the day, had no occasion to air them to Lord Brouncker of the Society, as was my hope. Yet expound I must, or burst. Elizabeth, then, at dinner made audience for me, whether she would or no. My spate at last exhausted, asked for her thoughts on't.

She said only that Holy Writ sufficed on the matter for her, whereat I could but make a sour face. To bed in some anger, and in fear lest the Royal Society prove as close-minded, which God prevent. Did He not purpose man to reason on the world around him, He should have left him witless as the sim.

May 24. To Gresham College this morning, to call on Lord Brouncker. He examined with great care the papers I had done up, his face revealing nought. Felt myself at recitation once more before a professor, a condition whose lack these last years I have not missed. Feared also he might not be able to take in the writing, it being done in such haste some short-hand characters may have replaced the common ones.

Then to my delight he declared he reckoned it deserving of a hearing at the Society's weekly meeting next. Having said so much, he made to dismiss me, himself being much occupied with devising a means whereby to calculate the relation of a circle's circumference to its diameter. I wish him joy of't. I do resolve one day soon, however, to learn the multiplication table, which me-seems should be of value at the Admiralty. Repaired there from the college, to do the work I had set by yesterday.

May 26. Watch these days Will and Peg with new eyes. I note for instance them using between themselves our deaf-man's signs, as well as to me and my wife. As well they might, them conveying far more subtler meanings than the bestial howlings and gruntings that are theirs in nature. Thus though they may not devise any such, they own the wit to see its utility.

I wonder would the shimpanse likewise?

A girl came today asking after the vacant maidservant's post, a pretty bit with red hair, white teeth and fine strong haunches. Thought myself she would serve, but Elizabeth did send her away. Were her looks liker to Peg's, she had I think been hired on the spot. But a quarrel on it not worth the candle, the more so as I have seen fairer.

May 28. This writ near cockcrow, in hot haste, lest any detail of the evening escape my recollection. Myself being a late addition, spoke last, having settled the title "A Proposed Explication of the Survival of Certain Beasts in America and Their Disappearance Hereabouts" on the essay.

The prior speakers addressed one the organs internal of bees and other the appearance of Saturn in the optic glass, both topics which interest me but little. Then called to the podium by Lord Brouncker, all aquiver as a virgin bride. Much wished myself in the company of some old soakers over roast pigeons and dumplings and sack. But a brave front amends for much, and so plunged in straightaway.

Used the remains of the hairy elephant presented here a sennight past as example of a beast vanished from these shores yet across the sea much in evidence. Then on to the deficiencies of sims as hunters, when set beside even the most savagest of men.

Thus far well-received, and even when noting the struggle to live and leave progeny that does go on among each kind and between the several kinds. But the storm broke, as I feared it should and more, on my drawing out the implications therefrom: that of each generation only so many may flourish and breed; and that each succeeding generation, being descended of these survivors alone, differs from that which went before.

My worse and fearfullest nightmare then came true, for up rose shouts of blasphemy. Gave them back what I had told Elizabeth on the use of reason, adding in some heat I had expected such squallings of my wife who is a woman and ignorant, but better from men styling themselves natural philosophers. Did they aim to prove me wrong, let them so by the reason they do profess to cherish. This drew further catcalling but also approbation, which at length prevailed.

Got up then a pompous little manikin, who asked how I dared set myself against God's word insofar as how beasts came to be. On my denying this, he did commence reciting at me from Genesis. When he paused for to draw breath, I asked most mildly of him on which day the Lord did create the sims. Thereupon he stood discomfited, his foolish mouth hanging open, at which I was quite heartened.

Would the next inquisitor had been so easily downed! A Puritan he was, by his somber cloak and somberer bearing. His questions took the same tack as the previous, but not so stupidly. After first enquiring if I believed in God, whereat I truthfully told him aye, he asked did I think Scripture to be the word of God. Again said aye, by now getting and dreading the drift of his argument. And as I feared, he bade me next point him out some place where Scripture was mistaken, ere supplanting it with fancies of mine own.

I knew not how to make answer, and should have in the next moment fled. But up spake to my great surprise Lord Brouncker, reciting from Second Chronicles, the second verse of the fourth chapter, wherein is said of Solomon and his Temple, *Also he made the molten sea of ten cubits from brim to brim, round in compass, and the height thereof was five cubits, and a line of thirty cubits did compass it round about.*

This much perplexed the Puritan and me as well, though I essayed not to show it. Lord Brouncker then proceeded to his explication, to wit that the true compass of a ten-cubit round vessel was not thirty cubits, but above one and thirty, I misremember the exact figure he gave. Those of the Royal Society learned in mathematics did agree he had reason, and urged the Puritan make the experiment for his self with cup, cord and rule, which were enough for to demonstrate the truth.

I asked if he was answered. Like a gentleman he owned he was, and bowed, and sat, his face full of troubles. Felt with him no small sympathy, for once one error in Scripture is admitted, where shall it end?

The next query was of different sort, a man in periwig enquiring if I did reckon humankind to have arisen by the means I described. Had to reply I did. Our forefathers might be excused for thinking otherwise, them being so widely separate from all other creatures they knew.

But we moderns in our travels round the globe have found the shimpanse, which standeth nigh the flame of reasoned thought; and more important still the sim, in whom the flame does burn, but more feebly than in ourselves. These bridging the gap twixt man and beast meseems do show mankind to be in sooth a part of nature, whose engenderment in some past distant age is to be explained through natural law.

Someone rose to doubt the variation in each sort of living thing being sufficient eventually to permit the rise of new kinds. Pointed out to him the mastiffe, the terrier, and the bloodhound, all of the dog kind, but become distinct through man's choice of mates in each generation. Surely the same might occur in nature, said I. The fellow admitted it was conceivable, and sat.

Then up stood a certain Wilberforce, with whom I have some small acquaintance. He likes me not, nor I him. We know it on both sides, though for civility's sake feigning otherwise. Now he spoke with smirking air, as one sure of the mortal thrust. He did grant my willingness to have a sim as great-grandfather, said he, but was I so willing to claim one as great-grandmother? A deal of laughter rose, which was his purpose, and to make me out a fool.

Had I carried steel, I should have drawn on him. As was, rage sharpened my wit to serve for the smallsword I left at home. Told him it were no shame to have one's great-grandfather a sim, as that sim did use to best advantage the intellect he had. Better that, quoth I, than dissipating the mind on such digressive and misleading quibbles as he raised. If I be in error, then I am; let him shew it by logic and example, not as it were playing to the gallery.

Came clapping from all sides, to my delight and the round dejection of Wilberforce. On seeking further questions, found none. Took my own seat whilst the Fellows of the Society did congratulate me and cry up my essay louder, I thought, than either of the other two. Lord Brouncker acclaimed it as a unifying principle for the whole of the study of life, which made me as proud a man as any in the world, for all the world seemed to smile upon me.

And so to bed.

A subtle, beautifully wrought fantasy, which seems at first to be concerned mainly with offering a Bradburyian nostalgia for a simpler time—until it slides imperceptibly into ever-intensifying horror. Richard Kearns, who teaches at Loyola Marymount University in Southern California, has been a writer of fiction, poetry, and advertisements, a critic, an aerobics instructor, a photographer, and half a dozen other highly miscellaneous things. He's working on a novel now.

GRAVE ANGELS

Richard Kearns

I first met Mr. Beauchamps when he dug Aunt Fannie's grave, the day before she died. I can remember it very clearly.

School was over, the heat of summer had finally settled in, withering the last of spring's magnolia blossoms, and I had just turned ten. Bobby, my older brother, and his friends had gone to the swimming hole down by the Dalton place, but I hadn't gone with them—not because I didn't want to. The last time I'd gone, they'd stolen my clothes. I figured it'd be at least another week before it'd be safe to go with them.

So I'd gone to the Evans Cemetery instead.

There were two cemeteries inside the Evans city limits—one for whites and one for blacks. It's still that way, as a matter of fact. But the white cemetery—the Evans Cemetery proper—had sixteen of the biggest oak trees in all of Long County, growing close enough together so you could move from one tree to the next without having to get down again. I liked to go there, especially on

277

hot days, and climb the trees, read, watch the motorcars hurry in and out of Evans like big black bugs. There was always a breeze in the oaks, and I was sure it never touched the earth.

I used to sit in those branches for hours at a time, like a meadowlark or a squirrel, listening to that breeze. Underneath me, I could feel the trees bend and sway, creaking and rattling and bumping into one another, as if they were all alive and talking among themselves, elbowing each other and laughing sometimes.

I remember it was a Saturday, and I remember I'd brought *Robinson Crusoe* with me to read. I'd read it before, but it was a story I enjoyed—I liked pretending that I was entirely alone, free to do whatever I wanted.

I had just gotten comfortable on my branch when I heard someone humming down underneath me, and the sound of wood being tossed into a pile on the ground. Quietly, I closed my book and turned around to spy.

There was an old black man standing with his back to me, maybe thirty feet away from the tree I was in. He was dressed in blue and white striped overalls and a white long-sleeved shirt. On his head was an engineer's cap like the men wore down in the railway yard—It had blue and white stripes in it too. Next to him was a wheelbarrow—old, rust- and dirt-encrusted, its contents spilled on the ground: several two-by-fours of different lengths, painted white; a big tan canvas, all folded up; and digging tools.

He took his cap off, mopped his head with a big red bandanna handkerchief—he was partly bald—put the hat back on, stuffed the handkerchief in his pocket, and studied the graves for a moment, fists on his hips.

Then he sighed, shook his head, and, mumbling and grunting, squatted and scooped up the pieces of lumber in his arms. Their ends flailed the air every which way as he stood again.

He made his way over by Great-Great-Grandpa Evans's grave— the one with the angel sculpted in red granite—where, after deciding on a spot, he spent a couple of minutes meticulously arranging the two-by-fours so they formed a perfect white rectangle against the green grass. He then retrieved the canvas, spread it next to the area he'd staked out, rolled up his sleeves, took out a shovel, and started digging up the sod.

I was fascinated. He worked all morning without a stop, carefully placing shovelfuls of the caramel brown earth on top of the canvas, making sure that as he dug, the sides of the hole were straight, swinging the pick-ax in big arcs over his head, or chiseling at the sides with it in tiny hammerlike strokes, slow and steady. He hummed to himself, sang songs I'd never heard before, grunted a lot, talked to himself whenever he thought there was a problem keeping the sides straight up and down, chuckling more and more as he got deeper.

He stopped when the sun was overhead and he had dug up to his thighs. I could tell he was hot.

He crawled out, put the pickax and shovel in the wheelbarrow, and then spent a couple of minutes inspecting his work. After that, he walked straight toward the oaks, pulling the wheelbarrow behind him.

I had been pleased with my spying. I had hardly moved all morning, even when I got bored watching him, and watched the cars on Route 85 instead, or the lazy crows circle overhead. I hadn't made a sound.

But he walked right to the tree I was hiding in, parked the wheelbarrow, looked up through the leaves like he knew I was there the whole time, cupped his hands over his mouth, and called out: "Timothy Evans, you come down from there right now!"

I was so scared I dropped *Robinson Crusoe*. I watched it fall, sickeningly, right into his wheelbarrow. It took a long time to get there.

I didn't move, hoping he'd go away. He didn't.

"Timothy!"

"What makes you think Timothy Evans is up here?" I yelled back, trying to disguise my voice.

"Well, now, I know who's up there and who ain't, so you get your rear down here, Timothy Evans. No games!"

I slithered down a couple of levels, where we could see each other better, and changed tactics. "Why?"

"It's lunchtime."

"I have mine," I countered, showing him my brown bag.

"Mine's better," he said, pulling a tan wicker basket out from under his wheelbarrow. "Besides, I do believe I'll go home with your book if you don't come and get it."

"How'd you do that?"

"Do what?"

"Where'd the basket come from?"

He smiled. It was a pleasant smile, and I felt I liked him right away. He set the basket on the grass, took his hat off, and mopped his forehead with his sleeve. "If you don't come down, you'll never find out—will you?" With that, he bent over, produced a big red and white checkered tablecloth from the basket, spread it out in the shade under the next tree, sat down, and began to unpack the food.

I could smell the chicken from where I sat. He had potato salad, iced lemonade, and baking powder biscuits with butter and honey. "Promise you won't hurt me if I come down?"

"I ain't promising anything," he said, eating a drumstick, " 'cept I'm going to eat all of this if you don't come down here and help me with it."

My stomach growled. Mama had made a peanut butter sandwich for me, with a couple of oranges for snacks. Fried chicken was a lot better. He looked old; I figured I could outrun him if I had to.

I came down in as expert and dignified a manner as possible, not slipping even once. From the bottom branch I dropped my lunch off to the side, swung by my hands briefly, and made a perfect landing by the wheelbarrow. Squatting next to it, I examined its underside, hoping to find the hook or shelf where the picnic basket had been hidden. There was nothing but pieces of rust caught in old cobwebs.

"Lunch is over here, boy," he yelled at me. I peered back at him over the top of the wheelbarrow. "You're not going to find anything to eat by looking over there." He laughed and went back to work on his drumstick.

I wiped my hands on my jeans, picked up my sack lunch, and retrieved *Robinson Crusoe* before I walked over to the tablecloth. I stood, book tucked under my arm, and watched him eat for a couple of seconds. "What's your name?" I asked.

He pulled a white paper napkin out of the basket, wiped his lips, chin, and fingers with it, and then looked up at me. "I am Mr. Beauchamps," he said, pronouncing it *bow-shomps*, like a foreigner, "and I am very pleased to meet you, Timothy." He took my hand and shook it, as if he were one of Papa's business partners.

His hand was huge around mine, and felt warm and dry and crusty with calluses.

"Have a seat," he told me, nodding, while he lifted the hinged basket lid and fished around briefly. "You can't eat standing up." He produced a second blue and white china plate, dumped a second drumstick and three biscuits on it, and slid it over to me.

The chicken was good. So was the lemonade. I broke open one of the biscuits, which was hot, smeared butter all over it with a plastic knife, and dribbled honey on top of that. "How come you call yourself mister?" I asked. "None of the colored men I know call themselves mister. Only whites."

He leaned toward me on one elbow and plopped a pile of potato salad on my plate. "Three reasons," he said, sticking a plastic spoon in the mound and then sitting up. "First, 'cause I am eighty-three years old, and there are only two people in the whole city of Evans that are older than I am. Second, 'cause no one knows my first name, and I'm not telling what it is, so there's nothing I can be called called *but* Mr. Beauchamps. Third," he said, leaning forward again, " 'cause I am the gravedigger here. I buried 657 people in my time—white and colored, rich and poor, all of them the same. Ain't no boy does anybody's gravedigging."

"Oh."

He smiled and took a final bite out of his drumstick. "You weren't expected to know that, of course."

"Mr. Beauchamps." I smiled back at him. He was as remarkable up close as he was from a distance. His skin was the blackest I'd ever seen, like baker's chocolate or chicory coffee. His face was leathery and full of wrinkles, and his hands looked like they might have been tree roots. He had white hair, white eyebrows, even one or two white whiskers that curled out on his face from where he had missed them shaving, I guess. They were easy to see because his skin was so dark.

I think the thing I remember most about him was his smile. His teeth weren't yellow, like most black folk I knew. They were bright white, and when he smiled, his whole face lit up, and all his wrinkles would mesh together and smile too.

"Isn't it kind of scary being a gravedigger?"

"Nope." He looked all around him. "Don't know what could

make a day like today scary. The sun's out, shining bright; the grass is green, just like always; and if you're quiet enough, you can hear the birds singing away, two counties over. No boss to stand around and give me a hard time, lots of long lunches—if you take my meaning—my own shovel and pick and wheelbarrow, and new kinds of flowers blooming practically every time I come out here. Can't think of any place I'd rather work.''

"But all those dead people—''

"Nonsense, Timothy. We're all going to be dead one day. I'm going to die, you're going to die, your mama and papa are going to die. It's part of life, part of living. The Lord says we can't enter the Kingdom of Heaven 'less we're born again. That's what dying is—being born again in God's Kingdom. We just can't see it so clear from this side.''

I looked past him, back to where he'd been working. The old stone angel was standing guard over the spot. "Whose grave you digging now?''

"I ain't saying.''

"How come?''

"I just ain't. 'Sides,'' he said, leaning back and stretching out on the grass, "it's your turn to do the talking now.''

"My turn?''

"Sure. Read to me from your book.''

So I read to him. I read the part where Robinson Crusoe found Friday—first in a dream, and then when he saved him from being eaten by other cannibals. Friday was the first human companion Robinson Crusoe had after living on the island by himself for years.

. . . never was a more faithful, loving, sincere servant than Friday was to me; without passions, sullenness, or designs; his very affections were tied to me, like those of a child to its father, and, I dare say, he would have sacrificed his life for my own, upon any occasion whatever.

I was greatly delighted with him, and made it my business to teach him everything that was proper and useful, and especially to make him speak, and understand me when I spoke. And he was a very apt scholar, and he was so merry, so diligent, and so pleased when he could understand me, or make me understand him, that it was very pleasant for me to talk to him. And now my life began to be very easy and happy.

Mr. Beauchamps chuckled when I finished reading, scratched his cheek, and said, "Now ain't that something."

"I like it. It's a good book."

"You would think Mr. Crusoe wanted a friend, after being lonely all the time."

"I think it would be fun to be alone like that."

"I see." He sat up and pawed through the picnic basket once again, but couldn't find anything for dessert, so each of us had an orange from my lunch. They were extra juicy, and we had a contest to see which one of us could spit the pits farther. Mr. Beauchamps won.

"Well," he said, sitting up and patting his stomach, "time for me to get back to work. Seeing as I found you, though, you're going to have to work with me, just like I was Mr. Crusoe."

"You found me!"

" 'Course I did. Spying on me from the trees, just like some kind of savage. I could call you Saturday."

"I'm not a savage! My name is Timothy—"

"*All* children are savages! You take my word for it. That's what growing up consists of—civilizing you. You can be Saturday Evans."

"No!"

He chuckled again. "Very well," he said, hooking his thumbs in his suspenders, "I'll be more civilized than Mr. Crusoe was and let you keep your own name. Just so long as you keep me company, if you catch my drift."

"I don't mind that," I said, getting to my feet. "Do I get to watch you dig up close?"

"Of course you do. But we have to clean up here first."

Everything got packed, including my peanut butter sandwich. Then Mr. Beauchamps made the basket disappear by hiding it behind his back. He laughed when I asked him where it went, and told me he didn't know himself, but it hardly mattered until he was hungry again.

I watched him dig the rest of the grave that afternoon. I sat with

my feet dangling in it sometimes, or lay on my stomach near the
edge of it. The earth smelled rich and damp and somehow clean.

He talked about gravedigging, how it was a craft, how you had
to know the earth, whether it was going to be wet enough to stay
packed, or if it was going to be mud four feet down, or sand, or
tree roots. He said early summer was the best time to dig, and told
me how hard it was to dig graves in winter, or in the middle of a
storm. But he said he couldn't stop digging graves just on account
of the weather.

We sang together, sometimes songs I knew, sometimes songs he
taught me. The breeze would brush by us every once in a while,
and when we weren't talking or singing, I would just listen to the
quiet, or to the sound of Mr. Beauchamps's shovel slicing through
the earth.

It was late in the afternoon. Just as Great-Great-Grandpa Evans's
angel started to touch the feet of the oaks with her shadow, we
finished. The grave was deep—deeper than Mr. Beauchamps was
tall.

He handed me the shovel, leaned the pickax in one corner of the
grave, and climbed up on on it like a stepladder. He hauled himself
out from there. Then he took the shovel back, neatly hooked the
head of the pickax with the back of the shovel's metal blade, and
pulled it up.

"I have to go home now, sir."

He tipped his hat and bowed slightly. "Have a good evening,
then, Saturday."

"That's Timothy."

"Timothy."

"You have a good evening, too, Mr. Beauchamps."

When I got home, I found my empty lunch bag folded up and
stuck between the pages of *Robinson Crusoe*. I was sure I had put it
in the picnic basket when we were cleaning up.

Aunt Fannie died Sunday afternoon.

At least that's when we found her. When we left for church that
morning, she was alive.

Aunt Fannie lived with us in one of the upstairs bedrooms, and
Mama looked after her, day and night. She was too sick to take
care of herself, and had been that way for years.

I was helping Mama carry the dinner tray upstairs. Aunt Fannie always ate before the rest of us did on Sunday, and if I helped, Mama usually let her give me a cookie or a piece of cake from the tray.

I noticed something different right away when we walked into the room, but Mama didn't. She went straight to the windows and opened them, just like she always did, and the wind billowed the white lace curtains like sails.

Aunt Fannie was all propped up on her pillows, and tucked in with a white quilt that had pink roses embroidered on it in every square. Her face was powdered—she always did that; she said she could go through the whole week just plain, but the least she could do was look pretty on the Lord's day—and there was just a little touch of pink on her cheeks.

She held a Bible in one hand loosely. The wind came in the room and lifted the filmy wisp of gray hair that had fallen on her cheek, pushing it back on her head and making it tremble, just for a moment.

She looked like she was asleep. I knew she wasn't. I knew because I couldn't hear her breathing.

Mama tried to wake her up several times. I didn't say anything. Then she told me to get Papa.

We buried her Tuesday morning, in the grave I had watched Mr. Beauchamps dig. The site was littered with wreaths and sprays of bright-petaled flowers, with weeping, long-faced adults dressed in black, most of them carrying Bibles; and with frightened children— Bobby and his friends included—who either clung to their parents singly, or stood together in groups of three or four, trying to understand what had happened.

I knew they were all seeing an illusion I couldn't see. The flowers, somber clothes, the prayers couldn't hide the clumps of uncut grass, the color and smell of the earth in the grave, the impressions left on the gravesides from the pickax or shovel, the black stone Mr. Beauchamps had tossed up on the canvas after digging around it and cursing for half an hour, the way the wind danced through the oak trees, inviting me to climb them. Or the way Aunt Fannie smiled when she died.

But more than all these things, I wondered how Mr. Beauchamps had known to dig her grave. I tried to spot him all the way through the funeral, even up to the point where it was my turn to throw a handful of dirt on Aunt Fannie's casket. He was nowhere to be seen. The granite angel was the only witness of the weekend's events; she stood silent, reigning over the proceedings, her eyes fixed on a point off on the horizon.

I stopped at the Evans Cemetery every day for two weeks after that, but I still couldn't find him. Where could he be, I wondered. How did he know?

I knew he had to have been there while I was gone: when I went to look for him Wednesday, after the funeral, the flowers were gone, and the canvas; the grave was filled up and the sod put back in place. There was a brand spanking new granite headstone to mark her grave, half as tall as I was. The front of it was polished shiny, and I could see my own faint image in it.

Mama had green eyes, and when she would watch me, I was sure she could see what I was thinking. I wasn't afraid of being watched, exactly—sometimes she would keep at it for weeks at a time, though it never would bring enough trouble to warrant Papa spanking me—but when she got that look and I knew she was watching, I knew I had to be good, or at least be careful.

And she watched me after the funeral.

Now, Mama would never say much to me while she was watching. Nothing out of the ordinary, that is; she would still say things like, "Timothy, sit up straight," or, "Timothy, pick your things up when you're through with them." Sometimes I would get a clue why she was watching me from what she didn't say.

But I never knew all the reasons for all the times she would watch. There would be times, after a bout of watching, when she would make up her mind about what she was thinking, and then tell me about it. But just as often, she would stop as quietly as she started, and never say what I did to bring it on, or why she stopped, or what she saw.

After Aunt Fannie's funeral was one of the times she decided to talk. I was in the kitchen at breakfast one morning, when Papa had left for the store but before Bobby was gone.

I knew something was up when I saw her making only one sack lunch instead of two for Bobby and me. I felt all queasy inside when she came over and put it on the table next to Bobby; I hunched over my cereal and pretended I hadn't seen, and that nothing out of the ordinary was happening.

"Timothy," she said, and I had to look up at her, "stay put for a while after you finish. I want to talk to you." She smiled at me—a quick, toothless twitch almost, which was supposed to let me know that everything was all right—but it didn't help.

"Yes, ma'am."

She walked back to the counter and began cleaning up, washing the knives, screwing the top on the peanut butter jar, packing up the bread, brushing the crumbs toward the sink. Her window was open, and from where I sat I could see the tops of the sweet peas in her garden out back; but no wind came blowing in the kitchen to flap the yellow checkered curtains, or stir the leaves on the two tiny plants she had growing in the pots on the sill.

Bobby stared at me over his cereal bowl, the spoon briefly frozen in his mouth—he had black curly hair and freckles, and people said he looked just like Papa when Papa was small; I was blond, and Mama had light brown hair, straight as rain when she didn't have it pinned up, so I guess I must have looked like her by default, though people didn't say that—and he applied himself to finishing quickly, not looking at me again until he stuck out his tongue at me as he grabbed his lunch and ran out back. The spring on the screen twanged as the door slammed shut behind him.

Mama came back to the table, took away our empty bowls and spoons, and washed them, untied and hung up her apron on its hook by the refrigerator, poured herself a cup of coffee, and then sat down in Bobby's chair.

"Timothy, you've been spending time down at the graveyard—haven't you?" She said it all casual-like, but her green eyes swung up at me, even though her head was tilted down at her coffee cup.

"Yes, ma'am."

Mama looked down again; carefully grasping her cup by its handle with her right hand, thumb on top, she slowly turned the saucer underneath with her left. "You know what your papa would do if he found out, don't you?"

"Yes, ma'am."

Her lips formed a thin, straight line across the bottom of her face, and she stopped turning the saucer. "Your Aunt Fannie loved *you* very much too.'' She glanced at me, almost like she was afraid I would say something, then took a deep breath and went on. ''You know, you were such a colicky baby, and so fussy, your Aunt Fannie was over here quite a bit after you were born. She said she felt like it was her duty, her being your godmother and all.''

Mama was silent for a moment. She hesitated briefly, then lifted the cup to her lips and sipped, setting it back with slow, graceful determination, still not looking at me. ''Your papa was having hard times at the store, so we couldn't afford hired help like we could with Bobby. Least, that's what he said; I could never tell the difference between the hard times and the good times there, just by going in and looking. I don't suppose that made it any less true, though.''

She looked at me now, and smiled her twitchy smile. ''There are times I used to wonder if there wasn't anything more to raising babies than feeding you, and washing your dirty diapers, and cleaning you up. And I used to wonder if you were ever going to be anything but hungry, or in pain, or just crabby. That's why your Aunt Fannie was such a godsend.'' Mama leaned back in her chair. ''You used to fuss so, and cry and cry and cry, and there was nothing anybody could do for you until Fannie came over. She knew lots of ways to quiet you, her raising a family that had been and gone already; but your favorite was her music box. She'd bring that little thing with her, and open it up and you'd be just all smiles and wonder. Not that it worked when anybody else played it, mind you. We tried that.'' Mama chuckled. ''You were just too smart for that, I guess.''

She sat forward and drank her coffee again. ''But you got better, and I got better, and business got better for your Papa, and Fannie got worse. That's the truth of it.'' Mama started to turn the saucer around again, sighed, and stopped, still holding it, though. ''They read your Aunt Fannie's will last week,'' she said, staring at her hands. ''She left money for you and Bobby to go to college, when the time comes. Not that we couldn't have sent you, of course; it'll just be easier now. We should be grateful for that.''

''Yes, ma'am,'' I said, my voice a whisper.

That startled Mama; I don't think she expected me to say anything. She studied me for a second, and then got up and went to her apron, digging her hand in its pocket as she brought it back to the table with her. "She willed me her gold locket," she said, pulling it out and putting it on the table in front of me. It spun when Mama put it down; I could see the delicate rose engraved on the front as it slowed. "Go ahead and open it," Mama said over her shoulder as she hung the apron up again. "Your papa said I could go down to the store and pick a chain for it later in the week."

There were pictures of me and Bobby and Papa on the inside. "It's pretty," I said.

"Yes, it is, isn't it?" Mama answered, sitting down again, this time putting a small wooden box in front of me, and setting three fat brass rollers on end next to it. The box was made of dark walnut, with nicks and dents worn smooth by age and polish; across the lid were inlaid two black stripes with red diamonds. Mama opened it, and delicious music came pouring out. I recognized Brahms's *Lullaby* right away. "Fannie left this for you," Mama said. "Your papa didn't think you should have it until you were older; he said you might break it. You'll be careful, won't you?"

"Yes, ma'am."

"Take it then, and keep it safe," she said. She showed me how to change the brass rollers so I could play four different songs. Their names were engraved on their insides: Beethoven's *Für Elise,* Bach's *Sarabande,* Mozart's *Minute Waltz,* and the lullaby by Brahms. We both listened to the Bach piece play all the way through, the somber minor chords twinkling so you could hear all the notes in a row.

Then it was over.

"Timothy," Mama said as I went upstairs to put the music box away, "I want you to keep away from Evans Cemetery for a while."

I leaned over the banister and looked at her, her figure a dim, hazy silhouette framed against the sunlit kitchen doorway. "Yes, ma'am."

"Just for a while," she said. "You can go back and visit your Aunt Fannie after the summer is over. It's just that there will be other people going to visit her now, and I'd rather they didn't find you there."

"Yes, ma'am."

She smiled. "Maybe you and I can go together and take flowers to her grave sometime. Would you like that?"

"Yes, ma'am."

We never went.

I gave up waiting for Mr. Beauchamps. But I still wasn't getting along too well with Bobby and the rest of the gang, so instead of hanging out at the cemetery, I would spend time over at the old Robinson house. I was safe there; the rest of the kids thought it was haunted.

It sat off by itself, on a hill along the road to Mariana Marsh, and there was a big dead gray tree in front of it with all the bark stripped off. None of the windows had any glass. Someone had tried to board them up a long time ago. But they had since been opened by brave adventurers like myself.

It might have been painted white or yellow once. Most of the paint had peeled or worn off over the years, and the wood underneath was the same color as the tree in front—gray. There were still patches of nondescript color that clung tenaciously to the outside, in a futile attempt to defy the elements. The roof over the front porch sagged, and would probably fall off soon. The outside steps were gone.

My favorite spot was up on the second floor, by the bay windows that faced south, toward town and Robinson's Woods. I made it my room. On clear mornings I could see Mama hanging laundry out behind our house, or watch the cars drive into town and park in front of Papa's store.

Every time I was there, I would clean up the new collection of dead branches and litter that had blown in through the open windows. I fixed up an old rocking chair I found in the basement of the house, replacing the tattered upholstery with a burlap bag that said "50 Lbs Net, Parkinson's Cabbage, Produce of U.S.A." I hid Aunt Fannie's music box in the window seat, and I could sit and rock and listen to it play while I looked out at town or over the woods. Or I could just read.

It was Mr. Beauchamps who found me, two months after the funeral, and it was in the Robinson house. There was a light rain outside, and I was in my rocker, listening to the music box play Mozart's waltz, thinking about having to go back to school again in a month and a half. The song ended, and I reached for the music box to start it over again.

"That was real pretty, Timothy."

I turned around and looked, real quick, but I already knew it was him from the voice. He had his own rocker, put together out of a dozen pieces of twisted cane, painted red. He smiled at me, rocking back and forth.

I wasn't going to let him know he scared me. "Hello, Mr. Beauchamps."

"Where did you get that music box?"

"From Aunt Fannie. She willed it to me."

"I see." He stopped rocking, and dug his hands into one of his overall pockets. "Here. Try this."

He tossed something at me, which I caught, examined long enough to realize it was identical to the other brass cylinders that had come with the box, and then fitted it into the machine. It was labeled Chopin's *Nocturne*. I turned the key as far as it would go, and then started it playing.

I could hear Mr. Beauchamps humming softly with the melody. "How did you know Aunt Fannie was going to die?" I asked without looking at him.

He stopped humming. "We're all going to die," he said huskily. "I told you that before."

"But how did you know when?"

He sighed wearily. "I just knew I had to dig the grave—that's all there was to it."

I turned around and looked at him. "Do you know when everybody's going to die?"

He chuckled and relaxed, and his rocking chair started to squeak in time with the music. "Not everybody," he said, after listening for several beats. "Strictly speaking, I'm just limited to the people in Evans. They managed to die without anybody knowing before I came, and will probably continue to do so after I'm gone."

"But how did you know to dig their graves?"

"I just knew." He chuckled again. "Take tomorrow, for instance."

"Somebody's going to die tomorrow?"

"Now, I didn't say that. I'm just saying I got a grave to dig over in the Quarters Cemetery. I want you to meet me there and help."

"So somebody's going to die over in Quarters! Who's it going to be?"

"I ain't saying."

"It's old Mammy Walker, isn't it? She's been sick for months."

"Nope."

"Sam DeLuth?"

"Nope."

"Will Atkins?"

"Nope."

I thought for a moment. "Jackson Hardich?"

Mr. Beauchamps looked startled for second, long enough to stop his chair. "I told you—I ain't saying." He fell back to rocking.

"It *is* Jackson—isn't it?" Everybody in Evans knew that Jackson Hardich was going to take on more trouble than he could handle one day. He was always picking fights out in the Quarters after dark, and there were several times recently when Sheriff Tucker had to be called to settle things down.

"Maybe yes and maybe no," Mr. Beauchamps said. "Whoever it is, it don't change the fact that there's a grave that's got to be dug." He leaned forward and squinted at me. "You going to be there tomorrow?"

I looked outside at the rain and then back at Mr. Beauchamps. "I can't come if it's going to be raining."

"Oh, then there's no problem. Tomorrow will be a fine day."

"If it is, I'll be there."

"Good."

There was a hot white flash and a thunderclap that made my chest rumble from being so close, and when my ears stopped ringing, I turned to ask Mr. Beauchamps more about Jackson Hardich, but he was gone, along with his rocking chair. I remember smiling to myself, rocking back and forth vigorously, watching the rain come down harder, listening to the music. It had been fairly easy to trick Mr. Beauchamps into revealing who the grave was for. Now that I knew who the dead man was, I could go see him before he died.

It took all day to dig the grave, the same as before. And it was a Saturday, the same as before. But the Quarters Cemetery wasn't as nice as the Evans Cemetery. The grave markers were smaller, most of them made out of wood, many of them cracked and gray and slowly falling over. There were fewer flowers, fewer trees, and the work was harder. I had to help Mr. Beauchamps pull up half a dozen huge stones before we were through; my hands were rubbed raw in spots from it.

It wasn't a bad day, though. We had our lunch together and fed biscuit crumbs to a family of meadowlarks who sang for us later. As a surprise, Mr. Beauchamps brought harmonicas for both of us; once I got through his "brief demonstration of the proper technique for the mouth organ," I was even able to keep up with him on a couple of the songs we had only sung last time. He said I was a quick learner, and taught me to play Chopin's *Nocturne,* just like my music box, though nowhere near as fancy, and with none of the right harmonies.

When we finished the digging, Mr. Beauchamps stood in the cool afternoon shadows that spilled into the bottom of the grave. He smiled. "This is good work, Timothy," he said. "Good, honest work. You should be proud of it." He grunted as he climbed out on his pickax, laboriously settling himself into a sitting position with his feet still dangling in Jackson's grave. "You go home now and eat a good dinner," he said. Then he leaned over and poked at me with his finger. "Take yourself a hot bath too. Hot, mind you." And he tapped his nose. "And you soak in it. We wouldn't want you to be stiff and sore like some old man before your time."

I left him while he was still laughing about that. But I didn't go home. Instead I headed for Potter's Drugstore, on the edge of the Quarters, to spy on Jackson Hardich.

He worked there for Mr. Potter most days, and on Saturdays he and his friends would meet there before taking off for the evening's festivities. Potter's was also the scene of the last two fights Jackson got into.

When I got there, Sheriff Tucker's squad car and an ambulance were there before me, pulled up crooked against the curb, their lights flashing, red and amber spots dancing up and down the outsides of the dingy frame houses huddled together on Sultana Street, the power lines off in the distance winking with an orange glow.

I hid by the gas station garage across the street, behind a pile of old tires. Potter's was closed, but there were lights on in the barbershop next door. A small crowd had begun to gather—mostly older black men, dressed in dark gray suits and hats, standing around the way people did at Aunt Fannie's funeral—when Sheriff Tucker came out of the alley behind Potter's and told everybody to get on home. Right behind him came two ambulance attendants carrying a litter with a white sheet-wrapped body on it. Whoever it was, it was plain to see he was dead. But I had to know who.

That was when I became aware I wasn't the only one hiding behind the garage.

I couldn't see his face. All I could tell was he was black, he was watching the attendants put the body into the ambulance, and there was a dark stain spreading high up on his left shirt sleeve, almost by his shoulder.

"You killed him—didn't you?"

"Who's that?" He whirled around, holding a knife in his right hand, his face all shiny with sweat. It was Ronnie Johnson. He couldn't see me.

"You killed Jackson Hardich."

"No!"

"You knifed him."

"No! It ain't true!"

"He made you fight him, and you stabbed him in the middle of it. I know it."

Ronnie began to move toward me, crouched. "You can't say that. You don't know nothing. Who's back there?"

"You're going to die for it too!"

Ronnie stood straight up. "No! He ain't dead!"

"He is!"

"You stop right where you are, boy!" It was Sheriff Tucker. He'd spotted Ronnie from across the street.

Ronnie took off down Sultana Street, running as fast as he could. The sheriff was right behind him.

They found him guilty. I knew that before anyone else did. Mr. Beauchamps dug Ronnie Johnson's grave while the jury was still deliberating.

As I got older, I got better at guessing whose grave we would be digging. And by the time I was in high school, I could get a sense of when Mr. Beauchamps was about to show up as well as who it was we'd have to go gravedigging for. He paid me for my help when I was in high school; he said I was doing my share of a man's work.

Bobby went off to Raleigh for college, and came back with a degree in business and a wife. Her name was Mary Sue Alders—Mary Sue Evans after she married Bobby. They got themselves a house in town, and Bobby started helping Papa with the business, supervising the clerks and keeping the inventory.

I was a loner all through high school, and the kids were happy to leave me to myself. I would watch the people in Evans, waiting; when I felt the time was right, I would go out to the old Robinson house and meet Mr. Beauchamps.

There came a time, though, when I was a senior, a month away from graduating, when he showed up at school to find me. I was out behind the gymnasium, skipping pebbles across the lagoon. He stepped out suddenly from behind one of the willow trees.

"Hello, Timothy."

I looked around to see if any of the other kids were in sight. "What are you doing here?"

He walked down to the shore, his big mud-crusted boots making the gravel crunch, stooped, picked up a stone, tossed it at the lagoon, and watched it skim the distance to the far shore. He looked pleased with himself. "Fancy that," he said, "and at my age too." He looked down at me where I was sitting. "I'll need your help tomorrow, Timothy."

I stood up, beat the dust out of my jeans, and then looked him square in the eye. "Who's it going to be this time?"

He chuckled. "You won't guess it. I can guarantee that."

"Well, then tell me the cemetery."

"Evans. Over by the oak trees."

"Evans. That means it's somebody white." I thought for a moment. "Couldn't be. Old Mrs. Forester is the sickest one of the lot, and even she's doing better, according to Doc Morrison."

"Ain't Mrs. Forester—you're right about that."

"All right. You just wait and see, I'll have it figured out by tomorrow morning when we start."

He took his engineer's hat off and held it over his heart, like the flag was passing by, and sticking out his jaw defiantly, said, "You won't neither, Timothy Evans. I know it."

I stayed awake past midnight, going through the phone book, trying to figure out who it could be. I made lists and tore them all up. I even called the two motels in town, to see if there were any elderly visitors I had somehow not heard about. In the end, I decided to give up graciously, and wait and see who was going to die, just like any other normal person.

The next morning, Mr. Beauchamps knew I hadn't figured it out, but he didn't say anything. He was more cheerful than usual, though.

It was a good gravedigging day: the sky was a clear, bright, cloudless blue; it was warm, but not so warm as to be uncomfortable; there was the tiniest of breezes that played with the grass tops as it came blowing across the cemetery to cool us off. Mr. Beauchamps let me do most of the work. He said if I had it in me, I ought to do it—like singing a song, building a house, or dancing.

I did the best job I could, but that didn't hurry the finish of it. Mr. Beauchamps inspected the entire grave very thoroughly when we were through. He was pleased with it, and paid me twenty dollars extra—my fair share, he said. So I headed home to start the vigil that would let me know who was going to die.

Mary Sue was waiting for me when I got in. She was the only one there. She sat down and told me that Mama and Papa had been in a serious automobile accident, and that Bobby was with them now over at the Long County Hospital. She said it didn't look good for either of them.

I went numb. I should have known, I told myself. I should have tried to stop them from going out. I should have warned them. I should have prevented it somehow.

I don't remember Mary Sue driving me to the hospital. I don't remember trying to find my parents in the emergency room, I don't remember Doc Morrison trying to calm me down. I don't remember being dragged away by the orderlies to the waiting room. Mary Sue told me about it later.

I do remember the waiting room. It was ugly. The furniture was white wrought iron with cushions, and you could see the shiny metal spots where other people had worn away the paint with worry, waiting.

Bobby and Mary Sue and I had cups of coffee from a machine all night, and we hardly said a word to one another. Bobby must have smoked four packs of cigarettes. Mary Sue sat next to him with her arm around him.

It wasn't fair—knowing that one of them was going to go for sure, and not knowing which. I didn't want to choose which one I'd rather have live, but I couldn't stop myself from choosing, over and over again. When morning came, we found out it was Mama that had survived, although she was paralyzed from the waist down. Papa had died in the operating room.

We buried him Monday morning. Bobby made me go to the funeral. I hadn't wanted to.

We buried a man I realized I never really knew—my father. As we lowered the casket into the grave I had dug, I wondered who he was, how he met my mama, whether he loved her right away when they met or whether it took time to get to know her, whether he was always good at business, whether he had ever sat up all night waiting for someone to die, whether he loved me.

I felt like a stranger to the whole world. I had spent years watching it, waiting for people to fall down like targets in a shooting gallery. And now, here I was, somehow back in it, and all the names and faces I had known were distant, mysterious and cold.

Mary Sue did her best to help. She and Bobby moved back into our house, and we put Mama up in Aunt Fannie's old room. Mary Sue and I took care of Mama—keeping her company more than anything else. We took her on walks. We went with her to the show. We sat with her in the garden, on the porch, in her room. I think she used to hate being crippled. Most of all, I think she missed Papa.

I dug up stacks of photographs Papa had taken and then hidden away in the attic, and Mama and I would spend evenings pasting them into newly bought albums.

Most of them were family picnics and Fourth of July gatherings, the lot of us scattered across the backyard, eating huge chunks of pink watermelon, lying on the grass or sitting in lawn chairs with various aunts and uncles and grandparents, before they all died.

I found a picture of myself in diapers, sitting on Grandma Larkins's lap, a blanket draped over my head while I drooled all over myself, white socks barely staying on my feet because they were too big to fit.

And there were pictures of Bobby and me. We had climbed trees together, peered around corners together, taken baths and swum in swimming pools together. There was one where we stood arm in arm, looking doubtfully at two live turkeys Papa had bought for Thanksgiving one year.

But the best pictures were of Mama. She was pretty, in a simple, open-air way. That was how Papa must have seen her. She didn't smile in most of the photographs, but rather appeared to be thoughtful, moody, elusive, quietly untame. One photograph Papa took of her I remember particularly: she was in the kitchen, and she must have just gotten up, because her hair was mussed and she was wearing her robe that had tiny white flowers embroidered in it near the top; she stood next to an old, scarred butcher-block table with a baby bottle on it, holding her hands together, and behind her I could see an old black telephone and a couple of cartons of empty cola bottles on the floor next to the refrigerator. But she looked so regal, so stately, like she owned the world. Her mouth curled in a little smile.

Mama would tell me stories about every single picture as we put it in an album. The only drawback to this was that Papa had always been the photographer and never the subject. I only heard about him. I never saw what he was like. I could see that it was painful for Mama to talk about him, now that he was gone.

I still dug graves for Mr. Beauchamps. But my purpose was different. I waited to know when we would start to dig Mama's grave.

We never talked about the accident, or Papa's death. He never brought the subject up, and neither did I. All we ever talked about was the proper digging of graves, and he remained just as cheerful as he had ever been.

Mama and I were together by ourselves one night. I think she arranged for it to be that way.

"Timothy," she said "you and I have to have a little talk."

"About what?"

"I think it's about time you should be getting to college."

I looked at her. She seemed a tiny woman now, and so old—even compared to the pictures Papa had taken just before their accident. "There's plenty of time for that," I said.

"There isn't!" she snapped, like she always did when she didn't want to hear any more about it. She regretted it right away, though. "I think it's wonderful," she said, "your staying here to take care of me and all, and it's meant a lot to me. I can't say it hasn't. But you're nearly a grown man, Timothy. You've got to start living your own life, finding out what it is that you want to do, and doing it. Why, it's not right for you to keep from putting yourself to good use. You've got intelligence. You've got talents. You've got money. With those three things, there's nothing you can't do."

"But—"

"I don't want to hear any buts!" She glared at me for a few seconds, and then looked down at her hands. "Oh, I thought so careful 'bout what I wanted to say, and it isn't coming out right." She started to cry. When I tried to comfort her, she waved me away, and pulled out one of those tiny rose-embroidered old-lady handkerchiefs and dabbed at her eyes with it.

She sniffed. "I'm sorry."

"That's all right, Mama."

She tried to smile at me, which prompted another, shorter crying spell, only this time she let me hold her hand. Neither one of us said anything for a couple of minutes. Then she pulled her hand away and started fidgeting with her handkerchief.

"I had a dream," she began, not looking at me. "And in that dream, there was an old colored man, dressed in a white tuxedo with a white top hat, who came to me. He said, 'Hello, Mrs. Evans, I've come to take you for a little walk.' I started to tell him I couldn't walk, when I found myself walking already, and since there wasn't much else to say, I didn't say anything.

"He seemed like such a nice man, and he brought me to the edge of a huge plowed field. 'I'll tell you a secret, Mrs. Evans,' he said. 'That isn't a field at all. It's angels' wings.' I wanted to tell him that was a bunch of nonsense, but I looked and saw feathers, growing up out of the ground.

"Oh, Timothy, they were so beautiful! They were all different colors, like they were made out of rainbows, and they grew huge right in front of me, without hardly any time passing at all. So I turned to the man and said, 'Mister, I do believe I'd like to go out there and lie down in those feathers.' And he smiled at me—such a nice smile—and said 'Why, of course you would. That's why we came here.'

"Then he helped me out into the field, and I found a spot I particularly liked, and sat down, and wrapped myself in feathers. They were soft and cozy. It was wonderful."

Mama took my hand and looked at me again. "When I turned around to thank the man, he wasn't there. Neither was anything else. The whole earth had kind of unfolded like, and I found myself riding on the wings of the biggest angel I ever imagined, tucked in just like a little baby, safe and sound and warm and secure. She smiled when she saw me looking at her."

Mama let go of my hand and started carefully folding her handkerchief. "That's all I remember."

"That was very pretty, Mama."

"No, it's not! Least, not in the way you're thinking. That dream meant something."

I swallowed because my mouth was dry, and asked her what.

She didn't answer me at first. She just sat there, folding and unfolding her handkerchief. The sound of crickets chirping came in through the open window. "I'm going to die, Son."

"No—"

"I am!" She waited for me to say something else, and when I didn't, she went on. "Maybe tomorrow, maybe years from now. But it's a fact. It's going to happen. And it's not your place to sit beside me while I'm going about it. That's all I'm saying."

"Maybe you're right."

"I'm right."

"Yes, ma'am."

We sat together and listened to the sounds the night was making. After an hour, a chill began to creep into the house, and I bade her good night and went to bed.

Mr. Beauchamps was waiting for me in his red rocker when I got to the Robinson house the next day. "Morning, Timothy," he said. "I'm going to need you tomorrow."

"I know." I pulled the music box out of its hiding place in the

window seat and let it play. Mr. Beauchamps started to play along
with it on his harmonica.

"It's Mama's grave—isn't it?"

"I never tell who I'm digging for," he said, picking up the
melody again when he finished talking.

I let the tune run out. "What if we don't dig it?"

"We have to dig it," he said.

"Well, what if we don't?"

He stopped rocking. "Timothy Evans, I swear to you, I won't
never pass up a grave that needs digging."

"Oh."

"You going to be there?"

I looked at him. "Yeah, I'll be there."

"I thought you would." He started rocking again, and played a
new song on his harmonica. The notes lingered in the air long after
he disappeared.

I met him in the morning, just like always. It was a cold day, and
the oaks waved their fire-colored autumn leaves at us, mocking. We
still had no problem working up a sweat as we dug, though.

Mr. Beauchamps was more given to humming than to conversation. He hardly said a word to me all day, or I to him. For lunch,
we sat huddled over his picnic basket like a couple of scavengers;
the wind was too brisk to lay out the tablecloth and take our time.

Still, even with a short meal, it was a long day of hard work that
sank into tones of gray as the afternoon wore on. The sky was
bleak, colorless and unrelieved. The dirt stuck to itself, almost like
clay, and it was hard to break up.

We finished. I climbed out first, and Mr. Beauchamps went on
his usual inspection tour. Then he walked over to the pickax, stood
on it, and started to pull himself out.

I swung the shovel for all I was worth. It sliced into his skull as
if it were slicing into a piece of clay, sounding much the same, and
then stuck there. I tugged on it—once, twice, and a third time
before it came loose, and Mr. Beauchamps tumbled back into the
grave. As he lay there, blood pooling around his head in a red
halo, he slowly smiled.

I shivered. The chill of the day penetrated me all at once, turning
my insides to ice, squeezing all the breath out of me, choking me. I

dropped to my knees, then to my hands, and let the shovel slip from my grasp into the open grave.

Slowly, quietly, tiny clods of dirt, on their own, began rolling down the graveside pile of earth. They trickled over the edge of the grave in twos and threes at first, sounding like summer hail as they hit bottom, or bounced off Mr. Beauchamps's body. They gathered numbers and strength and speed rapidly, forming a brown waterfall that covered him, and filled the air with growing thunder, until the heavens roared with it, and the ground shook with it, and I thought I would burst. I pressed my hands to my head and rocked back on my heels, dizzy.

Then there was quiet. Abruptly. I opened my eyes to see the pieces of sod slowly crawl off the canvas, like big green caterpillars, moving back to the spots where they belonged, settling in and weaving their edges together where we had cut them. A cold wind came up, whipping through the trees behind me and cutting through the wings of Great-Great-Grandpa Evans's stone angel, who stood a little ways off, aloof and praying.

I folded up the canvas, collected the two-by-fours, threw them into the wheelbarrow, hid them all in among the oak trees, and left.

Doc Morrison's car was parked outside our house when I got home, a silhouette in the gray shades of evening against our whitewashed front porch. I waited for him to come out and drive away before I went in.

I found Bobby and Mary Sue at the kitchen table, drinking coffee, Bobby's cigarette in the ashtray in front of him sending a long plume of smoke straight up until it curled away two feet over their heads. The fluorescent light made their faces pale, and Mary Sue looked like she'd been crying. They both stood up when I walked in, helplessly rooted in place for a moment. Then Mary Sue darted to the stove and poured me a cup of coffee.

"What happened?" I asked, cradling the coffee's warmth in my hands, trying to rid myself of the chill that had followed me inside. I left my jacket on.

Bobby realized he was staring at me; he sat down, reached for his cigarette with one hand, and rested his forehead in the other.

"Your mother had a stroke," Mary Sue said, sitting down again and putting her arm around Bobby's shoulder.

I wanted to shiver—out of hope, out of fear, hardly daring to give into one, lest the other should overcome me. Still holding the cup, I pulled a chair out with my foot and sat down, not bothering to scoot up to the table. "Is she going to be all right?"

Bobby took a final drag on his cigarette, sucked the smoke in deep, and then blew it out in a cloud of frustration. "She's paralyzed," he said. "Doc Morrison says by all rights she should have died."

Nobody spoke for a moment. We didn't look at each other either. "Then she's alive," I said, trying to hide my smile.

"She can't move," Bobby said. "She can't feed herself, she can't sit up, she can't move her arms or her hands, she can't talk. She's alive, all right, if you can call it that." He left the room. Mary Sue and I watched him go, watched the kitchen door swing slowly shut, listened to his footsteps pad down the hall and up the stairs to their bedroom. Mary Sue crushed out his still-burning cigarette.

"The doctor says it's still too early to tell the extent of the damage," she said. "Your mother could get better. She might recover the use of her arms, at least partially. He said she might learn to talk again. He wasn't sure her condition would be permanent. He'll call for a specialist Monday morning. We're supposed to bring her to the hospital then—"

"If she survives, you mean. He's waiting for her to die."

Mary Sue stared at the palms of her hands. "Yes," she said. "That seems to be just about the size of it." She looked up at me. "I'm sorry, Timothy. If you'd been here when the doctor came and heard what he'd said, maybe you'd think differently. As it is, just right now, she might as well stay home. There's nothing they can do for her at the hospital."

"Until Monday?"

"Until Monday."

"Well, she's not going to die," I said, the sweat trickling down under my arms, beading on my forehead.

"You don't know that, Timothy—"

"I do."

"But you can't—"

"I *know*," I said, staring her full in the face. Her eyes were brown, like Bobby's. It was something I had never noticed before.

"She won't die." I dropped my gaze and sipped at my coffee. The table seemed miles away.

Mary Sue sighed, sat back, and ran her fingers through her hair. "All right then. You know. More than me, more than your brother, more than the doctor. More than anybody. She won't die." She stood up, and her chair scraped across the floor the way Bobby's did. "I wish I wanted you to be right." With that she left.

I was so excited I could hardly contain myself. Mama was alive! She had made it! She would get better. We would bring her doctors, nurses, medicine—whatever she needed. It was only a matter of time before she got better. That was all. I drained my coffee cup and headed upstairs.

Mama's room was warm, and filled with a pale rosy glow from the nightlight—a frosted white hurricane lamp with pink flowers painted on it. Mama was asleep, so I contented myself with standing next to her bed, jacket draped over one shoulder, and watching her breathe. I had to stand still and observe carefully to do it. But the faint indications were there.

As I moved to leave and close the door behind me, I thought I noticed movement in the shadows on the far side of her bed. I froze. "No," I whispered at the darkness, "I won't do it." I flipped on the light switch, half expecting to see Mr. Beauchamps. But there was nothing. Only Mama's thin, wasted form, captured by the bedsheets and the quilt. Her eyes came open, staring at the ceiling first, then turning her head, slowly, searching for me, finding me. I turned out the light and knelt by her bed, my head close to hers.

"I will not dig your grave, Mama," I told her. "I won't do it."

But she stared at me, her green eyes pleading, unmoving. I took her limp hand in mine. "I won't. We don't know what can happen, Mama. We'll take you to the hospital Monday, and there'll be doctors, and special equipment, and medicine. We'll fix you, Mama. We'll make you better, and you'll talk and write and maybe even walk again. Who knows? But you're not going to die Mama— we've got that on our side."

There wasn't anything else I could say, or any way Mama could answer, so I tucked her in again, and went to bed. I dreamed about her green eyes staring, and about the cold all night.

In the morning I woke to find Mr. Beauchamps's pickax and

shovel in my room, propped against the wall next to my bed. They were wet with dew. I wiped them off with my bed sheets, so they wouldn't rust, and put them away in the garage.

Long County Hospital did what it could for Mama, reluctantly. For the two months she was there, I visited her during the days, sometimes with Bobby, sometimes with Mary Sue, most often by myself.

I would read to her—newspapers, poetry I knew she liked, Bible passages. We'd prop her up so she could see what I was reading, and follow along with me. She wouldn't, though. On good days, her green eyes would watch me wherever I went in the room; on bad days, she would just stare at nothing.

It was the same routine after we brought her home, once Doc Morrison and the hospital made it clear there was nothing that could be done for Mama, even if they had wanted to. We put her back in Aunt Fannie's room, hired a live-in nurse, bought a whirlpool bath, rented all sorts of fancy monitoring equipment—anything the experts asked for. Christmas came and went.

And the dance with Mr. Beauchamps's digging tools began to be an odd diversion, a game that wouldn't stop.

I was frightened of them at first, not sure if something worse was waiting to happen. No matter where I hid them, they would show up in my room mornings, always in the same spot, damp, but no dirt, no rust.

The novelty of it took over after the fear wore off. It was like having my own rabbit in a hat. I would hide them further and further away, or make it harder, to see if the trick would still work. I started in the garage at first; locked, chained, bolted, encased in cement out back. From there I went to the graveyards. And the Robinson house. The marsh. Long City, when I had the excuse to go.

I nearly got in trouble when I left them at the store—Bob Potter bought the pickax, and it vanished from his shed during the night. Bobby replaced it without saying anything, and I couldn't figure why. I couldn't ask, either. That was another game: discovery, hoping and fearing Mary Sue, Bobby, or Althea—Mama's nurse, Mammy Walker's girl who trained for medicine instead of midwifing, like Mammy—would find out. I tried to imagine what they would do if they knew.

Once the specialists started coming to our house to see Mama, after the first of the year, I let the pickax and shovel stay in my room on hooks. The playing got weary, tedious, losing its edge with each new prospect for Mama's recovery.

They all seemed cut from the same mold, the specialists—gray-suited, bald, bespectacled; embarrassed smiles on all their faces. They came to us from New York, Washington, Chicago, Los Angeles, more out of curiosity to see Mama like she was some kind of freak than because they thought she could be helped. They examined her, consulted, and we waited. She didn't get any better.

I kept reading to her anyway. I didn't feel like it was as much a matter of hope as it was a matter of time.

Bobby and Mary Sue adjusted rather quickly to Mama being home. They would help me with the reading, and Mary Sue and Althea worked as a team to take care of Mama—giving her baths, preparing her food, keeping records. Bobby took me with him to the store to teach me the business, which was fine as far as I was concerned; I was through with gravedigging, and willing to help out running things.

The situation lasted until February, when Bobby said he was tired of all the gloom and doom hanging over our heads, and he and Mary Sue started going out on the weekends. I stayed home with Mama.

Which was why Mary Sue asked me to help with a surprise birthday party for Bobby—she said she thought it would do us all some good to have regular people over at the house. I was hesitant at first, but she kept at it until I agreed to help.

My part in the plan was to take Bobby over to the county seat—to file some tax papers, ostensibly—and stall him while we were there. We weren't supposed to get home until eight o'clock. I called over to Jameson's Garage in Long City ahead of time and let them know what was going on, so when the car wouldn't start from the distributor cap being jimmied, they wouldn't give me away. They timed it just right, holding back from fixing the car until seven-thirty. None of them could tell me how the shovel and the pickax got in the back seat; they acted like it was somebody else's joke.

I raced home. After the first five minutes at eighty miles an hour, Bobby stopped asking me why. He just buckled the seat belts and wedged himself in the corner against the door and the seat, one arm over the top of the front seat, the other braced against the dash.

We first heard the sirens when we passed the Evans city limits. I screeched the car to a stop outside the circle of fire trucks, and it was plain to see the firemen were fighting a losing battle against the burning house. Our burning house.

Bobby tried to run inside, but that wasn't what held my attention. Rather, it was the bank of ambulances parked along the drive, one or two of them pulling away as we pulled up. There were burnt and charred bodies being loaded up and down the line, and moans filling the air above the roar of the fire and spitting of the hoses. I began opening the back doors of the ambulances nearest me, reeling in the sweet stench of cooked flesh that boiled out every time. They were all alive.

I found her in the fifth car. Mama had been burned beyond recognition, except for a single, lidless green eye that turned toward me.

I slammed the door shut, screaming, stumbling away. A pair of attendants carrying a squirming body on a litter ran past me. The world began to spin, and I could feel the heat from the fire reach for me, even as I heard the sound of the explosion.

I knew what I had to do. I grabbed the pickax and the shovel and ran for Evans Cemetery, as fast as I could, the moon lighting my way as I rushed across the open fields, trying to leave behind me the sounds of the fire, the smell of burning people.

I found the wheelbarrow where I left it, rolled it to the first spot, measured out a rectangle with my two-by-fours, and started digging. I wept until I couldn't see through my swollen eyelids, cursed and screamed until I was hoarse, swung the pickax at the defenseless earth with a vengeance until I was barely able to lift it, and the moon glared down at me like Mama's eye, lighting everything I did. When I finished the grave, I sat for a minute at the bottom, panting.

It was still night.

I picked up my boards and laid out the dimensions of the next grave. I went so much slower than the first, and now I began to regret killing Mr. Beauchamps, not out of guilt, but because I could have used his help.

The digging became painful; even in the moonlight I could see the bruises and cuts on my hands. My feet hurt. My back ached from the strain. I thought of Mr. Beauchamps digging graves even after he reached ninety, going slow and steady, and that gave me hope to go on.

I finally finished the second grave. I was barely able to crawl out. As I lay there, exhausted, I suddenly realized I had been listening to music.

It took me a minute to recognize the tune: Chopin's *Nocturne*, played on the silvery, tinkling tones of Aunt Fannie's music box.

And then I realized it was still night, and I was still looking at a scene illuminated by moonlight. I rolled over.

He was sitting on the shoulder of the old stone angel, dressed in a white tuxedo instead of his blue and white striped overalls, and his engineer's hat was replaced by a white silk top hat. "Hello, Timothy," he said. The music box sat in his lap, its lid open.

"Hello, Mr. Beauchamps," I croaked back.

"Save your strength," he said, pushing off from his perch and slowly floating to the ground. "You've got a lot of work ahead of you tonight."

"The moon—"

"Never you mind about the moon! I'm doing my part, and you do yours—there are lots of graves to dig before morning gets here. You can rest a little before you get started on the next one, though."

So I rested to Chopin. And dug to Mozart, Beethoven, and Brahms. Grave after grave, until the pain, the remorse, the revulsion drained away; and there was nothing left but the sound of the shovel, the shadows dancing with the moonlight that poured down from the sky, the crisp, brittle notes of the music box, and the gentle encouragement of Mr. Beauchamps. The sun came up as I finished digging the twenty-seventh grave.

There is no one left to get close to anymore. Except for Mr. Beauchamps. In addition to bringing me lunch when I'm working, he always comes by on special occasions—the anniversary of our meeting, my birthday, his birthday, the day I passed his gravedigging total of 743—and that was well over a decade ago.

I am ninety-six years old now, and have buried 915 people—my brother, my sister-in-law, my cousin, my nieces and nephews, the sheriff, the doctor, the black folk who lived down in the Quarters, the white folk who used to work for the Evans family business; people I never knew, or met, or even heard of. As I dug every one of their graves, I wondered who they all were, where they came from, and I was glad to give them their deaths, to help them step into the next Kingdom. But I am tired. I have been tired since the night I dug twenty-seven graves.

When there's a nice day and I don't have to go digging, I put flowers on Mama's grave, or on Mr. Beauchamps's. He was the first black man ever to be buried in Evans Cemetery, even if no one else knows about it.

And I keep hoping the next grave I dig will be my own.

Since the start of his remarkable career more than a decade ago, John Varley has been astonishing the science fiction world with the inventiveness, audacity, and velocity of his storytelling. This latest exploit in the equally remarkable career of Lunar policewoman Anna Louise Bach shows Varley at the top of his considerable form.

TANGO CHARLIE AND FOXTROT ROMEO

John Varley

The police probe was ten kilometers from Tango Charlie's Wheel when it made rendezvous with the unusual corpse. At this distance, the wheel was still an imposing presence, blinding white against the dark sky, turning in perpetual sunlight. The probe was often struck by its beauty, by the myriad ways the wheel caught the light in its thousand and one windows. It had been composing a thought-poem around that theme when the corpse first came to its attention.

There was a pretty irony about the probe. Less than a meter in diameter, it was equipped with sensitive radar, very good visible-light camera eyes, and a dim awareness. Its sentient qualities came from a walnut-sized lump of human brain tissue cultured in a lab. This was the cheapest and simplest way to endow a machine with certain human qualities that were often useful in spying devices. The part of the brain used was the part humans use to appreciate beautiful things. While the probe watched, it dreamed endless beautiful dreams. No one knew this but the probe's control, which was a computer that had not bothered to tell anyone about it. The computer did think it was rather sweet, though.

There were many instructions the probe had to follow. It did so religiously. It was never to approach the wheel more closely than five kilometers. All objects larger than one centimeter leaving the wheel were to be pursued, caught, and examined. Certain categories were to be reported to higher authorities. All others were to be vaporized by the probe's small battery of lasers. In thirty years of observation, only a dozen objects had needed reporting. All of them proved to be large structural components of the wheel which had broken away under the stress of rotation. Each had been destroyed by the probe's larger brother, on station five hundred kilometers away.

When it reached the corpse, it immediately identified it that far: it was a dead body, frozen in a vaguely fetal position. From there on, the probe got stuck.

Many details about the body did not fit the acceptable parameters for such a thing. The probe examined it again, and still again, and kept coming up with the same unacceptable answers. It could not tell what the body was . . . and yet it was a body.

The probe was so fascinated that its attention wavered for some time, and it was not as alert as it had been these previous years. So it was unprepared when the second falling object bumped gently against its metal hide. Quickly the probe leveled a camera eye at the second object. It was a single, long-stemmed, red rose, of a type that had once flourished in the wheel's florist shop. Like the corpse, it was frozen solid. The impact had shattered some of the outside petals, which rotated slowly in a halo around the rose itself.

It was quite pretty. The probe resolved to compose a thought-poem about it when this was all over. The probe photographed it, vaporized it with its lasers—all according to instruction—then sent the picture out on the airwaves along with a picture of the corpse, and a frustrated shout.

"Help!" the probe cried, and sat back to await developments.

"A puppy?" Captain Hoeffer asked, arching one eyebrow dubiously.

"A Shetland Sheepdog puppy, sir," said Corporal Anna-Louise Bach, handing him the batch of holos of the enigmatic orbiting object, and the single shot of the shattered rose. He took them, leafed through them rapidly, puffing on his pipe.

"And it came from Tango Charlie?"

"There is no possible doubt about it, sir."

Bach stood at parade rest across the desk from her seated superior and cultivated a detached gaze. I'm only awaiting orders, she told herself. I have no opinions of my own. I'm brimming with information, as any good recruit should be, but I will offer it only when asked, and then I will pour it forth until asked to stop.

That was the theory, anyway. Bach was not good at it. It was her ineptitude at humoring incompetence in superiors that had landed her in this assignment, and put her in contention for the title of oldest living recruit/apprentice in the New Dresden Police Department.

"A Shetland . . ."

"Sheepdog, sir." She glanced down at him, and interpreted the motion of his pipestem to mean he wanted to know more. "A variant of the Collie, developed on the Shetland Isles of Scotland. A working dog, very bright, gentle, good with children."

"You're an authority on dogs, Corporal Bach?"

"No, sir. I've only seen them in the zoo. I took the liberty of researching this matter before bringing it to your attention, sir."

He nodded, which she hoped was a good sign.

"What else did you learn?"

"They come in three varieties: black, blue merle, and sable. They were developed from Icelandic and Greenland stock, with infusions of Collie and possible Spaniel genes. Specimens were first shown at Cruft's in London in 1906, and in American—"

"No, no. I don't give a damn about Shelties."

"Ah. We have confirmed that there were four Shelties present on Tango Charlie at the time of the disaster. They were being shipped to the zoo at Clavius. There were no other dogs of any breed resident at the station. We haven't determined how it is that their survival was overlooked during the investigation of the tragedy."

"Somebody obviously missed them."

"Yes, sir."

Hoeffer jabbed at a holo with his pipe.

"What's this? Have you researched *that* yet?"

Bach ignored what she thought might be sarcasm. Hoeffer was pointing to the opening in the animal's side.

"The computer believes it to be a birth defect, sir. The skin is not fully formed. It left an opening into the gut."

"And what's this?"

"Intestines. The bitch would lick the puppy clean after birth. When she found this malformation, she would keep licking as long as she tasted blood. The intestines were pulled out, and the puppy died."

"It couldn't have lived anyway. Not with that hole."

"No, sir. If you'll notice, the forepaws are also malformed. The computer feels the puppy was stillborn."

Hoeffer studied the various holos in a blue cloud of pipe smoke, then sighed and leaned back in his chair.

"It's fascinatilng, Bach. After all these years, there are dogs alive on Tango Charlie. And breeding, too. Thank you for bringing it to my attention."

Now it was Bach's turn to sigh. She *hated* this part. Now it was her job to explain it to him.

"It's even more fascinating than that, sir. We knew Tango Charlie was largely pressurized. So it's understandable that a colony of dogs could breed there. But, barring an explosion, which would have spread a large amount of debris into the surrounding space, this dead puppy must have left the station through an airlock."

His face clouded, and he looked at her in gathering outrage.

"Are you saying . . . there are humans alive aboard Tango Charlie?"

"Sir, it has to be that . . . or some *very* intelligent dogs."

Dogs can't count.

Charlie kept telling herself that as she knelt on the edge of forever and watched little Albert dwindling, hurrying out to join the whirling stars. She wondered if he would become a star himself. It seemed possible.

She dropped the rose after him and watched it dwindle, too. Maybe it would become a rosy star.

She cleared her throat. She had thought of things to say, but none of them sounded good. So she decided on a hymn, the only one she knew, taught her long ago by her mother, who used to sing it for her father, who was a spaceship pilot. Her voice was clear and true.

> *"Lord guard and guide all those who fly*
> *Through Thy great void above the sky.*
> *Be with them all on ev'ry flight,*
> *In radiant day or darkest night.*
> *Oh, hear our prayer, extend Thy grace*
> *To those in peril deep in space."*

She knelt silently for a while, wondering if God was listening, and if the hymn was good for dogs, too. Albert sure was flying through the void, so it seemed to Charlie he ought to be deserving of some grace.

Charlie was perched on a sheet of twisted metal on the bottom, or outermost layer of the wheel. There was no gravity anywhere in the wheel, but since it was spinning, the farther down you went the heavier you felt. Just beyond the sheet of metal was a void, a hole ripped in the wheel's outer skin, fully twenty meters across. The metal had been twisted out and down by the force of some long-ago explosion, and this part of the wheel was a good place to walk carefully, if you had to walk here at all.

She picked her way back to the airlock, let herself in, and sealed the outer door behind her. She knew it was useless, knew there was nothing but vacuum on the other side, but it was something that had been impressed on her very strongly. When you go through a door, you lock it behind you. Lock it tight. If you don't, the breathsucker will get you in the middle of the night.

She shivered, and went to the next lock, which also led only to vacuum, as did the one beyond that. Finally, at the fifth airlock, she stepped into a tiny room that had breathable atmosphere, if a little chilly. Then she went through yet another lock before daring to take off her helmet.

At her feet was a large plastic box, and inside it, resting shakily on a scrap of bloody blanket and not at all at peace with the world, were two puppies. She picked them up, one in each hand—which didn't make them any happier—and nodded in satisfaction.

She kissed them, and put them back in the box. Tucking it under her arm, she faced another door. She could hear claws scratching at this one.

"Down, Fuchsia," she shouted. "Down, momma-dog." The

scratching stopped, and she opened the last door and stepped through.

Fuchsia O'Charlie Station was sitting obediently, her ears pricked up, her head cocked and her eyes alert with that total, quivering concentration only a mother dog can achieve.

"I've got 'em, Foosh," Charlie said. She went down on one knee and allowed Fuchsia to put her paws up on the edge of the box. "See? There's Helga, and there's Conrad, and there's Albert, and there's Conrad, and Helga. One, two, three, four, eleventy-nine and six makes twenty-seven. See?"

Fuchsia looked at them doubtfully, then leaned in to pick one up, but Charlie pushed her away.

"I'll carry them," she said, and they set out along the darkened corridor. Fuchsia kept her eyes on the box, whimpering with the desire to get to her pups.

Charlie called this part of the wheel The Swamp. Things had gone wrong here a long time ago, and the more time went by, the worse it got. She figured it had been started by the explosion—which, in its turn, had been an indirect result of The Dying. The explosion had broken important pipes and wires. Water had started to pool in the corridor. Drainage pumps kept it from turning into an impossible situation. Charlie didn't come here very often.

Recently plants had started to grow in the swamp. They were ugly things, corpse-white or dental-plaque-yellow or mushroom gray. There was very little light for them, but they didn't seem to mind. She sometimes wondered if they were plants at all. Once she thought she had seen a fish. It had been white and blind. Maybe it had been a toad. She didn't like to think of that.

Charlie sloshed through the water, the box of puppies under one arm and her helmet under the other. Fuchsia bounced unhappily along with her.

At last they were out of it, and back into regions she knew better. She turned right and went three flights up a staircase—dogging the door behind her at every landing—then out into the Promenade Deck, which she called home.

About half the lights were out. The carpet was wrinkled and musty, and worn in the places Charlie frequently walked. Parts of the walls were streaked with water stains, or grew mildew in leprous patches. Charlie seldom noticed these things unless she was looking through her pictures from the old days, or was coming up from the maintenance levels, as she was now. Long ago, she had tried to keep things clean, but the place was just to big for a little girl. Now she limited her housekeeping to her own living quarters—and like any little girl, sometimes forgot about that, too.

She stripped off her suit and stowed it in the locker where she always kept it, then padded a short way down the gentle curve of the corridor to the Presidential Suite, which was hers. As she entered, with Fuchsia on her heels, a long-dormant television camera mounted high on the wall stuttered to life. Its flickering red eye came on, and it turned jerkily on its mount.

Anna-Louise Bach entered the darkened monitoring room, mounted the five stairs to her office at the back, sat down, and put her bare feet up on her desk. She tossed her uniform cap, caught it on one foot, and twirled it idly there. She laced her fingers together, leaned her chin on them, and thought about it.

Corporal Steiner, her number two on C Watch, came up to the platform, pulled a chair close, and sat beside her.

"Well? How did it go?"

"You want some coffee?" Bach asked him. When he nodded, she pressed a button in the arm of her chair. "Bring two coffees to the Watch Commander's station. Wait a minute . . . bring a pot, and two mugs." She put her feet down and turned to face him.

"He did figure out there had to be a human aboard."

Steiner frowned. "You must have given him a clue."

"Well, I mentioned the airlock angle."

"See? He'd never have seen it without that."

"All right. Call it a draw."

"So then what did our leader want to do?"

Bach had to laugh. Hoeffer was unable to find his left testicle without a copy of *Gray's Anatomy*.

"He came to a quick decision. We had to send a ship out there *at once*, find the survivors and bring them to New Dresden with all possible speed."

"And then you reminded him . . ."

". . . that no ship had been allowed to get within five kilometers of Tango Charlie for thirty years. That even our probe had to be small, slow, and careful to operate in the vicinity, and that if it crossed the line it would be destroyed, too. He was all set to call the Oberluftwaffe headquarters and ask for a cruiser. I pointed out that A, we already *had* a robot cruiser on station under the reciprocal trade agreement with *Allgemein Fernsehen Gesellschaft*; B, that it was perfectly capable of defeating Tango Charlie without any more help; but C, any battle like that would *kill* whoever was on Charlie; but that in any case, D, even if a ship *could* get to Charlie there was a good reason for not doing so.''

Emil Steiner winced, pretending pain in the head.

''Anna, Anna, you should never list things to him like that, and if you do, you should *never* get to point D.''

''Why not?''

''Because you're lecturing him. If you have to make a speech like that, make it a set of options, which I'm sure you've already seen, sir, but which I will list for you, sir, to get all our ducks in a row. Sir.''

Bach grimaced, knowing he was right. She was too impatient.

The coffee arrived, and while they poured and took the first sips, she looked around the big monitoring room. This is where impatience gets you.

In some ways, it could have been a lot worse. It *looked* like a good job. Though only a somewhat senior Recruit/Apprentice Bach was in command of thirty other R/A's on her watch, and had the rank of Corporal. The working conditions were good: clean, high-tech surroundings, low job stress, the opportunity to command, however fleetingly. Even the coffee was good.

But it was a dead-end, and everyone knew it. It was a job many rookies held for a year or two before being moved on to more important and prestigious assignments: part of a routine career. When a R/A stayed in the monitoring room for five years, even as a watch commander, someone was sending her a message. Bach understood the message, had realized the problem long ago. But she couldn't seem to do anything about it. Her personality was too abrasive for routine promotions. Sooner or later she angered her commanding officers in one way or another. She was far too good for anything overtly negative to appear in her yearly evaluations. But there were ways such reports could be written, good things left un-said, a lack of excitement on the part of the reporting officer . . . all things that added up to stagnation.

So here she was in Navigational Tracking, not really a police function at all, but something the New Dresden Police Department had handled for a hundred years and would probably handle for a hundred more.

It was a necessary job. So is garbage collection. But it was not what she had signed up for, ten years ago.

Ten years! God, it sounded like a long time. Any of the skilled guilds were hard to get into, but the average apprenticeship in New Dresden was six years.

She put down her coffee cup and picked up a hand mike.

"Tango Charlie, this is Foxtrot Romeo. Do you read?"

She listened, and heard only background hiss. Her troops were trying every available channel with the same message, but this one had been the main channel back when TC-38 had been a going concern.

"Tango Charlie, this is Foxtrot Romeo. Come in, please."

Again, nothing.

Steiner put his cup close to hers, and leaned back in his chair.

"So did he remember what the reason was? Why we can't approach?"

"He did, eventually. His first step was to slap a top-priority security rating on the whole affair, and he was confident the government would back him up."

"We got that part. The alert came through about twenty minutes ago."

"I figured it wouldn't do any harm to let him send it. He needed to do something. And it's what I would have done."

"It's what you *did*, as soon as the pictures came in."

"You know I don't have the authority for that."

"Anna, when you get that look in your eye and say, 'If one of you bastards breathes a word of this to *anyone*, I will cut out your tongue and eat it for breakfast,' . . . well, people listen."

"Did I say that?"

"Your very words."

"No wonder they all love me so much."

She brooded on that for a while, until T/A3 Klosinski hurried up the steps to her office.

"Corporal Bach, we've finally seen something," he said.

Bach looked at the big semicircle of flat television screens, over three hundred of them, on the wall facing her desk. Below the screens were the members of her watch, each at a desk/console, each with a dozen smaller screens to monitor. Most of the large screens displayed the usual data from the millions of objects monitored by Nav/Track radar, cameras, and computers. But fully a quarter of them now showed curved, empty corridors where nothing moved, or equally lifeless rooms. In some of them skeletons could be seen.

The three of them faced the largest screen on Bach's desk, and unconsciously leaned a little closer as a picture started to form. At first it was just streaks of color. Klosinski consulted a datapad on his wrist.

"This is from camera 14/P/delta. It's on the Promenade Deck. Most of that deck was a sort of PX, with shopping areas, theaters, clubs, so forth. But one sector had VIP suites, for when people visited the station. This one's just outside the Presidential Suite."

"What's wrong with the picture?"

Klosinski sighed.

"Same thing wrong with all of them. The cameras are old. We've got about five percent of them in some sort of working order, which is a miracle. The Charlie computer is fighting us for every one."

"I figured it would."

"In just a minute . . . there! Did you see it?"

All Bach could see was a stretch of corridor, maybe a little fancier than some of the views already up on the wall, but not what Bach thought of as VIP. She peered at it, but nothing changed.

"No, nothing's going to happen now. This is a tape. We got it when the camera first came on." He fiddled with his data pad, and the screen resumed its multi-colored static. "I rewound it. Watch the door on the left."

This time Klosinski stopped the tape on the first recognizable image on the screen.

"This is someone's leg," he said, pointing. "And this is the tail of a dog."

Bach studied it. The leg was bare, and so was the foot. It could be seen from just below the knee.

"That looks like a Sheltie's tail," she said.

"We thought so, too."

"What about the foot?"

"Look at the door," Steiner said. "In relation to the door, the leg looks kind of small."

"You're right," Bach said. *A child?* she wondered. "Okay, Watch this one around the clock. I suppose if there was a camera in that room, you'd have told me about it."

"I guess VIP's don't like to be watched."

"Then carry on as you were. Activate every camera you can, and tape them *all*. I've got to take this to Hoeffer."

She started down out of her wall-less office, adjusting her cap at an angle she hoped looked smart and alert.

"Anna," Steiner called. She looked back.

"How did Hoeffer take it when you reminded him Tango Charlie only has six more days left?"

"He threw his pipe at me."

Charlie put Conrad and Helga back in the whelping box, along with Dieter and Inga. All four of them were squealing, which was only natural, but the quality of their squeals changed when Fuchsia jumped in with them, sat down on Dieter, then plopped over on her side. There was nothing that sounded or looked more determined than a blind, hungry, newborn puppy, Charlie thought.

The babies found the swollen nipples, and Fuchsia fussed over them, licking their little bottoms. Charlie held her breath. It almost looked as if she was counting her brood, and that certainly wouldn't do.

"Good dog, Fuchsia," she cooed, to distract her, and it did. Fuchsia looked up, said I haven't got time for you now, Charlie, and went back to her chores.

"How was the funeral?" asked Tik-Tok the Clock.

"Shut up!" Charlie hissed. "You . . . you big idiot! It's okay, Foosh."

Fuchsia was already on her side, letting the pups nurse and more or less ignoring both Charlie and Tik-Tok. Charlie got up and went into the bathroom. She closed and secured the door behind her.

"The funeral was very beautiful," she said, pushing the stool nearer the mammoth marble washbasin and climbing up on it.

Behind the basin the whole wall was a mirror, and when she stood on the stool she could see herself. She flounced her blonde hair out and studied it critically. There were some tangles.

"Tell me about it," Tik-Tok said. "I want to know *every* detail."

So she told him, pausing a moment to sniff her armpits. Wearing the suit always made her smell so gross. She clambered up onto the broad marble counter, went around the basin and goosed the 24-karat gold tails of the two dolphins who cavorted there, and water began gushing out of their mouths. She sat with her feet in the basin, touching one tail or another when the water got too hot, and told Tik-Tok all about it.

Charlie used to bathe in the big tub. It was so big it was more suited for swimming laps than bathing. One day she slipped and hit her head and almost drowned. Now she usually bathed in the sink, which was not quite big enough, but a lot safer.

"The rose was the most wonderful part," she said. "I'm glad you thought of that. It just turned and turned and turned . . ."

"Did you say anything?"

"I sang a song. A hymn."

"Could I hear it?"

She lowered herself into the basin. Resting the back of her neck on a folded towel, the water came up to her chin, and her legs from the knees down stuck out the other end. She lowered her mouth a little, and made burbling sounds in the water.

"Can I hear it? I'd like to hear."

"Lord guide and guard all those who fly . . ."

Tik-Tok listened to it once, then joined in harmony as she sang it again, and on the third time through added an organ part. Charlie felt the tears in her eyes again, and wiped them with the back of her hand.

"Time to scrubba-scrubba-scrubba," Tik-Tok suggested.

Charlie sat on the edge of the basin with her feet in the water, and lathered a washcloth.

"Scrubba-scrub beside your nose," Tik-Tok sang.

"Scrubba-scrub beside your nose," Charlie repeated, and industriously scoured all around her face.

"Scrubba-scrub between your toes. Scrub all the jelly out of your belly. Scrub your butt, and your you-know-what."

Tik-Tok led her through the ritual she'd been doing so long she didn't even remember how long. A couple times he made her giggle by throwing in a new verse. He was always making them up. When she was done, she was about the cleanest little girl anyone ever saw, except for her hair.

"I'll do that later," she decided, and hopped to the floor, where she danced the drying-off dance in front of the warm air blower until Tik-Tok told her she could stop. Then she crossed the room to the vanity table and sat on the high stool she had installed there.

"Charlie, there's something I wanted to talk to you about," Tik-Tok said.

Charlie opened a tube called "Coral Peaches" and smeared it all over her lips. She gazed at the thousand other bottles and tubes, wondering what she'd use this time.

"Charlie, are you listening to me?"

"Sure," Charlie said. She reached for a bottle labeled "The Glenlivet, Twelve Years Old," twisted the cork out of it, and put it to her lips. She took a big swallow, then another, and wiped her mouth on the back of her arm.

"Holy mackerel! That's real sippin' whiskey!" she shouted, and set the bottle down. She reached for a tin of rouge.

"Some people have been trying to talk to me," Tik-Tok said. "I believe they may have seen Albert, and wondered about him."

Charlie looked up, alarmed—and, doing so, accidentally made a solid streak of rouge from her cheekbone to her chin.

"Do you think they shot at Albert?"

"I don't think so. I think they're just curious."

"Will they hurt me?"

"You never can tell."

Charlie frowned, and used her finger to spread black eyeliner all over her left eyelid. She did the same for the right, then used another jar to draw violent purple frown lines on her forehead. With a thick pencil she outlined her eyebrows.

"What do they want?"

"They're just prying people, Charlie. I thought you ought to know. They'll probably try to talk to you, later."

"Should I talk to them?"

"That's up to you."

Charlie frowned even deeper. Then she picked up the bottle of Scotch and had another belt.

She reached for the Rajah's Ruby and hung it around her neck.

Fully dressed and made up now, Charlie paused to kiss Fuchsia and tell her how beautiful her puppies were, then hurried out to the Promenade Deck.

As she did, the camera on the wall panned down a little, and turned a few degrees on its pivot. That made a noise in the rusty mechanism, and Charlie looked up at it. The speaker beside the camera made a hoarse noise, then did it again. There was a little puff of smoke, and an alert sensor quickly directed a spray of extinguishing gas toward it, then itself gave up the ghost. The speaker said nothing else.

Odd noises were nothing new to Charlie. There were places on the wheel where the clatter of faltering mechanisms behind the walls was so loud you could hardly hear yourself think.

She thought of the snoopy people Tik-Tok had mentioned. That camera was probably just the kind of thing they'd like. So she turned her butt to the camera, bent over, and farted at it.

She went to her mother's room, and sat beside her bed telling her all about little Albert's funeral. When she felt she'd been there long enough she kissed her dry cheek and ran out of the room.

Up one level were the dogs. She went from room to room, letting them out, accompanied by a growing horde of barking jumping Shelties. Each was deliriously happy to see her, as usual, and she had to speak sharply to a few when they kept licking her face. They stopped on command; Charlie's dogs were all good dogs.

When she was done there were seventy-two almost identical dogs yapping and running along with her in a sable-and-white tide. They rushed by another camera with a glowing red light, which panned to follow them up, up, and out of sight around the gentle curve of Tango Charlie.

Bach got off the slidewalk at the 34strasse intersection. She worked her way through the crowds in the shopping arcade, then entered the Intersection-park, where the trees were plastic but the winos sleeping on the benches were real. She was on Level Eight. Up here, 34strasse was taprooms and casinos, second-hand stores, missions, pawn shops, and cheap bordellos. Free-lance whores, naked or in elaborate costumes according to their specialty, eyed her and sometimes propositioned her. Hope springs eternal; these men and women saw her every day on her way home. She waved to a few she had met, though never in a professional capacity.

It was a kilometer and a half to Count Otto Von Zeppelin Residential Corridor. She walked beside the slidewalk. Typically, it operated two days out of seven. Her own quarters were at the end of Count Otto, apartment 80. She palmed the printpad, and went in.

She knew she was lucky to be living in such large quarters on a T/A salary. It was two rooms, plus a large bath and a tiny kitchen. She had grown up in a smaller place, shared by a lot more people. The rent was so low because her bed was only ten meters from an arterial tubeway; the floor vibrated loudly every thirty seconds as the capsules rushed by. It didn't bother her. She had spent her first ten years sleeping within a meter of a regional air-circulation station, just beyond a thin metal apartment wall. It left her with a hearing loss she had been too poor to correct until recently.

For most of her ten years in Otto 80 she had lived alone. Five times, for periods varying from two weeks to six months, she shared with a lover, as she was doing now.

When she came in, Ralph was in the other room. She could hear the steady huffing and puffing as he worked out. Bach went to the bathroom and ran a tub as hot as she could stand it, eased herself in, and stretched out. Her blue paper uniform brief floated to the surface; she skimmed, wadded up, and tossed the soggy mass toward the toilet.

She missed. It had been that sort of day.

She lowered herself until her chin was in the water. Beads of sweat popped out on her forehead. She smiled, and mopped her face with a washcloth.

After a while Ralph appeared in the doorway. She could hear him, but didn't open her eyes.

"I didn't hear you come in," he said.

"Next time I'll bring a brass band."

He just kept breathing heavy, gradually getting it under control. That was her most vivid impression of Ralph, she realized; heavy breathing. That, and lots and lots of sweat. And it was no surprise he had nothing to say. Ralph was oblivious to sarcasm. It made him tiresome, sometimes, but with shoulders like his he didn't need to be witty. Bach opened her eyes and smiled at him.

Luna's low gravity made it hard for all but the most fanatical to aspire to the muscle mass one could develop on the Earth. The typical Lunarian was taller than Earth-normal, and tended to be thinner.

As a much younger woman Bach had become involved, very much against her better judgment, with an earthling of the species "jock." It hadn't worked out, but she still bore the legacy in a marked preference for beefcake. This doomed her to consorting with only two kinds of men: well-muscled mesomorphs from Earth, and single-minded Lunarians who thought nothing of pumping iron for ten hours a day. Ralph was one of the latter.

There was no rule, so far as Bach could discover, that such specimens had to be mental midgets. That was a sterotype. It also happened, in Ralph's case, to be true. While not actually mentally defective, Ralph Goldstein's idea of a tough intellectual problem was how many kilos to bench press. His spare time was spent brushing his teeth or shaving his chest or looking at pictures of himself in bodybuilding magazines. Bach knew for a fact that Ralph thought the Earth and Sun revolved around Luna.

He had only two real interests; lifting weights, and making love to Anna-Louise Bach. She didn't mind that at all.

Ralph had a swastika tattooed on his penis. Early on, Bach had determined that he had no notion of the history of the symbol; he had seen it in an old film and though it looked nice. It amused her to consider what his ancestors might have thought of the adornment.

He brought a stool close to the tub and sat on it, then stepped on a floor button. The tub was Bach's chief luxury. It did a lot of fun things. Now it lifted her on a long rack until she was half out of the water. Ralph started washing that half. She watched his soapy hands.

"Did you go to the doctor?" he asked her.

"Yeah, I finally did."

"What did he say?"

"Said I have cancer."

"How bad?"

"Real bad. It's going to cost a bundle. I don't know if my insurance will cover it all." She closed her eyes and sighed. It

annoyed her to have him be right about something. He had nagged
her for months to get her medical check-up.

"Will you get it taken care of tomorrow?"

"No. Ralph, I don't have time tomorrow. Next week, I promise.
This thing has come up, but it'll be all over next week, one way or
another."

He frowned, but didn't say anything. He didn't have to. The
human body, its care and maintenance, was the one subject Ralph
knew more about than she did, but even she knew it would be
cheaper in the long run to have the work done now.

She felt so lazy he had to help her turn over. Damn, but he was
good at this. She had never asked him to do it; he seemed to enjoy
it. His strong hands dug into her back and found each sore spot, as
if by magic. Presently, it wasn't sore anymore.

"What's this thing that's come up?"

"I . . . can't tell you about it. Classified, for now."

He didn't protest, nor did he show surprise, thought it was the
first time Bach's work had taken her into the realm of secrecy.

It was annoying, really. One of Ralph's charms was that he was
a good listener. While he wouldn't understand the technical side of
anything, he could sometimes offer surprisingly good advice on
personal problems. More often, he showed the knack of synthesizing and expressing things Bach had already known, but had not
allowed herself to see.

Well, she could tell him part of it.

"There's this satellite," she began. "Tango Charlie. Have you
ever heard of it?"

"That's a funny name for a satellite."

"It's what we call it on the tracking logs. It never really had a
name—well, it did, a long time ago, but GWA took it over and
turned it into a research facility and an Exec's retreat, and they just
let it be known as TC-38. They got it in a war with Telecommunion,
part of the peace treaty. They got Charlie, the Bubble, a couple
other big wheels.

"The thing about Charlie . . . it's coming down. In about six
days, it's going to spread itself all over the Farside. Should be a
pretty big bang."

Ralph continued to knead the backs of her legs. It was never a good idea to rush him. He would figure things out in his own way, at his own speed, or he wouldn't figure them out at all.

"Why is it coming down?"

"It's complicated. It's been derelict for a long time. For a while it had the capacity to make course corrections, but it looks like it's run out of reaction mass, or the computer that's supposed to stabilize it isn't working anymore. For a couple of years it hasn't been making corrections."

"Why does it—"

"A Lunar orbit is never stable. There's the Earth tugging on the satellite, the solar wind, mass concentrations of Luna's surface . . . a dozen things that add up, over time. Charlie's in a very eccentric orbit now. Last time it came within a kilometer of the surface. Next time it's gonna miss us by a gnat's whisker, and the time after that, it hits."

Ralph stopped massaging. When Bach glanced at him, she saw he was alarmed. He had just understood that a very large object was about to hit his home planet, and he didn't like the idea.

"Don't worry," Bach said, "there's a surface installation that might get some damage from the debris, but Charlie won't come within a hundred kilometers of any settlements. We got nothing to worry about on that score."

"Then why don't you just . . . push it back up . . . you know, go up there and do . . ." Whatever it is you do, Bach finished for him. He had no real idea what kept a satellite in orbit in the first place, but knew there were people who handled such matters all the time.

There were other questions he might have asked, as well. Why leave Tango Charlie alone all these years? Why not salvage it? Why allow things to get to this point at all?

All those questions brought her back to classified ground.

She sighed, and turned over.

"I wish we could," she said, sincerely. She noted that the swastika was saluting her, and that seemed like a fine idea, so she let him carry her into the bedroom.

And as he made love to her she kept seeing that incredible tide of Shelties with the painted child in the middle.

After the run, ten laps around the Promenade Deck, Charlie led the pack to the Japanese Garden and let them run free through the tall weeds and vegetable patches. Most of the trees in the Garden were dead. The whole place had once been a formal and carefully tended place of meditation. Four men from Tokyo had been employed full time to take care of it. Now the men were buried under the temple gate, the ponds were covered in green scum, the gracefully arched bridge had collapsed, and the flower beds were choked with dog turds.

Charlie had to spend part of each morning in the flower beds, feeding Mister Shitface. This was a cylindrical structure with a big round hole in its side, an intake for the wheel's recycling system. It ate dog feces, weeds, dead plants, soil, scraps . . . practically anything Charlie shoved into it. The cylinder was painted green, like a frog, and had a face painted on it, with big lips outlining the hole. Charlie sang The Shit-Shoveling Song as she worked.

Tik-Tok had taught her the song, and he used to sing it with her. But a long time ago he had gone deaf in the Japanese Garden. Usually, all Charlie had to do was talk, and Tik-Tok would hear. But there were some places—and more of them every year—where Tik-Tok was deaf.

" '. . . *Raise dat laig'* " Charlie puffed. " *'Lif dat tail, If I gets in trouble will you go my bail?'* "

She stopped, and mopped her face with a red bandanna. As usual, there were dogs sitting on the edge of the flowerbed watching Charlie work. Their ears were lifted. They found this *endlessly* fascinating. Charlie just wished it would be over. But you took the bad with the good. She started shoveling again.

" *'I gets weary, O' all dis shovelin'* . . .' "

When she was finished she went back on the Promenade.

"What's next?" she asked.

"Plenty," said Tik-Tok. "The funeral put you behind schedule."

He directed her to the infirmary with the new litter. There they weighed, photographed, X-rayed, and catalogued each puppy. The results were put on file for later registration with the American Kennel Club. It quickly became apparent that Conrad was going to be a cull. He had an overbite. With the others it was too early to tell. She and Tik-Tok would examine them weekly, and their standards were an order of magnitude more stringent than the AKC's.

Most of her *culls* would easily have best of breed in a show, and as for her breeding animals . . .

"I ought to be able to write Champion on most of these pedigrees."

"You must be patient."

Patient, yeah, she'd heard that before. She took another drink of Scotch. *Champion Fuchsia O'Charlie Station*, she thought. *Now that would really make a breeder's day.*

After the puppies, there were two from an earlier litter who were now ready for a final evaluation. Charlie brought them in, and she and Tik-Tok argued long and hard about points so fine few people would have seen them at all. In the end, they decided both would be sterilized.

Then it was noon feeding. Charlie never enforced discipline here. She let them jump and bark and nip at each other, as long as it didn't get *too* rowdy. She led them all to the cafeteria (and was tracked by three wall cameras), where the troughs of hard kibble and soft soyaburger were already full. Today it was chicken-flavored, Charlie's favorate.

Afternoon was training time. Consulting the records Tik-Tok displayed on a screen, she got the younger dogs one at a time and put each of them through thirty minutes of leash work, up and down the Promenade, teaching them Heel, Sit, Stay, Down, Come according to their degree of progress and Tik-Tok's rigorous schedules. The older dogs were taken to the Ring in groups, where they sat obediently in a line as she put them, one by one, through free-heeling paces.

Finally it was evening meals, which she hated. It was all human food.

"Eat your vegetables," Tik-Tok would say. "Clean up your plate. People are starving in New Dresden." It was usually green salads and yucky broccoli and beets and stuff like that. Tonight it was yellow squash, which Charlie liked about as much as a root canal. She gobbled up the hamburger patty and then dawdled over the squash until it was a yellowish mess all over her plate like baby shit. Half of it ended up on the table. Finally Tik-Tok relented and let her get back to her duties, which, in the evening, was grooming. She brushed each dog until the coats shone. Some of the dogs had already settled in for the night, and she had to wake them up.

At last, yawning, she made her way back to her room. She was pretty well plastered by then. Tik-Tok, who was used to it, made allowances and tried to jolly her out of what seemed a very black mood.

"There's *nothing* wrong!" she shouted at one point, tears streaming from her eyes. Charlie could be an ugly drunk.

She staggered out to the Promenade Deck and lurched from wall to wall, but she never fell down. Ugly or not, she knew how to hold her liquor. It had been ages since it made her sick.

The elevator was in what had been a commercial zone. The empty shops gaped at her as she punched the button. She took another drink, and the door opened. She got in.

She hated this part. The elevator was rising up through a spoke, toward the hub of the wheel. She got lighter as the car went up, and the trip did funny things to the inner ear. She hung on to the hand rail until the car shuddered to a stop.

Now everything was fine. She was almost weightless up here. Weightlessness was great when you were drunk. When there was no gravity to worry about, your head didn't spin—and if it did, it didn't matter.

This was one part of the wheel where the dogs never went. They could never get used to falling, no matter how long they were kept up here. But Charlie was an expert in falling. When she got the blues she came up here and pressed her face to the huge ballroom window.

People were only a vague memory to Charlie. Her mother didn't count. Though she visited every day, mom was about as lively as V.I. Lenin. Sometimes Charlie wanted to be held so much it hurt. The dogs were good, they were warm, they licked her, they loved her . . . but they couldn't hold her.

Tears leaked from her eyes, which was really a bitch in the ballroom, because tears could get *huge* in here. She wiped them away and looked out the window.

The moon was getting bigger again. She wondered what it meant. Maybe she would ask Tik-Tok.

She made it back as far as the Garden. Inside, the dogs were sleeping in a huddle. She knew she ought to get them back to their rooms, but she was far too drunk for that. And Tik-Tok couldn't do a damn thing about it in here. He couldn't see, and he couldn't hear.

She lay down on the ground, curled up, and was asleep in seconds.

When she started to snore, the three or four dogs who had come over to watch her sleep licked her mouth until she stopped. Then they curled up beside her. Soon they were joined by others, until she slept in the middle of a blanket of dogs.

A crisis team had been assembled in the monitoring room when Bach arrived the next morning. They seemed to have been selected by Captain Hoeffer, and there were so many of them that there was not enough room for everyone to sit down. Bach led them to a conference room just down the hall, and everyone took seats around the long table. Each seat was equipped with a computer display, and there was a large screen on the wall behind Hoeffer, at the head of the table. Bach took her place on his right, and across from her was Deputy Chief Zeiss, a man with a good reputation in the department. He made Bach very nervous. Hoeffer, on the other hand, seemed to relish his role. Since Zeiss seemed content to be an observer, Bach decided to sit back and speak only if called upon.

Noting that every seat was filled, and that what she assumed were assistants had pulled up chairs behind their principles, Bach wondered if this many people were really required for this project. Steiner, sitting at Bach's right, leaned over and spoke quietly.

"Pick a time," he said.

"What's that?"

"I said pick a time. We're running an office pool. If you come closest to the time security is broken, you win a hundred Marks."

"Is ten minutes from now spoken for?"

They quieted when Hoeffer stood up to speak.

"Some of you have been working on this problem all night," he said. "Others have been called in to give us your expertise in the matter. I'd like to welcome Deputy Chief Zeiss, representing the Mayor and the Chief of Police. Chief Zeiss, would you like to say a few words?"

Zeiss merely shook his hand, which seemed to surprise Hoeffer.

Bach knew he would never have passed up an opportunity like that, and probably couldn't understand how anyone else could.

"Very well. We can start with Doctor Blume."

Blume was a sour little man who affected wire-rimmed glasses and a cheap toupee over what must have been a completely bald head. Bach thought it odd that a medical man would wear such clumsy prosthetics, calling attention to problems that were no harder to cure than a hangnail. She idly called up his profile on her screen, and was surprised to learn he had a Nobel Prize.

"The subject is a female caucasoid, almost certainly Earthborn."

On the wall behind Hoeffer and on Bach's screen, tapes of the little girl and her dogs were being run.

"She displays no obvious abnormalities. In several shots she is nude, and clearly has not yet reached puberty. I estimate her age between seven and ten years old. There are small discrepancies in her behavior. Her movements are economical—except when playing. She accomplishes various hand-eye tasks with a maturity beyond her apparent years." The doctor sat down abruptly.

It put Hoeffer off balance.

"Ah . . . that's fine, doctor. But, if you recall, I just asked you to tell me how old she is, and if she's healthy."

"She appears to be eight. I said that."

"Yes, but—"

"What do you want from me?" Blume said, suddenly angry. He glared around at many of the assembled experts. "There's something badly wrong with that girl. I say she is eight. Fine! Any fool could see that. I say I can observe no health problems visually. For this, you need a doctor? Bring her to me, give me a few days, and I'll give you six volumes on her health. But videotapes . . . ?" He trailed off, his silence as eloquent as his words.

"Thank you, Doctor Blum," Hoeffer said. "As soon as—"

"I'll tell you one thing, though," Blume said, in a low, dangerous tone. "It is a disgrace to let that child drink liquor like that. The effects in later life will be terrible. I have seen large men in their thirties and forties who could not hold half as much as I saw her drink . . . *in one day!*" He glowered at Hoeffer for a moment. "I was sworn to silence. But I want to know who is responsible for this."

Bach realized he didn't know where the girl was. She wondered how many of the others in the room had been filled in, and how many were working only on their own part of the problem.

"It will be explained," Zeiss said, quietly. Blume looked from Zeiss to Hoeffer, and back, then settled into his chair, not mollified but willing to wait.

"Thank you, Doctor Blume," Hoeffer said again. "Next we'll hear from . . . Ludmilla Rossnikova, representing the GMA Conglomerate."

Terrific, thought Bach. He's brought GMA into it. No doubt he swore Ms. Rossnikova to secrecy, and if he really thought she would fail to mention it to her supervisor then he was even dumber than Bach had thought. She had worked for them once, long ago, and though she was just an employee she had learned something about them. GMA had its roots deep in twentieth-century Japanese industry. When you went to work on the executive level at GMA, you were set up for life. They expected, and received, loyalty that compared favorably with that demanded by the Mafia. Which meant that, by telling Rossnikova his "secret," Hoeffer had insured that three hundred GMA execs knew about it three minutes later. They could be relied on to keep a secret, but only if it benefited GMA.

"The computer on Tango Charlie was a custom-designed array," Rossnikova began. "That was the usual practice in those days, with BioLogic computers. It was designated the same as the station: BioLogic TC-38. It was one of the largest installations of its time.

"At the time of the disaster, when it was clear that everything had failed, the TC-38 was given its final instructions. Because of the danger, it was instructed to impose an interdiction zone around the station, which you'll find described under the label Interdiction on your screens."

Rossnikova paused while many of those present called up this information.

"To implement the zone, the TC-38 was given command of certain defensive weapons. These included ten bevawatt lasers . . . and other weapons which I have not been authorized to name or describe, other than to say they are at least as formidable as the lasers."

Hoeffer looked annoyed, and was about to say something, but

Zeiss stopped him with a gesture. Each understood that the lasers were enough in themselves.

"So while it is possible to destroy the station," Rossnikova went on, "there is no chance of boarding it—assuming anyone would even want to try."

Bach thought she could tell from the different expressions around the table which people knew the whole story and which knew only their part of it. A couple of the latter seemed ready to ask a question, but Hoeffer spoke first.

"How about canceling the computers's instructions?" he said. "Have you tried that?"

"That's been tried many times over the last few years, as this crisis got closer. We didn't expect it to work, and it did not. Tango Charlie won't accept a new program."

"Oh my God," Doctor Blume gasped. Bach saw that his normally florid face had paled. "Tango Charlie. She's on Tango Charlie."

"That's right, doctor," said Hoeffer. "And we're trying to figure out how to get her off. Doctor Wilhelm?"

Wilhelm was an older woman with the stocky build of the Earthborn. She rose, and looked down at some notes in her hand.

"Information's under the label Neurotropic Agent X on your machines," she muttered, then looked up at them. "But you needn't bother. That's about as far as we got, naming it. I'll sum up what we know, but you don't need an expert for this; there *are* no experts on Neuro-X.

"It broke out on August 9, thirty years ago next month. The initial report was five cases, one death. Symptoms were progressive paralysis, convulsions, loss of motor control, numbness.

"Tango Charlie was immediately quarantined as a standard procedure. An epidemiological team was dispatched from Atlanta, followed by another from New Dresden. All ships which had left Tango Charlie were ordered to return, except for one on its way to Mars and another already in parking orbit around Earth. The one in Earth orbit was forbidden to land.

"By the time the teams arrived, there were over a hundred reported cases, and six more deaths. Later symptoms included blindness and deafness. It progressed at different rates in different people, but it was always quite fast. Mean survival time from onset of symptoms was later determined to be forty-eight hours. Nobody lived longer than four days.

"Both medical teams immediately came down with it, as did a third, and a fourth team. *All* of them came down with it, each and every person. The first two teams had been using class three isolation techniques. It didn't matter. The third team stepped up the precautions to class two. Same result. Very quickly we had been forced into class one procedures—which involves isolation as total as we can get it: no physical contact whatsoever, no sharing of air supplies, all air to the investigators filtered through a sterilizing environment. They *still* got it. Six patients and some tissue samples were sent to a class one installation two hundred miles from New Dresden, and more patients were sent, with class one precautions, to a hospital ship close to Charlie. Everyone at both facilities came down with it. We *almost* sent a couple of patients to Atlanta."

She paused, looking down and rubbing her forehead. No one said anything.

"I was in charge," she said, quietly. "I can't take credit for not shipping anyone to Atlanta. We were going to . . . and suddenly there wasn't anybody left on Charlie to load patients aboard. All dead or dying.

"We backed off. Bear in mind this all happened in five days. What we had to show for those five days was a major space station with all aboard dead, three ships full of dead people, and an epidemiological research facility here on Luna full of dead people.

"After that, politicians began making most of the decisions—but I advised them. The two nearby ships were landed by robot control at the infected research station. The derelict ship going to Mars was . . . I think it's still classified, but what the hell? It was blown up with a nuclear weapon. Then we started looking into what was left. The station here was easiest. There was one cardinal rule: *nothing* that went into that station was to come out. Robot crawlers brought in remote manipulators and experimental animals. Most of the animals died. Neuro-X killed most mammals: monkeys, rats, cats—"

"Dogs?" Bach asked. Wilhelm glanced at her.

"It didn't kill *all* the dogs. Half of the ones we sent in lived."

"Did you know that there were dogs alive on Charlie?"

"No. The interdiction was already set up by then. Charlie

Station was impossible to land, and too close and too visible to nuke, because that would violate about a dozen corporate treaties. And there seemed no reason not to just leave it there. We had our samples isolated here at the Lunar station. We decided to work with that, and forget about Charlie.''

"Thank you, doctor."

"As I was saying, it was by far the most virulent organism we had ever seen. It seemed to have a taste for all sorts of neural tissue, in almost every mammal.

"The teams that went in never had time to learn anything. They were all disabled too quickly, and just as quickly they were dead. We didn't find out much, either . . . for a variety of reasons. My guess is it was a virus, simply because we would certainly have seen anything larger almost immediately. But we never *did* see it. It was fast getting in—we don't know how it was vectored, but the only reliable shield was several miles of vacuum—and once it got in, I suspect it worked changes on genetic material of the host, setting up a secondary agent which I'm almost sure we isolated . . . and then it went away and hid very well. It was still in the host, in some form, it *had* to be, but we think its active life in the nervous system was on the order of one hour. But by then it had already done its damage. It set the system against itself, and the host was consumed in about two days.''

Wilhelm had grown increasingly animated. A few times Bach thought she was about to get incoherent. It was clear the nightmare of Neuro-X had not diminished for her with the passage of thirty years. But now she made an effort to slow down again.

"The other remarkable thing about it was, of course, its infectiousness. Nothing I've ever seen was so persistent in evading our best attempts at keeping it isolated. Add that to its mortality rate, which, at the time, seemed to be one hundred percent . . . and you have the second great reason why we learned so little about it.''

"What was the first?" Hoeffer asked. Wilhelm glared at him.

"The difficulty of investigating such a subtle process of infection by remote control.''

"Ah, of course.''

"The other thing was simply fear. Too many people had died for there to be any hope of hushing it up. I don't know if anyone tried. I'm sure those of you who were old enough remember the uproar.

So the public debate was loud and long, and the pressure for extreme measures was intense . . . and, I should add, not unjustified. The argument was simple. Everyone who got it was dead. I believe that if those patients had been sent to Atlanta, everyone on *Earth* would have died. Therefore . . . what was the point of taking a chance by keeping it alive and studying it?''

Doctor Blume cleared his throat, and Wilhelm looked at him.

"As I recall, doctor," he said, "there were two reasons raised. One was the abstract one of scientific knowledge. Though there might be no point in studying Neuro-X since no one was afflicted with it, we might learn something by the study itself."

"Point taken," Wilhelm said, "and no argument."

"And the second was, we never found out where Neuro-X came from . . . there were rumors it was a biological warfare agent." He looked at Rossnikova, as if asking her what comment GMA might want to make about *that*. Rossnikova said nothing. "But most people felt it was a spontaneous mutation. There have been several instances of that in the high-radiation environment of a space station. And if it happened once, what's to prevent it from happening again?"

"Again, you'll get no argument from me. In fact, I supported both those positions when the question was being debated." Wilhelm grimaced, then looked right at Blume. "But the fact is, I didn't support them very hard, and when the Lunar station was sterilized, I felt a lot better."

Blume was nodding.

"I'll admit it. I felt better, too."

"And if Neuro-X were to show up again," she went on, quietly, "my advice would be to sterilize immediately. Even if it meant losing a city."

Blume said nothing. Bach watched them both for a while in the resulting silence, finally, understanding just how much Wilhelm feared this thing.

There was a lot more. The meeting went on for three hours, and everyone got a chance to speak. Eventually, the problem was outlined to everyone's satisfaction.

Tango Charlie could not be boarded. It could be destroyed. (Some time was spent debating the wisdom of the original interdiction order—beating a dead horse, as far as Bach was concerned—and questioning whether it might be possible to countermand it.)

But things could *leave* Tango Charlie. It would only be necessary to withdraw the robot probes that had watched so long and faithfully, and the survivors could be evacuated.

That left the main question. *Should* they be evacuated?

(The fact that only one survivor had been sighted so far was not mentioned. Everyone assumed others would show up sooner or later. After all, it was simply not possible that just one eight-year-old girl could be the only occupant of a station no one had entered or left for thirty years.)

Wilhelm, obviously upset but clinging strongly to her position, advocated blowing up the station at once. There was some support for this, but only about ten percent of the group.

The eventual decision, which Bach had predicted before the meeting even started, was to do nothing at the moment.

After all, there were almost five whole days to keep thinking about it.

"There's a call waiting for you," Steiner said, when she got back to the monitoring room. "The switchboard says it's important."

Bach went into her office—wishing yet again for one with walls—flipped a switch.

"Bach," she said. Nothing came on the vision screen.

"I'm curious," said a woman's voice. "Is this the Anna-Louise Bach who worked in The Bubble ten years ago?"

For a moment, Bach was too surprised to speak, but she felt a wave of heat as blood rushed to her face. She knew the voice.

"Hello? Are you there?"

"Why no vision?" she asked.

"First, are you alone? And is your instrument secure?"

"The instrument is secure, if yours is." Bach flipped another switch, and a privacy hood descended around her screen. The sounds of the room faded as a sonic scrambler began operating. "And I'm alone."

Megan Galloway's face appeared on the screen. One part of Bach's mind noted that she hadn't changed much, except that her hair was curly and red.

"I thought you might not wish to be seen with me," Galloway said. Then she smiled. "Hello, Anna-Louise. How are you?"

"I don't think it really matters if I'm seen with you," Bach said.

"No? Then would you care to comment on why the New Dresden Police Department, among other government agencies, is allowing an eight-year-old child to go without the rescue she so obviously needs?"

Bach said nothing.

"Would you comment on the rumor that the NDPD does not intend to effect the child's rescue? That, if it can get away with it, the NDPD will let the child be smashed to pieces?"

Still Bach waited.

Galloway sighed, and ran a hand through her hair.

'You're the most exasperating woman I've ever known, Bach," she said. "Listen, don't you even want to try to talk me out of going with the story?"

Bach almost said something, but decided to wait once more.

"If you want to, you can meet me at the end of your shift. The Mozartplatz. I'm on the *Great Northern*, suite 1, but I'll see you in the bar on the top deck."

"I'll be there," Bach said, and broke the connection.

Charlie sang the Hangover Song most of the morning. It was not one of her favorites.

There was penance to do, of course. Tik-Tok made her drink a foul glop that—she had to admit—did do wonders for her headache. When she was done she was drenched in sweat, but her hangover was gone.

"You're lucky," Tik-Tok said. "Your hangovers are never severe."

"They're severe enough for me," Charlie said.

He made her wash her hair, too.

After that, she spent some time with her mother. She always valued that time. Tik-Tok was a good friend, mostly, but he was so *bossy*. Charlie's mother never shouted at her, never scolded or lectured. She simply listened. True, she wasn't very active. But it was nice to have somebody just to talk to. One day, Charlie hoped, her mother would walk again. Tik-Tok said that was unlikely.

Then she had to round up the dogs and take them for their morning run.

And everywhere she went, the red camera eyes followed her. Finally she had enough. She stopped, put her fists on her hips, and shouted at a camera.

"You stop that!" she said.

The camera started to make noises. At first she couldn't understand anything, then some words started to come through.

"... lie, Tango ... Foxtrot ... in, please. Tango Charlie ..."

"Hey, that's my name."

The camera continued to buzz and spit noise at her.

"Tik-Tok, is that you?"

"I'm afraid not, Charlie."

"What's going on, then?"

"It's those nosy people. They've been watching you, and now they're trying to talk to you. But I'm holding them off. I don't think they'll bother you, if you just ignore the cameras."

"But why are you fighting them?"

"I didn't think you'd want to be bothered."

Maybe there was some of that hangover still around. Anyway, Charlie got real angry at Tik-Tok, and called him some names he didn't approve of. She knew she'd pay for it later, but for now Tik-Tok was pissed, and in no mood to reason with her. So he let her have what she wanted, on the principle that getting what you want is usually the worst thing that can happen to anybody.

"Tanto Charlie, this is Foxtrot Romeo. Come in, please. Tango—"

"Come in *where?*" Charlie asked, reasonably. "And my name isn't Tango."

Bach was so surprised to have the little girl actually reply that for a moment she couldn't think of anything to say.

"Uh ... it's just an expression," Bach said. "Come in ... that's radio talk for 'please answer.' "

"Then you should say please answer," the little girl pointed out.

"Maybe you're right. My name is Bach. You can call me Anna-Louise, if you'd like. We've been trying to—"

"Why should I?"

"Excuse me?"

"Excuse you for what?"

Bach looked at the screen and drummed her fingers silently for a short time. Around her in the monitoring room, there was not a sound to be heard. At last, she managed a smile.

"Maybe we started off on the wrong foot."

"Which foot would that be?"

The little girl just kept staring at her. Her expression was not amused, not hostile, not really argumentative. Then why was the conversation suddenly so maddening?

"Could I make a statement?" Bach tried.

"I don't know. Can you?"

Bach's fingers didn't tap this time; they were balled up in a fist.

"I shall, anyway. My name is Anna-Louise Bach. I'm talking to you from New Dresden, Luna. That's a city on the moon, which you can probably see—"

"I know where it is."

"Fine. I've been trying to contact you for many hours, but your computer has been fighting me all the time."

"That's right. He said so."

"Now, I can't explain why he's been fighting me, but—"

"I know why. He thinks you're nosy."

"I won't deny that. But we're trying to help you."

"Why?"

"Because . . . it's what we do. Now if you could—"

"Hey. Shut up, will you?"

Bach did so. With forty-five other people at their scattered screens, Bach watched the little girl—the *horrible* little girl, as she was beginning to think of her—take a long pull from the green glass bottle of Scotch whiskey. She belched, wiped her mouth with the back of her hand, and scratched between her legs. When she was done, she smelled her fingers.

She seemed about to say something, then cocked her head, listening to something Bach couldn't hear.

"That's a good idea," she said, then got up and ran away. She was just vanishing around the curve of the deck when Hoeffer burst into the room, trailed by six members of his advisory team. Bach leaned back in her chair, and tried to fend off thoughts of homicide.

"I was told you'd established contact," Hoeffer said, leaning over Bach's shoulder in a way she absolutely *detested*. He peered at the lifeless scene. "What happened to her?"

"I don't know. She said, 'That's a good idea,' got up, and ran off."

"I told you to keep her here until I got a chance to talk to her."

"I tried," Bach said.

"You should have—"

"I have her on camera nineteen," Steiner called out.

Everyone watched as the technicians followed the girl's progress on the working cameras. They saw her enter a room to emerge in a moment with a big-screen monitor. Bach tried to call her each time she passed a camera, but it seemed only the first one was working for incoming calls. She passed through the range of four cameras before coming back to the original, where she carefully unrolled the monitor and tacked it to the wall, then payed out the cord and plugged it in very close to the wall camera Bach's team had been using. She unshipped this camera from its mount. The picture jerked around for awhile, and finally steadied. The girl had set it on the floor.

"Stabilize that," Bach told her team, and the picture on her monitor righted itself. She now had a worm's-eye view of the corridor. The girl sat down in front of the camera, and grinned.

"Now I can see you," she said. Then she frowned. "If you send me a picture."

"Bring a camera over here," Bach ordered.

While it was being set up, Hoeffer shouldered her out of the way and sat in her chair.

"There you are," the girl said. And again, she frowned. "That's funny. I was sure you were a girl. Did somebody cut your balls off?"

Now it was Hoeffer's turn to be speechless. There were a few badly suppressed giggles; Bach quickly silenced them with her most ferocious glare, while giving thanks no one would ever know how close she had come to bursting into laughter.

"Never mind that," Hoeffer said. "My name is Hoeffer. Would you go get your parents? We need to talk to them."

"No," said the girl. "And no."

"What's that?"

"No, I won't get them," the girl clarified, "and no, you don't need to talk to them."

Hoeffer had little experience dealing with children.

"Now, please be reasonable," he began, in a wheedling tone. "We're trying to help you, after all. We have to talk to your parents, to find out more about your situation. After that, we're going to help get you out of there."

"I want to talk to the lady," the girl said.

"She's not here."

"I think you're lying. She talked to me just a minute ago."

"I'm in charge."

"In charge of what?"

"Just in charge. Now, go get your parents!"

They all watched as she got up and moved closer to the camera. All they could see at first was her feet. Then water began to splash on the lens.

Nothing could stop the laughter this time, as Charlie urinated on the camera.

For three hours Bach watched the screens. Every time the girl passed the prime camera Bach called out to her. She had thought about it carefully. Bach, like Hoeffer, did not know a lot about children. She consulted briefly with the child psychologist on Hoeffer's team and the two of them outlined a tentative game plan. The guy seemed to know what he was talking about and, even better, his suggestions agreed with what Bach's common sense told her should work.

So she never said anything that might sound like an order. While Hoeffer seethed in the background, Bach spoke quietly and reasonably every time the child showed up. "I'm still here," she would say. "We could talk," was a gentle suggestion. "You want to play?"

She longed to use one line the psychologist suggested, one that would put Bach and the child on the same team, so to speak. The line was "The idiot's gone. You want to talk now?"

Eventually the girl began glancing at the camera. She had a different dog every time she came by. At first Bach didn't realize this, as they were almost completely identical. Then she noticed they came in slightly different sizes.

"That's a beautiful dog," she said. The girl looked up, then started away. "I'd like to have a dog like that. What's its name?"

"This is Madam's Sweet Brown Sideburns. Say *hi,* Brownie."
The dog yipped. "Sit up for mommy, Brownie. Now roll over.
Stand tall. Now go in a circle, Brownie, that's a good doggy, walk
on your hind legs. Now *jump,* Brownie. Jump, jump, *jump!"* The
dog did exactly as he was told, leaping into the air and turning a
flip each time the girl commanded it. Then he sat down, pink
tongue hanging out, eyes riveted on his master.

"I'm impressed," Bach said, and it was the literal truth. Like
other citizens of Luna, Bach had never seen a wild animal, had
never owned a pet, knew animals only from the municipal zoo,
where care was taken not to interfere with natural behaviors. She
had had no idea animals could be so smart, and no inkling of how
much work had gone into the exhibition she had just seen.

"It's nothing," the girl said. "You should see his father. Is this
Anna-Louise again?"

"Yes, it is. What's your name?"

"Charlie. You ask a lot of questions."

"I guess I do. I just want to—"

"I'd like to ask some questions, too."

"All right. Go ahead."

"I have six of them, to start off with. One, why should I call you
Anna-Louise? Two, why should I excuse you? Three, what is the
wrong foot? Four . . . but that's not a question, really, since you
already proved you *can* make a statement, if you wish, by doing
so. Four, why are you trying to help me? Five, why do you want to
see my parents?"

It took Bach a moment to realize that these were the questions
Charlie had asked in their first, maddening conversation, questions
she had not gotten answers for. And they were in their original
order.

And they didn't make a hell of a lot of sense.

But the child psychologist was making motions with his hands,
and nodding his encouragement to Bach, so she started in.

"You should call me Anna-Louise because . . . it's my first
name, and friends call each other by their first names."

"Are we friends?"

"Well, I'd like to be your friend."

"Why?"

"Look, you don't have to call me Anna-Louise if you don't want to."

"I don't mind. Do I have to be your friend?"

"Not if you don't want to."

"Why should I want to?"

And it went on like that. Each question spawned a dozen more, and a further dozen sprang from each of those. Bach had figured to get Charlie's six—make that five—questions out of the way quickly, then get to the important things. She soon began to think she'd never answer even the *first* question.

She was involved in a long and awkward explanation of friendship, going over the ground for the tenth time, when words appeared at the bottom of her screen.

Put your foot down, they said. She glanced up at the child psychologist. He was nodding, but making quieting gestures with his hands. "But gently," the man whispered.

Right, Bach thought. Put your foot down. And get off on the wrong foot again.

"That's enough of that," Bach said abruptly.

"Why?" asked Charlie.

"Because I'm tired of that. I want to do something else."

"All right," Charlie said. Bach saw Hoeffer waving frantically, just out of camera range.

"Uh . . . Captain Hoeffer is still here. He'd like to talk to you."

"That's just too bad for him. I don't want to talk to him."

Good for you, Bach thought. But Hoeffer was still waving.

"Why not? He's not so bad." Bach felt ill, but avoided showing it.

"He lied to me. He said you'd gone away."

"Well, he's in charge here, so—"

"I'm warning you," Charlie said, and waited a dramatic moment, shaking her finger at the screen. "You put that poo-poo-head back on, and I won't come in ever again."

Bach looked helplessly at Hoeffer, who at last nodded.

"I want to talk about dogs," Charlie announced.

So that's what they did for the next hour. Bach was thankful she had studied up on the subject when the dead puppy first appeared. Even so, there was no doubt as to who was the authority. Charlie knew everything there was to know about dogs. And of all the experts Hoeffer had called in, not one could tell Bach anything about the goddamn animals. She wrote a note and handed it to Steiner, who went off to find a zoologist.

Finally Bach was able to steer the conversation around to Charlie's parents.

"My father is dead," Charlie admitted.

"I'm sorry," Bach said. "When did he die?"

"Oh, a long time ago. He was a spaceship pilot, and one day he went off in his spaceship and never came back." For a moment she looked far away. Then she shrugged. "I was real young."

Fantasy, the psychologist wrote at the bottom of her screen, but Bach had already figured that out. Since Charlie had to have been born many years after the Charlie Station Plague, her father could not have flown any spaceships.

"What about your mother?"

Charlie was silent for a long time, and Bach began to wonder if she was losing contact with her. At last, she looked up.

"You want to talk to my mother?"

"I'd like that very much."

"Okay. But that's all for today. I've got work to do. You've already put me way behind."

"Just bring your mother here, and I'll talk to her, and you can do your work."

"No. I can't do that. But I'll take you to her. Then I'll work, and I'll talk to you tomorrow."

Bach started to protest that tomorrow was not soon enough, but Charlie was not listening. The camera was picked up, and the picture bounced around as she carried it with her. All Bach could see was a very unsteady upside-down view of the corridor.

"She's going into Room 350," said Steiner. "She's been in there twice, and she stayed a while both times."

Bach said nothing. The camera jerked wildly for a moment, then steadied.

"This is my mother," Charlie said. "Mother, this is my friend, Anna-Louise."

The Mozartplatz had not existed when Bach was a child. Construction on it had begun when she was five, and the first phase was finished when she was fifteen. Tenants had begun moving in soon after that. During each succeeding year new sectors had been opened, and though a structure as large as the Mozartplatz would never be finished—two major sectors were currently under renovation—it had been essentially completed six years ago.

It was a virtual copy of the Soleri-class arcology atriums that had sprouted like mushrooms on the Earth in the last four decades, with the exception that on Earth you built up, and on Luna you went down.

First dig a trench fifteen miles long and two miles deep. Vary the width of the trench, but never let it get narrower than one mile, nor broader than five. In some places make the base of the trench wider than the top, so the walls of rock loom outward. Now put a roof over it, fill it with air, and start boring tunnels into the sides. Turn those tunnels into apartments and shops and everything else humans need in a city. You end up with dizzying vistas, endless terraces that reach higher than the eye can see, a madness of light and motion and spaces too wide to echo.

Do all that, and you still wouldn't have the Mozartplatz. To approach that ridiculous level of grandeur there were still a lot of details to attend to. Build four mile-high skyscrapers to use as table legs to support the mid-air golf course. Crisscross the open space with bridges having no visible means of support, and encrusted with shops and homes that cling like barnacles. Suspend apartment buildings from silver balloons that rise half the day and descend the other half, reachable only by glider. Put in a fountain with more water than Niagara, and a ski slope on a huge spiral ramp. Dig a ten-mile lake in the middle, with a bustling port at each end for the luxury ships that ply back and forth, attach runways to balconies so residents can fly to their front door, stud the interior with zeppelin ports and railway stations and hanging gardens . . . and you still don't have Mozartplatz, but you're getting closer.

The upper, older parts of New Dresden, the parts she had grown up in, were spartan and claustrophobic. Long before her time Lunarians had begun to build larger when they could afford it. The newer, lower parts of the city were studded with downscale versions of Mozartplatz, open spaces half a mile wide and maybe fifty levels deep. This was just a logical extension.

She felt she ought to dislike it because it was so overdone, so fantastically huge, such a waste of space . . . and, oddly, so standardized. It was a taste of the culture of old Earth, where Paris looked just like Tokyo. She had been to the new Beethovenplatz at Clavius, and it looked just like this place. Six more arco-malls were being built in other Lunar cities.

And Bach liked it. She couldn't help herself. One day she'd like to live here.

She left her tube capsule in the bustling central station, went to a terminal and queried the location of the *Great Northern*. It was docked at the southern port, five miles away.

It was claimed that any form of non-animal transportation humans had ever used was available in the Mozartplatz. Bach didn't doubt it. She had tried most of them. But when she had a little time, as she did today, she liked to walk. She didn't have time to walk five miles, but compromised by walking to the trolley station a mile away.

Starting out on a brick walkway, she moved to cool marble, then over a glass bridge with lights flashing down inside. This took her to a boardwalk, then down to a beach where machines made four-foot breakers, each carrying a new load of surfers. The sand was fine and hot between her toes. Mozartplatz was a sensual delight for the feet. Few Lunarians ever wore shoes, and they could walk all day through old New Dresden and feel nothing but different types of carpeting and composition flooring.

The one thing Bach didn't like about the place was the weather. She thought it was needless, preposterous, and inconvenient. It began to rain and, as usual, caught her off guard. She hurried to a shelter where, for a tenthMark, she rented an umberella, but it was too late for her paper uniform. As she stood in front of a blower, drying off, she wadded it up and threw it away, then hurried to catch the trolley, nude but for her creaking leather equipment belt and police cap. Even this stripped down, she was more dressed than a quarter of the people around her.

The conductor gave her a paper mat to put on the artificial leather seat. There were cut flowers in crystal vases attached to the sides of the car. Bach sat by an open window and leaned one arm outside in the cool breeze, watching the passing scenery. She craned her neck when the *Graf Zeppelin* muttered by overhead. They said it was an exact copy of the first world-girdling dirigible, and she had no reason to doubt it.

It was a great day to be traveling. If not for one thing, it would be perfect. Her mind kept coming back to Charlie and her mother.

She had forgotten just how big the *Great Northern* was. She stopped twice on her way down the long dock to board it, once to buy a lime sherbet ice cream cone, and again to purchase a skirt. As she fed coins into the clothing machine, she looked at the great metal wall of the ship. It was painted white, trimmed in gold. There were five smokestacks and six towering masts. Midships was the housing for the huge paddlewheel. Multi-colored pennants snapped in the breeze from the forest of rigging. It was quite a boat.

She finished her cone, punched in her size, then selected a simple above-the-knee skirt in a gaudy print of tropical fruit and palm trees. The machine hummed as it cut the paper to size, hemmed it and strengthened the waist with elastic, then rolled it out into her hand. She held it up against herself, it was good, but the equipment belt spoiled it.

There were lockers along the deck. She used yet another coin to rent one. In it went the belt and cap. She took the pin out of her hair and shook it down around her shoulders, fussed with it for a moment, then decided it would have to do. She fastened the skirt with its single button, wearing it low on her hips, south-seas style. She walked a few steps, studying the effect. The skirt tended to leave one leg bare when she walked, which felt right.

"Look at you," she chided herself, under her breath. "You think you look all right to meet a worlds-famous, glamorous tube personality? Who you happen to despise?" She thought about reclaiming her belt, then decided that would be foolish. The fact was it was a glorous day, a beautiful ship, and she was feeling more alive than she had in months.

She climbed the gangplank and was met at the top by a man in an outlandish uniform. It was all white, covered everything but his face, and was festooned with gold braid and black buttons. It looked hideously uncomfortable, but he didn't seem to mind it. That was one of the odd things about Mozartplatz. In jobs at places like the *Great Northern*, people often worked in period costumes, though it meant wearing shoes or things even more grotesque.

He made a small bow and tipped his hat, then offered her a hibiscus, which he helped her pin in her hair. She smiled at him.

Bach was a sucker for that kind of treatment—and knew it—perhaps because she got so little of it.

"I'm meeting someone in the bar on the top deck."

"If madame would walk this way . . ." He gestured, then led her along the side rail toward the stern of the ship. The deck underfoot was gleaming, polished teak.

She was shown to a wicker table near the rail. The steward held the chair out for her, and took her order. She relaxed, looking up at the vast reaches of the arco-mall, feeling the bright sunlight washing over her body, smelling the salt water, hearing the lap of waves against wood pilings. The air was full of bright balloons, gliders, putt-putting nano-lights, and people in muscle-powered flight harnesses. Not to far away, a fish broke the surface. She grinned at it.

Her drink arrived, with sprigs of mint and several straws and a tiny parasol. It was good. She looked around. There were only a few people out here on the deck. One couple was dressed in full period costume, but the rest looked normal enough. She settled on one guy sitting alone across the deck. He had a good pair of shoulders on him. When she caught his eye, she made a hand signal that meant "I might be available." He ignored it, which annoyed her for a while, until he was joined by a tiny woman who couldn't have been five feet tall. She shrugged. No accounting for taste.

She knew what was happening to her. It was silly, but she felt like going on the hunt. It often happened to her when something shocking or unpleasant happened at work. The police headshrinker said it was compensation, and not that uncommon.

With a sigh, she turned her mind away from that. It seemed there was no place else for it to go but back into that room on Charlie Station, and to the thing in the bed.

Charlie knew her mother was very sick. She had been that way "a long, long time." She left the camera pointed at her mother while she went away to deal with her dogs. The doctors had gathered around and studied the situation for quite some time, then issued their diagnosis.

She was dead, of course, by any definition medical science had accepted for the last century.

Someone had wired her to a robot doctor, probably during the final stages of the epidemic. It was capable of doing just about anything to keep a patient alive and was not programmed to understand brain death. That was a decision left to the human doctor, when he or she arrived.

The doctor had never arrived. The doctor was dead, and the thing that had been Charlie's mother lived on. Bach wondered if the verb "to live" had ever been so abused.

All of its arms and legs were gone, victims of gangrene. Not much else could be seen of it, but a forest of tubes and wires entered and emerged. Fluids seeped slowly through the tissue. Machines had taken over the function of every vital organ. There were patches of greenish skin here and there, including one on the side of its head which Charlie had kissed before leaving. Bach hastily took another drink as she recalled that, and signaled the waiter for another.

Blume and Wilhelm had been fascinated. They were dubious that any part of it could still be alive, even in the sense of cell cultures. There was no way to find out, because the Charlie Station computer— Tik-Tok, to the little girl—refused access to the autodoctor's data outputs.

But there was a very interesting question that emerged as soon as everyone was convinced Charlie's mother *had* died thirty years ago.

"Hello. Anna-Louise. Sorry I'm late."

She looked up and saw Megan Galloway approaching.

Bach had not met the woman in just over ten years, though she, like almost everyone else, had seen her frequently on the tube.

Galloway was tall, for an Earth woman, and not as thin as Bach remembered her. But that was understandable, considering the recent change in her life. Her hair was fiery red and curly, which it had not been ten years ago. It might even be her natural color; she was almost nude, and the colors matched, though that didn't have to mean much. But it looked right on her.

She wore odd-looking silver slippers, and her upper body was traced by a quite lovely filigree of gilded, curving lines. It was some sort of tattoo, and it was all that was left of the machine called the Golden Gypsy. It was completely symbolic. Being the Golden Gypsy was worth a lot of money to Galloway.

Megan Galloway had broken her neck while still in her teens. She became part of the early development of a powered exoskeleton, research that led to the hideously expensive and beautiful Golden Gypsy, of which only one was ever built. It abolished wheelchairs and crutches for her. It returned her to life, in her own mind, and it made her a celebrity.

An odd by-product to learning to use an exoskeleston was the development of skills that made it possible to excel in the new technology of emotional recording: the "feelies." The world was briefly treated to the sight of quadriplegics dominating a new art form. It made Galloway famous as the best of the Trans-sisters. It made her rich, as her trans-tapes out-sold everyone else's. She made herself extremely rich by investing wisely, then she and a friend of Bach's had made her fabulously rich by being the first to capture the experience of falling in love on a trans-tape.

In a sense, Galloway had cured herself. She had always donated a lot of money to neurological research, never really expecting it to pay off. But it did, and three years ago she had thrown the Golden Gypsy away forever.

Bach had thought her cure was complete, but now she wondered. Galloway carried a beautiful crystal cane. It didn't seem to be for show. She leaned on it heavily, and made her way through the tables slowly. Bach started to get up.

"No, no, don't bother," Galloway said. "It takes me a while but I get there." She flashed that famous smile with the gap between her front teeth. There was something about the woman; the smile was so powerful that Bach found herself smiling back. "It's so good to walk I don't mind taking my time."

She let the waiter pull the chair back for her, and sat down with a sigh of relief.

"I'll have a Devil's Nitelite," she told him. "And get another of whatever that was for her."

"A banana Daquiri," Bach said, surprised to find her own drink was almost gone, and a little curious to find out what a Devil's Nitelite was.

Galloway stretched as she looked up at the balloons and gliders.

"It's great to get back to the moon," she said. She made a small gesture that indicated her body. "Great to get out of my clothes. I always feel so free in here. Funny thing, though. I just *can't* get used to not wearing shoes.'' She lifted one foot to display a slipper. "I feel too vulnerable without them. Like I'm going to get stepped on.''

"You can take your clothes off on Earth, too," Bach pointed out.

"Some places, sure. But aside from the beach, there's no place where it's *fashionable*, don't you see?''

Bach didn't, but decided not to make a thing out of it. She knew social nudity had evolved in Luna because it never got hot or cold, and that Earth would never embrace it as fully as Lunarians had.

The drinks arrived. Bach sipped hers, and eyed Galloway's, which produced a luminous smoke ring every ten seconds. Galloway chattered on about nothing in particular for a while.

"Why did you agree to see me?" Galloway asked, at last.

"Shouldn't that be my question?''

Galloway raised an eyebrow, and Bach went on.

"You've got a hell of a story. I can't figure out why you didn't just run with it. Why arrange a meeting with someone you barely knew ten years ago, and haven't seen since, and never liked even back then?''

"I always liked you, Anna-Louise," Galloway said. She looked up at the sky. For a while she watched a couple pedaling a skycycle, then she looked at Bach again. "I feel like I owe you something. Anyway, when I saw your name I thought I should check with you. I don't want to cause you any trouble.'' Suddenly she looked angry. "I don't *need* the story, Bach. I don't need *any* story, I'm too big for that. I can let it go or I can use it, it makes no difference.''

"Oh, that's cute," Bach said. "Maybe I don't understand how you pay your debts. Maybe they do it different on Earth.''

She thought Galloway was going to get up and leave. She had reached for her cane, then thought better of it.

"I gather it doesn't matter, then, if I go with the story.''

Bach shrugged. She hadn't come here to talk about Charlie, anyway.

"How is Q.M., by the way?" she said.

Galloway didn't look away this time. She sat in silence for almost a minute, searching Bach's eyes.

"I thought I was ready for that question," she said at last. "He's living in New Zeland, on a commune. From what my agents tell me, he's happy. They don't watch television, they don't marry. They worship and they screw a lot.''

"Did you really give him half of the profits on that . . . that tape?''

"Did give him, am giving him, and will continue to give him until the day I die. And it's half the *gross*, my dear, which is another thing entirely. He gets half of every Mark that comes in. He's made more money off it than I have . . . and he's never touched a tenthMark. It's piling up in a Swiss account I started in his name.''

"Well, he never sold anything.''

Bach hadn't meant that to be as harsh as it came out, but Galloway did not seem bothered by it. The thing she had sold . . .

Had there ever been anyone as thoroughly betrayed as Q.M. Cooper? Bach wondered. She might have loved him herself, but he fell totally in love with Megan Galloway.

And Galloway fell in love with him. There could be no mistake about that. Doubters are referred to *Gitana de Oro* catalog #1, an emotional recording entitled, simply, ''Love.'' Put it in your trans-tape player, don the headset, punch PLAY, and you will experience just how hard and how completely Galloway fell in love with Q.M. Cooper. But have your head examined first. GDO #1 had been known to precipitate suicide.

Cooper had found this an impediment to the course of true love. He had always thought that love was something between two people, something exclusive, something private. He was unprepared to have Galloway mass-produce it, put it in a box with liner notes and a price tag of LM14.95, and hawk copies in every trans-tape shop from Peoria to Tibet.

The supreme irony of it to the man, who eventually found refuge in a minor cult in a far corner of the Earth, was that the tape itself, the means of his betrayal, his humiliation, was proof that Galloway had returned his love.

And Galloway had sold it. Never mind that she had her reasons, or that they were reasons with which Bach could find considerable sympathy.

She had sold it.

All Bach ever got out of the episode was a compulsion to seek lovers who looked like the Earth-muscled Cooper. Now it seemed she might get something else. It was time to change the subject.

"What do you know about Charlie?" she asked.

"You want it all, or just a general idea?" Galloway didn't wait for an answer. "I know her real name is Charlotte Isolde Hill Perkins-Smith. I know her father is dead, and her mother's condition is open to debate. Leda Perkins-Smith has a lot of money—if she's alive. Her daughter would inherit, if she's dead. I know the names of ten of Charlie's dogs. And, oh yes, I know that, appearances to the contrary, she is thirty-seven years old."

"Your source is very up-to-date."

"It's a very good source."

"You want to name him?"

"I'll pass on that, for the moment." She regarded Bach easily, her hands folded on the table in front of her. "So. What do you want me to do?"

"Is it really that simple?"

"My producers will want to kill me, but I'll sit on the story for at least twenty-four hours if you tell me to. By the way," she turned in her seat and crooked a finger at another table. "It's probably time you met my producers."

Bach turned slightly, and saw them coming toward her table.

"These are the Myers twins, Joy and Jay. Waiter, do you know how to make a Shirley Temple and a Roy Rogers?"

The waiter said he did, and went off with the order while Joy and Jay pulled up chairs and sat in them, several feet from the table but very close to each other. They had not offered to shake hands. Both were armless, with no sign of amputation, just bare, rounded shoulders. Both wore prosthetics made of golden, welded wire and powered by tiny motors. The units were one piece, fitting over their backs in a harnesslike arrangement. They were quite pretty—light and airy, perfectly articulated, cunningly wrought—and also creepy.

"You've heard of amparole?" Galloway asked. Bach shook her head. "That's the slang word for it. It's a neo-Moslem practice. Joy and Jay were convicted of murder."

"I have heard of it." She hadn't paid much attention to it, dismissing it as just another hare-brained Earthling idiocy.

"Their arms are being kept in cryonic suspension for twenty years. The theory is, if they sin no more, they'll get them back.

Those prosthetics won't pick up a gun, or a knife. They won't throw a punch.''

Joy and Jay were listening to this with complete stolidity. Once Bach got beyond the arms, she saw another unusual thing about them. They were dressed identically, in loose bell-bottomed trousers. Joy had small breasts, and Jay had a small mustache. Other than that, they were absolutely identical in face and body. Bach didn't care for the effect.

"They also took slices out of the cerebrums and they're on a maintenance dosage of some drug. Calms them down. You don't want to know who they killed, or how. But they were proper villains, these two.''

No, I don't think I do, Bach decided. Like many cops, she looked at eyes. Joy and Jay's were calm, placid . . . and deep inside was a steel-gray coldness.

"If they try to get naughty again, the amparole units go on strike. I suppose they might find a way to kill with their feet.''

The twins glanced at each other, held each other's gaze for a moment, and exchanged wistful smiles. At least, Bach hoped they were just wistful.

"Yeah, okay,'' Bach said.

"Don't worry about them. They can't be offended with the drugs they're taking.''

"I wasn't worried.'' Bach said. She couldn't have cared less what the freaks felt; she wished they'd been executed.

"Are they really twins?'' she finally asked, against her better judgment.

"Really. One of them had a sex change, I don't know which one. And to answer your next question, yes they do, but only in the privacy of their own room.''

"I wasn't—''

"And your other question . . . they are *very* good at what they do. Who am I to judge about the other? And I'm in a highly visible industry. It never hurts to have conversation pieces around. You need to get noticed.''

Bach was starting to get angry, and she was not quite sure why. Maybe it was the way Galloway so cheerfully admitted her base motives, even when no one had accused her of having them.

"We were talking about the story,'' she said.

"We need to go with it," Joy said, startling Bach. Somehow, she had not really expected the cyborg-thing to talk. "Our source is good and the security on the story is tight—"

"—but it's dead certain to come out in twenty-four hours," Jay finished for her.

"Maybe less," Joy added.

"Shut up," Galloway said, without heat. "Anna-Louise, you were about to tell me your feeling on the matter."

Bach finished her drink as the waiter arrived with more. She caught herself staring as the twins took theirs. The metal hands were marvels of complexity. They moved just as cleverly as real hands."

"I was considering leaking the story myself. It looked like things were going against Charlie. I thought they might just let the station crash and then swear us all to secrecy."

"It strikes me," Galloway said, slowly, "that today's developments give her an edge."

"Yeah. But I don't envy her."

"Me, either. But it's not going to be easy to neglect a girl whose body may hold the secret of eternal life. If you do, somebody's bound to ask awkward questions later."

"It may not be eternal life," Bach said.

"What do you call it, then?" Jay asked.

"Why do you say that?" Joy wanted to know.

"All we know is she's lived thirty years without growing any older—externally. They'd have to examine her a lot closer to find out what's actually happening."

"And there's pressure to do so."

"Exactly. It might be the biggest medical breakthrough in a thousand years. What I think has happened to her is not eternal life, but extended youth."

Galloway looked throughtful. "You know, of the two, I think extended youth would be more popular."

"I think you're right."

They brooded over that in silence for a while. Bach signaled the waiter for another drink.

"Anyway," she went on, "Charlie doesn't seem to need protection just now. But she may, and quickly."

"So you aren't in favor of letting her die."

Bach looked up, surprised and beginning to be offended, then she remembered Doctor Wilhelm. The good Doctor was not a monster, and Galloway's question was a reasonable one, given the nature of Neuro-X.

"There has to be a way to save her, *and* protect ourselves from her. That's what I'm working toward, anyway."

"Let me get this straight, then. You were thinking of leaking the story so the public outcry would force the police to save her?"

"Sure I thought . . ." Bach trailed off, suddenly realizing what Galloway was saying. "You mean you think—"

Galloway waved her hand impatiently.

"It depends on a lot of things, but mostly on how the story is handled. If you start off with the plague story, there could be pressure to blast her out of the skies and have done with it." She looked at Jay and Joy, who went into a trance-like state.

"Sure, sure," Jay said. "The plague got big play. Almost everybody remembers it. Use horror show tapes of the casualties . . ."

". . . line up the big brains to start the scare," Joy said.

"You can even add sob stuff, after it gets rolling."

"What a tragedy, this little girl has to die for the good of us all."

"Somber commentary, the world watches as she cashes in."

"You could make it play. No problem."

Bach's head had been ping-ponging between the two of them. When Galloway spoke, it was hard to swing around and look at her.

"Or you could start off with the little girl," Galloway prompted.

"*Much* better," Joy said. "Twice the story there. Indignant exposé stuff: 'Did you know, fellow citizens . . .' "

" '. . . there's this little girl, this innocent child, swinging around up there in space and she's going to *die!*' "

"A *rich* little girl, too, and her dying mother."

"Later, get the immortality angle."

"Not too soon," Joy cautioned. "At first, she's ordinary. Second lead is, she's got money."

"Third lead, she holds the key to eternal youth."

"Immortality."

"Youth, honey, youth. Who the fuck knows what living forever is like? Youth you can sell. It's the *only* thing you can sell."

"Megan, this it the biggest story since Jesus."

"Or at least we'll *make* it the biggest story."

"See why they're so valuable?" Galloway said. Bach hardly heard her. She was re-assessing what she had thought she knew about the situation.

"I don't know what to do," she finally confessed. "I don't know what to ask you to do, either. I guess you ought to go with what you think is best."

Galloway frowned.

"Both for professional and personal reasons, I'd rather try to help her. I'm not sure why. She is dangerous, you know."

"I realize that. But I can't believe she can't be handled."

"Neither can I." She glanced at her watch. "Tell you what, you come with us on a little trip."

Bach protested at first, but Galloway would not be denied, and Bach's resistance was at a low ebb.

By speedboat, trolley, and airplane they quickly made their way to the top of Mozartplatz, where Bach found herself in a four-seat PTP—or point-to-point—ballistic vehicle.

She had never ridden in a PTP. They were rare, mostly because they wasted a lot of energy for only a few minutes' gain in travel time. Most people took the tubes, which reached speeds of three thousand miles per hour, hovering inches above their induction rails in Luna's excellent vacuum.

But for a celebrity like Galloway, the PTP made sense. She had trouble going places in public without getting mobbed. And she certainly had the money to spare.

There was a heavy initial acceleration, then weightlessness. Bach had never liked it, and enjoyed it even less with a few drinks in her.

Little was said during the short journey. Bach had not asked where they were going, and Galloway did not volunteer it. Bach looked out one of the wide windows at the fleeting moonscape.

As she counted the valleys, rilles, and craters flowing past beneath her, she soon realized her destination. It was a distant valley, in the sense that no tube track ran through it. In a little over an hour, Tango Charlie would come speeding through, no more than a hundred meters from the surface.

The PTP landed itself in a cluster of transparent, temporary domes. There were over a hundred of them, and more PTP's than Bach had ever seen before. She decided most of the people in and around the domes fell into three categories. There were the very wealthy, owners of private spacecraft, who had erected most of these portable Xanadus and filled them with their friends. There were civic dignitaries in city-owned domes. And there were the news media.

This last category was there in its teeming hundreds. It was not what they would call a *big* story, but it was a very visual one. It should yield spectacular pictures for the evening news.

A long, wide black stripe had been created across the sundrenched plain, indicating the path Tango Charlie would take. Many cameras and quite a few knots of pressure-suited spectators were situated smack in the middle of that line, with many more off to one side, to get an angle on the approach. Beyond it were about a hundred large glass-roofed touring buses and a motley assortment of private crawlers, sunskimmers, jetsleds and even some hikers: the common people, come to see the event.

Bach followed along behind the uncommon people: Galloway, thin and somehow spectral in the translucent suit, leaning on her crystal cane; the Myers twins, whose amparolee arms would not fit in the suits, so that the empty sleeves stuck out, bloated, like crucified ghosts; and most singular of all, the wire-sculpture arm units themselves, walking independently, on their fingertips, looking like some demented, disjointed mechanical camel as they lurched through the dust.

They entered the largest of the domes, set on the edge of the gathering nearest the black line, which put it no more than a hundred meters from the expected passage.

The first person Bach saw, as she was removing her helmet, was Hoeffer.

He did not see her immediately. He, and many of the other people in the dome, were watching Galloway. So she saw his face as his gaze moved from the celebrity to Joy and Jay . . . and saw amazement and horror, far too strong to be simple surprise at their weirdness. It was a look of recognition.

Galloway had said she had an excellent source.

She noticed Bach's interest, smiled, and nodded slightly. Still struggling to remove her suit, she approached Bach.

"That's right. The twins heard a rumor something interesting might be going on at NavTrack, so they found your commander. Turns out he has rather odd sexual tastes, though it's probably fairly pedestrian to Joy and Jay. They scratched his itch, and he spilled everything."

"I find that . . . rather interesting," Bach admitted.

"I thought you would. Were you planning to make a career out of being a R/A in Navigational Tracking?"

"That wasn't my intention."

"I didn't think so. Listen, don't touch it. I can handle it without there being any chance of it backfiring on you. Within the week you'll be promoted out of there."

"I don't know if . . ."

"If what?" Galloway was looking at her narrowly.

Bach hesitated only a moment.

"I may be stiff-necked, but I'm not a fool. Thank you."

Galloway turned away a little awkwardly, then resumed struggling with her suit. Bach was about to offer some help, when Galloway frowned at her.

"How come you're not taking off your pressure suit?"

"That dome up there is pretty strong, but it's only one layer. Look around you. Most of the natives have just removed their helmets, and a lot are carrying those around. Most of the Earthlings are out of their suits. They don't understand vacuum."

"You're saying it's not safe?"

"No. But vacuum doesn't forgive. It's trying to kill you *all* the time."

Galloway looked dubious, but stopped trying to remove her suit.

Bach wandered the electronic wonderland, helmet in hand.

Tango Charlie would not be visible until less than a minute before the close encounter, and then would be hard to spot as it would be only a few seconds of arc above the horizon line. But there were cameras hundreds of miles downtrack which could already see it, both as a bright star, moving visibly against the background, and as a jittery image in some very long lenses. Bach watched as the wheel filled one screen until she could actually see furniture behind one of the windows.

For the first time since arriving, she thought of Charlie. She wondered if Tik-Tok—no, dammit, if the Charlie Station Computer had told her of the approach, and if so, would Charlie watch it. Which window would she choose? It was shocking to think that, if she chose the right one. Bach might catch a glimpse of her.

Only a few minutes to go. Knowing it was stupid, Bach looked along the line indicated by the thousand cameras, hoping to catch the first glimpse.

She saw Megan Galloway doing a walk-around, followed by a camera crew, no doubt saying bright, witty things to her huge audience. Galloway was here less for the event itself than for the many celebrities who had gathered to witness it. Bach saw her approach a famous TV star, who smiled and embraced her, making some sort of joke about Galloway's pressure suit.

You can meet him if you want, she told herself. She was a little surprised to discover she had no interest in doing so.

She saw Joy and Jay in heated conversation with Hoeffer. The twins seemed distantly amused.

She saw the countdown clock, ticking toward one minute.

Then the telescopic image in one of the remote cameras began to shake violently. In a few seconds, it had lost its fix on Charlie Station. Bach watched as annoyed technicians struggled to get it back.

"Seismic activity," one of them said, loud enough for Bach to hear.

She looked at the other remote monitor, which showed Tango Charlie as a very bright star sitting on the horizon. As she watched, the light grew visibly, until she could see it as a disc. And in another part of the screen, at a site high in the lunar hills, there was a shower of dust and rock. That must be the seismic activity, she thought. The camera operator zoomed in on this eruption, and Bach frowned. She couldn't figure out what sort of lunar quake could cause such a commotion. It looked more like an impact. The rocks and dust particles were fountaining up with lovely geometrical symmetry, each piece, from the largest boulder to the smallest mote, moving at about the same speed and in a perfect mathematical trajectory, unimpeded by any air resistance, in a way that could never be duplicated on Earth. It was a dull gray expanding dome shape, gradually flattening on top.

Frowning, she turned her attention to the spot on the plain where she had been told Charlie would first appear. She saw the first light of it, but more troubling, she saw a dozen more of the expanding domes. From here, they seemed no larger than soap bubbles.

Then another fountain of rock erupted, not far from the impromptu parking lot full of tourist buses.

Suddenly she knew what was happening.

"It's shooting at us!" she shouted. Everyone fell silent, and as they were still turning to look at her, she yelled again. "Suit up."

Her voice was drowned out by the sound every Lunarian dreads: the high, haunting shriek of escaping air.

Step number one, she heard a long-ago instructor say. See to *your own* pressure integrity *first*. You can't help anybody, man, woman or child, if you pass out before you get into your suit.

It was a five-second operation to don and seal her helmet, one she had practiced a thousand times as a child. She glimpsed a great hole in the plastic roof. Debris was pouring out of it, swept up in the sudden wind: paper, clothing, a couple of helmets . . .

Sealed up, she looked around and realized many of these people were doomed. They were not in their suits, and there was little chance they could put them on in time.

She remembered the next few seconds in a series of vivid impressions.

A boulder, several tons of dry lunar rock, crashed down on a bank of television monitors.

A chubby little man, his hands shaking, unable to get his helmet over his bald head. Bach tore it from his hands, slapped it in place, and gave it a twist hard enough to knock him down.

Joy and Jay, as good as dead, killed by the impossibility of fitting the mechanical arms into their suits, holding each other calmly in metallic embrace.

Beyond the black line, a tour bus rising slowly in the air, turning end over end. A hundred of the hideous gray domes of explosions growing like mushrooms all through the valley.

And there was Galloway. She was going as fast as she could, intense concentration on her face as she stumbled along after her helmet, which was rolling on the ground. Blood had leaked from one corner of her nose. It was almost soundless in the remains of the dome now.

Bach snagged the helmet, and hit Galloway with a flying tackle. Just like a drill: put helmet in place, twist, hit three snap-interlocks, then the emergency pressurization switch. She saw Galloway howl in pain and try to put her hands to her ears.

Lying there she looked up as the last big segment of the dome material lifted in a dying wind to reveal . . . Tango Charlie.

It was a little wheel rolling on the horizon. No bigger than a coin.

She blinked.

And it was *here*. Vast, towering, coming directly at her through a hell of burning dust.

It was the dust that finally made the lasers visible. The great spokes of light were flashing on and off in millisecond bursts, and in each pulse a trillion dust motes were vaporized in an eyeball-frying purple light.

It was impossibles that she saw it for more than a tenth of a second, but it seemed much longer. The sight would remain with her, and not just in memory. For days afterward her vision was scored with a spiderweb of purple lines.

But much worse was the awesome grandeur of the thing, the whirling menace of it as it came rushing out of the void. That picture would last much longer than a few days. It would come out only at night, in dreams that would wake her for years, drenched in sweat.

And the last strong image she would carry away from the valley was of Galloway, turned over now, pointing her crystal cane at the wheel, already far away on the horizon. A line of red laser light came out of the end of the cane and stretched away into infinity.

"Wow!" said Charlotte Isolde Hill Perkins-Smith. "Wow, Tik-Tok, that was great! Let's do it again."

Hovering in the dead center of the hub, Charlie had watched all of the encounter. It had been a lot like she imagined a roller-coaster would be when she watched the films in Tik-Tok's memory. If it had a fault—and she wasn't complaining, far from it—it was that the experience had been too short. For almost an hour she had watched the moon get bigger, until it no longer seemed round and the landscape was rolling by beneath her. But she'd seen that much before. This time it just got larger and larger, and faster and faster, until she was scooting along at about a zillion miles an hour. Then there was a lot of flashing lights . . . and gradually, the ground got farther away again. It was still back there, dwindling, no longer very interesting.

"I'm glad you liked it," Tik-Tok said.

"Only one thing. How come I had to put on my pressure suit?"

"Just a precaution."

She shrugged, and made her way to the elevator.

When she got out at the rim, she frowned. There were alarms sounding, far around the rim on the wheel.

"We got a problem?" she asked.

"Minor," Tik-Tok said.

"What happened?"

"We got hit by some rocks."

"We must of passed *real* close!"

"Charlie, if you'd been down here when we passed, you could have reached out and written your name on a rock."

She giggled at that idea, then hurried off to see to the dogs.

It was about two hours later that Anna-Louise called. Charlie was inclined to ignore it, she had so much to do, but in the end, she sat down in front of the camera. Anna-Louise was there, and sitting beside her was another woman.

"Are you okay, Charlie?" Anna wanted to know.

"Why shouldn't I be?" Damn, she thought. She wasn't supposed to answer a question with another question. But then, what right did Anna have to ask her to do that?

"I was wondering if you were watching a little while ago, when you passed so close to the moon."

"I sure was. It was great."

There was a short pause. The two women looked at each other, then Anna-Louise sighed, and faced Charlie again.

"Charlie, there are a few things I have to tell you."

As in most disasters involving depressurization, there was

not a great demand for first aid. Most of the bad injuries were fatal.

Galloway was not hearing too well and Bach still had spots before her eyes; Hoeffer hadn't even bumped his head.

The body-count was not complete, but it was going to be high.

For a perilous hour after the passage, there was talk of shooting Tango Charlie out of the sky.

Much of the advisory team had already gathered in the meeting room by the time Bach and Hoeffer arrived—with Galloway following closely behind. A hot debate was in progress. People recognized Galloway, and a few seemed inclined to question her presence here, but Hoeffer shut them up quickly. A deal had been struck in the PTP, on the way back from the disaster. The fix was in, and Megan Galloway was getting an exclusive on the story. Galloway had proved to Hoeffer that Joy and Jay had kept tapes of his security lapse.

The eventual explanation for the unprovoked and insane attack was simple. The Charlie Station Computer had been instructed to fire upon any object approaching within five kilometers. It had done so, faithfully, for thirty years, not that it ever had much to shoot at. The close approach of Luna must have been an interesting problem. Tik-Tok was no fool. Certainly he would know the consequences of his actions. But a computer did not think at all like a human, no matter how much it might sound like one. There were rigid hierarchies in a brain like Tik-Tok. One part of him might realize something was foolish, but be helpless to over-ride a priority order.

Analysis of the pattern of laser strikes helped to confirm this. The hits were totally random. Vehicles, domes, and people had not been targeted; however, if they were in the way, they were hit.

The one exception to the randomness concerned the black line Bach had seen. Tik-Tok had found a way to avoid shooting directly ahead of himself without violating his priority order. Thus, he avoided stirring up debris that Charile Station would be flying through in another few seconds.

The decision was made to take no reprisals on Tango Charlie. Nobody was happy about it, but no one could suggest anything short of total destruction.

But action had to be taken now. Very soon the public was going to wonder why this dangerous object had not been destroyed before the approach. The senior police present and the representatives of the Mayor's office all agreed that the press would have to be let in. They asked Galloway if they could have her cooperation in the management of this phase.

And Bach watched as, with surprising speed, Megan Galloway took over the meeting.

"You need time right now," she said, at one point. "The best way to get it is to play the little-girl angle, and play it hard. You were not so heartless as to endanger the little girl—and you had no reason to believe the station was any kind of threat. What you have to do now is tell the truth about what we know, and what's been done."

"How about the immortality angle?" someone asked.

"What about it? It's going to leak someday. Might as well get it out in front of us."

"But it will prejudice the public in favor of . . ." Wilhelm looked around her, and decided not to finish her objection.

"It's a price we have to pay," Galloway said, smoothly. "You folks will do what you think is right. I'm sure of that. You wouldn't let public opinion influence your decision."

Nobody had anything to say to that. Bach managed not to laugh.

"The big thing is to answer the questions before they get asked. I suggest you get started on your statements, then call in the press. In the meantime. Corporal Bach has invited me to listen in on her next conversation with Charlie Perkins-Smith, so I'll leave you now."

Bach led Galloway down the corridor toward the operations room, shaking her head in admiration. She looked over her shoulder.

"I got to admit it. You're very smooth."

"It's my profession. You're pretty smooth, yourself."

"What do you mean?"

"I mean I owe you. I'm afraid I owe you more than I'll be able to repay."

Bach stopped, honestly bewildered.

"You saved my *life*," Galloway shouted. *"Thank you!"*

"So what if I did? You don't owe me anything. It's not the custom."

368 / John Varley

"What's not the custom?"

"You can be grateful, sure. I'd be, if somebody pressurized me. But it would be an insult to try to pay me back for it. Like on the desert, you know, you have to give water to somebody dying of thirst."

"Not in the deserts I've been to," Galloway said. They were alone in the hallway. Galloway seemed distressed, and Bach felt awkward. "We seem to be at a cultural impasse. I feel I owe you a lot, and you say it's nothing."

"No problem." Bach pointed out. "You were going to help me get promoted out of this stinking place. Do that, and we'll call it even."

Galloway was shaking her head.

"I don't think I'll be able to, now. You know that fat man you stuffed into a helmet, before you got to me? He asked me about you. He's the Mayor of Clavius. He'll be talking to the Mayor of New Dresden, and you'll get the promotion and a couple of medals and maybe a reward, too."

They regarded each other uneasily. Bach knew that gratitude could equal resentment. She thought she could see some of that in Galloway's eyes. But there was determnation, too. Megan Galloway paid her debts. She had been paying one to Q.M. Cooper for ten years.

By unspoken agreement they left it at that, and went to talk to Charlie.

Most of the dogs didn't like the air blower. Mistress Too White O'Hock was the exception. 2-White would turn her face into the stream of warm air as Charlie directed the hose over her sable pelt, then she would let her tongue hang out in an expression of such delight that Charlie would usually end up laughing at her.

Charlie brushed the fine hair behind 2-White's legs, the hair that was white almost an inch higher than it should be on a champion Sheltie. Just one little inch, and 2-White was sterilized. She would have been a fine mother. Charlie had seen her looking at puppies whelped by other mothers, and she knew it made 2-White sad.

But you can't have everything in this world. Tik-Tok had said that often enough. And you can't let all your dogs breed, or pretty soon you'll be knee deep in dogs. Tik-Tok said that, too.

In fact, Tik-Tok said a lot of things Charlie wished were not true. But he had never lied to her.

"Were you listening?" she asked.

"During your last conversation? Of course I was."

Charlie put 2-White down on the floor, and summoned the next dog. This was Engelbert, who wasn't a year old yet, and still inclined to be frisky when he shouldn't be. Charlie had to scold him before he would be still.

"Some of the things she said," Tik-Tok began. "It seemed like she disturbed you. Like how old you are."

"That's silly," Charlie said, quickly. "I knew how old I am." This was the truth . . . and yet it wasn't everything. Her first four dogs were all dead. The oldest had been thirteen. There had been many dogs since then. Right now, the oldest dog was sixteen, and sick. He wouldn't last much longer.

"I just never added it up," Charlie said, truthfully.

"There was never any reason to."

"But I don't grow up," she said, softly. "Why is that, Tik-Tok?"

"I don't know, Charlie."

"Anna said if I go down to the moon, they might be able to find out."

Tik-Tok didn't say anything.

"Was she telling the truth? About all those people who got hurt?"

"Yes."

"Maybe I shouldn't have got mad at her."

Again, Tik-Tok was silent. Charlie had been very angry. Anna and a new woman. Megan, had told her all these awful things, and when they were done Charlie knocked over the television equipment and went away. That had been almost a day ago, and they had been calling back almost all the time.

"Why did you do it?" she said.

"I didn't have any choice."

Charlie accepted that. Tik-Tok was a mechanical man, not like her at all. He was a faithful guardian and the closest thing she had to a friend, but she knew he was different. For one thing, he didn't have a body. She had sometimes wondered if this inconvenienced him any, but she had never asked.

"Is my mother really dead?"

"Yes."

Charlie stopped brushing. Engelbert looked around at her, then waited patiently until she told him he could get down.

"I guess I knew that."

"I thought you did. But you never asked."

"She was someone to talk to," Charlie explained. She left the grooming room and walked down the promenade. Several dogs followed behind her, trying to get her to play.

She went into her mother's room and stood for a moment looking at the thing in the bed. Then she moved from machine to machine, flipping switches, until everything was quiet. And when she was done, that was the only change in the room. The machines no longer hummed, rumbled, and clicked. The thing on the bed hadn't changed at all. Charlie supposed she could keep on talking to it, if she wanted to, but she suspected it wouldn't be the same.

She wondered if she ought to cry. Maybe she should ask Tik-Tok, but he'd never been very good with those kind of questions. Maybe it was because he couldn't cry himself, so he didn't know when people ought to cry. But the fact was, Charlie had felt a lot sadder at Albert's funeral.

In the end, she sang her hymn again, then closed and locked the door behind her. She would never go in there again.

"She's back," Steiner called across the room. Bach and Galloway hastily put down their cups of coffee and hurried over to Bach's office.

"She just plugged this camera in," Steiner explained, as they took their seats. "Looks a little different, doesn't she?"

Bach had to agree. They had glimpsed her in other cameras as she went about her business. Then, about an hour ago, she had entered her mother's room again. From there, she had gone to her own room, and when she emerged, she was a different girl. Her hair was washed and combed. She wore a dress that seemed to have started off as a woman's blouse. The sleeves had been cut off and bits of it had been inexpertly taken in. There was red polish on her nails. Her face was heavily made up. It was overdone, and completely wrong for someone of her apparent age, but it was not the wild, almost tribal paint she had worn before.

Charlie was seated behind a huge wooden desk, facing the camera.

"Good morning, Anna and Megan," she said, solemnly.

"Good morning, Charlie," Galloway said.

"I'm sorry I shouted at you," Charlie said. Her hands were folded carefully in front of her. There was a sheet of paper just to the left of them; other than that, the desk was bare. "I was confused and upset, and I needed some time to think about the things you said."

"That's all right," Bach told her. She did her best to conceal a yawn. She and Galloway had been awake for a day and a half. There had been a few catnaps, but they were always interrupted by sightings of Charlie.

"I've talked things over with Tik-Tok," Charlie went on. "And I turned my mother off. You were right. She was dead, anyway."

Bach could think of nothing to say to that. She glanced at Galloway, but could read nothing in the other woman's face.

"I've decided what I want to do," Charlie said. "But first I—"

"Charlie," Galloway said, quickly, "could you show me what you have there on the table?"

There was a brief silence in the room. Several people turned to look at Galloway, but nobody said anything. Bach was about to, but Galloway was making a motion with her hand, under the table, where no one but Bach was likely to see it. Bach decided to let it ride for the moment.

Charlie was looking embarrassed. She reached for the paper, glanced at it, then looked back at the camera.

"I drew this picture for you," she said. "Because I was sorry I shouted."

"Could I see it?"

Charlie jumped down off the chair and came around to hold the picture up. She seemed proud of it, and she had every right to be. Here at last was visual proof that Charlie was not what she seemed to be. No eight-year-old could have drawn this fine pencil portrait of a Sheltie.

"This is for Anna," she said.

"That's very nice, Charlie," Galloway said. "I'd like one, too."

"I'll draw you one!" Charlie said happily . . . and ran out of the picture.

There was angry shouting for a few moments. Galloway stood her ground, explaining that she had only been trying to cement the friendship, and how was she to know Charlie would run off like that?

Even Hoeffer was emboldened enough to take a few shots, pointing out—logically, in Bach's opinion—that time was running out and if anything was to be done about her situation every second was valuable.

"All right, all right, so I made a mistake. I promise I'll be more careful next time. Anna, I hope you'll call me when she comes back." And with that, she picked up her cane and trudged from the room.

Bach was surprised. It didn't seem like Galloway to leave the story before it was over, even if nothing was happening. But she was too tired to worry about it. She leaned back in her chair, closed her eyes, and was asleep in less than a minute.

Charlie was hard at work on the picture for Megan when Tik-Tok interrupted her. She looked up in annoyance.

"Can't you see I'm busy?"

"I'm sorry, but this can't wait. There's a telephone call for you."

"There's a . . . *what*?"

But Tik-Tok said no more. Charlie went across the room to the phone, silent these thirty years. She eyed it suspiciously, then pressed the button. As she did, dim memories flooded through her. She saw her mother's face. For the first time, she felt like crying.

"This is Charlotte Perkins-Smith," she said, in a childish voice. "My mother isn't . . . my mother . . . may I ask who's calling, please?"

There was no picture on the screen, but after a short pause, there was a familiar voice.

"This is Megan Galloway, Charlie. Can we talk?"

When Steiner shook Bach's shoulder, she opened her eyes to see Charlie sitting on the desk once more. Taking a quick sip of the hot coffee Steiner had brought, she tried to wipe the cobwebs from her mind and get back to work. The girl was just sitting there, hands folded once more.

"Hello, Anna," the girl said. "I just wanted to call and tell you I'll do whatever you people think is best. I've been acting silly. I hope you'll forgive me; it's been a long time since I had to talk to other people."

"That's okay, Charlie."

"I'm sorry I pissed on Captain Hoeffer. Tik-Tok said that was a bad thing to do, and that I ought to be more respectful to him, since he's the guy in charge. So if you'll get him, I'll do whatever he says."

"All right, Charlie. I'll get him."

Bach got up and watched Hoeffer take her chair.

"You'll be talking just to me from now on," he said, with what he must have felt was a friendly smile. "Is that all right?"

"Sure," Charlie said, indifferently.

"You can go get some rest now, Corporal Bach," Hoeffer said. She saluted, and turned on her heel. She knew it wasn't fair to Charlie to feel betrayed, but she couldn't help it. True, she hadn't talked to the girl all that long. There was no reason to feel a friendship had developed. But she felt sick watching Hoeffer talk to her. The man would lie to her, she was sure of that.

But then, could she have done any different? It was a disturbing thought. The fact was, there had as yet been no orders on what to do about Charlie. She was all over the news, the public debate had begun, and Bach knew it would be another day before public officials had taken enough soundings to know which way they should leap. In the meantime, they had Charlie's cooperation, and that was good news.

Bach wished she could be happier about it.

"Anna, there's a phone call for you."

She took it at one of the vacant consoles. When she pushed the Talk button, a light came on indicating the other party wanted privacy, so she picked up the handset and asked who was calling.

"Anna," said Galloway, "come at once to room 569 in the Pension Kleist. That's four corridors from the main entrance to NavTrack, level—"

"I can find it. What's this all about? You got your story."

"I'll tell you when you get there."

The first person Bach saw in the small room was Ludmilla Rossnikova, the computer expert from GMA. She was sitting in a chair across the room, looking uncomfortable. Bach shut the door behind her, and saw Galloway sprawled in another chair before a table littered with electronic gear.

"I felt I had to speak to Tik-Tok privately," Galloway began, without preamble. She looked about as tired as Bach felt.

"Is that why you sent Charlie away?"

Galloway gave her a truly feral grin, and for a moment did not look tired at all. Bach realized she loved this sort of intrigue, loved playing fast and loose, taking chances.

"That's right. I figured Ms. Rossnikova was the woman to get me through, so now she's working for me."

Bach was impressed. It would not have been cheap to hire Rossnikova away from GMA. She would not have thought it possible.

"GMA doesn't know that, and it won't know, if you can keep a secret," Galloway went on. "I assured Ludmilla that you could."

"You mean she's spying for you."

"Not at all. She's not going to be working against GMA's interests, which are quite minimal in this affair. We're just not going to tell them about her work for me, and next year Ludmilla will take early retirement and move into a dacha in Georgia she's coveted all her life."

Bach looked at Rossnikova, who seemed embarrassed. So everybody has her price, Bach thought. So what else is new?

"Turns out she had a special code which she withheld from the folks back at NavTrack. I suspected she might. I wanted to talk to him without anyone else knowing I was doing it. Your control room was a bit crowded for that. Ludmilla, you want to take it from there?"

She did, telling Bach the story in a low voice, with reserved, diffident gestures. Bach wondered if she would be able to live with her defection, decided she'd probably get over it soon enough.

Rossnikova had raised Charlie Station, which in this sense was synonymous with Tik-Tok, the station computer. Galloway had talked to him. She wanted to know what he knew. As she suspected, he was well aware of his own orbital dynamics. He knew he was going to crash into the moon. So what did he intend to do about Charlotte Perkins-Smith? Galloway wanted to know.

What are you offering? Tik-Tok responded.

"The important point is, he doesn't want Charlie to die. He can't do anything about his instruction to fire on intruders. But he claims he would have let Charlie go years ago but for one thing."

"Our quarantine probes," Bach said.

"Exactly. He's got a lifeboat in readiness. A few minutes from impact, if nothing has been resolved, he'll load Charlie in it and blast her away, after first killing both your probes. He knows it's not much of a chance, but impact on the lunar surface is no chance at all."

Bach finally sat down. She thought it over for a minute, then spread her hands.

"Great," she said. "It sounds like all our problems are solved. We'll just take this to Hoeffer, and we can call off the probes."

Galloway and Rossnikova were silent. As last, Galloway sighed.

"It may not be as simple as that."

Bach stood again, suddenly sure of what was coming next.

"I've got good sources, both in the news media and in city hall. Things are not looking good for Charlie."

"I can't *believe* it!" Bach shouted. "They're ready to let a little girl die? They're not even going to try to save her?"

Galloway made soothing motions, and Bach gradually calmed down.

"It's not definite yet. But the trend is there. For one thing, she is *not* a little girl, as you well know. I was counting on the public perception of her as a little girl, but that's not working out so well."

"But all your stories have been so positive."

"I'm not the only newscaster. And . . . the public doesn't always determine it anyway. Right now, they're in favor of Charlie, seventy-thirty. But that's declining, and a lot of that seventy percent is soft, as they say. Not sure. The talk is, the decision makers are going to make it look like an unfortunate accident. Tik-Tok will be a great help there; it'll be easy to provoke an incident that could kill Charlie."

"It's just not right," Bach said, gloomily. Galloway leaned forward and looked at her intently.

"That's what I wanted to know. Are you still on Charlie's side, all the way? And if you are, what are you willing to risk to save her?"

Bach met Galloway's intent stare. Slowly, Galloway smiled again.

"That's what I thought. Here's what I want to do."

Charlie was sitting obediently by the telephone in her room at the appointed time, and it rang just when Megan had said it would. She answered it as she had before.

"Hi there, kid. How's it going?"

"I'm fine. Is Anna there too?"

"She sure is. Want to say hi to her?"

"I wish you'd tell her it was you that told me to—"

"I already did, and she understands. Did you have any trouble?"

Charlie snorted.

"With *him*? What a doo-doo-head. He'll believe anything I tell him. Are you sure he can't hear us in here?"

"Positive. Nobody can hear us. Did Tik-Tok tell you what all you have to do?"

"I think so. I wrote some of it down."

"We'll go over it again, point by point. We can't have any mistakes."

When they got the final word on the decision, it was only twelve hours to impact. None of them had gotten any sleep since the close approach. It seemed like years ago to Bach.

"The decision is to have an accident," Galloway said, hanging up the phone. She turned to Rossnikova who bent, hollow-eyed, over her array of computer keyboards. "How's it coming with the probe?"

"I'm pretty sure I've got it now," she said, leaning back. "I'll take it through the sequence one more time." She sighed, then looked at both of them. "Every time I try to re-program it, it wants to tell me about this broken rose blossom and the corpse of a puppy and the way the wheel looks with all the lighted windows." She yawned hugely. "Some of it's kind of pretty, actually."

Bach wasn't sure what Rossnikova was talking about, but the important thing was the probe was taken care of. She looked at Galloway.

"My part is all done," Galloway said. "In record time, too."

"I'm not even going to guess what it cost you," Bach said.

"It's only money."

"What about Doctor Blume?"

"He's with us. He wasn't even very expensive. I think he wanted to do it, anyway." She looked from Bach to Rossnikova, and back again. "What do you say? Are we ready to go? Say in one hour?"

Neither of them raised an objection. Silently, they shook each other's hands. They knew it would not go easy with them if they were discovered, but that had already been discussed and accepted and there seemed no point in mentioning it again.

Bach left them in a hurry.

The dogs were more excited than Charlie had ever seen them. They sensed something was about to happen.

"They're probably just picking it up from you," Tik-Tok ventured.

"That could be it," Charlie agreed. They were leaping and running all up and down the corridor. It had been *hell* getting them all down here, by a route Tik-Tok had selected that would avoid all the operational cameras used by Captain Hoeffer and those other busybodies. But here they finally were, and there was the door to the lifeboat, and suddenly she realized that Tik-Tok could not come along.

"What are you going to do?" she finally asked him.

"That's a silly question, Charlie."

"But you'll *die!*"

"Not possible. Since I was never alive, I can't die."

"Oh, you're just playing with words." She stopped, and couldn't think of anything good to say. Why didn't they have more words? There ought to be more words, so some of them would be useful for saying goodbye.

"Did you scrubba-scrub?" Tik-Tok asked. "You want to look nice."

Charlie nodded, wiping away a tear. Things were just happening so *fast*.

"Good. Now you remember to do all the things I taught you to do. It may be a long time before you can be with people again, but I think you will, someday. And in the meantime, Anna-Louise and Megan have promised me that they'll be very strict with little girls who won't pick up their rooms and wash their hair."

"I'll be good," Charlie promised.

"I want you to obey them just like you've obeyed me."

"I will."

"Good. You've been a very good little girl, and I'll expect you to continue to be a good girl. Now get in that lifeboat, and get going."

So she did, along with dozens of barking Shelties.

There was a guard outside the conference room and Bach's badge would not get her past him, so she assumed that was where the crime was being planned.

She would have to be very careful.

She entered the control room. It was understaffed, and no one was at her old chair. A few people noticed her as she sat down, but no one seemed to think anything of it. She settled down, keeping an eye on the clock.

Forty minutes after her arrival, all hell broke loose.

It had been an exciting day for the probe. New instructions had come. Any break in the routine was welcome, but this one was double good, because the new programmer wanted to know *everything*, and the probe finally got a chance to transmit its poetry. It was a hell of a load off one's mind.

When it finally managed to assure the programmer that it understood and would obey, it settled back in a cybernetic equivalent of wild expectation.

The explosion was everything it could have hoped for. The wheel tore itself apart in a ghastly silence and began spreading itself wildly to the blackness. The probe moved in, listening, listening . . .

And there it was. The soothing song it had been told to listen for, coming from a big oblong hunk of the station that moved faster than the rest of it. The probe moved in close, though it had not been told to. As the oblong flashed by the probe had time to catalog it (LIFEBOAT, type 4A; functioning) and to get just a peek into one of the portholes.

The face of a dog peered back, ears perked alertly.

The probe filed the image away for later contemplation, and then moved in on the rest of the wreckage, lasers blazing in the darkness.

Bach had a bad moment when she saw the probe move in on the lifeboat, then settled back and tried to make herself inconspicuous as the vehicle bearing Charlie and the dogs accelerated away from the cloud of wreckage.

She had been evicted from her chair, but she had expected that. As people ran around, shouting at each other, she called room 569 at the Kleist, then patched Rossnikova into her tracking computers. She was sitting at an operator's console in a corner of the room, far from the excitement.

Rossnikova was a genius. The blip vanished from her screen. If everything was going according to plan, no data about the lifeboat was going into the memory of the tracking computer.

It would be like it never existed.

Everything went so smoothly, Bach thought later. You couldn't help taking it as a good omen, even if, like Bach, you weren't superstitious. She knew nothing was going to be easy in the long run, that there were bound to be problems they hadn't thought of . . .

But all in all, you just had to be optimistic.

The remotely-piloted PTP made rendezvous right on schedule. The transfer of Charlie and the dogs went like clockwork. The empty lifeboat was topped off with fuel and sent on a solar escape orbit, airless and lifeless, its only cargo a barrel of radioactive death that should sterilize it if anything would.

The PTP landed smoothly at the remote habitat Galloway's agents had located and purchased. It had once been a biological research station, so it was physically isolated in every way from lunar society. Some money changed hands, and all records of the habitat were erased from computer files.

All food, air, and water had to be brought in by crawler, over a rugged mountain pass. The habitat itself was large enough to accommodate a hundred people in comfort. There was plenty of room for the dogs. A single dish antenna was the only link to the outside world.

Galloway was well satisfied with the place. She promised Charlie that one of these days she would be paying a visit. Neither of them mentioned the reason that no one would be coming out immediately. Charlie settled in for a long stay, privately wondering if she would *ever* get any company.

One thing they hadn't planned on was alcohol. Charlie was hooked bad, and not long after her arrival she began letting people know about it.

Blume reluctantly allowed a case of whiskey to be brought in on the next crawler, reasoning that a girl in full-blown withdrawal would be impossible to handle remotely. He began a program to taper her off, but in the meantime Charlie went on a three-day bender that left her bleary-eyed.

The first biological samples sent in all died within a week. These were a guinea pig, a rhesus monkey and a chicken. The symptoms were consistent with Neuro-X, so there was little doubt the disease was still alive. A dog, sent in later, lasted eight days.

Blume gathered valuable information from all these deaths, but they upset Charlie badly. Bach managed to talk him out of further live animal experiments for at least a few months.

She had taken accumulated vacation time, and was living in a condominium on a high level of the Mozartplatz, bought by Galloway and donated to what they were coming to think of as the Charlie Project. With Galloway back on Earth and Rossnikova neither needed nor inclined to participate further, Charlie Project was Bach and Doctor Blume. Security was essential. Four people knowing about Charlie was already three too many, Galloway said.

Charlie seemed cheerful, and cooperated with Blume's requests. He worked through robotic instruments, and it was frustrating. But she learned to take her own blood and tissue samples and prepare them for viewing. Blume was beginning to learn something of the nature of Neuro-X, though he admitted that, working alone, it might take him years to reach a breakthrough. Charlie didn't seem to mind.

The isolation techniques were rigorous. The crawler brought supplies to within one hundred yards of the habitat and left them sitting there on the dust. A second crawler would come out to bring them in. Under no circumstances was anything allowed to leave the habitat, nor to come in contact with anything that was going back to the world—and, indeed, the crawler was the only thing in the latter category.

Contact was strictly one-way. Anything could go in, but nothing could come out. That was the strength of the system, and its final weakness.

Charlie had been living in the habitat for fifteen days when she started running a fever. Doctor Blume prescribed bed rest and aspirin, and didn't tell Bach how worried he was.

The next day was worse. She coughed a lot, couldn't keep food down. Blume was determiend to go out there in an isolation suit. Bach had to physically restrain him at one point, and be very firm with him until he finally calmed down and saw how foolish he was being. It would do Charlie no good for Blume to die.

Bach called Galloway, who arrived by express liner the next day.

By then Blume had some idea what was happening.

"I gave her a series of vaccinations," he said, mournfully. "It's so standard . . . I hardly gave it a thought. Measles-D1, the Manila-strain mumps, all the normal communicable diseases we have to be so carefull of in a Lunar environment. Some of them were killed viruses, some were weakened . . . and they seem to be attacking her."

Galloway raged at him for a while. He was too depressed to fight back. Bach just listened, withholding her own judgment.

The next day he learned more. Charlie was getting things he had not inoculated her against, things that could have come in as hitch-hikers on the supplies, or that might have been lying dormant in the habitat itself.

He had carefully checked her thirty-year-old medical record. There had been no hint of any immune system deficiency, and it was not the kind of syndrome that could be missed. But somehow she had acquired it.

He had a theory. He had several of them. None would save his patient.

"Maybe the Neuro-X destroyed her immune system. But you'd think she would have succumbed to stray viruses there on the station. Unless the Neuro-X attacked the viruses, too, and changed them."

He mumbled things like that for hours on end as he watched Charlie waste away on his television screen.

"For whatever reason . . . she was in a state of equilibrium there on the station. Bringing her here destroyed that. If I could understand how, I still might save her . . ."

The screen showed a sweating, gaunt-faced little girl. Much of her hair had fallen out. She complained that her throat was very dry and she had trouble swallowing. She just keeps fighting, Bach thought, and felt the tightness in the back of her own throat.

Charlie's voice was still clear.

"Tell Megan I finally finished her picture," she said.

"She's right here, honey," Bach said. "You can tell her yourself."

"Oh." Charlie licked her lips with a dry tongue, and her eyes wandered around. "I can't see much. Are you there, Megan?"

"I'm here."

"Thanks for trying." She closed her eyes, and for a moment Bach thought she was gone. Then the eyes opened again.

"Anna-Louise?"

"I'm still right here, darling."

"Anna, what's going to happen to my dogs?"

"I'll take care of them," she lied. "Don't you worry." Somehow she managed to keep her voice steady. It was the hardest thing she had ever done.

"Good. Tik-Tok will tell you which ones to breed. They're good dogs, but you can't let them take advantage of you."

"I won't."

Charlie coughed, and seemed to become a little smaller when she was through. She tried to lift her head, could not, and coughed again. Then she smiled, just a little bit, but enough to break Bach's heart.

"I'll go see Albert," she said. "Don't go away."

"We're right here."

She closed her eyes. She continued breathing raggedly for over an hour, but her eyes never opened again.

*   *   *

Bach let Galloway handle the details of cleaning up and covering up. She felt listless, uninvolved. She kept seeing Charlie as she had first seen her, a painted savage in a brown tide of dogs.

When Galloway went away, Bach stayed on at the Mozartplatz, figuring the woman would tell her if she had to get out. She went back to work, got the promotion Galloway had predicted, and began to take an interest in her new job. She evicted Ralph and his barbells from her old apartment, though she continued to pay the rent on it. She grew to like Mozartplatz even more than she had expected she would, and dreaded the day Galloway would eventually sell the place. There was a broad balcony with potted plants where she could sit with her feet propped up and look out over the whole insane buzz and clatter of the place, or prop her elbows on the rail and spit into the lake, over a mile below. The weather was going to take some getting used to, though, if she ever managed to afford a place of her own here. The management sent rainfall and windstorm schedules in the mail and she faithfully posted them in the kitchen, then always forgot and got drenched.

The weeks turned into months. At the end of the sixth month, when Charlie was no longer haunting Bach's dreams, Galloway showed up. For many reasons Bach was not delighted to see her, but she put on a brave face and invited her in. She was dressed this time, Earth fashion, and she seemed a lot stronger.

"Can't stay long," she said, sitting on the couch Bach had secretly begun to think of as her own. She took a document out of her pocket and put it on a table near Bach's chair. "This is the deed to this condo. I've signed it over to you, but I haven't registered it yet. There are different ways to go about it, for tax purposes, so I thought I'd check with you. I told you I always pay my debts. I was hoping to do it with Charlie, but that turned out . . . well, it was more something I was doing for myself, so it didn't count."

Bach was glad she had said that. She had been wondering if she would be forced to hit her.

"This won't pay what I owe you, but it's a start." She looked at Bach and raised one eyebrow. "It's a start, whether or not you accept it. I'm hoping you won't be too stiff-necked, but with loonies—or should I say Citizens of Luna?—I've found you can never be too sure."

Bach hesitated, but only for a split second.

"Loonies, Lunarians . . . who cares?" She picked up the deed. "I accept."

Galloway nodded, and took an envelope out of the same pocket the deed had been in. She leaned back, and seemed to search for words.

"I . . . thought I ought to tell you what I've done." She waited, and Bach nodded. They both knew, without mentioning Charlie's name, what she was talking about.

"The dogs were painlessly put to sleep. The habitat was depressurized and irradiated for about a month, then reactivated. I had some animals sent in and they survived. So I sent in a robot on a crawler and had it bring these out. Don't worry, they've been checked out a thousand ways and they're absolutely clean."

She removed a few sheets of paper from the envelope and spread them out on the table. Bach leaned over and looked at the pencil sketches.

"You remember she said she'd finally finished that picture for me? I've already taken that one out. But there were these others, one with your name on it, and I wondered if you wanted any of them?"

Bach had already spotted the one she wanted. It was a self-portrait, just the head and shoulders. In it Charlie had a faint smile . . . or did she? It was that kind of drawing; the more she looked at it, the harder it was to tell just what Charlie had been thinking when she drew this. At the bottom it said. "To Anna-Louise, my friend."

Bach took it and thanked Galloway, who seemed almost as anxious to leave as Bach was to have her go.

Bach fixed herself a drink and sat back in "her" chair in "her" home. That was going to take some getting used to, but she looked forward to it.

She picked up the drawing and studied it, sipping her drink. Frowning, she stood and went through the sliding glass doors onto her balcony. There, in the brighter light of the atrium, she held the drawing up and looked closer.

There was somebody behind Charlie. But maybe that wasn't right, either, maybe it was just that she had started to draw one thing, had erased it and started again. Whatever it was, there was another network of lines in the paper that were very close to the picture that was there, but slightly different.

The longer Bach stared at it, the more she was convinced she was seeing the older woman Charlie had never had a chance to become. She seemed to be in her late thirties, not a whole lot older than Bach.

Bach took a mouthful of liquor and was about to go back inside when a wind came up and snatched the paper from her hand.

"Goddamn weather!" she shouted as she made a grab for it. But it was already twenty feet away, turning over and over and falling. She watched it dwindle past all hope of recovery.

Was she relieved?

"Can I get that for you?"

She looked up, startled, and saw a man in a flight harness, flapping like crazy to remain stationary. Those contraptions required an amazing amount of energy, and this fellow showed it, with bulging biceps and huge thigh muscles and a chest big as a barrel. The metal wings glittered and the leather strap creaked and the sweat poured off him.

"No thanks," she said, then she smiled at him. "But I'd be proud to make you a drink."

He smiled back, asked her apartment number, and flapped off toward the nearest landing platform. Bach looked down, but the paper with Charlie's face on it was already gone, vanished in the vast spaces of Mozartplatz.

Bach finished her drink, then went to answer the knock on her door.

1986, THE SF AND FANTASY YEAR IN REVIEW

Charles N. Brown

1986 was the year we drowned in books. *Locus* counted 1,502 titles published in America that could be considered sf and fantasy—and that didn't include near future thrillers, many "magic realism" fantasies, and other borderland items. There were 846 brand new titles—another record. That's 2.32 new sf books per day. If you read sixteen books per week, and never take a day off, you could almost keep up.

Unsurprisingly, sales were not as good as in 1985. There were more books returned by booksellers—not only because of lower sales per book but also because of lack of room. Thus the time a specific book was on sale also went down, leading to lower sales, etc. It's a downward-moving spiral hard to break unless the publishers concentrate on fewer books. Indeed, the top of each list sold well, and the minor books hardly sold at all. Several publishers have cut their lists, but others are more than willing to take up the slack. Science fiction accounts for some 10 percent of the fiction titles, a slightly higher percentage of the sales, and an even higher percentage of the profit, because it has a longer shelf life and better reissue potential. One hundred forty-six publishers (another record) did sf books last year.

1986 BOOKS

There were 294 science fiction novels published, and the quality as well as the quantity was high. Outstanding titles included *Founda-*

tion and Earth by Isaac Asimov (Doubleday), the latest attempt by the old master to tie all his books together; *Heart of the Comet* by Gregory Benford and David Brin (Bantam), a story of the next passing of Halley's Comet and how it changes mankind; *Speaker for the Dead* by Orson Scott Card (Tor), a sequel to his award-winning *Ender's Game* and an even better book; *Chanur's Homecoming* by C. J. Cherryh (Phantasia/DAW), breathless space opera and the conclusion to an excellent series; *The Songs of Distant Earth* by Arthur C. Clarke (Del Rey), minor Clarke but still excellent reading; *When Gravity Fails* by George Alec Effinger (Arbor/Bantam), one of the best futuristic hardboiled mysteries of recent years; *Count Zero* by William Gibson (Arbor/Ace), the semi-sequel to *Neuromancer; The Moon Goddess and the Son* by Donald Kingsbury (Baen), a near future saga which had some genuine insights into our relations with the Soviets; *The Coming of the Quantum Cats* by Frederik Pohl (Bantam), with some amazing twists on the alternate-world story; *Star of Gypsies* by Robert Silverberg (Donald I. Fine), an introspective space opera; and *Marooned in Realtime* by Vernor Vinge (Bluejay), my favorite of the year—a book with some genuinely new ideas.

There were 263 new fantasy novels—a 50 percent increase over 1985. Sixty-one of those were horror; many of the others were the beginnings or middles of interchangeable trilogies; but there was still some outstanding work. *The Folk of the Air* by Peter Beagle (Del Rey) brings magic to Berkeley in several ways; *Homunculus* by James P. Blaylock (Ace) is a lively romp through an alternate past; *Wizard of the Pigeons* by Megan Lindholm (Ace) successfully combines magic and modern Seattle; *Godbody* by Theodore Sturgeon (Donale I. Fine), the last, unfinished pure Sturgeon, is both fascinating and unsuccessful; *Soldier of the Mist* by Gene Wolfe (Tor), the first of a new saga, is a historical novel such as only Wolfe could write; and *Blood of Amber* by Roger Zelazny (Arbor/Avon), the seventh book in the Amber pentology, continues a very popular series.

It was a good year for first novelists. There were 47 of them, with sf predominating over fantasy. Some were finished products; most were more interesting for the future they promise. The six that impressed me most were *Shards of Honor* by Lois McMaster Bujold (Baen), *Windmaster's Bane* by Tom Dietz (Avon), *Wrack &*

Roll by Bradley Denton (Questar), *Fire Sanctuary* by Katharine Eliska Kumbriel (Questar), *The Hercules Text* by Jack McDevitt (Ace), and *A Hidden Place* by Robert Charles Wilson (Bantam). Some of these authors will be the stars of tomorrow.

It was an excellent year for collections. Among the 67 published were a baker's half-dozen of outstanding work by authors who have never published collections before: *In Alien Flesh* by Gregory Benford (Tor), *The River of Time* by David Brin (Dark Harvest/Bantam), *Visible Light* by C. J. Cherryh (Phantasia/DAW), *Burning Chrome* by William Gibson (Arbor House), *Artificial Things* by Karen Joy Fowler (Bantam), *The Planet on the Table* by Kim Stanley Robinson (Tor), and *Howard Who?* by Howard Waldrop (Doubleday). The Gibson, Fowler, and Robinson collections are especially interesting for their look at three of the "hot" authors of the seventies.

Two anthologies, *L. Ron Hubbard Presents Writers of the Future: Vol. II* edited by Algis Budrys (Bridge) and *Mirrorshades: The Cyberpunk Anthology* edited by Bruce Sterling (Arbor), are also of interest to those who want to look at the newer names in sf.

There were several 1986 works which should be added to your permanent reference shelf. *Trillion Year Spree: The History of Science Fiction* by Brian Aldiss with David Wingrove (Atheneum), a revision of an earlier work, is the best one-volume critical history of sf. *Science Fiction, Fantasy, and Weird Magazines* edited by Marshall Tymn and Mike Ashley (Greenwood) is the best historical reference book on the magazines. It is *not* a bibliography or list of stories, but a collection of essays on each magazine plus publishing data. *Twentieth-Century Science Fiction Writers, 2nd Edition*, edited by Curtis C. Smith (St. James') is the best one-volume reference on modern authors. It has essays on and bibliography/biography of approximately 600 authors.

HEADLINERS

Douglas Adams got $3 million for British and American rights to his next two books. The first, *Dirk Gently's Holistic Detective Agency*, will be published by Simon & Schuster in 1987.

Marion Zimmer Bradley got $2.5 million for two historical

fantasy novels. The first, *The Firebrand*, will be published in 1987 by Simon & Schuster.

Robert A Heinlein got around $2 million for *To Sail Beyond the Sunset*, to be published by Putnam on July 7, 1987, Heinlein's 80th birthday.

Dean R. Koontz got a mere $1 million from Berkley for two new novels, plus a rewritten older book.

Arthur C. Clarke hit seven figures for book and movie rights to *Cradle*, a collaboration with scientist Gentry Lee.

Jean Auel's *The Mammoth Hunters* had a first printing by Crown of a million copies—the largest fiction first printing ever. It headed the American and British bestseller lists for most of the year, and even made the Swedish list without benefit of translation.

Eve Paige Spenser, who, as Evelyn Paige and Evelyn Paige Gold, was managing editor of *Galaxy* and *Beyond* from 1950 to 1957, spun a wheel in the California Lottery and won $15.2 million, the largest U.S. prize so far.

Six-figures sums, once the province of only general bestseller authors, were earned by William Gibson, Gregory Benford, Poul and Karen Anderson, Katherine Kurtz, Clive Barker, Piers Anthony (from two different publishers!), Joe Haldeman, C. J. Cherryh, Jack Chalker, Frederik Pohl, Robert Silverberg, Joan Vinge, and probably others too bashful to talk about it.

Ian Ballantine celebrated his 70th birthday but only placed second in an over-60 skiing contest.

Jane Yolen sold her 100th book.

Harlan Ellison had a busy year. He quit *The Twilight Zone* over network censorship, won the Milford Award for lifetime achievement in editing, and took over the *Hour 25* radio program in Los Angeles. He did not turn in *The Last Dangerous Visions*.

PUBLISHING

This was the year where big fish were swallowed by bigger fish. Bertelsmann, the German owner of Bantam, bought Doubleday, Dell, Delacorte, and the Literary Guild (which includes the Science Fiction Book Club) and formed Bantam Doubleday Dell Publishing. Penguin, the British owner of Viking/Penguin, bought New

American Library (which also distributes DAW books) and Dutton. Macmillan, the British company that owns St. Martin's Press (but not the American Macmillan, which swallowed Scribner's, Atheneum, and G. K. Hall/Twayne/Gregg Press) bought Tor Books from owner/founder Tom Doherty. Barnes & Noble, the third-largest bookstore chain, bought B. Dalton, the second-largest. The reasons behind these mergers were given as foreign investment (we're the foreigners[!]), economies of scale, and vertical integration. The last is specially important to authors who prefer hard/soft contracts where they get to keep 100% of the royalties. Will this feeding frenzy affect science fiction? Not much. The biggest authors, the ones who make the *New York Times* bestseller list, will probably make more money. The rest of us will be unaffected. Science fiction is best published by individuals who work within a company as combination editor/publisher/art director/marketing expert. It's more important that NAL hired an experienced sf editor than that the company was sold. As long as Tom Doherty can run Tor (and St. Martin's was buying his expertise as well as the company) independently, except for financial arrangements, there should be no problem.

Bluejay Books, the specialty publishing house formed by Jim Frenkel in 1983, has suspended operations. It didn't go bankrupt, but didn't make enough money on each book to cover overhead. Other publishers have taken over the Bluejay titles. Some of the major sf publishers—Berkley, Bantam, and DAW—cut their lists in 1986. Others—Tor, Baen, NAL, Warner—expanded. And others— Avon, Arbor House—started major programs. Sf publishers are a hardy breed. If one vanishes, two take its place.

THE SMALL PRESS

Sf also has a vigorous small press. Indeed, the line between the larger small-press operations and the smaller publishers is disappearing. Instead of just doing limited editions and fine books, several small presses are originating books, keeping them in print, and selling rights to the major publishers. Small-press books. especially limited signed editions, should be ordered directly from the publishers. Write them for availablilty of past books and for advance notice of future works. All books mentioned below are full-size hardcover first editions, unless otherwise noted.

Arkham House (Sauk City, WI 53583), the oldest of the specialty presses, did two excellent collections last year: *Dreams of Dark and Light* by Tanith Lee, and *Tales of the Quintana Roo* by James Tiptree, Jr.

Donald Grant Publisher (West Kingston, RI 02892) did at least nine books last year in horror, collections, and non-fiction. Outstanding titles included *The Curious Quests of Brigadier Ffellowes*, a collection by Sterling E. Lanier; *The Long Night of the Grave* and *The Dark Cry of the Moon*, horror novels by Charles L. Grant; *Yellow Fog*, a vampire novel by Les Daniels; *One Who Walked Alone: Robert E. Howard, the Final Years*, a memoir by Howard's only girlfriend; and more volumes in the special editions of Howard's "Conan" series. All Donald Grant books are heavily illustrated.

Phantasia Press (5536 Crispin Way, West Bloomfield, MI 48033) did two volumes by C. J. Cherryh, *Chanur's Homecoming* (they have the entire "Chanur" series available in hardcover) and *Visible Light*, a collection. They also produced a special limited, signed hardcover reprint of the Hugo and Nebula winning novel *Neuromancer* by William Gibson, and the final volume in the "Spellsinger" series by Alan Dean Foster. They have the entire series available in special hardcover first editions.

Underwood-Miller (651 Chestnut St., Columbia, PA 17512) did two original Jack Vance collections, *The Dark Side of the Moon* and *The Augmented Agent*, plus a limited, signed hardcover reprint of *Blood of Amber* by Roger Zelazny.

Dark Harvest (Box 48134, Niles, IL 60648) did two excellent collections, *Blue Champagne* by John Varley and *The River of Time* by David Brin, plus two very good horror anthologies, *Black Wine* edited by Douglas E. Winter, and *Night Visions 3* edited by George R. R. Martin.

Kerosina Books (Plovers Barrow, School Road, Nomansland, Salisbury, Wilts., SP5 2B4, United Kingdom) is a new British small press doing special editions of British writers. The books sell mostly to the American market. Last year, their first, they produced *Kaeti & Company* by Keith Roberts, and *Shades of Darkness* by Richard Cowper.

NESFA Press (Box G, MIT Branch, Cambridge, MA 02139)

produces short story collections honoring guests of honor at conventions. *Out of My head* by Robert Bloch and *Between Two Worlds* by Terry Carr/*Messages Found in an Oxygen Bottle* by Bob Shaw (a back-to-back volume) were their 1986 books.

W. Paul Ganley: Publisher (Box 149, Amherst Branch, Buffalo, NY 14226) does Lovecraft-inspired fiction. *Ship of Dreams* by Brian Lumley was his main 1986 book.

The small press used to be the only source of science fiction reference books. University presses and library publishers are doing most of these now, but some of the best non-fiction books are still coming from the small press publishers. Serconia Press (Box 1786, Seattle, WA 98111) did *. . . And the Lurid Glare of the Comet*, a collection of essays by Brian Aldiss which includes a major part of his autobiography; AC Projects (Rt. 4, Box 137, Franklin, TN 37064) produced *The John W. Campbell Letters*, a fascinating look at a famous editor; Advent: Publishers (Box A3228, Chicago, IL 60690) did *Galaxy Magazine: The Dark and the Light Years* by David L. Rosheim, an issue-by-issue discussion of *Galaxy*; Locus Press (Box 13305, Oakland, CA 94661) produced *Science Fiction in Print: 1985* by Charles N. Brown and William G. Contento, an index to all books and stories published in 1985.

MAGAZINES

It was pretty much a flat year for the magazines. Circulation was up slightly for *Amazing, Analog*, and *F&SF*, down for *Isaac Asimov's SF Magazine* and for *Twilight Zone. Omni* published twenty sf stories and had unchanged circulation—still greater than all the sf magazines combined.

Gardner Dozois had his first full year as editor of *Isaac Asimov's SF Magazine*. He did an impressive job, but the circulation still dropped. I'm beginning to fear that Asimov's name, a fine way to start the magazine, is now a limiting factor because it's associated with more traditional values than *Asimov's* present state-of-the-art fiction.

Patrick Lucien Price replaced George Scithers at *Amazing Stories*, raised the rates, and revamped the look of the magazine's interior. It's too early to say what changes there may be in the fiction.

Tappan King replaced Michael Blaine at *The Twilight Zone* and totally redesigned the magazine. He moved the fiction toward more traditional work in fantasy, horror, and even sf.

Analog and *Fantasy & Science Fiction* were unchanged during the year.

Far Frontiers, the paperback magazine edited by Jerry Pournelle and Jim Baen, managed three issues and then was folded into a resurrected *New Destinies* edited by Jim Baen. *Stardate*, the mixed media sf magazine, went out of business. A resurrected *If* had one issue, and then vanished. *L. Ron Hubbard's To the Stars* was canceled without ever leaving the starting gate.

Aboriginal SF, edited by Charles C. Ryan, a tabloid-size full-color magazine, published two issues in 1986. the 11" × 17" size made it nearly impossible to display, and it may shrink to a magazine size in 1987.

Weird Tales, which has had more incarnations than Shirley MacLaine, will be resurrected in 1987 by George Scithers, a former editor of *Asimov's* and *Amazing*.

Another magazine, called just *sf*, has been announced by a new Canadian publisher.

OBITUARIES

The three most important deaths of 1986 took place early in the year and were reported here in 1986. They should be mentioned again.

Frank Herbert, 65, author of *Dune*, died February 11, 1986 after cancer surgery. Although he wrote over two dozen books, his reputation rests on *Dune* (1965) and its many sequels. The series has an estimated 25 million copies in print. *Dune* is probably the best selling sf novel of all time and usually heads the list of all-time best sf novels. *Children of Dune* (1976) was the first genuine sf bestseller—75,000 copies in hardcover. Herbert became the first of the sf authors able to command a million-dollar advance. He was an excellent didactic writer whose books are filled with ideas and concepts frequently tinged with mysticism. Herbert's best work, outside the "Dune" series, includes *The Dragon in the Sea* (1956),

Whipping Star (1964), *The Dosadi Experiment* (1977), and the non-sf novel *Soul Catcher* (1972).

Judy-Lynn del Rey, 43, publisher of Del Rey Books, died February 20, 1986, after four months in a coma following a stroke. She began her editorial career in 1965 at *Galaxy* magazine. She became Balantine sf editor in 1974 and, with her husband, Lester, as fantasy editor, launched the most successful sf and fantasy publishing list of all time. She had an unerring eye for commercial fiction and was a genius at promotion. She recognized *Star Wars* before the movie appeared and sold four million copies of the movie tie-in. Del Rey Books has had more bestselling sf books than nearly all the other lines combined.

L. Ron Hubbard, 74, Golden Age sf writer, founder of Dianetics and Scientology, and recently a bestselling sf writer, died of a stroke on January 24, 1986. A prodigious pulp writer in the thirties and forties, he turned to sf in the late thirties and was a mainstay for *Astounding* and *Unknown* until 1950, when he invented Dianetics, the Science of Mental Health, which later blossomed into Scientology and the Church of Scientology. He returned to sf in 1982 with *Battlefield Earth* and completed a ten-part novel, *Mission Earth*, before he died. The first six volumes have appeared. He also sponsored the "Writers of the Future" contest, which may have a lasting effect on the field.

Robert P. Mills, 65, two-time Hugo-winning editor of *The Magazine of Fantasy and Science Fiction* (1958–1962) and well-known literary agent, was found dead of a heart attack on February 8, 1986.

Manly Wade Wellman, 82, old-time pulp writer, died April 5, 1986, from numerous medical problems. He broke into the pulps in 1927 and turned out a lot of fiction up to the end of World War II. He then turned to non-fiction and turned out many books on the Civil War. *Rebel Boast* (1956) was a Pulitzer Prize nominee; *Dead and Gone* (1954) won a 1955 Edgar. He returned to fantasy in the seventies, mostly with southern regional fantasy stories about John the balladeer, hero of *Who Fears the Devil* (1963). He won a World Fantasy Award in 1975 for his collection *Worse Things Waiting*, and also won the Life Achievement Award in 1980.

Chesley Bonestell, 98, died June 11, 1986, at his home in Carmel, California. Bonestell had a number of successful careers—

architect, Hollywood background artist, painter of space scenes, landscape painter, and historical painter, but it was as a space and science fiction (a label he disliked and denied) artist that he was most influential and will be most rememberd. His lifetime more than spanned the era between the beginnings of aviation (his early astronomical paintings were destroyed in the 1906 San Francisco earthquake!) and the space age. He was an architect between 1910 and 1937, working on such projects as the Golden Gate Bridge and the Chrysler Building. In 1938, at the age of 50, he became a Hollywood special effects artist. He did matte paintings for many movies, including *Citizen Kane* (1941), *The Hunchback of Notre Dame* (1939), and *The Fountainhead* (1949). Bonestell took his new expertise on camera angles, combining it with his architectural background and his love for astronomy, and drew Saturn as it would look from each of its major satellites. *Life* bought the unsolicited package, and in 1944, at the age of 56, when most men are thinking of retirement, Bonestell embarked on his most rewarding career, as space expert. He did paintings for all the leading general magazines as well as covers for the science fiction magazines. He collaborated with Willy Ley on *The Conquest of Space* (1949), the first visual tour of the solar system. Many more books followed, with collaborators such as Werner von Braun, Fred Whipple, and Arthur C. Clarke. He teamed up with Robert A Heinlein for the first realistic space movie, *Destination Moon* (1950), which won an Oscar for special effects. He also did *When Worlds Collide* (1951), *War of the Worlds* (1953), and *The Conquest of Space* (1953). His books and movies inspired not only an entire generation of science fiction authors, but also the generation of scientists that finally took us into space. In 1956, he did a 10' × 40' mural of the lunar surface for the Boston Museum of Space. When it proved to be inaccurate, he replaced it with a mural of our galaxy. It was painted in 1968, when he was 80, and was his last major work in astronomy. He received a special Hugo in 1974 and was one of the few artists ever to have a one-man show at the Smithsonian. In 1972, at the age of 84, he embarked on another career—historical painting. He produced *The Golden Age of the Missions* (1984), a view of the 21 California missions as they would have looked in the early 19th century. He worked from architectural plans, old photographs, and written descriptions. He held his last one-man show in Carmel, California, at the age of 96.

Other deaths included Thomas N. Scortia, 59, sf author and co-author of a series of bestselling disaster novels and movies; Robert F. Young, 71, short story writer; Russell M. Griffin, 42, sf novelist; Mike Hodel, 46, sf talk show host; Harry Otto Fischer, 75, co-inventer with Fritz Leiber of the fantasy heroes Fafhrd and the Grey Mouser; Jorge Luis Borges, 86, world-famous short story writer of enigmatic fiction and winner of the 1979 World Fantasy Award for Life Achievement; R. Glenn Wright, 54, professor and guiding force behind the Clarion sf writers' workshop; and John D. MacDonald, 70, minor sf and major mystery writer.

MOVIES

Sf films grossed substantially less in 1986 than in the two preceding years. There were just two big hits, *Star Trek IV* with a box-office of more than $81,000,000 (it should top a hundred million dollars with 1987 box office included) and *Aliens* with $78,000,000. Behind these movies, sixth and seventh in the year's top ten, was #10, *The Golden Child*, panned by the critics but grossing $52,000,000 by the end of the year. Critical hits which didn't make the top ten included *Peggy Sue Got Married*, *The Fly*, and *Little Shop of Horrors*. *Poltergeist II* was more popular with moviegoers than with the critics. Box office losers included *Howard the Duck* (which cost $30 million to make and grossed half that), *Labyrinth*, *Psycho III*, *Legend*, *Big Trouble in Little China*, Stephen Kings's *Maximum Overdrive*, *Invaders from Mars*, *Highlander*, and *Vamp*; and the year's big losers, *Clan of the Cave Bear*, *Solarbabies*, *King Kong Lives*, and *From Beyond*, none of which reached $2 million gross.

In all, sf and fantasy accounted for more than a quarter of the gross among the top ten films, and 15 percent of the total for all films—not that bad a performance. And box office figures don't represent a film's total sales. Sf is doing well in home video rentals and sales, which bring new life to theater failures like *Dune* and *2010* (both selling well to home viewers).

As for television, the *Twilight Zone* revival was cancelled, but sf fans got better news as well—a new series, *Star Trek: The Next Generation* is set to begin filming in 1987, with David Gerrold as consultant.

AWARDS

Tim Powers won the Philip K. Dick Memorial Award for best original paperback of 1985 with *Dinner at Defiant's Palace*—the second time he's won this award. Runner-up was Richard Grant for his first novel, *Saraband of Lost Time*.

The John W. Campbell Memorial Award for best novel of 1985 went to David Brin for *The Postman*.

The 1985 Nebula Awards were presented at a banquet at the Claremont Hotel in Berkeley, California, April 26, 1986. Winners were: Best Novel, *Ender's Game* by Orson Scott Card; Best Novella, "Sailing to Byzantium" by Robert Silverberg; Best Novelette, "Portraits of His Children" by George R. R. Martin; Best Short Story, "Out of All Them Bright Stars" by Nancy Kress. The Grand Master Award went to Arthur C. Clarke. The Nebula Awards are nominated and voted on by members of the Science Fiction Writers of America.

The 1986 Locus Awards were announced on May 21st, 1986, in Oakland, California. Winners were: Best sf Novel, *The Postman* by David Brin; Best Fantasy Novel, *Trumps of Doom* by Roger Zelazny; Best First Novel, *Contact* by Carl Sagan; Best Novella, "The Only Neat Thing to Do" by James Tiptree, Jr.; Best Novelette, "Paladin of the Lost Hour" by Harlan Ellison; Best Short Story, "With Virgil Oddum at the East Pole" by Harlan Ellison; Best Collection, *Skeleton Crew* by Stephen King; Best Anthology, *Medea: Harlan's World* edited by Harlan Ellison; Best Non-Fiction/Reference, *Benchmarks: Galaxy Bookshelf* by Algis Budrys; Best Artist, Michael Whelan; Best Magazine, *Locus*; Best Publisher, Ballantine/Del Rey. The Locus Awards are chosen by subscribers to *Locus* magazine. There are more nominations for the Locus Awards than for the Hugos and Nebulas combined.

The 1986 Hugo Awards were presented in Atlanta, Georgia, on August 30th. Winners were: Best Novel, *Ender's Game* by Orson Scott Card; Best Novella, "24 Views of Mount Fuji, by Hokusai" by Roger Zelazny; Best Novelette, "Paladin of the Lost Hour" by Harlan Ellison; Best Short Story, "Fermi and Frost" by Frederik Pohl; Best Non-Fiction, *Science Made Stupid* by Tom Weller; Best Dramatic Presentation, *Back to the Future*; Best Professional Editor, Judy-Lynn del Rey [refused by Lester del Rey]; Best Professional Artist, Michael Whelan; Best Semi-Prozine, *Locus*, edited by Charles N. Brown; Best Fanzine, *Lan's Lantern*, edited by George Lankowski; Best Fan Writer, Mike Glyer; Best Fan Artist, Joan Hanke-Woods. The John W. Campbell Award for best new writer went to Melissa Scott. Nominations and voting for the Hugo Awards and the Campbell Awards are open to any member of the World Science Fiction Convention in the year of presentation.

The 1986 World Fantasy Awards were presented at the 12th World Fantasy Convention Banquet, November 2, 1986, at the Biltmore Plaza Hotel in Providence, Rhode Island. Winners were: Life Achievement, Avram Davidson; Best Novel, *Song of Kali* by Dan Simmons; Best Novella, "Nadelman's God" by T.E.D. Klein; Best Short Story, "Paper Dragons" by James Blaylock; Best Anthology/Collection, *Imaginary Lands* edited by Robin McKinley' Best Artist (tie), Jeff Jones, Thomas Canty; Special Award (Professional), Pat LoBrutto; Special Award (Non-Professional), Douglas E. Winter; Special Convention Award, Donald A. Wollheim. The winners are chosen by a panel of judges.

CONVENTIONS

Confederation, the 44th World Science Fiction Convention, held in Atlanta, Georgia, August 28–September 1, 1986, had one extra feature never before seen at a science fiction convention—the Marriott Marquis Hotel. Imagine a 50-story lobby shaped halfway between the props for H. G. Wells' *Things to Come* and the inside of *Alien*, and you might come close to the convention hotel. The glass elevators crawling up a central pillar, the huge red banners displayed a third of the way up the atrium, created for the first time a setting completely appropriate for a science fiction convention. The 5,500 attendees enjoyed a very pleasant, hospitable convention. Even the weather cooperated. Ray Bradbury was gracious, sincere, and easily approachable. He never seemed to run out of enthusiastic energy, and his Guest of Honor speech was partially a love letter to science fiction and to science fiction fans. Fan Guest of Honor Terry Carr also talked about the wonders of fandom, and Toastmaster Bob Shaw was very witty. The most serious note of the convention came when Owen Lock, acting for Lester del Rey, turned down the Best Editor Hugo awarded posthumously to Judy-Lynn del Rey. Lester del Rey's letter pointed out that she won partially because of her death, and he could not accept that. Oddly enough, the audience seemed equally in favor of the award for Judy-Lynn del Rey as for the rejection by Lester del Rey. It was an excellent convention, and the Atlanta committee deserves a standing ovation.

The 45th World Science Fiction Convention, Conspiracy '87, will be held in Brighton, England, August 27–September 2, 1987. Guests of Honor will be Doris Lessing, Alfred Bester, Arkady and Boris Strugatsky, Jim Burns, Joyce and Ken Slater, David Langford, and Brian W. Aldiss. For information, write to Conspiracy '87, P.O. Box 43, Cambridge, England CB1 3JJ; American agents: Bill and Mary Burns, 23 Kensington Court, Hempstead, NY 11550.

The 1987 North American SF Convention, Cactuscon, will be held in Phoenix, Arizona, September 3–6, 1987, with Guests of Honor including Hal Clement and Marjii Ellers. For information, write to Cactuscon, Box 27201, Temple, AZ 85282.

The 1988 World Science Fiction Convention, Nolacon II, will be held in New Orleans, Louisiana, September 1–5, 1988, with Guests of Honor including Donald A. Wollheim, Roger Sims, and Mike Resnick. For information, write Nolacon II, 921 Canal St., Suite 831, New Orleans, LA 70112.

Noreascon III, the 47th World Science Fiction Convention, will be held in Boston, Massachusetts, August 31–September 4, 1989, with guests including Andre Norton, Ian and Betty Ballantine, and The Stranger Club. For information, write Noreascon III, Box 46, MIT Branch P.O., Cambridge, MA 02139.

TRENDS

The 1986 trends included Cyberpunk, pro and con; the expansion of shared-world anthologies, fantasy trilogies, and horror novels;

problems with oversize conventions; publishers merging; and chain bookstore expansion problems. I fearlessly predict that some of these trends will continue, some will not—and there will be new ones for 1987.

—Charles N. Brown

Charles N. Brown is the editor of Locus, *the newspaper of the science fiction field. Sample copies are $2.50 each anywhere in the world. Subscriptions in the United States are $24.00 for twelve issues, $45.00 for twenty-four issues, via second-class mail. First-class subscriptions in the U.S. or Canada are $32.00 for twelve issues, $61.00 for twenty-four issues. Overseas subscriptions are $27.00 for twelve issues, $51.00 for twenty-four issues, via sea mail. Airmail overseas subscriptions to Europe and South America are $45.00 for twelve issues, $85.00 for twenty-four issues; airmail to Australia, Asia, and Africa is $50.00 for twelve issues, $95.00 for twenty-four issues. All subscriptions are payable in U.S. funds to Locus Publications, P.O. Box 13305, Oakland, CA 94661.*

RECOMMENDED READING

Terry Carr

VANCE AANDAHL: "Born from the Beast." *Fantasy and Science Fiction*, August 1986.

LOIS McMASTER BUJOLD: "Aftermaths." *Far Frontiers*, Vol. 5.

RONALD ANTHONY CROSS: "Hotel Mind Slaves." *Universe 16*, edited by Terry Carr.

JOHN DALMAS: "A Field to Play On." *Far Frontiers*, Vol. 6.

PAUL DiFILIPPO: "Skintwister." *Fantasy and Science Fiction*, March 1986.

TERRY DOWLING: "Time of the Star." *Aphelion Science Fiction Magazine*, Winter 1986.

DORIS EGAN: "Timerider." *Amazing Stories*, March 1986.

NANCY ETCHEMENDY: "The Ladies of Wahloon Lake." *Fantasy and Science Fiction*, August 1985.

MICHAEL F. FLYNN: "Eifelheim." *Analog*, November 1986.

LISA GOLDSTEIN: "Scott's Cove." *Amaxing Stories*, September 1986.

CHARLES L. HARNESS: "The Picture by Dora Gray." *Analog*, December 1986.

STEPHEN KING: "The End of the Whole Mess." *Omni*, October 1986.

TOM MADDOX: "Snake Eyes." *Omni*, April 1986.

SEAN McMULLEN: "The Deciad." *Omega Science Digest*, November 1986.

402 / Terry Carr

PAT MURPHY: "In the Abode of the Snows," *Isaac Asimov's Science Fiction Magazine*, Mid-December 1986.

REBECCA BROWN ORE: "Projectile Weapons and Wild Alien Water." *Amazing Stories*, May 1986. "The Tyrant That I Serve." *Amazing Stories*, September 1986.

JOHN SHIRLEY: "What It's Like to Kill a Man." *Stardate*, January-February 1986.

JAMES STEVENS: "Into That Good Night." *Afterlives*, edited by Pamela Sargent and Ian Watson.

SOMTOW SUCHARITKUL: "Fiddling for Waterbuffaloes." *Analog*, April 1986.

HARRY TURTLEDOVE: "Around the Salt Lick." *Analog*, February 1986. "The Iron Elephant." *Analog*, May 1986.

KATE WILHELM: "The Girl Who Fell into the Sky." *Isaac Asimov's Science Fiction Magazine*, October 1986.

F. PAUL WILSON:"Dydeetown Girl." *Far Frontiers*, Vol. 4.

DONALD WISMER: "Safe Harbor." *Tin Stars*, edited by Isaac Asimov, Martin H. Greenberg, and Charles G. Waugh.

GEORGE ZEBROWSKI: "The Idea Trap." *Universe 16*, edited by Terry Carr.

ROGER ZELAZNY: "Permafrost." *Omni*, April 1986.